Deep Water

A Brooks & Banks Novel

PJ Mouchet

Paul Mouchet Publishing

Contents

Dedication   VII

Preface   VIII

1. Officer Kent Dade   1

2. Officer Mike Reeves   6

3. Willow   14

4. Jackson   21

5. Willow   28

6. Jackson   36

7. Willow   45

8. Jackson   52

9. Willow   61

10. Jackson   69

11. Willow   77

12. Jackson   86

13. Willow   94

14. Jackson   101

15. Willow   109

16. Jackson   117

17. Willow   123

18. Jackson   130

19. Willow   137

20. Jackson   144

21. Willow   149

22. Jackson   155

23. Willow   164

24. Jackson   172

25. Willow   183

26. Jackson   195

27. Willow   201

28. Jackson   208

29. Willow   216

30. Jackson   224

31. Willow   231

32. Jackson   236

33. Willow   244

34. Jackson   252

35. Willow   259

36. Jackson   263

37. Willow   271

38. Jackson   277

39. Willow   286

40. Reeves   292

41. Willow   300

42. Jackson   308

43. Reeves   315

44. Jackson   324

45. Willow   330

46. Jackson   336

47. Mason   340

48. Reeves   344

49. Willow   348

50. Jackson   352

51. Mason   356

52. Willow   361

53. Jackson   370

54. Willow   375

55. Jackson   381

56. Willow   391

57. Jackson   398

Afterword   403

Also By   404

To my wife, who believes in me, even when I struggle to believe in myself. Without her support and infinite patience, I would have never realized my dream of becoming an author.
And, to my big sister Louise, thank you for helping me bring my stories to life.

Preface

In the winter of 2025, I took my first trip to Beaufort, South Carolina. My wife, Candice, our golden retriever, Gizmo, and I stayed in a cozy house just ten minutes from the beach on Fripp Island.

Like my novel *Violent Echoes*, the city of Beaufort is more than just a backdrop. I wanted to capture the lowcountry's charm and reflect the spirit of this gem of a city. Many of the places and restaurants mentioned are real, drawn from our experiences during that unforgettable stay.

That said, this is a work of fiction. Any resemblance to real persons, living or dead, is purely coincidental, even if certain characters or events may have been inspired by real life. While I've done my best to honor the feel of Beaufort, I've also taken creative liberties—adjusting details of the county and its surroundings where the story required.

My hope is that this blend of authenticity and imagination brings Beaufort to life on the page, deepens the mystery, and draws you into its streets. And if you ever find yourself there, I hope you'll discover the same charm and character that inspired this story.

Cheers,
Paul

Chapter One

Officer Kent Dade

Monday, December 9, 4:43 AM.
  Beaufort, South Carolina
  Officer Kent Dade balled up the waxy food wrapper and tossed it onto the floor of his cruiser. The third night in a row eating Taco Bell. The third night of acid reflux burning a hole through his stomach. He had sworn to himself he'd eat better, but, almost seven hours into a twelve-hour shift, good intentions meant jack shit.

He had just taken another bite when his radio crackled to life. *"Unit 247, we've got a 10-39 on Port Republic Street. Caller reports hearing a woman screaming from residence 400."*

"Seriously?" he answered through the mouthful of food. "That's the third time in eight days she's called in a complaint about her neighbor."

"I hear you," the dispatcher replied. "But Mrs. Hargrove reporting hearing screams is new though. You'd best check it out."

Kent's gut gurgled, a warning he'd learned not to ignore. He looked down at the half-eaten burrito clutched in his left hand and swallowed. "10-4," he responded, voice gravelly from fatigue. "It's probably a couple of racoons fighting. I'll be there in ten. I need to hit the can first."

"Roger that," the dispatcher said with a laugh. "You really need to cut back on the fast food, Kent. You're not going to fit behind the wheel if you keep it up."

You're hilarious.

Kent clipped his mic back on its holder and tossed the remains of his burrito out the window. The rapidly increasing distress in his lower intestines told him there was no time to waste.

The sodium vapor streetlights cast sickly yellow pools across his windshield as he made the turn toward the Shell station. His dashboard clock read 4:47 AM. There was no way he was going to meet his ten-minute estimated time of arrival.

He didn't care. He had more pressing business to attend to.

The gas station bathroom reeked of industrial cleaner and something much worse, something the disinfectant couldn't mask. The lock was busted, and the toilet sat too far from the door to brace with his foot. Despite being in a fully enclosed room, he felt exposed. Kent kept one hand on his holstered weapon as he relieved himself. Twenty-three years on the force had taught him never to let his guard down, especially with his pants pooled around his ankles.

Back in the cruiser, he popped two antacids and let them dissolve on his tongue. He gagged as the chalky taste mingled with the still-lingering ghost of cheap Mexican Food. Another rumble churned in his gut, and he debated hitting the can again.

No more Taco Bell.

Kent started his engine and slammed the shifter into drive. He needed to deal with this call, even if it was going to be another goose chase.

The radio stayed quiet as he sped through the empty streets of Beaufort's historic district. Centuries-old live oaks laden with Spanish moss stretched across the narrow roads, creating a pitch-black tunnel. As he approached the address, he noticed a white panel van parked in the laneway, its engine running. Kent deliberately kept his gaze forward and continued past. He made a slow circuit around the neighboring blocks before returning. He groaned when he saw the van was still present, as well as a silver Toyota Camry parked on the street that hadn't been there earlier.

Dade parked his cruiser behind the Camry and waited. While trying to decide what to do, he rolled down the window and took a deep breath of the frosty night air.

At 5:19 AM, as he was about to pull away, another call came in over the radio.

Unit 247, be advised, a second 911 call was placed regarding your location. The caller didn't identify himself, but he is in the house and requested an ambulance. He said a woman has been stabbed. The line went dead before the 911 operator could get additional details. An EMT has been dispatched and should be on scene in fifteen minutes.

The fact that someone had called 911 from inside the house confused the shit out of Kent. "Roger that," he replied. "I'm on scene now, preparing to enter."

After waiting several long moments, Kent stepped out of his cruiser and drew his weapon with a hand that wouldn't quite steady. His mouth went dry as he made his way toward the side of the house, taking the long route around a hedge. Each step became heavier than the last.

As he walked past the rear of the white van, security flood lights sprang to life, illuminating the front of the house and the side door. Kent flinched and dropped to one knee. While his pulse raced out of control, sweat trickled between his shoulder blades despite the uncharacteristic December chill.

"Shit, shit, shit," he whispered. He looked back to his cruiser, wishing he'd never left the safety of his bathroom stall.

Kent patted his vest pocket for his backup magazine, then checked it again. With his weapon trembling slightly in his right hand, he moved to the side entrance and pounded on the door.

"This is Officer Kent Dade of the Beaufort Police Department! Open the door!" The last word caught in his throat. He waited almost a full minute, shuffling his feet, before repeating his actions with less conviction than before.

When his second knock went unanswered, he tried the doorknob, secretly hoping it would be locked. The door swung inward to a darkened vestibule, illuminated only by the overhead flood lights from outside.

Kent clutched his weapon with both hands now, fighting the nervous tremor. He flicked a glance toward the white panel van. His belly suddenly churned with something far worse than Taco Bell regret. He clicked the send button on his mic. "Dispatch, be advised. I'm entering the residence after repeated knocks. I'm going to conduct a wellness check."

"10-4," dispatch replied. "Two additional units are enroute. ETA, nine minutes."

"Officer Dade, Beaufort PD," he called, his announcement coming out in a quavering whisper. He cleared his throat. "I'm... I'm entering the house."

A gurgle from deep in Kent's intestines told him he'd best hurry, or better yet, retreat. Sweat soaked his undershirt and gathered along his hairline. Each passing second seemed to tighten an invisible noose around his neck.

He pushed open the swinging door with the barrel of his gun, wincing at the slight squeak of the hinges. He took a hesitant step into the dining room.

"It burns!" a woman screamed, sending Kent retreating into the kitchen. "Oh God, take it out. Please make it stop. It burns!"

"Don't," a man yelled back. "Jane, you'll die. Jesus, Jane. No!"

The woman screamed again, loud enough to make Kent look for an exit. His finger slipped dangerously close to the trigger as he stumbled over the threshold, barely catching himself on the doorframe. He checked his watch. It had been five minutes since he'd arrived.

Backup will be here soon. Come on Kent, get a grip.

He forced himself to move into the dining room. Several chairs had been knocked over, and a tablecloth was on the floor. In the dim edge of the room, he could see a woman sprawled on the floor, and a man pinning her down.

Kent turned his flashlight on the pair, the beam wavering noticeably. The light caught the butcher knife in the man's hand, poised to strike, blood dripping from the blade and down his arm. Kent's eyes widened and relief swept through him as the man's face came into view. He tightened his grip on his handgun and took careful aim.

"D-drop the knife," he stammered before stealing himself. "Drop it now, or I'll shoot you dead."

Even to his own ears, the threat sounded hollow.

Chapter Two

Officer Mike Reeves

December 9, 7:23 AM.

Florence, Alabama

"Surveillance just intercepted a call." The radio crackled in Officer Mike Reeves's earpiece, tension bleeding through Operations' usually controlled tone. "The bomb is at the home you're watching."

"Roger that," Mike said, excitement coursing through his veins. He had been sitting on this house for over six hours through the wee hours of the night. Zeus, his German Shepherd K9, had slept most of the time, but he hopped to his feet at the sound of his handler's voice. "We'll hold until bomb squad gets here."

"You may not have time," Operations said. "Timer's hot. Fifteen minutes to detonation."

Mike reached for Zeus's fur, steadying himself rather than his dog. "What's the status of the bomb squad?" Mike kept his voice low, even though he hadn't seen anyone since shortly after 2 AM.

"Eleven minutes out, minimum." A pause filled with unspoken implications. "The cell phone conversation we intercepted confirms two hostiles and one device. A dirty bomb, cesium-137. Current wind patterns project the fallout will hit downtown at the height of rush hour. We've estimated casualties in the tens of thousands."

Mike closed his eyes. Eleven minutes until the bomb squad arrived. Fifteen minutes until detonation. Simple math with devastating consequences.

"Command is green lighting your infiltration." Another pause, heavier this time. "You're our best shot at preventing mass casualties, but if you'd rather wait until the bomb techs arrive..."

Mike's throat constricted, his damp shirt clinging like a straitjacket. Thousands of lives were at stake. Zeus's warmth pressed against his leg, steady and sure. Mike dreaded what lay ahead, but this was precisely what they had trained for.

Time to put that training into action.

"Negative." He drew his weapon and took a deep breath. "Zeus and I are engaging. We'll neutralize the target before the techs get here."

"Roger that," operations replied. Mike could almost hear Command's grimace.

"Listen closely, Mike. According to our intel, the two hostiles are on the main floor, and they've placed the device on the second floor to ensure maximum fallout after detonation. You have fourteen minutes to locate and neutralize the target."

"Copy." Mike turned to Zeus, whose dark eyes watched him with absolute focus. "No room for error this time, buddy."

They crossed the manicured lawn in short bursts, using decorative bushes for cover. His body had grown stiff waiting all night, making his movements sluggish despite his athletic build. The humidity made it difficult to breathe and sweat dampened the dark curls beneath his cap. Beside him, Zeus moved like liquid shadow, every muscle coiled with pent up energy and an insatiable desire to do his job.

The side door's lock yielded to Mike's picks in under thirty seconds. Zeus's nose worked constantly, sampling air currents as they slipped inside. The house smelled of lemon cleaner and something astringent, something chemical that made Zeus's nostrils flare.

Side by side, they cleared the mud room, the laundry room, and the half-bath. Each empty space ratcheted Mike's tension higher. Where were the zealots? Intel had put them on the main floor. Had they heard him breaking in? Had they moved upstairs to protect the device? Or worse, detonate it early?

A creak overhead shattered his thoughts. Mike's head snapped up, but the dog maintained his focused forward movement. Mike forced himself to breathe.

Focus. Slow is smooth. Smooth is fast.

The zealots were the priority. Take them out first, then let the bomb tech deal with the device. Movement caught his eye. The kitchen doorway.

Mike pivoted, acquiring his target. The figure stood partially concealed behind the door frame, weapon raised. The officer's training took over. Two controlled pairs: *pop-pop, pop-pop.* Center mass. The hostile dropped. He quickly checked his watch.

One down. Ten minutes until detonation. Six minutes until back-up arrived.

They pushed forward, Zeus leading them deeper into the house. The dog's breathing changed, becoming shorter, faster sniffs.

A shadow detached itself from a darkened doorway in the main hall. Mike engaged before the second hostile could level his weapon. Another clean drop.

Two down. Intel confirmed. Nine minutes.

Mike clicked his radio. "Code four. We're clear. I'm going to look for the bomb." He waited for a reply that never came. Did they have a scrambler in the home, something to prevent communication? He considered stepping outside to contact Control, but the bomb squad was still five minutes out. That gave him and Zeus plenty of time to locate the bomb.

"Find it," he said as he stepped over the dead body and into the living room. The staircase to the second floor lay ahead. Early morning light flooded through a transom window over the front entrance, leaving the rest of the room in relative darkness.

Zeus's nose lifted, sampling a new current of air. The dog's head swiveled toward a closed closet door. A low rumble built in his chest.

Mike noted the signal but kept moving toward the staircase. Intel had identified the bomb was on the second floor, and it was the only priority now. That timer was still counting down, and the chemical scent was growing stronger. Zeus was just picking up residual traces, or maybe it was... The closet door burst open, gunfire erupting. Bullets hammered Mike's chest. Zeus lunged as another muzzle flash erupted from the darkness.

Oh God, intel was wrong. There was a third. I got us both—

"EXERCISE TERMINATED."

As reality crashed back in, Mike stood frozen, his weapon still raised. Not real bullets. No radiation. No deaths. Just the cold sting of failure as his vest's impact sensors flashed angry red, each light marking where he should have died.

Fuck!

***

FBI Special Agent Jackson Brooks groaned and scrubbed the back of his neck as fluorescent lights flooded the training space, harsh and unforgiving. He glanced at his partner, FBI Special Agent Willow Banks, standing next to him. She frowned and shook her head, saddened by what she had to do next.

"Officer Reeves." Willow's voice cut through the speakers like a blade. Even through the observation booth's tinted glass, her tall frame commanded attention as she leaned forward, blonde hair catching the light as she shook her head in disappointment. "You and your K9 partner are both dead. Zeus gave you multiple clear indicators of an immediate threat, which you ignored because it didn't match your intel. Would you like to know what that would have cost your city?"

Mike lowered his weapon and hung his head, sweat dripping along his clean-shaven jaw. SBI Special Agent Baker, the third zealot, emerged from the closet, looking grim behind his protective mask. Zeus sat beside Mike, posture perfect, eyes alert. Unlike his handler, the dog had done everything right.

"If this had been real," Willow continued, her tone carrying the weight of someone who'd learned these lessons the hard way, "you'd have died before warning the bomb squad about the third hostile. They'd have entered with bad intel, and the device would have detonated before they could disarm it. Thousands would be dead, because you trusted the voice in your ear over your partner at your side."

"Report to observation," Jackson's voice joined Willow's. "Bring Zeus with you."

In the observation booth above, Jackson set down his tablet with a quiet sigh, his six-foot-three frame unfolding from the chair as he stood to get a better view of the monitors. He watched Mike holster his training weapon, his movements stiff with embarrassment.

"Jesus, Jax," Willow said, sounding defeated. She was Mike's trainer, and his failure was as much hers as it was his. "Zeus knew that closet was wrong the moment they entered the main hallway." Her voice was tight, and Jackson knew she was seeing a different scene, remembering a different mistake. "I don't know why my brother sent him to us. He's clearly not ready. I doubt he ever will be. Zeus tried to tell him three separate times, but Reeves was so focused on that intel brief..."

"Two confirmed hostiles," Jackson said. "The perfect trap. Feed responders exactly what they expect, make them think they've solved the puzzle..."

"Then hit them when they stop looking for threats." Willow's jaw tightened. "Zeus wasn't checking that closet for bomb residue. He was trying to tell his partner someone was hiding in there. Someone intel said shouldn't exist."

"And in real life, they'd both be dead." Jackson stood as footsteps approached. "Along with God knows how many others, because the next team in would be working from the same bad intel."

After a curt knock, the operations door opened. Mike entered with Zeus still in perfect heel position, his face flushed with a mixture of shame and frustration. His vest's impact sensors continued to flash, each red light marking what would have been a fatal wound.

"Have a seat, Officer Reeves." Willow's tone was carefully neutral as he gestured to an empty chair. "Let's talk about why the bad guys would want you to think you know exactly what you're walking into. And then let's talk about why your partner was trying to tell you different."

Zeus settled at Mike's feet, alert and ready despite his handler's failure.

Mike cleared his throat. "The intel—"

"The intel was wrong," Willow cut in. "Intel can be manipulated. Intel can be exactly what someone wants you to see." She leaned forward. "But you know what can't be fooled? What can't be tricked by false information or misleading evidence?" She pointed toward Zeus. "Your partner was trying to save your life in there, and you refused to listen."

Outside the observation booth, the training facility hummed with activity as other teams prepared for their own scenarios.

"We'll send our report to your chief," Willow said. "But if you don't mind me being blunt, you're not meant to be a handler, at least, not in this capacity. When the pressure is on, you turn inward and become too self-reliant. You forget that you are a member of a team. Your K9 isn't a tool. He's your partner."

Jackson watched Willow debriefing the officer. Just eight months ago, she'd been in Mike's position, receiving the same wisdom from Jackson's mother, an expert trainer in her own right. Willow had excelled beyond expectation. She wasn't just a quick study; she was intuitive and open, but more importantly, she was empathetic. As soon as she accepted that she shared a bond with her dog, she understood what it meant to have one as a partner.

"I'll practice," Mike said. He glanced down at Zeus, who was sitting calmly at his side. "I want this more than I can say. I'll take more courses. I'll pay better attention. Please, don't write me off as a lost cause."

"That's not up to us," Jackson said. He felt for the young man, but instincts couldn't be taught. They would provide feedback to Officer Reeve's supervisor. What she chose to do with it was her call. "But I'll be sure to include your willingness to learn."

The buzz of Willow's phone interrupted the conversation. "It's Cooper," she said to Jackson, waggling her cell phone at him. "He's likely looking for an update on his officer." She accepted the call and tucked a loose strand of wavy blonde hair behind her ear. "Hey Coop. We just finished our evaluation of Officer Reeves."

Willow's expression turned dark, and she stepped out of the room with Ranger, her Belgian Malinois K9, at her side. The call had offered Jackson a welcome interruption. He didn't like being the bearer of bad news, but he also knew that if he fudged the report, it could cost lives. "That's all, Officer. You've got an amazing dog, and I truly hope you two find a way to work together."

Mike offered a curt nod and gave a sharp tug on his dog's leash to let him know they were leaving. Zeus immediately complied and locked his eyes on his handler, awaiting his next command. The pair exited the debriefing room without looking back. While Jackson waited for his partner's return, he gathered up his paperwork and tidied the observation station for the next group coming in. The Alabama State Bureau of Investigation had graciously lent them their training facility for today's session, and Jackson didn't want to abuse their hospitality by leaving the place a mess.

When Willow returned, she looked ill. "I've got to go home," she said. The color drained from her face as she stared at her phone's screen. Ranger pressed against her leg, responding to the sudden tension in her body.

"Is there a problem at the house?" Jackson asked, fear welling up inside him. He'd left his Golden Retriever K9, Ruby, at home this morning. She hadn't quite been herself, and he figured she needed a break after a particularly rigorous training session the day before. He had asked his vet, Dr. Jason Simmons, to check in on her. "Did something happen to Ruby?"

Willow swallowed hard, her voice coming out hollow. "Not our home." She looked up, her expression a particular mix of hurt and dread. "To where I grew up. To Beaufort, South Carolina."

Chapter Three

Willow

The phone trembled in Willow's hand as she pressed it against her ear. Amid the commotion around her, she hoped she'd misunderstood her brother's words. She stuck her finger in her left ear, attempting to block the ambient noise.

"Cooper? Can you repeat that? I don't think I heard you correctly."

Her brother's voice was tight and shaky in a way that made her heart clench. "You heard me right, Will. Mason's been arrested. For murder."

The words crashed into her, causing her knees to buckle. She leaned against the wall for support, her breath catching in her throat. Mason? Murder? The two concepts refused to align in her mind, like magnets repelling each other. Willow hadn't spoken to her eldest brother in almost three years, not since the day he'd destroyed her engagement to Matt Carver. Even knowing her brother had acted to protect her didn't make the memory any less painful. It had been a terrible season of loss that had hardened something inside her. First her parents and Mason's wife died in a car accident, followed by her breakup with Matt a few weeks later.

"What? That's impossible..."

"I'm looking at the crime scene right now." Cooper's voice dropped lower. "It's bad, sis. It's really bad. Hunter's with Mason at the police station. I've already sent him the murder-scene photos. I know he's a corporate lawyer, but at least he can make sure Mason's treated properly until we can get him a real criminal defense attorney."

Willow closed her striking blue eyes, fighting to keep her voice steady. "Tell me everything."

As Cooper detailed the scene, each word made her grip the phone tighter. Blood. A knife. A patrol officer witness. Mason in handcuffs. It was too much to cope with. Ranger leaned into her, responding to her rising distress. "You need to get down here, Will. I mean, Mason's fucked, and we don't have the resources to fully investigate. At least, not well enough to clear him."

"It's outside our jurisdiction," Willow said. "It's not a federal case."

"I'm inviting you to investigate. Isn't that good enough?" He sounded desperate, something that was not in her brother's nature. It seemed a lot was happening that wasn't in either of her brothers' natures.

"Your chief would need to invite us, and even then, it'd go through Charleston unless I get SAC clearance." Silence followed. Willow knew Cooper was trying to devise a plan that would get her involved, but he was coming up short. "Look. Talk to Chief Stevens to see if it's even a possibility. Whether or not we're officially involved, Jax and I will come down and do what we can to help."

"In the meantime," Cooper said with a strained and weary voice. "I'm going to coordinate with Hunter to line up a proper defense attorney. I'm not sure how we're going to afford someone decent, but I'll remortgage my house if I have to."

"Don't worry about the price," Willow said. "Have you contacted Wade and Colten? We'll all kick in to help." She desperately hoped Jackson wouldn't object to her offer.

Her response had been automatic. Her resentment for Mason momentarily forgotten.

"I called Colten, and he told Wade. They were together when I called. Colten said they'll come east as soon as possible, but they're in the middle of *something* that they couldn't tell me about."

Colten and Wade were older than Cooper but younger than Hunter. They had moved to California to work on an IT startup. Last Willow had heard they were doing okay but neither shared much about specifics. Wade had once mentioned an NSA contract, which Colten had quickly denied. They were likely under an NDA, so she hadn't pressed them for details. Willow understood what it was like to not be able to share with her siblings.

"There's no reason for them to make the trip," Willow said, doing her best to ignore the ever-increasing commotion around her. "We can keep them up to speed as we learn things." She turned her back to a group of officers who were discussing the scenario they were planning. "Listen. I've got to go right now, but I'll be there as soon as I can be."

"Love you, sis. I'll touch base again as soon as I have more details." Cooper disconnected before Willow could respond. Her breath caught as cold dread spread through her body.

"I've got to go home," she said as she rejoined Jackson, her voice hollow. The training facility suddenly felt too bright, too loud.

"Is there a problem at the house?" Jackson had already gathered his belongings, concern etched on his features. "Did something happen to Ruby?"

She swallowed hard. "Not our home." She looked up, meeting his dark brown eyes, knowing she couldn't hide how deeply this had shaken her. "To where I grew up. To Beaufort, South Carolina. My brother's been arrested for murder."

"Your brother?" Jackson's brow furrowed. "Which one?"

"Mason." The name tasted like ash in her mouth. She hadn't forgiven him, not by a long shot, but he was family, and she wouldn't turn her back on him. "Cooper just called. He's already contacted Hunter." She drew a steadying breath. "We need to go home, pack, and head to Beaufort as soon as we can."

"Of course. We'll leave immediately."

That was one of the many things she loved about her fiancé, he knew when to act and when to let her take the reins.

In the two months since he'd proposed, she'd never seen him hesitate when she needed him.

Sometimes the guilt of keeping secrets from him, especially about her previous engagement, weighed heavily on her. How could she explain the broken relationship with her brother without revealing the painful truth about Matt? Opening up about that night would mean reliving the worst period of her life. No doubt, she'd have to come clean, but she feared the potential repercussions. She had tried to bring it up before, but the timing never felt right.

The drive home was mercifully short, but every passing minute felt like an hour. Willow's mind raced with memories of the last time she'd seen Mason, the night he'd shown her the truth about Matt. He'd been right to intervene, but the way he'd done it had shattered their relationship. Now here she was, engaged again, keeping secrets about her past, and her eldest brother was in handcuffs.

Jackson's phone rang just as they pulled onto their street. He answered it on speaker, Dr. Simmons's familiar voice filling the car.

"Good news," the vet said, chuckling. "I figured out why Ruby's been a bit off lately." He let the comment hang there for several seconds. "Congratulations! You're going to be a grandfather."

Jackson's eyebrows shot up. "You're saying..."

"Yup. She's pregnant. Healthy as can be, but she'll need to take it easy for a while."

Despite everything, Willow felt a tiny smile tugging at her lips as Jackson ended the call. He faced her, his eyes bright with pride.

"We're going to be grandparents," he said, his grin fading slightly as he remembered why they were rushing home. "Though I suppose we have more pressing matters right now."

"Ruby's going to be a mom," she said softly. "At least there's one piece of good news today." She looked over her shoulder into the back seat. "Ranger! You dog, you!" Her K9 tilted his head to the side, unsure what his handler was saying to him. "I guess we didn't do a good job of keeping you two separated while Ruby was in heat."

"They spend all their time together," Jackson said with a chuckle. "Nature will find a way."

"And so will a horn-dog," Willow replied. "After she has her litter, we're going to have to do a better job of keeping them apart. I don't plan on having a house filled with... whatever kind of puppies these two are going to make."

"They're going to be adorable," Jackson said. "Just like our kids will be."

Her heart stopped.

"You want to have kids?" Willow asked, her mind momentarily shifting gears from her brother's crisis. The question caught her off guard, stirring a mix of emotions she hadn't expected to navigate today. Having children was something she'd thought about abstractly, but between her demanding career and the trauma of her past losses, she'd never allowed herself to seriously consider it. Then again, she had never expected to have a man like Jackson in her life. "It's not something we've ever talked about."

"I'd like to be a dad," he said, the memory of his own childhood in rural Alabama coming to mind, the way his father had taught him to track through the woods long before FBI training was even a thought. "Growing up with all that space, all that freedom... I want to give a kid that kind of foundation. But if that's not where you see our future together, I can adjust. We'll always have our fur-babies. Although, Momma might be disappointed if we don't give her real grandbabies."

Willow turned away and looked out the window. Their relationship had been unexpected, a whirlwind, and the happiest eight months of her life. She loved Jackson dearly, and his parents were the kindest, most giving people she had ever known. They had opened their house to her and made her feel at home from the very first day. She had wanted her and Jackson to get their own place, but his parents had insisted they stay with them and not rush into a purchase. Homes in the area were either pricey, or they were falling apart, or both.

"Will? Are you okay?" Jackson's hand settled over hers, giving it a light squeeze. "Having kids... I know it's not something we talked about, and now is the worst possible time to bring it up. It just kind of... slipped out."

Jackson had the same soulful brown eyes as Ruby, and it shattered her heart to look at him. Not because of the impromptu discussion about children, but because she needed to share a piece of her past that she had buried away. "Of course I want children."

The words fell out of her mouth before she could fully process them, surprising even herself. Jackson lit up like a Christmas tree, and Willow felt a flutter of both warmth and anxiety at his reaction. She wasn't lying, she did want children, but the possibility suddenly felt both wonderful and terrifying. "Maybe we can hold off discussing it until we get through my brother's arrest. He's going to need my undivided attention."

"You know we're not going to be allowed to investigate, right?" Jackson gripped Willow's hand. "It's not a federal case, and even if we're invited to assist, there's no way Alice is going to let you be involved. You're too close."

"Like you were too close to your best friend's murder?" Willow shot back, heat rising in her face. She pulled her hand away. "Alice Baldwin might be our SAC, but she's also my friend, and she knows I can keep a level head, just like you did when we investi-gated Tanner's murder."

"But you were in charge," Jackson said, his voice soft and caring. "Remember? You insisted, because I was too close to be objective."

"Fine," Willow said, taking Jackson's hand again. "You lead this time, and I'll give you advice on the locals. I'll talk to Cooper and ask if he can smooth the way with Chief Stevens. If we can get her to officially invite the FBI into the investigation, I'm sure we can get Alice to approve us taking the lead."

"Why would your brother have sway with the chief, even if he's a sergeant with the PD? I expect she'll have the same concern about letting a family member investigate."

"I think the Beaufort PD is short on detectives."

Jackson pulled into their laneway and slipped the shifter into park. "Let's worry about that when we get there. For now, let's focus on getting ourselves to South Carolina."

Willow agreed, the momentary distraction fading as her mind returned to her brother's situation. She began mentally cataloging what they'd need to pack. "Do you think your parents will be okay with looking after Ruby and Ranger while we're gone? We might be a while."

"Why wouldn't the dogs come with us? If we're going to be investigating, we're going to need them both."

"Can Ruby travel in her condition?" Willow had never dealt with a pregnant dog before, and she had no idea what to expect.

"She'll be fine," Jackson said, "but if you're worried, I'll check with Jason, just to be certain."

Chapter Four

Jackson

Jackson glanced at Willow as she gripped the wheel of their new Suburban. They'd just passed through Atlanta, GA, and she hadn't said a word in the four hours since leaving Florence, AL. Clearly, she was worried about her brother and the murder charges he was facing. Their two dogs, Ruby and Ranger, were sleeping on the back seat, their noses almost touching. He resisted the urge to reach out and pet them. He'd never had newborn puppies before, and the idea of training them from day one thrilled him. If his parents didn't allow the puppies to live in their house with them, he'd either have to make some adjustments to the kennels, or he and Willow would have to move up their house-hunting schedule.

"We're going to figure this out," he said. "It's got to be a mistake." Jackson wasn't sure he believed what he was saying. A patrol officer had found Mason straddling the murder victim, holding a butcher knife in his hand.

A curt nod was all Willow gave in response. Jackson was sure she was running every possible scenario through her head, working out every conceivable angle. But he was also certain that there was something more going on. When they had a case, they talked it through. They had always worked out their plans together, bouncing ideas off each other and making sure every base was covered.

"Talk to me, Will. Let me in."

A tear tumbled down Willow's cheek. She swiped it away, immediately replaced by another.

"I hate him," she said. "But he's my brother, and I also love him." Her expression crumbled and tears continued to spill. "I have things... things I need to tell you. Things I should have told you months ago, but..." She turned away and focused her attention on the road ahead of her.

"Whatever it is, Will. We'll get through it." Jackson's words were punctuated by Ranger's whining. "There isn't anything I won't do for you."

"Jesus Christ, Jax!" she shouted. "You're not helping."

Jackson recoiled. He knew Willow to be fiery, but never towards him, at least not when he was trying to help.

A sob escaped Willow's lips. Her eyes were locked on the road, and her breathing was far too quick. "Damn it. I'm sorry, okay? I don't mean to snap at you, but sometimes I wish you weren't so goddamned nice to me. I'm not worthy of it."

"Well, that's just fucking ridiculous," Jackson said, throwing in some vulgar language. He never swore, or at least he tried not to. When Willow snort-laughed, he knew his choice of words had had the desired effect.

Before she faced him, Willow breathed deeply and wiped her cheeks one more time. "I used to be engaged," she blurted. The way her face was contorted, it seemed like speaking the words aloud had caused her unbearable pain. "There. I said it. That's my secret that I have wanted to share with you, but somehow never found the right time."

Jackson's mouth went dry, and his mind blanked. The sadness in Willow's expression morphed into worry and then fear.

"Do you hate me?" she asked, her voice thick with emotion. "I know I should have told you a long time ago..."

"Hate you?" It took a few moments, but Jackson eventually got his emotional feet beneath himself. "Never. I mean, we both had lives before we met last April. I just wish you had trusted me enough to tell me sooner, but I get it. What I don't get is, why tell me now, and why do you hate Mason? Is he the reason you and your fiancé broke up?"

"Oh, Jesus." Willow turned back to watch the road, the soft hum of the wheels and the rumble of the engine filling the void. "His name was Matt Carver. He was Mason's best friend growing up. When I turned seventeen, Matt asked me out. Mason nearly beat him to death when he found out."

"How much older was he?" Jackson asked. "You have five older brothers, and Mason's the oldest, so Matt had to be at least..."

"He's seven years older than me," Willow said. "He was twenty-four at the time."

"I can understand your brother's reaction then." The idea that a twenty-four-year-old thought it was okay to ask out a teenager... it made Jackson's blood boil.

"I had thought it was the age thing too," Willow said. "But there was more. I didn't find out how much more until years later." She shuddered, like she was trying to rid herself of the filth. "I didn't see Matt again until I joined the FBI and was posted to the Charleston field office. I didn't even know that Matt had also joined the FBI. I nearly dropped my coffee when I bumped into him in the elevator."

Jackson could imagine it, and he didn't like the coincidence. Even if Willow was a grown woman at that point, the guy still sounded like a predator.

"A few days later, Matt invited me out for lunch. He spent the entire time apologizing for his stupidity." Willow raised a shoulder. "He was handsome, witty, and utterly charming. Over the next few weeks, lunches became dinners, and dinners became..." She turned away, seemingly no longer able to look Jackson in the face. "Before I knew it, we were engaged and planning a spring wedding."

"And Mason objected?"

"He didn't just object," Willow said, her mouth drawn into a thin line. "He pestered me every night with endless phone calls, telling me that Matt was a bad man, that he was a womanizer, and that he only wanted me because he couldn't have me when I was seventeen."

Jackson grimaced. From everything he knew of Willow, she didn't take to being told what to do. She was a strong, independent woman who said what she wanted and did what she wanted. "I'm guessing that didn't go well."

"Ya think? It got so bad that I started ducking his calls and ignoring his texts. After I ghosted him, I got a text from my niece, Ivy, telling me that her dad needed to speak with me. The next morning, Mason drove from Beaufort up to Charleston to apologize. At least that's what I thought he was doing."

"What do you mean?" Jackson had no idea what her brother might have done, but the tone in Willow's voice suggested it was unforgivable.

"It was the week before my wedding day," Willow said. Her breath hitched, then slowed as she steeled herself. "He showed up at my apartment, and suggested we go out for breakfast. He said he wanted to apologize to me over eggs benedict at my favorite hotel restaurant. He wanted to make things right so that I'd let him walk me down the aisle. I was touched by the gesture. Not having my father..." The words fell away as she struggled to finish the sentence.

"That was nice." When Willow gave Jackson a death stare, he cocked an eyebrow. "Wasn't it?"

"It would have been, had he not had an ulterior motive." Willow's gaze returned to the road ahead. "The motherfucker set the whole thing up. Matt's bachelor party had been at the same hotel the night before. While Mason and I were having breakfast, Matt showed up in the dining room with a girl on each arm. All three reeked of sex and cheap hotel soap."

"Oh, not good," Jackson said. He wasn't sure how she could have smelled them from across the dining room, but he wasn't about to challenge her assertion.

"Ya think?" Willow repeated as her nostrils flared. "I marched up to Matt and the two bimbos ready to lay into him when bimbo number one said '*You're going to have to wait your turn. We're not finished with him yet.*'" Jackson cringed at the thought of what happened next. "So, I grabbed the stupid twat by the hair and bounced her nose off my knee. Then I stormed out, but not before I kicked Matt in the balls hard enough to lift him off the ground."

"I'm so sorry you went through that, Will." Jackson chuckled. Truly, he felt bad for her, but he was having no trouble picturing how it all played out. "I'm surprised you let him off with a field goal kick to his testes."

"I might have smashed up his car a little as well on my way out." She looked at Jackson and grinned. "I also wrote *Cheating man-whore* on his windows with my lipstick. At least I didn't use my key to gouge the sides of the car like in Carrie Underwood's song, *Before He Cheats.*" Her grin turned into a full-on smile.

"I still think he got off easy." Jackson was trying hard to suppress a laugh. It wasn't funny, but he'd seen Willow unleash her wrath on people, and she could be more than a little scary when she got her dander up. "But I don't get why you're angry at Mason over that."

"While I was letting the air out of Matt's tires, the cheating bastard showed up." A crease formed between Willow's eyebrows and her lips turned into a snarl. "The stupid prick said it wasn't his fault. He whined it was a setup, that the girls were Mason's gift to the bachelor party. Like that made it okay."

"Oh." It was the only thing Jackson could think of saying. First, he was speechless over the fact that Matt thought Mason's actions were a reasonable excuse for his own behavior, and second, he wasn't sure that what Mason had done was a bad thing, not if it protected his sister from a monster.

"Fucking right, oh!"

Both Ruby and Ranger were now up and competing to nuzzle Willow's neck. She took turns petting each dog, letting them provide some much-needed canine therapy.

"Outside of some necessary interactions to gather my belongings from Matt's house, I haven't spoken with either of them since." Willow turned back to Jackson and raised her eyebrows. "Don't you think that is a good reason to hate them? Well?"

Jackson stared at Willow, wide-eyed. He didn't know what to say or do. He wanted to hug her and say that everything would be okay. He also wanted to say that Matt got what he deserved, but he couldn't fault Mason. Not entirely, at least. From what Willow had said, her brother had tried to warn her many times, but she had refused to listen. It had left Mason with few choices. Unfortunately, he chose the nuclear option.

"Jesus Christ!" Willow bellowed, loud enough to make the two dogs whine and back away from her. "You agree with what Mason did. Fucking men. You're all alike. You think we need your help, even when we don't ask for it."

Jackson crossed his arms over his chest. He'd had enough of this. "If our daughter was marrying a creep, I'd burn the world down to stop it. Wouldn't you?" Fury burbled up from somewhere inside of him, somewhere primal. "If someone you loved was putting themselves in a position to irreparably hurt themselves, would you sit by and do nothing?"

Willow's eyes narrowed and her lips parted, like she was working up the exact words to effectively eviscerate and emasculate him. He found himself holding his breath waiting for the onslaught that was sure to follow. Before she could begin, her phone rang through the SUV's speakers with Hunter Banks's name appearing on the Suburban's display screen.

The conversation wasn't over. Not by a longshot.

Chapter Five

Willow

Willow was grateful for her brother's call. It kept her from lashing out at Jackson with words she didn't mean, and he didn't deserve. He wasn't wrong to ask how she'd have handled it if the tables had been turned. Truth was, she didn't know. But that didn't matter. She'd hated Mason for so long that there was no room for forgiveness. No room to consider that maybe, just maybe, she'd been wrong all along. Matt's betrayal had scarred her, and she'd been punishing everyone since. Including Jackson.

"Talk to me," Willow said after punching the answer button on her steering wheel. "Tell me you're going to get Mason out of this."

"Hey, Willow," Hunter's voice crackled through. "I'm out of my depth," he added after a long pause. "I think it's best we meet at Mason's house. He's worried about the girls, and he'd like you there when they get home from school. After we get the kids settled, I'll fill you in on what I know."

"Fill me in now," Willow shot back. "We're three hours out, unless I floor it. I need to formulate a plan, and I don't want to do that with the kids around."

"Fine," Hunter said, resigned to giving his sister what she wanted. "But I don't have anything definitive right now."

"Tell us what you've got," Jackson added, his voice calm but with an edge of impatience. "Your sister's crawling out of her skin."

"Jackson? Is that you?"

"Yes," Willow said. "Why are you stalling? What the hell is going on?"

Hunter exhaled, a long, pained breath. "Mason was arrested early this morning. A police officer responded to a 911 call from a neighbor. She'd heard screaming next door. When the patrolman arrived, he found Mason..."

"Yes, I know all that," Willow interrupted. "Coop filled me in on the arrest. I want to know what's happened since. I'm assuming he's already been booked by the Beaufort PD, and that you prevented them from questioning him? Who was the arresting officer?"

Another long pause. "Um... Officer Kent Dade. He said he walked into a bloodbath and caught Mason red-handed."

"That fat fuck?" Willow spat. "The man's a lazy-ass prick just coasting toward retirement. Did he properly Mirandize Mason? Have you had a chance to interview him?"

Hunter's voice was stiff. "He said he did. Cooper, however, exercised due diligence when Mason was brought into the station." Hunter's speech slowed, becoming more formal. "He documented verbal confirmation, and had Mason sign the appropriate forms to create a complete record. They logged all his personal effects, specifically his phone and keys. No wallet or additional items were present. They conducted standard evidence collection protocols, including swabbing for trace evidence and photographic documentation of the apparent injuries."

"Injuries?" Willow's heart skipped. "What kind of injuries? Had Mason been defending himself and that's why he stabbed her?"

"Unlikely," Hunter replied. There was something in his voice that made Willow pause. Normally blunt and unfiltered, her brother was suddenly cautious, measured. "He had scratches on his face, neck, and back. He was covered in blood, so they bagged his clothes, gave him a jumpsuit, and put him in holding."

"Tell me about the scratches," Willow pressed. "Does it look like she fought him off?"

"Sort of," Hunter muttered. "The ones on his face and neck... yeah, it looks like she was fighting him. The ones on his back though." He trailed off, the hesitation in his voice making Willow's chest tighten.

"You think they had sex? And then Mason killed her?" Willow's eyes flicked to Jackson. He'd mostly remained quiet, but now he was staring out the window, his arms crossed. Even he seemed to think Mason was guilty, and Jackson always tried to see the best in people.

"I haven't had much time to discuss it with Mason yet, but yeah," Hunter finally said. "That's exactly what it looked like. He said he'd had relations with her earlier that night. He had left his wallet behind. When he came back to the house to grab it, he found her on the floor with a knife in her chest."

Willow blew out a breath and thanked a god she had no faith in. She couldn't believe that her eldest brother could be a murderer, but now there was at least a plausible explanation for what had happened. Still, something nagged at her. She hadn't asked the most obvious question yet.

"Did you ask him about the scratches?" she said, ignoring Hunter's obvious desire to wrap up the conversation. She needed more details. More answers.

"I'll tell you more later," Hunter said quickly. "I've gotta go now. Mason's being transported to another facility."

"That makes no sense," Willow blurted out. "The DA's already moving him to Beaufort County Detention Center? Why the rush?"

"Not there," Hunter replied, the same cagey tone creeping back into his voice. "He's being taken to MCAS Beaufort for processing."

"To the Marine Corps Air Station?" Willow yelled, her voice incredulous. "What the hell?"

"The victim was a naval petty officer," Hunter explained, voice tight. "NCIS has claimed jurisdiction. They're transferring him now."

Hunter's tone shifted, now pleading. "Look, Willow, I need to go. I'm following the investigator to make sure Mason's processed properly. We'll talk more later. I'll meet you at Mason's. We'll figure out what's next then."

***

It was almost 6pm by the time Willow and Jackson arrived. A pile-up on the interstate had forced them to take smaller highways, along with hundreds of other vehicles.

The Christmas lights wrapped around the porch railings flickered in sync with Willow's heartbeat as she pulled the Suburban into the circular driveway. Mason's house, her childhood home, loomed before them, its antebellum architecture a stark reminder of everything she'd been running from. The wraparound porch where she'd spent countless summer evenings reading was now festooned with garland and twinkling white lights. A massive Fraser Fir stood in the front window, its decorations visible even through the gauzy curtains.

"Aunt Willow!" The screen door slammed open with enough force to rattle the wreaths hanging on the double front doors. Three girls burst onto the porch, their excited squeals piercing the crisp December air.

"Oh God," Willow whispered, squeezing her eyes tight. "I didn't. I can't."

Jackson's hand covered hers. "You can. They need you."

The youngest, eight-year-old Sarah, practically flew down the steps, her golden curls bouncing with each bound. Behind her, twelve-year-old Emma and fourteen-year-old Ivy moved with marginally more restraint, though their faces shone with the same desperate excitement.

"Dogs!" Sarah shrieked, spotting Ruby and Ranger in the back seat. "Daddy didn't tell us you had dogs!"

Willow's throat constricted. She hadn't seen the girls in person since her break-up with Matt. She tried to have regular Zoom calls with them, but they wanted more from her. They didn't understand why she stopped coming by. It had made Willow feel like she had abandoned them because she was too wrapped up in her own pain to consider theirs.

"Ranger," she said, her voice taut as she spoke to her K9. "Easy." But the Belgian Malinois was already wagging his tail, pressing his nose against the window as Sarah approached.

The girls surrounded the SUV before Willow could even unbuckle her seatbelt. She caught a glimpse of Hunter standing on the porch, his expression a mix of relief and concern, before Sarah yanked open the SUV's back door.

"Sorry we're late." Willow's apology and explanation were cut short.

"Sarah Katherine Banks!" Hunter's shout carried across the yard. "You ask before you approach dogs."

"It's okay," Willow called back, though her heart raced as Sarah threw her arms around Ranger's neck. The dog, trained to take down armed suspects, responded by enthusiastically licking the girl's cheek.

Ivy reached the driver's side door just as Willow stepped out. The teenager hesitated for a fraction of a second before launching herself into her aunt's arms.

"We missed you so much," she whispered, her words muffled against Willow's shoulder. "Why didn't you ever visit?"

The question took Willow's breath away. "I... I meant to..."

Before she could form a response, Emma joined the hug, sandwiching her between them. "Is it true you moved to Alabama? Do you still catch bad guys? Is that why you're here? To catch a bad guy?"

Willow's throat tightened. The girls knew nothing of what was happening. They needed to know before their friends found out. Beaufort was a small city, and news, especially rich gossipy news, traveled like wildfire. A leaden weight settled in her gut. She needed to tell them tonight.

"Girls," Hunter called from the porch. "Let your aunt breathe. And someone should probably rescue that poor man from Sarah and the dogs."

Jackson was surrounded by both dogs and Willow's youngest niece, all competing for his attention. Sarah was chattering non-stop about her own dog, a rescue named Pickle, while simultaneously trying to hug both Ruby and Ranger.

"That's Jackson," Willow said, disentangling herself from the older girls. "He's my fiancé."

"You're getting married?" Ivy's eyes widened. "Does Dad know?"

The innocent question twisted something in Willow's chest. Of course, Mason didn't know. She hadn't told him anything since that morning at the hotel almost three years ago.

"Let's get inside," Hunter said, finally joining them in the driveway. "It's freezing out here, and I need to talk to your aunt about some things."

The foyer was exactly as Willow remembered, down to the scuff mark on the baseboards where she'd once crashed her bike trying to ride it down the stairs. Her eyes burned at the familiar Christmas scents of pine needles, cinnamon, and her mother's recipe for mulled cider.

Sarah was still focused entirely on the dogs, now trying to convince Jackson to let them meet Pickle. "He's in the backyard because Uncle Hunter said he might be too excited with visitors coming. Please, please, please can I bring him in?"

"Tell you what," Jackson said, kneeling to her level. "How about we let Ruby and Ranger get settled first? They've had a long drive, and Ruby needs to be extra careful because she's going to have puppies."

"Puppies?" All three girls squealed in unison, bouncing on their toes with wide-eyed delight.

Their laughter echoed through the house; a burst of joy so pure it tugged at something deep in Willow's soul. For a moment, she just watched her nieces, their bright little lives untouched by the weight of everything that had happened.

Then, as if the mood had shifted on a breeze, Ivy turned toward the front room. "Gramma's tree," she said softly, her voice quieter than before. "Dad puts it up every year, exactly the way she did. Even uses all her old ornaments."

Willow moved closer, drawn by the familiar decorations. There, near the top, was the salt dough handprint she'd made in second grade. Below it hung the delicate glass angel their mother had bought the year Ivy was born. Every branch held a memory, each one more painful than the last.

"I'm sorry," she whispered, touching the angel with trembling fingers. "I'm so sorry I stayed away."

"You're here now," Emma said, slipping her hand into Willow's. "That's what matters."

Hunter cleared his throat. "Girls, why don't you show Jackson and the dogs where they can get settled? I need to talk to your aunt about some legal stuff."

"Can we take them to the backyard to meet Pickle?" Sarah bounced on her toes, her little hands pressed together in prayer. "Please?"

Jackson looked to Willow, who inclined her head. "Go ahead," she said. "Ranger, with Jackson." The dog immediately moved to Jackson's side, while Ruby was already being led away by Emma.

Sarah skipped her way out of the room while Ivy folded her arms over her chest and sat at the dining room table.

As the happy chatter faded toward the back of the house, Hunter's expression grew serious. "Ivy, honey. Can you give us a minute? I really need to talk with Aunt Willow. In private."

"Fine," she said, adding a dramatic eyeroll for effect. "I know when I'm not wanted." She flashed a smile. "I'm just glad you're here."

"I'm going to take Ranger to meet Pickle," Jackson said. "Can you wait until I get back?"

"Sure thing," Willow said, even though every second of waiting was ratcheting up her anxiety.

As soon as Jackson and the girls were all outside, Hunter turned to Willow. "I've got some news that you're not going to like."

Willow squared her shoulders. "We'll wait for Jax."

Chapter Six

Jackson

After Jackson had ensured the children and the dogs were getting along, he suggested they postpone the discussion until he could prepare some dinner. Hunter had suggested they order pizza or some other fast food, but Willow nixed the idea. Jackson believed she had wanted a chance to ground herself before hearing everything about her eldest brother being a murderer.

The sizzle of chicken hitting the hot oil provided Jackson a welcome distraction from the tension radiating off Willow. Through the kitchen window, he watched the girls racing around the backyard with the dogs. Even Ranger, who was usually all business, had abandoned his training to play chase with Sarah. Ruby trotted along more sedately, accepting gentle pets from Emma while Ivy threw a tennis ball for an enthusiastic, if somewhat rotund, dachshund. While the chicken fried, Jackson prepared coffee. It was going to be a long night.

"Okay," Willow said, her voice tight as she leaned against the kitchen counter. "Walk us through it. From the beginning." She accepted the cup of coffee Jackson handed her and moved to the kitchen table across from Hunter.

Hunter ran a hand through his hair, exhaustion evident in every movement. "Mason's been renovating that antebellum house on Port Republic for the past nine months. He was hired by the owner, Liam Fitzpatrick, to convert it into a B&B." He offered a grateful nod when Jackson handed him a mug of black coffee. "Shortly after the work began, the owner insisted on having on-site security because of the equipment and materials stored there. That's how Mason met Jane, the murder victim. She was the security guard on duty."

Jackson caught Willow's eye. Based on her expression, they were thinking the same thing. Mason had been working with Jane for nine months, and when it came to crimes of passion, the attacker was almost always someone close to the victim. He flipped the chicken sizzling in the pan, desperately searching for a new angle that might exonerate his fiancée's brother.

Nothing came to mind.

The pieces were all fitting together, but in the worst possible way.

"You said Mason had been scratched," Jackson said, grasping for a thread, something that might lead in a different direction. "Have you gotten anything back from the medical examiner's office yet?"

"Nothing yet from the ME's office," Hunter said, with a sigh. He rubbed the back of his neck, an obvious delay tactic. He had information that he didn't want to share, but Willow's earnest expression said that she'd wring every last detail out of her brother. "But they're definitely from Jane. Mason confirmed it."

Willow splayed her hands across the table as she leaned in. "What aren't you saying? What's the catch?"

"There's no catch!" he bellowed back. "That's the problem. Nothing I can find offers any possible alternative to what we're all afraid of admitting. I don't want to believe it, but everything points to Mason having done it."

Willow tightly wrapped her arms around herself and dropped her head onto the table.

"She scratched his face during sex?" Jackson asked, trying not to lose hope. "Is that... even a thing people do?"

"No," Hunter said, his expression turned dark. "The way Mason explained it, they had been arguing all day yesterday. He had said things he regretted. After their shift was over, he came back to the site to apologize and..."

"Ya, ya," Willow said. "We get it. They had rough makeup sex, and she raked his back. What about the scratches on his face and neck?"

"I was getting to it, Will." Hunter's voice raised, his face becoming flushed. Again, he glanced over his shoulder at the back door. "After they... did it... Mason went home. He was getting ready for bed when he realized he didn't have his wallet. He checked everywhere, including his truck. He figured he'd dropped it at the worksite and drove back to look."

"He couldn't wait until he went back to work?" Jackson asked.

"Monday mornings he takes the girls out for breakfast before school," Hunter said. "He's been doing that since..."

"Since Mason's wife and our parents were killed in a car crash," Willow said. "He had wanted to create new routines for them, ways for the girls to..." Her brow furrowed and her breathing slowed. Seeing that she was unable to continue, Hunter pushed on.

"Anyway," he said, his voice husky. "When Mason got to the house he found Jane on the dining room floor with a knife in her chest. He called 911 immediately. He thought she was dead. Then, out of the blue, she started screaming saying that her chest was burning. She wanted to pull the knife out, and Mason tried to stop her. She must've thought he was her attacker because she fought him off, scratching his face and neck. At some point, she pulled the knife out and blood started spurting from the wound. Mason took the knife from her and tried to staunch the bleeding. That's when Officer Dade came and arrested him."

"Jesus Christ." Willow looked to Jackson, her blue eyes silently pleading for him to... he didn't know what she wanted. He moved across the kitchen, gave her a hug and whispered that everything would be okay.

"What's NCIS got to do with this?" Willow asked, pushing Jackson aside. "You said they took him into custody."

Her actions didn't bother Jackson. When she was on a case, Willow was intense. She was also completely self-sufficient and didn't like to be babied. He made his way back to the counter and resumed preparations for dinner.

"Jane was a naval petty officer," Hunter said. "When the BPD found her credentials, they immediately contacted NCIS."

"Navy? You said she was a security guard." Willow's forehead crinkled. "She was moonlighting?"

"I guess," Hunter said. "To be honest, I didn't put that together." He scratched his head. "I should have, but... I'm not trained for this. I do contract law, not this criminal shit. The only reason I'm doing any of this is to help our brother from being railroaded into saying or doing something he shouldn't. Cooper and I have been trying to line someone up, but we're not having any luck. Apparently, everyone is busy with other cases."

Jackson stirred the sauce, processing the details. That no lawyer would take the case didn't sound right to him at all, but then again, he didn't know much about how law firms handled their affairs. He had never been on the defense's side of a case.

"Tell me about the NCIS transfer," Willow said, seemingly too focused on the case to be concerned with finding a lawyer. "Did they treat him well?"

Hunter's hesitation was subtle but noticeable. "As good as could be expected, I guess. They swooped in and insisted on redoing everything. Said they were concerned that Cooper's involvement had compromised the BPD's investigation."

"Cooper wouldn't..." Willow started, unable to finish her thought.

"No, never," Hunter said, anger in his voice. "Coop's the most straight-shooting guy I've ever known. Even more than dad was. When Mason was brought into the station, Coop made sure that he was properly mirandized. He didn't want to leave any room for a technical loophole. It was the other officers who told him to lighten up, that they'd protect Mason like he was one of their own."

Willow banged her head on the table and laughed, but there was no humor in it.

Jackson added minced garlic to the pan sauce, letting the familiar routine of cooking anchor him as Willow and Hunter continued discussing the events. While he stirred, he stared out the back window, watching the children laughing and playing with the dogs.

The kitchen fell silent except for the bubbling sauce.

"Do you think there's any chance NCIS will let us help with the investigation?" Willow asked, breaking the awkward pause in the conversation.

"Unlikely," Hunter replied.

Jackson stopped stirring and stared at Hunter. There was something off in his tone, almost like he was being cagey.

"There's no real reason to make this an interdepartmental investigation," Jackson said. The devastated expression on Willow's face broke his heart. "But I'll talk to the lead investigator tomorrow and explain the situation. We have two highly trained K9s with us, and that might make the difference."

Hope sprang in Willow's eyes. She looked to Hunter, silently seeking his opinion on the matter.

"It's not going to happen, Will," he said. He stepped away from the table, like he was intentionally putting some distance between himself and his sister.

"What the fuck did you do, Hunter?" Willow asked. She obviously saw it, too. "Have you poisoned us with NCIS?"

With his hands held up in a defensive pose, Hunter warded off his sister's growing anger. "Not me," he said, cringing. His gaze jumped between Willow and Jackson. "You did. Three years ago, when you broke off your engagement with Matt Carver and tanked his career with the FBI."

Deep wrinkles appeared on Willow's forehead while she tried to understand what her brother had said. "I didn't do any such thing. He quit the FBI. I figured it was because he couldn't bear to deal with us sharing office space in the same building. But what does that have to do with NCIS?"

The question hung in the air like a great stink. Hunter's gaze shifted to Jackson for a moment before locking onto Willow. Realization struck and her expression shifted from confusion to fury in a blink.

"You've got to be fucking kidding me." Her hands curled into tight fists. "Matt joined NCIS? Matt *fucking* Carver is the lead investigator?"

Hunter pressed his lips together into a tight line. "He told me that after you broke things off, your boss, ASAC Alice Baldwin, forced him to leave the FBI. According to Matt, she had given him two options, and neither was good. Alice had made it clear that he could leave the bureau with a glowing letter of recommendation, or he could stay and she'd make sure he'd never see another promotion. He said she was protecting you because the two of you were close. That she used to be your ex-partner's partner... Kate something?"

Willow's eyes narrowed. "Her name was Kate Wilmington. She was my FBI partner. Alice was her life partner, before Kate was killed in the line of duty." Kate had also been Ranger's handler, and she had died taking a bullet to protect her dog. At the time, Willow couldn't fathom how anyone could do such a thing, but eight months after taking over as Ranger's handler, she understood completely.

Hunter nodded, sheepish. "Right. That's what he said. That Alice had it out for him the second things ended between you two."

"Of course Matt would say that," Willow muttered. "The truth is, he got bounced because the morning I caught the cheating bastard, I... let's just say I got a bit of revenge on him. When the Charleston police showed up, they found one of Matt's bimbos flashing his FBI credentials. Later, it came out that he had let her use them to fake-arrest people in the hotel lobby so that she could *pat them down*. Then Matt had used his position to quash the complaints with the hotel manager."

At least, that's what Alice had told her about what had happened to him. She'd also said that it was the Office of Professional Responsibility that had forced him to resign. Willow wondered if the truth lay somewhere in the middle of those two stories. At the time, she hadn't questioned her friend's words.

"Well," Hunter said with a doubtful look, "Matt also said he was a well-decorated agent and that Alice's recommendation letter got him hired by NCIS. He also said that he had received multiple offers, but he'd chosen NCIS because it kept him closer to home."

Willow scoffed at the comment. Matt may have been well-decorated, but as an agent, he was average at best. He had coasted on his looks and charm. Both of which he had in spades.

A crash from the back door interrupted the conversation. Three girls and three dogs tumbled into the kitchen, bringing with them the scent of crisp winter air and fresh excitement.

"Oh my god, what smells so amazing?" Ivy inhaled deeply.

"Is that chicken marsala?" Emma asked, already reaching for plates. "I'm starving!"

Sarah had Pickle tucked under one arm, the dachshund's stubby legs dangling contentedly. She stood on her tiptoes to get a look at what was on the stove. "Can the dogs have some too? Pickle loves chicken!"

"I can see that," Jackson said, eyeing the particularly portly pup with amusement. Ruby and Ranger sat perfectly at attention, though their eyes tracked every movement of the serving spoon.

"Girls," Hunter started, "we're discussing—"

"Dinner first," Willow cut in, her voice gentler than it had been all day. "Everything else can wait."

Jackson watched as she helped Sarah get Pickle's feet back on the ground, noting how her hands trembled slightly. He wanted to pull her close, to promise everything would be okay, but he knew better. Instead, he turned back to the stove and said, "Emma, want to help me plate this up?"

While the girls set the table, Jackson pulled out his phone and sent a quick text to Alice Baldwin, the new SAC at the Birmingham field office. Their field office. *Willow and I need emergency leave. I will explain later.* Almost instantly, he received a thumbs-up emoji. Their SAC was extremely supportive, but she'd want details sooner rather than later.

"Jackson?" Sarah tugged at his sleeve. "Can Ruby and Ranger sit with us? Pickle always eats with us at dinner time."

"Sarah Katherine," Hunter admonished, "these are working dogs."

"Of course they can," Jackson said, earning a grateful look from Willow. "They're family too."

As everyone settled around the table, Jackson couldn't help but notice how Willow's eyes kept drifting to the empty chair at the head of the table. Mason's chair. Her hand found Jackson's under the table, squeezing tight enough to hurt.

He squeezed back, trying to convey everything he couldn't say aloud. They would figure this out. They would find the truth. And if Matt Carver thought he could use this investigation to hurt Willow's family, well... Jackson had learned a few things about dealing with dirty investigators during his years with the Bureau.

But those were thoughts for later. Right now, there were three girls who needed normalcy, three dogs angling for chicken scraps, and a woman he loved trying desperately to hold herself together. Jackson served another helping of pasta and asked Ivy about her science project, letting the simple act of sharing a meal push back the darkness, if only for a moment.

Sarah looked at the empty chair. "Where's Daddy? Uncle Hunter said he'd be late tonight, but he's never this late. And he was gone before we got up. We missed Monday Breakfast."

Willow closed her eyes and squeezed Jackson's hand again. "Your dad got held up at work today," she said. "We can talk about it later."

"Don't let your dinner get cold," Jackson said, searching the children's eyes. They all seemed content with the vague explanation for now. "Can someone pass me the garlic cheese bread?"

Chapter Seven

Willow

Willow rinsed the last of the dishes, focusing on the sound of running water gurgling down the drain. She lingered at the sink, unsure if she was avoiding the inevitable or just needing time to breathe. Her mind was muddled, forced to process too many details, too many emotions. This time yesterday, she was happy. Content. Looking forward to spending Christmas with Jackson's parents. Looking forward to her spring wedding, or maybe summer. They hadn't set a date yet.

She dried her hands on a dish towel and glanced out the window. The floodlights illuminated the yard, washing everything in bright, stark light. Sarah was running around with Pickle, the little dog's legs barely keeping up with her excited bouncing. Ranger and Ruby flanked the child, like personal bodyguards. Emma and Ivy were by the old swing set, deep in conversation. Ivy looked too serious. She caught Willow's eye and pressed her lips into a thin line before returning to her conversation with Emma.

Willow's chest tightened. They weren't stupid. All through dinner they'd been waiting for news about their father. When it never came, their demeanor continued to deteriorate. Ivy had picked up on it first but chose to remain quiet.

Hunter and Jackson were still at the kitchen table, their voices low, hashing out legal strategies and planning ways to get past

NCIS roadblocks. When Willow thought the Beaufort PD was handling the case, she'd expected Cooper would have talked his chief into letting them in on the investigation. Chief Janet Stevens was a reasonable woman and an excellent leader. Willow had met her on multiple occasions, and they got along. If it had been up to her, Willow and Jackson would already have access to the crime scene.

But it wasn't up to Chief Stevens, and the universe had a perverse sense of humor, putting Willow's cheating, good for nothing ex in charge of the investigation. But this wasn't about Willow. It was about those girls. They were the ones getting the shit end of the stick. Nearly three years ago, they lost their mother. Now they were losing their father, too. She swallowed hard, knowing she needed to tell the girls tonight. They were going to find out, one way or another. It was best if they learned the news from family.

"I'll tell them." Hunter's voice cut through her thoughts, clear and decisive.

Willow clutched the dish towel and shook her head. "No, it's gotta be me," she said, not turning around. "He's my brother, too." The words tasted bitter, but she needed to do this. She refused to abandon her nieces a second time.

Hunter's exhale was heavy with tension. "You need to be careful how you tell them, Will. They still trust you. Don't break that."

The implicit accusation in his words, that she'd broken trust by staying away so long, hung in the air. Willow didn't respond. She already felt like she was breaking everything just by being there, carrying this news that would devastate her nieces.

Jackson's steady presence moved beside her and leaned against the counter. "If you want backup, I'm here. But if you need to do this alone, I get it." His voice carried the same quiet understanding that had drawn her to him in the first place.

Sarah's laughter carried inside as she attempted to teach Pickle new tricks, her golden curls bouncing with each exaggerated hand gesture. Emma and Ivy were both staring at Willow. Even from this distance, she could see the worry in their postures. They were old enough to sense something was wrong.

Willow stepped onto the porch, hugging her arms against the evening chill. The scent of pine and wood smoke lingered in the air, mixing with the faintest traces of Low Country pluff mud—the briny, slightly rotten smell of the salt marsh. To locals, it was the scent of home. Christmas lights cast a soft glow over the porch railing, making the yard appear deceptively warm. Deceptively safe.

Her pulse picked up as she formulated the right words. Willow knew how to interrogate suspects, when to push and when to let off. Except this wasn't an interrogation, and these weren't suspects. They were three children about to have their world shattered.

"Girls," she called, forcing her voice to stay even. "Come inside for a minute."

Sarah skidded to a stop, looking at her sisters for direction. Emma frowned, but Ivy was already moving, wiping her hands on her jeans as she headed toward the house.

One by one, they filed past Willow. Sarah came first, Pickle trotting close behind with his tail tucked low, picking up on the tension. Then Emma, her eyes scanning Willow's face with a quiet intelligence that seemed far older than twelve. Ivy came last, already five foot nine and nearly eye to eye with Willow, her long, wavy blonde hair a near match to Willow's own. The familiar strawberry scent of Ivy's shampoo clung to the air, stirring memories of a younger Willow who'd used the same brand. Ivy had always said she loved that smell. Now it felt like a relic from another life.

The two K9s stayed back, perhaps sensing they weren't needed. Ranger's eyes were focused on Willow, waiting for a command.

"Good boy," Willow murmured. "Look after your baby momma."

Willow slipped through the back door and into the house, still working out how she'd break the news.

The living room was dim except for the Christmas tree, its twinkling white lights creating soft shadows that danced across their faces as they settled onto the oversized couch. Pickle jumped up next to Sarah, snuggling against her side as if trying to shield her from what was coming.

Willow's carefully prepared words deserted her. She stood before them, feeling Hunter and Jackson's watchful presence in the doorway behind her. She sat down on the coffee table, leaning forward with her elbows on her knees.

"I need to tell you something important," she finally managed. "About your dad."

Ivy's shoulders immediately stiffened. At fourteen, she was old enough to recognize the tone that preceded bad news. Emma leaned forward, clasping her hands tightly in her lap. Sarah's little arms tightened around Pickle, confusion clouding her young face. "Is he coming home soon?"

Willow forced herself to continue, each word feeling like glass in her mouth. "Your dad... There was an incident this morning, and the police think that he was involved." She watched their expressions shift, trying to gauge how much to say at once. "We don't believe he did anything wrong, and we're going to help him, but things are going to be hard for a little while."

The silence that followed was absolute, broken only by Pickle's anxious whine.

Ivy found her voice first. Her posture stiffened, and she crossed her arms over her chest. Anger and suspicion threaded through her words. "He's in trouble, isn't he? What kind of *incident*? Why are you only telling us now?"

The breath Willow took barely made it into her lungs. They already knew. Maybe not the details, but the kids weren't stupid. They saw the way the adults were hesitating. The way no one had said Mason's name at dinner. The way Hunter, their unshakable uncle, had been tense all night.

"Did someone hurt Daddy?" Emma's lip trembled as she spoke.

Sarah's whisper was barely audible. "I want my daddy."

That simple question triggered a memory Willow had tried to bury. She was thrown back to the fateful night, standing in this same house as Cooper delivered the news about their parents and Maggy, Mason's wife. The children's mother. She remembered the cold finality of those moments, the way Mason had somehow held it together for everyone else while falling apart inside. She could still see him gathering his daughters close, explaining that Mommy was never coming home.

This was different, Willow told herself firmly. Their father was alive. But that old grief mixed with the present moment made it difficult to breathe. She swallowed, steadying herself.

"Your dad was arrested this morning," Willow said carefully. "They think he hurt someone. They think he... killed someone."

Ivy shot to her feet. "Dad wouldn't do something like that. He wouldn't hurt anyone. Why would they think he did?" Her voice rose with each question.

"We know it's not true," Willow said, cutting off Ivy's exit. "And we're going to prove it."

"If he didn't do anything, why can't he come home?" Emma's confusion was tinged with desperation.

Sarah's small voice cut through their questions. "Where is he? I want my daddy."

Willow wished she had better answers. "He's with people who are making sure everything is fair," she said, knowing how inadequate it sounded. "I don't know when he'll be home, but I promise you, we're doing everything we can to make sure he's okay."

Ivy's jaw clenched. "So, now you care? You couldn't be bothered to visit after Mom died, and now you're going to swoop back in and make everything right?" She shoved Willow aside and stormed up the stairs. "It's not fair! Dad didn't hurt anybody!"

The sharp crack of her bedroom door echoed through the house. A pain gripped Willow's heart, and her vision narrowed. Why had she taken her anger with Mason out on the girls? They hadn't deserved that, especially after they'd just lost their mother. They had needed Willow more than ever, and she wrapped herself in her work, shielding herself from a family that had done nothing but love her.

"Then why did they take him?" Emma's lip wobbled. "Ivy is right. It's not fair." She hesitated only a moment before following, her quiet footsteps a counterpoint to her sister's anger. She paused at the top of the stairs. "Is Daddy scared?"

The question nearly broke Willow. "I don't know," she admitted, moving to the bottom of the staircase. "But I know he's thinking about you."

It seemed that's all that Emma needed. She silently turned and disappeared into her bedroom.

Sarah remained on the couch, clutching Pickle for dear life. Her eyes were wide, her face wet with silent tears. "I want my daddy. When's he coming home?"

Willow's heart ached. She wanted to say soon. She wanted to promise tomorrow. But she couldn't lie to any of them.

"I don't know, sweetheart," she said softly, taking a seat beside her on the couch. "But I promise we're trying."

"Promise?" The child's voice was barely more than a squeak.

Jackson knelt beside the couch, rubbing Sarah's back. "It's okay to be scared, kiddo. But your dad's tough. And he's got all of us looking out for him."

Sarah nodded, let Pickle go, and crawled onto her aunt's lap. Willow stroked her hair and rocked the child to sleep.

After putting the tiny girl to bed, Willow sank onto the couch, exhaustion pressing down on her shoulders. She rubbed her temples, trying to ease the tension headache building behind her eyes. Jackson settled beside her, close enough that she could feel his warmth but not touching, giving her space and time to process her feelings. Jesus, she loved the man. He seemed to know exactly what she needed. After a moment, she leaned into him slightly, accepting the quiet support he offered.

Hunter's appearance in the doorway broke the moment. "Matt just called," he said, his expression grim. "He wants to meet you first thing in the morning. Both of you."

Willow straightened, her mind shifting into FBI mode despite her fatigue. "We're going to be invited to help with the case?"

"No clue. He just said he wanted to see you." Hunter paused. "I don't think he knows anything about Jackson, other than him being an FBI K9 handler. He said he wanted to see him too."

Willow felt Jackson tense slightly beside her, but his hand found hers in the shadows, squeezing gently. She wasn't ready for this, but it didn't matter. Tomorrow morning, she was walking straight into a room to the man she once thought she'd marry, the man who had burned her trust to the ground. And if Matt Carver thought he could use this case to settle old scores, he was in for a hell of a surprise. For now, they had three broken hearts upstairs to tend to, and a long night ahead.

One way or another, tomorrow would change everything.

Chapter Eight

Jackson

"Hey, Alice," Jackson said while driving through downtown Beaufort. "I just wanted to let you know what's going on here." He looked over at Willow who was staring out the passenger window of their SUV. "I can't get into too many details yet, but Willow's brother has been arrested for murder. We're working with NCIS. The murder victim was a navy petty officer."

"Uh-huh," Alice said, her voice filled with revulsion. "And by NCIS, you mean...?"

Jackson exhaled, not surprised she caught his meaning. "Yup. Matt Carver. He brought us in."

Silence. Then a clipped, "I see. You and Willow take as much time as you need. Family comes first."

"Thanks, Alice," Jackson said as he pulled into the parking lot of the Beaufort Marina. It was the nearest major parking lot to the downtown Beaufort restaurant. "We'll let you know how things are going when we learn more." He punched the 'end call' button.

Willow hopped out from the passenger seat and started making her way to Bay Street. As Jackson neared, she leaned into his shoulder "It's good having friends at the top. I was really worried she'd pull the plug on our involvement."

They walked in silence until they arrived at their destination. Jackson held the door for Willow as they entered the Blackstone

Café. The aroma of fresh coffee and sizzling bacon filled the air, mixing with the unmistakable scent of buttery grits that seemed to permeate every breakfast spot in the south. Around them, the gentle clink of plates and murmured conversations created a deceptively peaceful backdrop. Even still, it was only 8:00 AM, and already the day felt like it had stretched on for weeks.

Military personnel dotted the tables, some in crisp uniforms, others in civilian clothes, their bearing giving them away regardless of what they wore. The café's brick walls, adorned with framed photographs of local fishing boats and Marines on deployment, spoke to Beaufort's dual identity as both a military town and a slice of Low Country charm. Somewhere in the background, a radio played country music just loud enough to hear but not quite loud enough to make out the words.

The drive over had been tense. Leaving Ruby and Ranger at home hadn't been their first choice, but Cooper's wife, Genevieve, had shown up to stay with the girls, and that had sparked its own minor crisis. Ivy had planted herself in the foyer, arms crossed, insisting they didn't need a babysitter. "I can watch Emma and Sarah myself," she'd declared, her voice carrying that particular mixture of teenage defiance and wounded pride. Ever since hearing her father had been arrested, she had become increasingly hostile and belligerent.

Willow, already wound tight as a spring, had barely engaged. She'd simply stated they wouldn't be gone long and walked out, leaving Jackson to handle the fallout. He'd stepped closer to Ivy, keeping his voice low and steady. "Aunt Genevieve being here isn't about you," he'd explained. "It's about making sure you can focus on helping your dad when the time comes." Ivy's posture had softened slightly, but the resentment still simmered beneath the surface. Jackson chose to count that as a win.

Now, as they entered Blackstone's, Willow spotted Matt Carver immediately. He was sitting at a corner table, a steaming cup of coffee and three manila folders laid out in front of him like props in a play. He stood as Willow approached, an almost reflexive gesture that he seemed to regret as soon as he'd made it. His NCIS badge and sidearm were clearly visible on his belt, despite his casual attire. Jackson noted how Matt's eyes continuously tracked Willow's every movement, hungry for recognition she wasn't about to give. His eyes flicked to the engagement ring on her finger and something in his posture instantly shifted.

"Agent Carver," Jackson said, extending his hand in greeting. "I'm Special Agent Jackson Brooks, and I believe you already know Agent Banks."

Matt shook Jackson's hand, his grip strong and sure. "Please, sit. I've already eaten, but feel free to order," his voice smooth and deep.

Had Jackson not known what Matt had done to his fiancée, he'd have taken an instant liking to the man. There was something undeniably charming about him. When Jackson took his seat, Matt followed suit and motioned for Willow to sit across from him.

She didn't sit right away. She stood frozen, her shoulders tight and spine stiff, torn between staying and walking out. Finally, Willow pulled out a chair and took a seat, her voice clipped when she spoke. "Let's get this over with."

A middle-aged waitress, who looked like she'd worked there her entire life, showed up with menus, two mugs, and a carafe of coffee. "Morning. I'll give y'all a few minutes to settle in before I take your order. No rush. Just holler if you need me."

While Jackson thanked the woman, Willow poured two mugs of coffee and took a careful sip of her own.

Matt, either missing or ignoring the warning in her tone, attempted to make small talk. "You're still drinking your coffee black, huh?"

"Let's skip the nostalgia." Willow's response could have frozen the coffee in their cups.

Matt sighed, shifting in his seat. "Look, Willow—"

"Maybe we should start with why you asked us here," Jackson interrupted, recognizing the need to redirect before things deteriorated beyond repair. This meeting wasn't just about Mason's case, that much was clear, but they couldn't afford to let old wounds derail this opportunity.

Matt exhaled slowly, nodding. "Right." He straightened in his seat, his professional mask sliding into place. "Here's the situation. Our NCIS office here in Beaufort is small. We're stretched thin, handling multiple cases with limited resources. We don't have K9 units, and frankly, your expertise, both of yours, could be invaluable to this investigation."

Jackson listened carefully, noting what wasn't being said. The explanation felt convenient, perhaps too convenient. If Matt truly needed their help, why stage this meeting at a public café instead of the NCIS office? Something about it felt off, like Matt was manufacturing reasons to keep Willow close.

When he didn't get a reaction, Matt continued. "I'm pushing for your official involvement, and so far, no one's objected. It's not finalized yet, but I'm working on it."

Willow's arms crossed over her chest. "And in return?"

"You do what you do best." Matt leaned forward slightly, his coffee forgotten.

"Which is?" Willow leaned back in her chair, putting distance between them.

"Find the truth." Matt's gaze never wavered from Willow's face. "For Mason. For Petty Officer Jane Gamble. Before it gets buried under bureaucracy. I'm already getting pressured to close the case and hand it over to the federal prosecutor. It's hard to disagree. All the evidence points at Mason."

"He'd never do this," Willow said, lurching forward in her chair, looking like she was ready to peel Matt's face from his skull.

"I know," Matt said, pulling away, defensively throwing his hands up. "Mason and I have been friends since we were kids. Before our... falling out, we were inseparable." He blew out a long, slow breath. "The reason I'm on this case is because it's well known that Mason hates me. My boss figures I'll use that to put him away, ASAP. I don't want to do that. I mean, if he's guilty I'll make sure he pays, but if he's not, I'm not going to let him get railroaded into serving a life sentence for something he didn't do."

Jackson glanced at Willow, trying to gauge her reaction. He expected her to push back, to challenge Matt's obvious manipulation. Instead, she reached for one of folders on the table. Matt pinned it down for a second before releasing it to her grip. The entire time, he kept watching her face, like he was waiting for something more. The heavy silence settled over them, filled only by the background noise of the café and the soft rustle of papers as Willow opened the folder.

Jackson couldn't shake the feeling that the NCIS agent was holding back. His offer made sense on the surface, they could certainly help with the investigation, but there was an undertone that set his instincts on edge. He'd learned to trust his intuition over his years with the FBI, and right now, it was telling him that Matt Carver wasn't showing all his cards.

Matt pushed a folder toward Jackson before he pulled out a photograph and slid it onto the table. A young woman in crisp dress whites smiled back at them, her dark hair neatly tucked into a regulation bun.

"Jane Gamble," Matt said. "Twenty-seven. Petty Officer Second Class in the Navy, a Master-at-Arms. Basically, the navy's version of military police. She was originally from Pennsylvania." He paused, letting the image sink in. "She was stationed at MCAS Beaufort two years ago. Ever since her posting, she'd been assigned to gate duty where she'd checked IDs and monitored who came and went. According to her supervisor, she requested that task specifically. It allowed her to study during the long stretches of downtime at the gate."

"To study what?" Willow asked.

"Apparently, she was taking online courses. She made it clear to everyone that navy life was not for her and that she was working toward a position with the Bureau of Intelligence and Research in the State Department."

And she used the post to learn who came and went from the base every day, but for what exactly?

"She was an MP who wanted a job in the INR," Jackson said as he studied the photo, noting the intelligence and determined look in Jane's eyes.

Matt continued, "In her off time, she moonlighted as a security guard for Maritime Defense Solutions, a private security firm run by a guy named Sean Fitzpatrick."

Jackson immediately recognized that name, Fitzpatrick. Hunter had said the house was owned by Liam Fitzpatrick. It couldn't have been a coincidence.

"Moonlighting?" Willow's eyebrow raised. "That's allowed?"

"With proper authorization, yes." Matt's fingers drummed once on the table. "She was swimming in student loan debt, to the tune of one hundred thousand bucks. Jane had high aspirations, but she wasn't too bright."

Jackson found that hard to believe. A candidate for the INR would need to be exceptionally intelligent. "What led you to that conclusion?"

"She filed multiple complaints against Maritime Workforce Solutions," he said.

The cocky challenge in his voice grated on Jackson's nerves. He looked at Willow, whose expression appeared to be carved from granite. Whatever emotion she was feeling, she locked it away for no one to see.

"Maritime Workforce Solutions," Matt continued, "is owned by Michael Fitzpatrick, Sean Fitzpatrick's older brother. The home where she was working as a security guard is owned by Liam Fitzpatrick, their eldest brother. She was literally biting the hand that fed her."

Jackson watched Matt's face, looking for tells, but the man's expression remained carefully neutral. Willow's fingers tightened almost imperceptibly on her coffee cup. She, too, had caught the contradiction in Matt's statement. Jane wasn't stupid. If she was stirring the pot, she had been doing it for a reason. Whatever that reason was, it had died with her.

"Is that everything you've got?" Willow asked, a keen edge to her words.

"So far," Matt said, unable to hide his annoyance at the question. "The case is barely a day old, and like I said, our office is small."

"Why haven't you received more help then?" Willow shot back. "You've got a dead petty officer and you're the only one assigned to the case. Are you saying NCIS couldn't spare anyone from Charleston to come down and help out?"

"The case looks open and shut," Matt said. "Of course the brass isn't going to waste resources trying to prove something everyone already knows. I was told to wrap it up, not dig into it. Even so, I'm digging into it as a courtesy to my oldest friend, and as a favor to you."

"A favor?" Willow stood. "A fucking favor. To me?"

"Do you think we can get access to the house?" Jackson said, gently placing his hand on Willow's forearm. She glared at him for an instant before forcibly calming herself. "We can pick up the dogs and be there in twenty minutes."

"The NCIS response team is at the crime scene now," Matt said, closing his notebook. "I can't promise you access, but if you show up..." He shrugged. "I doubt anyone will throw you out."

It was a tenuous opening at best, and Jackson could see Willow recognized it for what it was. She leaned across the table, her voice low and threatening. "If this is about me, don't waste my time."

"This is about Jane Gamble. And Mason." Matt held her stare. "That's all."

Jackson stayed quiet, watching the exchange. He could see that Willow was barely holding it together by the rigid set of her spine, and the way her fingers flexed against the table. And Matt, for all his efforts to stay professional, couldn't quite hide his personal stake in this. His offer of help felt genuine enough, but there was clearly something self-serving beneath the razor-thin veneer.

"If we're doing this," Jackson finally said, "we need everything you've got."

Matt dipped his chin once without looking away from Willow. "It's all in the folders I gave you. The entire transcript of my conversation with Mason is in there too. I assumed you'd want to see that, too."

Willow closed her folder with deliberate care, tapping it once against the table's surface. "I want to talk with my brother," she said. "Without you."

"I can arrange that," Matt said, "but it will likely get me in hot water with my boss. She's going to hear Mason had *guests* and the sign-in log is going to show it was you." As his gaze drifted between the two FBI special agents, a small, awkward chuckle escaped his lips. "But it won't be the first time I ruffle some feathers. I'll meet you at the provost marshal's office at ten."

When Matt didn't get the reaction he was clearly hoping for, he rose from the table. "It was a pleasure to meet you, Agent Brooks." He turned to Willow and inclined his head slightly. "I hope we can find some time to talk. I have a lot to tell you."

"I'm sure you do," Willow said. "And whatever it is, you can keep it the fuck to yourself. I'm here to help my brother and that's all."

"Are y'all ready to order?" the waitress asked before dropping her voice low. "I don't know what's going on here, and I don't care, but whatever tiff you two are having, you can take it outside. I'll not have a scene. Do you understand me?"

"Yes," Willow said, her voice turning to the waitress. "I'd like an order of shrimp and grits, rye toast on the side."

Not until Matt had left did Jackson give his breakfast order. He had no appetite, but he expected it was going to be a very long day, so he made sure to order a hearty meal. For the next forty-five minutes, the two agents ate in relative silence, each of them processing the interaction and the file folders in front of them.

When it was time to go, Jackson paid the bill and left a sizable tip for the waitress as an apology for any distress they may have caused her.

"He's up to something," Willow said as they stepped out of the café. She stormed down the street, forcing Jackson to take long strides to keep up. She didn't speak again until they reached the vehicle, letting out a sharp exhale as she yanked open the driver's door.

"Clearly," Jackson said, sliding into the passenger seat. "And I think you're the only reason we're on this case."

Willow tossed the file onto the dashboard with more force than necessary. "Let's go talk to Mason." Her voice carried the weight of someone preparing for battle, and Jackson couldn't shake the feeling that their breakfast meeting had been just the opening salvo of a much larger conflict.

Chapter Nine

Willow

The Provost Marshal's Office at MCAS Beaufort wasn't built to impress. A squat, utilitarian building of weathered brick and narrow windows, it served its purpose without pretense. Willow felt the weight of every step as she approached the entrance, Jackson's steady presence at her side doing little to calm the storm brewing in her chest.

Matt Carver stood at the front desk, flipping through his phone like he had all the time in the world. His NCIS badge caught the fluorescent light. The deliberate display of authority made Willow's jaw clench.

The processing paperwork had been completed yesterday, which meant Mason had already been interviewed by NCIS. By Matt. The thought made her stomach turn.

An MP stepped out from behind a nondescript gray door, his expression impassive. "He's ready," he said, directing the words at Matt. His gaze flicked over the group. "There are only four chairs in the room. Do you want me to grab another?"

Matt shook his head and led the way. "I'll be standing during this interview."

"I want to speak with him alone," Willow stated, wondering who the fifth person in the room would be. "That was our agreement."

Matt ignored the comment and continued forward.

The MP used an RFID badge hanging from his belt to get past the entry lock. He held the door for them, but there was no kindness in his eyes. Willow's brother had been arrested for killing one of their own. Not something the marines were known for letting go of easily.

The interview room was just as sterile and lifeless as the rest of the building. Mason sat behind a metal table, wrists bound to a chain bolted at the center. Dark circles shadowed his eyes, stubble roughening his jaw, but his posture hadn't lost its old, unshakable pride. The moment Willow entered, his gaze locked onto hers, and for a heartbeat, she was seventeen again, standing in their parents' kitchen, the echo of screaming matches about Matt still ringing in her ears.

In the quiet moment that followed, Willow saw the sorrow in Mason's eyes. Was it for what he'd done to her, or that he was caught in a situation where he needed her help?

Matt closed the door with a deliberate click, taking up position against the wall. "I'll be observing."

Mason's eyes flickered to Matt. "Back for round two? You didn't believe me the first time?"

"I'm not the one asking the questions this time," Matt stated, motioning with his head to Willow.

He had kept his voice professional, but she could feel the tension behind the words. Willow took the seat across from Mason, grateful for Jackson's silent presence beside her as he settled into the adjacent chair. Hunter, who Willow hadn't even noticed until now, was sitting quietly next to their older brother. He acknowledged her presence with a curt nod.

"Didn't think you'd come." Mason's voice was rough, like he hadn't slept or that he'd been waiting for her.

"You're my brother, Mason." The words came automatically, but even now, they didn't sit right. Because deep down, she wasn't sure what hurt her more, the way Matt had betrayed her, or the way Mason had rammed the ugly truth of her ex-fiancé's infidelity down her throat. "But that doesn't mean I don't still hate you."

A ghost of a smile touched his lips, familiar and painful. "Fair enough."

Hunter cleared his throat, adjusting his tie. "In the interest of efficiency, I suggest we redirect our focus to the pertinent facts of the case."

Willow gave him a nod before turning her attention to her eldest brother. "Tell me why you were at the house so late at night."

Mason closed his eyes and groaned. "Like I've said, over and over, to get my wallet."

"This is the first time I'm hearing it," Willow said. She wanted to reach across the table and punch him in the face. "The people you told before weren't me, and I want to hear it directly from you. Don't give me an abridged version. I want every single detail."

"Fine," he said, giving in to his sister's demand. "When I came into the house, I called out to let Jane know I was there. There were lights on and I could see a dining room chair flipped over. I went to fix it and that's when I saw Jane lying on the floor with a knife in her chest. Her shirt was open, and she was covered in blood." His breaths came in short bursts. "She wasn't moving. I called 911. I don't remember what I said, but while I was talking to the operator, Jane moved. I hung up and dropped down beside her."

Mason lifted his head, his gaze boring into Willow's eyes. "I swear to God, she just lost it. One second she wasn't moving, and the next she was clawing at my face in complete hysterics. She must have thought I was the person who attacked her." He touched his face where three ugly red welts cut across his cheek. "I grabbed her wrist to stop her. I didn't want her to move. I think that's when she saw the knife and started screaming that it was burning and that she needed to get it out. I tried to stop her, but I was too slow."

Deep lines formed across his brow and his face contorted with revulsion. "She yanked it out and blood gushed from the wound. I took the knife away from her. I was afraid she'd try to stab me with it. I think that's when the cop showed up. I don't remember much after that."

Everything he said tracked with what Cooper had told her, and with what was in Matt's report. But hearing it from Mason himself, watching the way his jaw clenched and his fingers curled into fists, made it harder to stay detached. He looked shaken. Maybe even guilty. But not like a killer.

Willow exhaled slowly, forcing her voice to stay steady. "Tell me about Petty Officer Jane Gamble and your relationship with her."

His expression hardened. "We didn't have a relationship. We had sex. One time."

Matt stepped closer. "You told me that you two argued a lot."

Willow spun in her chair and glared at her ex.

So much for observing.

Matt rolled his eyes and returned to his place against the wall.

Mason exhaled, the chain rattling as he shifted in his chair. "She was always asking questions. Bothering my workers. Slowing us down." His jaw tightened. "She was bothering my crew *and* the migrant workers, the ones training for when the B&B opened. She was forever taking notes."

"Who'd the migrants work for?" Willow asked.

"How would I know? Ask the owner, Liam Fitzpatrick." Frustration crept into his voice. "I had more than enough work to do. I had no business with the staff, other than them cleaning and cooking us food."

"They cooked for you?" Willow leaned forward, catching the slight shift in Mason's expression. Something about this detail mattered, though she couldn't yet say why.

"Yes, they cooked for everyone." Mason shifted in his seat, the cuffs clinking against the chain. "Like I said, they were training to work at the B&B. They did everything but renovations." His brow furrowed. "Well, except for the gardeners... they worked non-stop preparing the grounds. Watching them was exhausting. They barely even took time to eat before they were back at it. If they stopped, they looked nervous."

Willow leaned in, catching something in his tone. "What do you mean?"

"At first, I didn't think much of it," Mason admitted, his gaze unfocused. "The men worked themselves to exhaustion, while some of the women spent more time practicing English with my crew than doing their jobs. Jane was the one who noticed they seemed afraid. Especially when their supervisor showed up. She insisted something was off."

Jackson frowned beside her. "Did she say why?"

Mason shook his head, the movement clipped and frustrated. "No. But, like every other concern, she wouldn't let it go. That was our last fight before..." His gaze slid away, fixing on the blank wall. "Before we hooked up."

Willow's mind raced with possibilities, each more troubling than the last. "So, she thought they were being mistreated?"

"Maybe." Mason's shoulders lifted in a half-shrug.

The implications made Willow's stomach churn. Her voice turned sharp, cutting through the room's stale air. "And instead of figuring out why she was so damn interested, you slept with her?"

Mason's head snapped up, his eyes blazing. "What? Are you suddenly the morality police? Matt was screwing around on you for months." He glared at the NCIS agent. "I told you, and told you, and yet, you were still willing to marry him." His voice trailed off, gaze shifting between Willow and Matt. "You know what? Never mind. It doesn't matter anymore. You already threw his sorry ass to the curb."

Matt exhaled through his nose, the tension in his shoulders tightening. "You think I give a damn about that right now?" His voice was measured but clipped, like he was forcing himself to stay professional. "Let's stay focused on Jane, shall we?"

Mason barked out a humorless laugh. "Oh, I think we should. You're the one running this show now, aren't you? It must feel pretty damn good, you finally holding all the cards. That's what this is, isn't it? Payback for proving to my sister that you're a lowlife scumbag who can't keep his dick in his pants?"

Matt's expression darkened, his jaw tight. "I'm running this case because NCIS assigned it to me."

"Enough. Both of you." Willow's hands curled into fists against the metal table. "Mason, I need facts, not your bullshit."

Mason shook his head, the chain rattling with the movement. "Fine. You want facts? Here's one for you. I don't know why Jane gave a damn about those workers, but it wasn't just curiosity. She was looking for something. And she was nervous."

Hunter leaned forward, his lawyer's instincts engaged. "Nervous how?"

"She didn't say," Mason admitted, frustration evident in every line of his body. "But she kept saying something wasn't right."

"You didn't mention this earlier," Matt said, stepping in between Willow and Jackson. He pressed his hands against the table and leaned across. "Maybe twenty-four hours in holding gave you time to concoct some lame excuses. Why did she keep saying something wasn't right and not tell you what?"

"Fuck you," Mason shot back.

"You're going to spend the rest of your life in prison," Matt spat.

Willow stood, grabbed Matt by the shoulder and shoved him away from the table.

"We're done here." Jackson's voice cut through the tension like a knife.

Willow spun to face him, heat rising in her cheeks. "Excuse me?"

His expression remained calm, but his tone left no room for argument. "We're getting nowhere. You're fighting Mason, Mason's fighting Matt, and we're not going to get anything new out of this interview."

"And what do you suggest?" Willow's words came out more condescending than intended.

Jackson crossed his arms, meeting her glare steadily. "I go with Matt to the crime scene. You go to the ME's office."

The suggestion hung in the air for a moment before understanding dawned. He was trying to keep her and Matt apart. And despite her irritation, she felt a surge of gratitude. They gathered their things, the scrape of chairs and rustle of papers filling the silence. As Willow reached for the door, Mason's voice stopped her.

"Will?"

She hesitated, hand on the handle.

His voice was quieter now, almost vulnerable. "You believe me, right? You know I wouldn't do this."

The words twisted something deep inside her. Mason had betrayed her trust before. But murder? No. Not that. She exhaled, staring at the door handle like it held all the answers.

"I know you didn't kill her." It was the only truth she could offer. And the only thing she was sure of. "If I had any doubt, I wouldn't be here." She stepped out of the room.

"Are the girls okay?" Mason called out.

"They're struggling," she said, turning to face him. Her anger wavered at the sight of his concern. "Ivy is trying to be strong, Sarah doesn't understand, and Emma..." Willow stepped back into the room, and her voice softened. "They're all scared. In one night, they lost their mother and their grandparents, and now they're afraid they're losing you too."

For the first time, Willow saw fear in her brother's eyes. "You'll look after them, right? You'll help them through this?"

The question twisted Willow's gut. She loved her nieces with all her heart, and it killed her to not have seen them for so long.

"Promise me you'll help them through this. They look up to you. All of them. Ivy has never stopped asking how you are and why you don't come visit."

Willow's throat tightened. She needed to leave before she broke down. "I'll do what I can to watch over them until I can get you out."

Mason folded his hands together and bent over at the waste. He held that pose for several seconds before responding. "Thank you, Willow. Knowing you're there means the world to them. To me."

Chapter Ten

Jackson

Jackson reviewed Officer Kent Dade's report while he sat in the Beaufort PD's interrogation room. Matt was supposed to be taking him to visit the crime scene, but the NCIS forensic team didn't want anyone there until they had finished their investigation. Rather than sit on their hands, Jackson suggested they have a talk with the officer. Cooper had set it up to have access to the police station and its resources.

Nerves flooded Jackson, making him jumpy. He needed Kent's words to match Mason's, for Willow's sake. She wouldn't admit it, but if the cracks widened and Mason's story didn't hold, it would break something inside her. Jackson wasn't about to let that happen.

He blew out a long breath as he flipped the page. Nothing in the officer's report suggested anything other than Mason's guilt. From an outsider's perspective, it appeared open and shut, but in Jackson's experience, nothing was ever that cut and dry. It was also commonplace for officers to include only what they deemed necessary in their report, and he was hoping to unearth something meaningful.

Reviewing the report had the added bonus of avoiding a conversation with the NCIS agent who had hurt his fiancée.

"How long have you been with Willow?" Matt asked, breaking the awkward silence.

"Excuse me?" Jackson replied, setting the report down, his gaze intensifying. The casual tone, the way Matt leaned back like this was some friendly chat, set Jackson's teeth on edge.

"How long have you been partners with her?" Matt asked. "I heard what happened to Kate. I know that wasn't long ago."

Jackson's fingers curled around the edge of the file. Willow still had nightmares about Kate, about the raid, the gunfire, the split-second decision she'd made that had changed everything. She had rushed in when Kate had told her to hold. Ranger, Kate's K9, had followed. If Kate hadn't thrown herself in harm's way, the dog would be dead. Instead, Kate had made the ultimate sacrifice and took the bullet that ended her life. Willow still blamed herself. Probably always would.

"And how the hell would you know about Kate's death?" Jackson said through clenched teeth.

Matt shrugged, too nonchalant. "I know things."

Of course he did. Jackson forced himself to take a slow breath. "Are you stalking her?"

Matt shifted uncomfortably in his chair. "No," he said defensively. "I still have friends in the bureau. They told me Kate had been killed. You, of all people, should know that these aren't just people you work with. They are people who become a part of your life. A part of your family." He crossed his arms over his chest. "Obviously Willow told you about us."

"Obviously," Jackson said. He already had his nose buried in the NCIS reports. His emotions were on the verge of bubbling over, so he thought it was best to avoid continuing the conversation. That decision lasted about three seconds. "Why did you invite us to assist? NCIS typically circles the wagons when they've got a case. Unless there is a specific reason to involve outside federal agencies, they keep things internal."

"I owed it to them," Matt said, his voice quieter. He seemed to struggle to maintain eye contact. "To both of them. I fucked up, as I'm sure you already know. I torched their trust. I burned it to the ground. This might be my only shot to rebuild it."

"And you think this makes it all go away?" Jackson leaned back and mirrored Matt, crossing his arms over his chest.

"Of course not..." Matt moved to the door, using his body to block anyone from coming in. "I was ordered to wrap this case up fast. Gather what I could to build a clean case against Mason, and hand it over to the federal prosecutor. No complications. No alternate theories. Just make it fit."

Matt's mouth twisted, his voice tightening. "My boss doesn't want questions. Just a conviction."

Jackson had seen cases like this before: rushed, railroaded, and built to convict rather than uncover the truth. The pattern was all too familiar. But hearing it from Matt, the man who had wrecked Willow, made his blood run hot.

Matt stared intently at his shoes. "Mason is the best man I've ever known. The guy's a fucking boy scout. He'd take a bullet to protect someone he didn't even know. There is no way he'd kill that woman. It's fucking impossible."

Jackson looked at Matt in a new light. His current behavior didn't excuse his past, but he was clearly going out of his way to make reparations. "Does your boss know you've invited us to help?"

"Not yet," he said, stuffing his hands in his pockets. "But my SSA's no idiot. Vicky Davidson's a bulldog, and she'll sniff this out soon enough. I had to get special clearance to get the FBI onto the base. She's close friends with the provost marshal. I doubt he'd go running to her with the news, but I'm sure it'll come up in conversation."

The door banged into Matt's back, earning a grunt from whoever was trying to enter. "Officer Dade?" he asked as he moved aside.

"Were you expecting someone else?" Dade said, scratching his oversized belly. "I got a call telling me to haul my ass over here. I was in bed. I work the night shift, you know."

"Take a seat, Officer," Matt said.

"We'd just like to review what happened yesterday morning," Jackson said. Matt's gaze snapped towards him, his mouth hard. He had told Jackson, in no uncertain terms, that he was an observer for this interview.

"It's all in my report," Dade said. "You can read it as many times as you like." He reached for the doorknob.

"Sit," Matt said. "You're going to tell us in your own words what transpired yesterday. We have questions."

Jackson didn't know what this policeman's issue was, but his attitude was equal parts arrogance and belligerence. He yanked a chair out and plopped himself into it. "Ask away."

"In your report," Matt said, snatching the folder away from Jackson's hand, "you stated that you received a call from dispatch at 4:43 AM regarding a 911 call, and you immediately headed to 400 Port Republic Street. Is that correct?"

"Mmhmm," Dade replied. He had the attitude of a spoiled twelve-year-old, and it grated on Jackson. Matt, surprisingly, didn't even seem to notice.

"Interesting," Matt said, his eyes narrowing. "According to the dispatcher's log, you were contacted again at 05:19 AM, and you hadn't made entry into the home yet. Where were you when the first call came in?"

Dade's maintained his disconnected demeanor, but his upper lip twitched at the question. "Same route as always," he muttered, scratching at his belly. "I don't keep a log of every damn minute. I was patrolling, doing my normal rounds."

"Funny that you don't remember," Matt said. "How's about I refresh your memory. According to your dispatcher, you were at the Taco Bell on Sea Island Parkway, and according to Google

Maps, you were about seven minutes away. At that time of night, with lights and sirens, you should have been able to make it there in under five. So, my question is, why the delay?"

Dade crossed his arms, resting them on his fat belly. "There was no rush. There never is when old lady Hargrove calls in an emergency."

"Have you been cleared by the chief to decide which 911 calls you can ignore?" Matt's tone sharpened. "So what is it, Officer? Are you lazy, incompetent, or just flat-out lying to me?"

"I'm none of those things!" Dade shifted in his chair and looked to Jackson for help. "I had to take a dump. End of mystery. What did you expect me to do? I had the shits, and the woman has been calling in complaints ever since renovations started on the house next door. If it's not one thing, it's another. She stands outside and watches, all day, every day. I think she's looking to jam up Fitzpatrick because he wants to turn the house into a bed and breakfast."

Jackson didn't agree with the officer's choosing to delay visiting the site, but if this woman was a habitual crank caller, he could sympathize.

"Are you referring to Liam Fitzpatrick, the property owner?" Matt asked. "Why would you think that?"

Dade got a conspiratorial look about him, and he leaned forward. "Old Lady Hargrove's been gunning for Fitzpatrick ever since he fast-tracked that B&B permit," Dade's voice became biting, like he was sharing critical intelligence. "She claims it's illegal. Says the board shut it down, but Fitzpatrick pulled strings."

"I take it this Fitzpatrick fellow is rich and well connected?" Jackson asked.

Matt and Dade nodded in unison. "His father, Liam Fitzpatrick Sr, was a self-made multi-millionaire. He owned several hotels and a dozen rental houses in Beaufort County," Matt said. "Along with a small fleet of shrimp and fishing boats, a security firm, and a placement agency. After he was executed by an ex-marine, his sons took over the operations. All indications suggest that they are even better businessmen than Liam Sr. was."

"Executed?" Jackson asked. "What do you mean?"

"It was two years ago," Matt said. "It made national news. Liam Fitzpatrick Sr. got busted for cocaine possession with intent to distribute. He had nearly thirty kilos worth. Nobody had ever suspected he was a criminal, right up until, in a strange twist of fate, he got caught because of a random fisheries inspection. They wanted to see what fish he had brought in and found a boatload of coke instead. He had promised to testify in exchange for full immunity. According to Fitzpatrick, he was just a middleman, and that there were much bigger fish to catch. He was to meet with the State's Attorney on the morning of his arraignment. When he stepped out of the transport vehicle, his killer opened fire. Fitzpatrick Sr., along with two state prison officials, died on scene."

"Do you know who hired the assassin?" Jackson asked.

"We never found out," Matt said with a shrug. "State police shot and killed him on scene."

"Did it lead to any other arrests?" Jackson asked, growing frustrated with the never-ending dead-ends.

"No," Matt said. "The shooter had no ties to Beaufort or anyone in the area. He lived in Miami for most of his post-military life."

"Is there anything else you need from me..." Dade said. When Matt didn't respond, he shifted his bulk and rose from the chair. "Okay then, it's been a pleasure chatting with you." The words dripped with over-stated sarcasm.

"Sit," Jackson said, his voice firm and authoritative. "I'm not done with you yet."

"We're done," Matt said. "I got what I wanted."

"I didn't," Jackson said, glaring at the other agent. "Tell me what you saw when you found Mr. Banks and the victim together."

"It's in my report," Dade said, his annoyed demeanor rising to the surface again. "The perp was straddling the woman holding a knife, and she was screaming her lungs out. Blood was pumping out of her chest like a geyser."

"What did the *suspect* do when you announced your presence?" Jackson asked.

"I ordered the *perp* to drop his weapon, or I'd shoot him dead."

Jackson wanted to smack the officer upside the head for his refusal to refer to Mason by the proper term, but it wasn't a hill to die on. Not yet anyway. He stepped closer and dropped his voice low. "You didn't answer my question. I asked what Mr. Banks did when you announced yourself. I didn't ask what you said."

Confusion spread across Dade's face. "He dropped the knife?"

"Are you asking me or telling me, Officer?" Jackson said. "What did he do when you announced yourself? What was his reaction? Did he look frightened or worried? Did he look guilty?"

Dade scratched his head. "None of those things, I guess." He looked away, searching his memory. "He threw the knife aside, well out of reach. He didn't even fight it." His forehead creased. "If anything... he almost looked relieved. Like... like he wanted to be caught."

"Did he say anything?" Jackson pushed.

"Not really," Dade said with a shrug. "He got off the woman, and I cuffed him to the banister. After that, I radioed the precinct, asking for backup and the medical examiner."

"You didn't render aid to the victim?" Matt jumped in. "Why not?"

"She was dead. There wasn't anything anyone could do for her."

"Are you a doctor?" Matt said. "First you decide what 911 calls are important, and then you decide whether or not a victim needs medical attention."

"I know an arterial spray when I see one," Dade said, pushing to his feet. "By the time I had cuffed the perp, she had stopped gushing. Her heart had stopped. Maybe if I was a fucking surgeon in an operating room, I could have done something. Could you, Special Agent Matt Carver? Could you have saved her?"

"Are you sure Mr. Mason didn't say anything?" Jackson said, stepping in between the two men. At six-foot-three, he was a good head taller than the patrolman. Dade ignored Jackson and glared at Matt. "Answer my question, Officer."

"Yeah," he snapped. "He said for me to call Sergeant Cooper Banks. I told him I'm not a fucking messenger service. When I called it in, I said who I had. If dispatch chose to call Banks, that was up to them."

"You recognized the suspect?" Jackson asked.

"Sure," Dade said with a shrug. "I've seen him around. Beaufort's not that big and the Banks family has lived here as long as I can remember."

"Did you read him his rights?" Jackson asked.

The steam in Dade's fury leaked out, and his shoulders sagged. "I might have. I don't remember. I frisked him, checking to make sure he didn't have any weapons or drugs on him."

"And?" Jackson said. "What did you find on his person?"

"Keys," Dade said. "I found his keyring filled with keys."

"Nothing else?" Jackson asked. "No wallet?"

Dade shook his head. "No. Just keys."

"I'm done now," Jackson said to Matt. "If your CSI team hasn't cleared the scene, I'd like to talk with the neighbor. If she's got a friendly ear, she might have a lot more to share with us."

Chapter Eleven

Willow

As Willow pushed through the double doors, the stench slammed into her—a revolting mix of antiseptic cleanser, decomposing flesh, and the metallic tang of blood. The morgue at MCAS Beaufort was small but efficient, its white walls and stainless-steel counters bathed in fluorescent light, refrigeration units humming steadily in the background.

Dr. Aaron Patel barely looked up from his paperwork. His scrubs had the faded softness of fabric washed a hundred times, and his salt-and-pepper hair stuck up in weary disarray. He reminded her of other medical examiners she'd worked with before—competent, no-nonsense, and perpetually tired.

"Special Agent Willow Banks," she said, flashing her credentials. "I'd like to ask you some questions regarding Petty Officer Gamble."

"Didn't expect the FBI on this one," he said, finally meeting her eyes. His tone wasn't hostile, just wary. "NCIS is protective of their cases."

"Special conditions," Willow said, tucking away her badge. "Joint operation."

Patel's eyebrow rose slightly, but he didn't push. "Banks?" he said, skepticism evident in the word. "Any relation to the suspect, Mason Banks?"

"He's my brother," Willow replied. She had hoped he wouldn't have noticed.

"And you're here to gather information that will exonerate your brother?" He walked over to his computer and paused. "Is that why you're here?"

"If my brother is guilty," Willow said, meaning it completely, "I expect him to be punished. But I also won't allow him to be railroaded if he's innocent."

"Fair enough," Patel said. "But I don't understand why you're here to speak with me. I've already sent my preliminary autopsy results to Agent Carver. If you're working in a joint operation, why hasn't he shared them with you already?"

"That's a good question," Willow said, her annoyance rising. "But my partner and I were only read in this morning. I guess Agent Carver neglected to include your report in our briefing material. Can you help me out or do you need confirmation from NCIS?"

"Unnecessary," Patel said as he logged into his computer. "If you didn't have permission to be here, you'd never have made it into my morgue." He opened a folder that contained photos of the dead petty officer.

Willow's breath hitched before she could stop it. Jane Gamble's body was a map of violence. The images highlighted her bruises, defensive wounds, and the fatal stab wound that turned her white skin into a canvas of red. She forced her hands to stay loose, not curl into fists. She had seen worse. Dealt with worse. But this was different. This was her brother's life on the line.

"She was stabbed with an eight-inch kitchen blade," Patel began, his voice taking on the detached tone medical examiners used when discussing the dead. He hesitated before adding, "The suspect's fingerprints are all over it, but that doesn't always mean what people think."

The hair on Willow's neck stood on end. "Meaning?"

Patel sighed, scrubbing a hand over his face. "You're not here to confirm what we already know, are you?"

"I'm here for the truth," Willow replied.

"That's what I'm trying to give you," Patel said, clicking to the next photo. "And the truth is... it's messy." He gestured to one particularly graphic image. "The blade nicked the ascending aorta, likely on the way in, but that's educated conjecture." He pointed to a closeup of the artery. "See here, the smooth cut along the vessel's edge. It didn't kill her immediately. And see here," he said, referencing a ragged edge beside the smooth cut. "The blood pressure eventually ruptured the artery completely. After that, she had maybe twenty seconds before she completely exsanguinated."

"According to the suspect," Willow said, trying to remain detached, "he called 911 as soon as he found her, before the knife was removed from her chest."

"Even if the EMTs had arrived immediately," the ME said with a grimace. "Unless they were cardiac surgeons, I don't think it would have mattered. Like I said, she bled out almost instantly."

The nature of Jane Gamble's death didn't tell Willow anything useful. Mason admitted he was there, and he didn't refute the eyewitness account that he was holding the knife.

"You said fingerprints on the weapon doesn't always mean what people think," Willow said. "Was there something about them that gave you pause to believe my brother had murdered this woman?"

The ME studied her for a long moment, then turned back to the photos. "The attack itself was brutal, but not chaotic. Whoever did this knew exactly where to put that knife. One precise strike." He met her eyes again. "Look at the angle of the blade." He flipped through the photos until he got to an external image, pre-autopsy. "If the suspect had been straddling her, the blade's angle would have likely been vertical. This was horizontal, designed to slip between her ribs. In my professional experience, that's not how crimes of passion usually play out. The positioning of the palm print left on the blade don't line up the way I'd expect."

"So, you think my brother's innocent?" Willow asked, trying not to get ahead of herself. "Because of how he was holding the knife?"

Dr. Patel sighed. "It's not conclusive by any stretch, but it raises questions. It's entirely possible that the suspect stabbed the victim, she fell away, and then he pulled out the knife using an overhand grip. With the amount of smeared blood on the weapon, it would be impossible to pull any latent prints."

"Fair enough," Willow said. Even if it wasn't conclusive, it was something to work with. Circumstantial evidence, in sufficient quantity, can easily exonerate a suspect. "What else can you tell me about the victim?"

"Physically," he said with a shrug. "She had a bad case of psoriasis on her hands and forearms."

"Is that important to the investigation?"

"No," the doctor said, not in and of itself. "But what is important is that she fought back. Hard."

The next series of photos showed defensive wounds including bruised wrists, and a darkened cheek. "Based on the pattern of bruising on her wrists, I believe her attacker was male with very large hands. He beat her and restrained her," Patel continued. "We found blood and skin under her fingernails. Whoever did this had grabbed her arms before he bound her wrists together. The transfer of Jane's medicated hand lotion might have resulted in easily identifiable fingerprints at the scene."

Willow shot him a questioning look. It was, at best, a long shot. If the killer was a professional like the stabbing suggested, he'd have been wearing gloves.

The look wasn't lost on the doctor. "I know," he said with a sympathetic tone. "It's not much, but DNA analysis might offer some insights. There was a significant amount of tissue under the petty officer's nails. There is no doubt she scratched your brother, but if she also scratched her killer, it would give you a better chance of identifying him. But, as I'm sure you're well aware, it will be a while before we get the results."

A while... could be days or even weeks. It was unlikely they had a lab on base. Willow figured it'd go to Charleston, where everyone in this area sent their samples for analysis. She was certain they'd have put a rush on it, but so did everyone else.

Willow understood. She let out a small breath, trying to maintain professional decorum. When Patel switched to the sexual assault evidence, her composure cracked.

"There was bruising and tearing around the anal region," he said softly, more gently than before. "Consistent with sexual assault." He highlighted another note on his screen. "But we also found vaginal lubricant and spermicide jelly, which suggests consensual intercourse as well."

Willow exhaled sharply, shaking her head.

"Jesus."

It wouldn't hold up in court, but no way had her brother slept with Jane and then returned an hour later to rape her. A good attorney might be able to use these details to create doubt in the jury, but it likely wouldn't be enough for a not guilty verdict.

"Mason's DNA?" Willow forced herself to ask. "I know you won't get any results back for a while, but..."

"No sperm was found in or around her anus," Patel replied, then added carefully, "Though that doesn't clear him. He could've used a condom."

Willow's fingernails dug into her palms. The evidence was a twisted maze. Some pointing to Mason's guilt, and some suggesting his innocence.

"Dr. Patel," she started, then paused, choosing her words carefully. "In your experience, does this feel like a crime of passion? Or something more... deliberate?"

"If someone had come to deliberately kill her," he replied. "He'd have either used a gun, or a blade of his own choosing. The use of a kitchen knife makes it look more like a weapon of opportunity."

The implication hung heavy in the air.

"Let's look at the lab analysis," Patel said, clicking through to another set of reports. "We've got tissue, fiber, stomach contents, and blood work all running. Early results show no drugs or alcohol in her system." He paused, squinting at the screen. "Last meal was pepperoni pizza, probably eaten about three hours before death."

"That matches the timeline Mason gave," Willow noted, more to herself than Patel. Her phone buzzed in her pocket, but she chose to ignore it. She wanted to stay focused on the task at hand.

"Fiber evidence is interesting," he continued, enlarging an image. "We're still waiting on complete analysis, but preliminary findings show multiple types, including some synthetic ones." He gestured to a particular section. "These don't appear to match the work clothes the suspect was wearing, but it's something else for us to look at more closely."

He switched to another file, and Willow recognized her brother's booking photos. "Now, about Mason Banks." Patel's voice took on a more measured tone. "When he was brought in, he was in shock but otherwise physically unharmed. Except for the scratches."

The photos showed angry red marks across Mason's face and neck, but what caught Willow's attention was a separate set of images showing his back.

"Two distinct sets," Patel explained. "The ones on his face and neck were fresh and consistent with the timeline of his arrest. But these wounds," he said, pointing to Mason's back, "were already scabbing. At least three hours old."

"What does all this tell you?" Willow asked. Her pulse was racing, while a dull ache was pushing behind her eyes.

Patel carefully closed the file. "I think it means there are questions that need answering."

"Can you call me when you get any of the lab results back?" she asked in a hopeful tone. "I'd really appreciate it."

***

The cold December air outside the morgue felt like a slap, but Willow welcomed it. She needed the shock to clear her head. The autopsy report was worse than she'd imagined. Mostly because it offered conflicting evidence.

Her phone buzzed again, and this time she answered. "Hey."

"How'd it go?" Jackson's voice was steady, grounding.

Willow rubbed her forehead, fighting back the growing tension headache. "Jane fought back, she was raped, and she bled out in under a minute." The clinical facts were easier to say than what she was really thinking.

"Raped?" Jackson said with disbelief. "Mason said they had sex. Could it have been to cover up that he had raped her?"

"I don't think so," Willow said, inwardly upset with herself for not having seen that possibility herself. She was too close to the case, and it was obvious to her that she wasn't seeing things clearly. She didn't care. She was seeing clearly enough to conduct a thorough investigation, and she had Jackson there to keep her honest. "Every indication is that there had been consensual intercourse, but there is also evidence that Gamble had been violently sodomized. Listen, Jax. I know he's my brother and that I'm not seeing things as clearly as I should, but this doesn't add up."

Jackson went quiet for a moment. When he spoke again, his voice was softer. "I trust you completely, and the fact that you're questioning your integrity tells me that you won't allow your point of view to be skewed."

"Thank you," Willow said, her heart ready to explode in her chest. God, she loved this man. "How did it go at the crime scene?"

"We couldn't get access," Jackson said. "CSI team was still on site. We spoke with the arresting officer instead. We uncovered some inconsistencies in his report, like him sitting on the 911 call for fifteen minutes. Had he done his job, the victim might still be alive."

"Fuck me," Willow said. "That lazy bastard."

"We're on our way to visit the neighbor, the one who'd made the original 911 call. Do you want to join in?"

She was desperate to get more facts, anything that she could grasp onto to prove her brother's innocence. She didn't know if she could maintain a professional rapport with Matt, though.

"I can do it on my own," Jackson said, reading her silence. "I get it, Will. No need to explain."

"Fuck that," she said. Her need to clear her brother was more important than her hurt feelings. "Do you want the dogs to come? Ranger's pretty good at *convincing* people to talk. He and Ruby can play *bad dog, good dog.*"

Jackson's unfiltered laughter was like music to her ears.

"I don't think they'll be needed," he said. "Not with this woman. She's got an ax to grind, and I think she's dying to spill her guts to anyone willing to listen to her."

"I'll be there in twenty," she said, curious about who this witness was. "I'm going to swing by the house and check in on the girls. Does that work for you?"

"See you in twenty," Jackson said. The tone in his voice said that he understood.

Willow ended the call and stared at the building she'd just left. The morgue's windows reflected the gray winter sky, making the whole structure look like it was made of steel and clouds. Somewhere inside, Jane Gamble's body held answers they desperately needed. The fiber evidence, the timing of the scratches, and the precise nature of the fatal wound all painted a picture of something more complicated than a simple crime of passion.

Willow pulled her coat tighter and headed for her SUV. They had leads to follow, and the clock was ticking. Somewhere in the tangle of threads was the truth about what had happened to Jane Gamble.

And hopefully, so was the proof that her brother wasn't a killer.

Chapter Twelve

Jackson

Jackson shifted his weight against the SUV's cold metal fender, watching Matt Carver pace while he fidgeted with his NCIS badge. The afternoon air carried the scent of that distinctive Low Country salt marsh pluff mud, as the locals called it. Willow had warned him of the distinctive aroma the night before. To Willow, it was the scent of home, but he thought it smelled more like a sewage processing plant.

Above them, Port Republic Street's ancient oaks dripped Spanish moss onto the neighbor's pristinely kept yard. Though the lawn and bushes were in their winter hibernation state, the estate still maintained its stately antebellum heritage.

"I can't remember the last time we had a cold snap like this," Matt offered, clearly uncomfortable with the silence. "Polar vortex, or some shit like that, coming down from the north. We might even get some snow." He gave a fake shiver, like snow was a foreign thing.

Back home, in northern Alabama, snow wasn't common, but they got a little almost every winter. He could do without it, but the dogs loved it, and he enjoyed watching them lose their minds playing in it, even when it was just a light dusting.

"Yeah." Jackson kept his eyes on the road, watching for Willow's vehicle. He checked his watch again. It had been nearly thirty minutes since they'd called her about the neighbor interview. The trip to Mason's house was taking longer than expected, and every minute standing here seemed to stretch for an eternity.

Matt cleared his throat. "You don't like me much, do you?"

Jackson turned slowly, studying the man who'd nearly married Willow. Who'd betrayed her trust in the worst way possible. The badge in Matt's hands caught the weak sunlight, glinting as his fingers worried its edges, a nervous tic that spoke volumes.

"It's not my job to like you." Jackson's voice was level and calm. He'd dealt with plenty of uncomfortable situations in his career, but this one scratched at something deeper. The way Willow's voice still caught when she mentioned Matt's name. The shadows that crossed her face when she thought no one was looking.

Matt shifted, badge slipping in his grip. "I get it," he muttered, eyes dropping. "I messed up bad, and she's got every right to be pissed at me." His voice trailed off, heavy with something unsaid, but he stopped short of more.

Jackson's jaw tightened. Whatever Matt was fishing for, he wasn't biting. Not here, not now. He turned back to the road, focusing on a cardinal that had landed in the neighbor's neatly trimmed azaleas.

The crunch of tires on gravel saved him from further conversation. Willow's SUV pulled up, and Jackson straightened, noting her slightly disheveled appearance. The visit with the girls had clearly taken its toll. She offered him a weak smile before opening the Suburban's rear door. Ranger immediately bounded out. He scanned the area before returning his gaze to Willow. He was followed by a significantly more sedate Ruby.

Worry crinkled Jackson's forehead. The vet had said she was in good health and okay to travel, but she looked exhausted and lacked her usual exuberance.

"Thought they might help." Willow's tone was casual, but her eyes met Jackson's with a hint of challenge. He'd questioned bringing the dogs earlier, suggesting they keep things low-key, but looking at her now, the way her fingers unconsciously sought Ranger's head for stability, she likely brought them as an additional buffer.

Jackson raised a shoulder, a slight smile touching his lips. He strode over to meet her, and to check on Ruby. "Everything okay at home?" he quietly asked as he neared.

"As good as can be expected," Willow said, her voice cracking faintly as she turned away, shoulders hunching. "Sarah and Pickle were running Ruby ragged, so I brought them both along."

It was a good explanation for Ruby's sedate behavior, but Jackson also assumed it was Willow's way of deflecting the conversation away from Ivy and Emma, who had likely given her a hard time. As Matt approached, Ranger focused on him. He hadn't growled, or made any other overt actions, but his body language spoke volumes. The agent stepped back, hands sliding into his pockets.

"Did Dr. Patel have anything useful?" Jackson asked, falling into step beside Willow as they approached the front door. He noticed how she angled slightly away from Matt, maintaining careful distance.

"Later," she murmured, just as Ruby's head snapped up, nose twitching toward the crime house. She had picked up the scent of old blood, maybe, or something fresher on the breeze. Jackson felt the shift in both dogs' energy, the sudden alertness, and the way Ranger's ears pricked forward. Something about the murder house had caught their attention, perhaps a scent or sound carried on the marsh wind.

Matt reached for the doorbell, but Jackson caught his arm.

"Wait." He watched Ranger work the perimeter of the neighbor's porch, nose low, tail stiff. Ruby, despite her pregnancy, mirrored him, her calm giving way to focused intensity. Their behavior sent a prickle up Jackson's spine, the one that said this wasn't going to be a routine witness interview after all.

The front curtain twitched ever so slightly, telling Jackson their presence had already been noticed.

"Maybe we should—" Matt started, but a shrill voice cut him off from inside.

"Who are you?" Evelyn Hargrove demanded, peering through the cracked door, her eyes narrowed. "I don't take kindly to strangers pokin' around my property. I've got a scatter gun, and I ain't afraid to use it."

"Mrs. Hargrove?" Matt answered back. "I'm Special Agent Matthew Carver, NCIS. I'm with Special Agents Brooks and Banks of the FBI. We'd like to ask you some questions regarding the 911 call you made about the screams you heard next door."

"Show me your badges," she yelled. "I don't believe you." The curtains pulled back, and a sharp-eyed woman peered at the edge of the window. The three of them presented their badges, but Jackson wasn't certain she was even looking. Her eyes were locked on Ruby and Ranger.

A moment later, the door swung open and the spritely woman in her late sixties knelt down.

"Oh, aren't you beauties!" she exclaimed, her gaze jumping between the dogs. "Can I give them a treat?" Before anyone could respond, her hand disappeared into a bulging jacket pocket, producing a pair of small Milk-Bones. "Always carry 'em. Dogs are everywhere 'round here." The ancient porch boards creaked beneath her feet as she stepped closer, treats extended.

"It's okay," Jackson said. Ruby approached carefully, taking the offered biscuit with her characteristic gentleness. Ranger held back, maintaining his alert pose until Willow gave an almost imperceptible nod. The dog moved forward then, sniffing the treat before snatching it from her fingers.

"You two look so cute in your FBI uniforms," she said, reaching into her pocket for more treats. "I know federal K9s when I see them." She tossed a cookie to each of the dogs before turning her attention back to the agents standing on her front porch.

"May we come in?" Willow asked, earning a frown from Evelyn. "If you don't mind."

She pulled the door closed behind her. "I do mind. You have no need to see the inside of my home."

Jackson looked at the binoculars tucked into the cushion of the chair on her front porch. He recalled the widow's walk at the top of the home when he had walked up the laneway. Something told him that Evelyn wasn't using it to wait for her husband to return from the sea. "Ma'am," he said, putting as much gentlemanly charm as he could into his voice. "I understand that you are a concerned citizen, and you make a point of caring about the health and safety of your neighbors." He nodded towards the binoculars. "If we were to enter your home, would we find more evidence of your neighborly concern?"

"Beaufort isn't the safe little community it once was," she said. "The local police do what they can with the budget that they have, but it's up to us to help any way possible." Her eyes lifted to the heavens. "I do what I can to help."

"And from your rooftop perch, you see the world with a unique perspective," Jackson said. "I'm sure the local law enforcement appreciates your efforts."

"Not as much as you might think," she said, annoyance in her voice. "Some of them, like that fat oaf Officer Dade, believe me to be a nuisance."

"Ma'am," Willow said, lightly touching Evelyn's bone-thin hand. "I can assure you that we appreciate your vigilance. Anything you can tell us about the night of the murder..." She placed her other hand over her heart.

Evelyn stood straighter. "Come inside," she said, opening the door. "I've got extensive notes, dates, times... I see all sorts of strange things going on next door. I saw a van arrive in the wee hours the night that sweet young woman was killed." She waved them in, eyes gleaming. "High time someone listened."

The agents exchanged glances but followed her inside. Evelyn's living room was a time capsule of floral upholstery, porcelain figurines, and lace doilies—except for the massive corkboard that dominated one wall. Newspaper clippings, sticky notes, and color-coded pins formed a chaotic web of speculation.

"I track patterns," she announced proudly, adjusting her glasses. "These folks don't think I notice, but I've been watching that house for months. Something wasn't right in there. Still isn't."

She spoke without pause, diving into details that ranged from odd noises and license plates to grocery deliveries and midnight visitors. Jackson's curiosity piqued when she spoke of fishing boats coming on moonless nights, and black people either coming off the boat or being taken to the boat. She added that large vans came and left at all times of day, either picking up or dropping off the black people working at the home. At first, Jackson suspected her fixation on the black workers might have been racially motivated, but the more she spoke, the more it seemed she was simply recounting what she saw without prejudice, but with her own brand of blunt honesty.

"You mentioned Officer Dade," Jackson said, "and that he didn't appreciate your concern."

A scowl immediately appeared on Evelyn's face.

"Did you see him at the house on the night of the murder?" Jackson asked.

"I certainly did," she said. "I watched everything that happened that night. I saw him arrive, and drive away, and then come back a while later. Then he sat in his car while God knows what was going on inside. It took him forever to get his fat arse out of his vehicle. I've got it all detailed in my notebook."

Matt's phone binged. He seemed pleased with the interruption. "The CSI team is done and is ready to head out. We're going to miss them if we don't move this along."

"Evelyn?" Willow asked gently. "Do you think we could borrow your notebook? I'd love an opportunity to look at it more closely. You may have captured information that will be integral to our investigation."

The elderly woman sat straighter and raised her chin. "My notebook is my property, and you have no right to take it."

"We aren't taking it," Jackson said, his tone earnest. "I promise that once we have a chance to review it in detail, it will be immediately returned to you."

She pursed her lips while she considered the agents' words. Her trepidation at giving up her prized notes seemed to vanish when Ruby whined and rested her head on the woman's lap. Jackson couldn't surmise what had triggered the dog to do that, but the way Evelyn's expression softened made him glad that Ruby had stepped in.

"Will you bring your pups with you when you return my property to me?"

Jackson exchanged a quick glance with Willow, both silently acknowledging the small victory. Evelyn's notebook was valuable, and her observations had opened some unexpected lines of inquiry. And now, Officer Dade had moved to the top of Jackson's list.

"Gladly," Willow said. "It appears they've grown quite attached to you."

"You don't need to butter me up, Missy," Evelyn said with a coy smile. "They like me because my pockets are full of treats, but I appreciate you saying it, nonetheless."

After giving Evelyn a signed receipt for her notebook, the team left the house and made their way next door. Two CSI team members were busy loading plastic evidence bags into the back of their van. Matt waved down a third member, a lanky woman with an annoyed look on her face. She turned away from the van, tapping continuously on her digital tablet.

"This is Caroline Richter," Matt said to Jackson. "She's the NCIS forensic team's supervisor. Caroline, these are Special Agents Willow Banks and Jackson Brooks, FBI."

The lead technician approached, her clipped hair matching her brusque manner. "We're done collecting, but the crime scene stays sealed. SSA Davidson's orders." She cast a pointed look at Matt, clearly expecting immediate compliance.

"Did you bring K9s when you searched the residence?" Matt asked.

The woman's brow furrowed. "No. We processed it like we always do. You think we missed something?"

"Wouldn't be the first time," Matt said evenly. "I think we should double check your work."

Her lips thinned. "SSA Davidson is already pissed that you let them near the suspect. If you go in now, she'll have your ass, and I'll fucking dance in the street!"

Matt flashed a boyish grin. "Wouldn't be the first time she's angry with me." He blew the CSI investigator a kiss. "I'll sweet talk my way out of it, just like I always do."

Caroline rolled her eyes at the comment and walked away. "It's your funeral, and I'll be the first to spit on your grave."

Ruby whined and took a tentative step toward the house. Her nostrils flared, inhaling a scent on the wind. She wasn't just interested, she was locked onto something. Unease crept up Jackson's spine. Whatever was going on inside, Ruby knew before he did.

Chapter Thirteen

Willow

Willow and Ranger trailed a good distance behind Jackson, Ruby, and Matt. At first, it bothered her, seeing her fiancé walking next to her ex, but then she realized Jackson was doing it for her. By keeping close to Matt, he spared her the discomfort of walking beside him.

"Do you see what I see?" she murmured to Ranger, spotting several security cameras mounted along the building's exterior. The idea of asking Matt for the footage left a bitter taste in her mouth. She briefly considered asking Jackson to act as a go-between, then scolded herself for the thought. She needed to grow a pair and face Matt herself.

"I'll do better later," she whispered to Ranger as she entered through the front door, unlike the others, who had gone in through the side. She could've sworn her dog cocked an eyebrow at her.

Willow paused in the living room, marveling at the elaborate woodwork and hand-carved moldings. Her father had been a master craftsman, capable of breathing new life into old buildings. Her brother had inherited the same talent.

The ME and CSI forensic team had come and gone, leaving the home in reasonably tidy condition. She had entered other crime scenes that had been left in a shambles, like a tornado had swept through, not caring about the property they had invaded.

While Ranger stood at attention beside Willow, Ruby seemed agitated. There was still a large puddle of blood on the floor in the dining room where the victim's body had been. The tables and chairs had been pushed to the side to give the ME space to do his work. Willow wished she could have seen things as they had been prior to being disrupted.

"Can you ask your CSI friend for her preliminary findings?" Willow asked. It burned her ass to ask anything from Matt, but her brother's freedom was at stake. The hopeful look in Matt's eyes as he pulled out his cellphone made her stomach churn. "And can you ask her about the video cameras outside? I'd like to see last night's footage."

"Hey, Caroline," Matt said, voice dropping into that smooth, all-too-easy warmth. "Can you send me everything you've got so far, photos, videos, inventory, the works?"

It was the same tone that used to make Willow's knees weak. It had been his good looks that had caught her eye, sure. But it was his voice, that smooth, rich cadence, that had sucked her in. Watching him use it to get what he wanted, clear as fucking day... she hated herself for ever having fallen for it.

"Thanks, hon," he said, flashing a thumbs up. "You're the best." Matt strutted closer, looking like he had just scored a major victory. She had asked him to do something for her, and he complied. Now he'd want something in return.

"Jax," Willow said, doing her best to ignore Matt. "You and Ruby have got the main floor covered. I'm going to look around upstairs."

Jackson's brow was furrowed when he gave a dismissive way. He was fully engrossed with Ruby's odd behavior.

"I'll come with you," Matt said. "I haven't been upstairs yet either."

Ranger's head snapped towards him, a low rumble in his chest. He had picked up on Willow's anxiety, and he wasn't afraid to respond in kind. "I've got this. Ranger works best without distractions."

It was a complete lie. Her Belgian Malinois could do a thorough search with guns and bombs going off around him. He would never be the search dog that Ruby was, but Willow had been working with him every day to improve his skills. It was one of the few activities that actually tired him out. Her K9 was an athlete in every sense of the word. He could do physical tasks all day long without ever slowing down. Nose work, on the other hand, fully engaged his brain, and the required level of concentration completely drained him.

"Ranger, heel," she said. The dog moved into lockstep beside her as they climbed the wide, picturesque staircase to the second floor. The remnants of fingerprint dust on the railing caught her attention. Instinctively, she stuffed her hands into her pockets to stop herself from inadvertently touching anything.

At the top of the stairs, a mezzanine stretched out in either direction. Immediately in front of her, an open set of double doors exposed a huge empty room with grand windows that overlooked the Beaufort River, gleaming hardwood floors, and the same wood paneling and plaster moldings as on the main floor. She stepped inside and blew out a low whistle. The home was being refurbished to turn it into a B&B hotel. At twenty by thirty feet, she couldn't imagine what this room would be used for. Formal parties, perhaps. Pushing the thought aside, Willow stepped closer to a pair of double doors that led to a large balcony. It overlooked a narrow ribbon of saltwater marsh, split by a floating dock that extended sixty or seventy feet out into the water.

"Caroline's preliminary report just came in," Matt called.

Willow's shoulders stiffened. His voice still had that smooth, confident ring, like he thought she'd be impressed—like she had so many times before. She forced herself to step into view.

He was smiling. Holding up his phone like it was a goddamn trophy.

"Great," she left the room and turned down the hall towards three open doors. "Forward the report to Jackson and me. I'll look it over while Ranger does his thing." In her peripheral vision, she caught the disappointment on Matt's face. The satisfaction it brought made Willow feel petty. She didn't care.

The next room was empty, like the grand hall, but it was smaller, cozier. It had a little closet and a small but lavish ensuite bathroom. The fixtures were all brand new, but they still maintained an air of old-world charm. No doubt, more of Mason's handywork.

As she entered the third room, her phone chimed, letting her know she had an email.

"Ranger, down," she said, opening the attachment labeled Inventory. She flipped through the list of items they had noted, photographed, and/or bagged. Each item identified as to where it had been located and who had logged it. Nothing of note stood out to her, except that much of the list appeared to be Jane Gamble's personal property.

Willow stepped back into the hallway, noting the open door at the far end of the mezzanine, and the messy room it opened into.

"Heel," she said, striding forward. Where every other room in the home appeared to have been treated with respect, this room was a disaster. There was a small dresser with every drawer pulled and thrown on the floor. The twin mattress had been flipped off the bed, the linens in a rumpled mess beside it. Books and clothes were strewn across the room. It baffled Willow as to why the CSI team had been so disrespectful. They hadn't been gathering evidence, they were searching for something. Something important.

A small writing desk caught her eye. It held a laptop dock and an external monitor. Large hardback books laid on the floor beside it. Willow moved closer to read the spines: *Advanced Investigative Techniques, Intelligence Gathering Methodology,* and *Pattern Analysis in Criminal Investigations.*

Not exactly light reading for a security guard or a naval petty officer. The woman clearly had higher aspirations.

Willow pulled out her phone and started looking through the list of items cataloged in this room. It was what she didn't find that got her blood pumping. There was no laptop, and there was no notebook. Mason had said Jane took copious amounts of notes.

It wasn't the CSI team who'd ransacked her room. It was her killer. He had obviously taken the laptop, but he might have overlooked her notebook. She wanted Ranger to search for it, but she had no target scent to give him. Everything in the room would smell of Jane.

Willow pulled on a pair of latex gloves and began her search. Ranger stood next to her, keenly interested in everything she was doing. Step by step, she searched, looking in places that she hoped weren't obvious. She looked under the boxspring, one of the few things not thrown aside. A smile pulled at her lips. She hadn't found a notebook, but she did find a bottle of medicated hand lotion on the floor.

Willow uncapped it, remembering Dr. Patel's observation about Jane's skin condition. Her notebook would have the scent all over it. So would everything else she touched, but at least she now had a clear target for Ranger. It was also possible that residue could have transferred onto her killer's hand, and a lotion-infused fingerprint could easily identify him. Or at least narrow things down. It was something else she'd need to bring up later on.

"Here, boy." She held the bottle low, letting the dog inhale deeply. "Find it."

Ranger immediately began quartering the room, nose working furiously. He alerted on the bed first, which was expected given how much time Jane would have spent there. Then the desk chair. The closet. Each time, Willow praised him briefly but kept him working. "Find it."

The dog was finding too many things with the lotion's scent, and Willow could sense his growing frustration. He wanted to please her but wasn't sure what specific item she wanted. Still, she kept him searching while she looked in places too high for her K9's nose to reach.

Ranger barked, drawing her attention to the fireplace. The dog's nose worked overtime, and then he did something unusual. He stepped into the cold hearth itself, sniffing the ashes. When Willow didn't immediately respond, his barking became insistent.

"Okay, okay, I hear you." She knelt beside the fireplace, examining the historical brickwork. Some of the mortar was crumbling, creating natural hiding spaces. Mason hadn't finished with this room, likely because Jane was living there. She began probing carefully, but Ranger's barking only grew more urgent. Finally, he thrust his nose toward the ashes themselves, maintaining eye contact with her in a way that meant he'd found something important.

Willow shifted her attention to the ash bed. At first glance, it looked undisturbed, but... there. A slight rectangular impression, as if something had been recently buried. She pulled out her cell phone and took several pictures, each from a different angle. Using her pen, she then carefully scraped away the top layer of ash.

A plastic sandwich bag emerged, containing a small spiral notebook.

"Good boy!" The praise burst from her automatically, and she quickly pulled out Ranger's favorite toy, a well-worn blue stuffed puppy that traveled everywhere in Willow's cargo pocket. The dog took it gleefully, shaking it with proud enthusiasm while Willow examined her find.

The notebook was protected by the plastic, but there may have been trace evidence on it as well. She pulled out an evidence bag and slipped the notebook inside. Double wrapped the way it was, she could barely open the notebook. Its pages were dense with handwriting, confirming what her brother had said.

Voices from downstairs made her pause. New voices, not just Matt and Jackson. She tucked the notebook into her jacket pocket and retrieved Ranger's toy, heading for the main floor. Two CSI techs were coming through the front door, carrying additional equipment. They stopped short when they saw her.

"Are the bodies upstairs?" Caroline, the lead CSI tech asked.

Bodies?

Jackson's gaze met hers, serious. "Ruby found something," he said with an ominous tone.

Willow's stomach dropped. "What?"

"Two bodies... Ruby found them hidden in the crawl space behind the dining room wall. Judging by the state of decomp... they've been there a day or two."

Chapter Fourteen

Jackson

Jackson followed Ruby through the dining room, watching the pregnant Golden Retriever with careful attention. Her behavior had shifted dramatically from the moment they'd entered the house. While Willow and Ranger were investigating Jane's room upstairs, Ruby had become increasingly agitated, circling the dining room and repeatedly returning to the same spot along the rear wall, pressing her muzzle against the baseboard, tail straight and rigid.

"She's just picking up Jane's scent," Matt said dismissively, gesturing toward the dark, brownish stain that marred the hardwood floor, the spot where Officer Kent Dade had found Jane bleeding out a day earlier. "Or maybe Jane was held against that wall before she was killed."

Jackson kept his eyes on Ruby, noting how she ignored the blood stain. In their years together, he'd learned to read her signals. Ruby wasn't confused or distracted, she was zeroed in on something specific. But what, exactly?

"How many times have you worked with K9 units?" Jackson asked, his voice deliberately neutral despite his irritation with Matt's dismissive attitude.

Matt shifted his weight, his leather shoes creaking against the floor. "Never. Not directly, anyway. I've seen them in action but haven't personally worked with them."

"That explains it," Jackson muttered, keeping his tone just loud enough for Matt to hear. He crouched beside Ruby, who had pressed her nose against the wainscoting again, her golden-brown eyes darting toward him with unmistakable urgency. "You have a camera scope in your SUV?" he asked. "I'd like to get a look at what's behind this wall."

"No," Matt replied, checking his watch with obvious impatience. His earlier eagerness to involve Jackson and Willow seemed to be fading. "But I can call the CSI team back. They won't be happy about it."

"Do I look like I care if they're upset?" Jackson asked. He couldn't see what Willow had once seen in the man. Matt's behavior was odd, like he'd rather be someplace else. A soft creak from the floor above reminded Jackson exactly where Willow was, and where Matt would rather be.

"Not really," Matt conceded, the corner of his mouth twitching. "I just wanted to see how committed you were to having them here. If they find something behind that wall, they're going to kick us out while they investigate."

Jackson studied the NCIS agent for a long moment. For all the man's personal failings, and there were many, he wasn't an idiot. Matt clearly saw the value of a proper investigation, even if it meant aggravating his own team. That didn't mean Jackson had to like him. The thought of what Matt had done to Willow, the pain he'd caused her, made his jaw clench involuntarily.

"Make the call," Jackson said, eyes still on Ruby. She hadn't moved an inch.

Matt stepped into the foyer, his phone already in hand. Left alone with Ruby, Jackson exhaled slowly, allowing his shoulders to drop. Maintaining a professional demeanor around Matt drained him more than he'd realized, and his obvious interest in Willow bothered him more than it should.

"Alright, girl," he murmured to Ruby, who tilted her head attentively. "Let's figure out what you're trying to tell me."

Ruby's pregnancy had slowed her down considerably over the past weeks, but nothing dampened her working instincts. If anything, her tracking abilities seemed sharper, more focused, as though her impending motherhood had heightened her already acute senses.

"Seek," Jackson commanded, his voice low and firm.

Ruby's ears perked up instantly, her body language shifting from anxious to purposeful. She traveled methodically along the wall until she reached the corner, nose skimming inches from the baseboards. At the end of the wall, she turned the corner, hesitated for a split second, then headed back to where she'd started.

Jackson followed, mentally mapping her path. Back at the starting point, Ruby tracked the scent to the next corner, continued around it, and exited through the doorway into the kitchen. Despite this being an active renovation site, the kitchen was immaculate. The only thing out of place was an open pizza box on the counter, and two remaining slices.

In the kitchen, Ruby maintained her focus, nose skimming along the cabinet bottoms without pause until she reached another wall. There, she stopped abruptly, lay down, and scratched at the surface with her paw. Jackson recognized her cadaver training signal immediately. She'd found a dead body.

He knelt beside Ruby, running his fingers along the ornate molding, feeling for anomalies. The woodwork was exquisite, with subtle curves and precise joints that blended seamlessly with the historic character of the house. Jackson pressed lightly at the edges, searching methodically. The plaster wall felt solid under his touch.

Ruby whined impatiently, her tail thumping against the floor in rhythmic agitation. Her soulful brown eyes never left the spot she'd identified.

Jackson stepped back, bringing the section of wall into full view. There was a faint outline of a passage, something easily overlooked if you weren't searching for it. A servants' corridor, hidden in plain sight, blending seamlessly into the house's decorative moldings. Clever. Practical. And, right now, deeply unsettling.

Jackson pressed again at different points along the molding, applying firmer pressure. A hidden latch gave way with a muted *click* that seemed deafening in the quiet kitchen. The panel shifted inward about half an inch, revealing its true nature.

"Good girl," he whispered to Ruby, rewarding her with gentle strokes along her golden coat. She sprang up, shoving her nose into the gap, urging Jackson to open it wider.

Jackson pressed against the edge of the panel and pushed it open further. Immediately, a wave of fetid air hit him. The unmistakable, primal stench of human decomposition was a smell that, once experienced, was never forgotten. It was simultaneously sweet and putrid, with undertones that triggered an instinctive revulsion.

"Matt," Jackson barked. "Get back here. Now!"

Jackson flicked on his cell phone's flashlight and peered inside. Ruby was nowhere to be seen. He stepped into the corridor, noting the electrical, plumbing, and HVAC pipework. Like the kitchen, the space was surprisingly clean and tidy. He scanned the walls nearest the door, searching for a light switch. The staff wouldn't be moving about these passages in the dark.

"Jesus Christ," Matt said as soon as he appeared. He buried his nose in the crook of his elbow. "Is that what Ruby was smelling?"

Jackson flipped the light switch, bathing the corridor in soft white light. "Let's see where her nose leads us," he said. Ruby barked twice, sharp and high pitched.

"Or we can follow her voice," Matt said.

The agents followed the corridor until it turned left, likely following the outside shape of the home. Twenty feet ahead, Jackson spotted Ruby lying down with her head on the ground beside two shirtless men sitting propped against the wall, huddled together. As he approached, Ruby moved aside, giving Jackson room to examine the bodies.

The older man clutched the younger against him. His face was slack and mouth slightly open, as if caught mid-breath. The younger man's fingers were curled, stiff in death, dark stains caked beneath his nails.

"No obvious wounds or bruising," Jackson said. "But, the bluish tinge of their lips is odd."

"The old guy looks like a laborer," Matt chimed in. "Look at how heavily calloused his hands are. They look like they just sat down and died. It's the strangest thing I've ever seen. Do you think they're part of the house staff?"

"No idea," Jackson said. "But we need to get out of here. We've corrupted the scene enough as it is. Call your CSI team and let them know what we've found. You had better call your boss as well. I'm going to do the same."

Matt left the kitchen while Jackson called SAC Alice Baldwin. He punched in her number and pressed his cell phone to his ear.

"Hey, Alice," he said when she answered.

"Jackson," she replied with a heavy sigh. "How's Willow holding up?"

"She's managing," Jackson said, choosing his words carefully. "Keeping her focus on the case."

"How are you doing? You sound stressed."

"Stressed? That would be one word for it," he said with a dry laugh, turning to face the corridor entrance. He dropped his voice to a whisper. "Things have gotten more complicated. We've uncovered two more bodies in the house. I doubt they're related to the original murder investigation, but I don't want to make assumptions. Based on their ethnicity and clothing, they're likely migrant workers."

"You need to call Beaufort PD," she said with a firm voice. "This is their jurisdiction. Just because NCIS invited the FBI to assist in the murder investigation, it doesn't mean we'd take on this other case. Proximity isn't a valid reason to push them out."

Jackson clenched his jaw. "I'll call them. I'm guessing it's going to turn into a jurisdictional nightmare."

"No doubt," Alice replied. "I'll call Charleston to let them know what's happening. If you can convince BPD to let us in, I'll make sure you have a team ready to assist."

"Thanks, Alice. You're okay if we're here longer than we expected?"

"Did I tell you to get back to Florence?" she asked, a hint of humor in her words. "Take care of yourselves, and keep me updated."

Voices from outside the kitchen told Jackson the CSI team had already arrived. "I will, and thanks again. I have to go."

"Give Willow a hug for me, will you?"

"Can do, boss. Can do."

***

Jackson rubbed his arms to stay warm while he, Willow, and Matt waited for the ME and the CSI team to do their work. It felt like a waste of time to stand around doing nothing, but they all wanted to hear the results from inside. Willow had called Cooper to bring the BPD in, but his boss had said it would be a while before they got clearance to be at the site. Until NCIS were satisfied that the two new victims were unrelated, they continued to claim jurisdiction.

The crunch of tires on gravel drew their attention as a sleek black Range Rover pulled up. The vehicle slowed to a stop, and a tall man in his early forties stepped out, his tailored cashmere coat and polished oxfords utterly incongruous against the crime scene tape fluttering in the breeze.

"That's Liam Fitzpatrick," Matt muttered under his breath. "Owner of this property."

The man's confident stride faltered slightly at the sight of the ME's truck and the NCIS forensic van parked at his house. His expression remained neutral, but Jackson caught the momentary tightening around his eyes.

"Agents," Liam said, his Low Country accent refined in a way that declared him to be in charge. "I understand there's been an incident on my property. I came as soon as I could."

"Mr. Fitzpatrick," Willow said, stepping forward. "Your home is the scene of an active homicide investigation. More than one, actually."

If the pluralization surprised him, Liam didn't show it. "How unfortunate. I've been in Charleston since last week, overseeing another project. My brother mentioned some trouble with the security guard, but..." His eyes drifted toward the house, then back to Willow. A slight hint of confusion marred his otherwise perfect mask. "More than one, you said?"

Ruby moved forward, her nose working the air near Liam's shoes. The man took an involuntary step back, his composure cracking for just a moment.

"We found two bodies concealed in the walls," Jackson said bluntly, watching Liam's face. "We are working under the assumption that they were a part of your staff. Any idea how they might have ended up there, Mr. Fitzpatrick?"

Liam's expression hardened, all pretense of polite concern vanishing. "I hire my brother Michael's company to manage staffing. I don't interact with the workers directly. And I certainly don't appreciate the implication."

"No one's implying anything yet," Jackson replied, noting how Ranger had positioned himself between Willow and Liam without command. "But it's your property, and your renovation. And the bodies are in your walls."

"My attorney will be handling all further communications." Liam's voice was ice. "I suggest you focus your investigation on Mason Banks. He's the one who was caught red-handed." He turned to leave, then paused. "And I'll need a copy of the warrant that allowed you to search beyond the areas relevant to Jane Gamble's death."

Matt stepped forward. "That's not how this works."

"That's exactly how this works, Agent." Liam's smile was unnerving. "My family has been in Beaufort for generations, and I know exactly how things work here. I'm surprised that you don't."

As Liam returned to his vehicle, Jackson watched Ruby's eyes follow him, her posture rigid with alertness.

"He's worried," Jackson said quietly to Willow. "And not just about the renovation schedule."

"Agreed," Willow said, her gaze fixed on the departing Range Rover. "Notice he didn't ask a single question about the victims. Not who they were, how they died. Nothing."

"Because he already knew," Jackson replied. It bothered him that Liam Fitzpatrick had referred to the three of them as *agents*. All three of them were wearing coats that covered their badges. "Just like he knew we were feds. Mr. Fitzpatrick is more informed than he should be."

"I told you," Matt said, stuffing his hands into his pockets. "The Fitzpatricks are extremely well connected."

Chapter Fifteen

Willow

Willow fumed that Matt had asked for the dogs to be put in the Suburban's cargo area. Jackson had offered to let him take the front seat, but Matt had declined the invitation after receiving a death stare from Willow. As far as she was concerned, he could sit in his own fucking car.

She was going to have words with Jackson about this later.

The air inside the SUV was thick with tension as Willow, Jackson, and Matt sat in silence, watching NCIS personnel stream in and out of the house. Yellow crime scene tape fluttered in the gentle breeze, a stark reminder of the horror they'd discovered inside. Two more bodies. Two more lives snuffed out in what was becoming a far more complex case than anyone had initially imagined.

Willow's mind raced, her thoughts returning to the notebook she'd secured from Jane's room. She shifted in her seat, reaching into her jacket pocket to retrieve the evidence bag.

"Matt," she said, breaking the silence, annoyed that she needed to speak with him. Her hatred for the man had been simmering in the back of her head, and each time she was forced to see his smug face, it came closer to the forefront. It took all of her self-control not to let her emotions boil over. "I have something you should see." She held up the sealed bag containing Jane's notebook, almost challenging him to berate her for taking evidence from the crime scene. "I found this. I would have given it to you sooner, but things got a bit chaotic when I came downstairs."

Matt's eyes widened slightly as he registered what she was holding. "Where exactly did you find it? We searched the home from top to bottom."

"Hidden in the ashes of the fireplace in Jane's room," Willow explained, watching his reaction carefully. "Ranger picked up the scent from her medicated lotion."

A hint of professional respect crossed Matt's face as he pulled latex gloves from his pocket and snapped them on. He unsealed Willow's evidence bag first, then carefully removed the Ziplock bag that contained the notebook itself. The acrid scent of ash filled the SUV's interior. Taking it by its metal ring binding to minimize contact, he extracted it and carefully opened the cover.

Willow waited for him to say something, but he just kept flipping pages, reading to himself.

"There had been a laptop," Willow said to Jackson. "NCIS didn't include it in the evidence log, suggesting someone had taken it before they got there."

"Or she forgot it at work," Matt said, his eyes never leaving the notebook. "We've put in a request to her commanding officer to search her office."

Willow shook her head at Jackson. "I doubt she forgot it. Jane's bedroom was ransacked. I mean, it was completely tossed. Unless it was the crime scene team, someone else had been there. Jane had abrasions on her wrists, likely from her attacker while he searched the place. When he couldn't find it... he beat her and raped her. When she still wouldn't talk, he stabbed her with a single thrust to the heart."

"Jesus," Matt said. "I had thought she might have been raped, the way her shirt and panties had been torn. Did the ME give any indication on whether he believed Mason had done it?"

"No," Willow said. "But he pointed out that whoever had killed Jane knew what he was doing. The murderer slipped the blade between her ribs. The strike was precise. Mason's fingerprints on the blade suggested he was holding the weapon with an overhand grip. The way he was straddling her, it would have been nearly impossible for him to turn the blade sideways to stab her. Mason didn't do this. I'm almost certain of it."

It dawned on Willow, at that very moment, that there were security cameras around the exterior of the home. "Was the security footage at the house found? I saw multiple cameras, but I don't remember seeing anything about them in the CSI report."

"The cameras at the house store their data to a central repository," Matt said, shaking his head. "We found the DVR in a cabinet in a service nook off the kitchen, but the SD card had been removed."

"What about cloud storage?" Jackson asked. "Surely the owner didn't rely on a single point of failure when protecting his multi-million-dollar home."

"We've already issued a subpoena to the service provider," Matt said, "but they're fighting it. It could be weeks or months until we get access."

"What about Fitzpatrick?" Willow asked. "Can't he give us access? Surely, he wants the killer found. His house is an active crime scene, and no work will take place until the case is closed."

"You'd think," Matt said, "but apparently, he's not the owner of the devices. They're owned by his brother Sean Fitzpatrick, or more precisely, by his company, Maritime Defense Solutions. Surprisingly, since it was their employee, and the home they were protecting, they're not in a hurry to air their dirty laundry."

"But what about the SD card?" Jackson asked. "The place has been locked down ever since Dade walked in on Mason."

"There may never have been one," Matt said with a look of sympathy. "With automated cloud storage, and with how cagey they're being about sharing the video, maybe they didn't bother with a physical device."

"Maybe whoever killed Jane took it," Willow said. "There was a third person at the house. I'm certain of it. If the cameras caught him coming into the house, it makes sense that he'd have taken it."

"Maybe," Jackson said. "But it's going to be tough to prove without any evidence."

"There might be evidence in here," Matt said, flipping aimlessly through the notebook's pages. "The victim took extremely detailed notes. There are dates, times, descriptions… looks like she was tracking the arrivals and departures of fishing boats and delivery trucks as well as…" he grunted, "the comings and goings of the workers."

"Can you lean forward so we can all look at the book together?" Willow asked. "It's a bit frustrating that we can't all see it."

Matt glanced up. He had a gleam in his eye that made Willow's skin crawl. "Why don't you come into the back seat with me? We can look at it together more comfortably."

Jackson frowned and glared at Willow. "Actually, I have a better idea," he said. "Let's go to Willow's house where we can spread out and check in on Mason's girls at the same time."

"That's a great idea," Matt said, his expression brightening. "It's been a few years since I've seen them. How are the girls doing?"

Willow's jaw tightened. "That works for me, but only if I can read the notebook while we're driving. Otherwise, Matt, you can go fuck yourself." She hadn't intended to say those words out loud, but they hadn't fazed him at all. The prick smirked at her, a hint of their complicated history flashing across his face.

"Still the same Willow," he said with a crude chuckle. He held out the notebook. "Passionate as always. I hope your new fiancé can handle you."

"My personal life is none of your fucking business." She regretted taking the bait as soon as the words left her mouth. Matt flashed his boyish grin at her; the same one he'd used whenever he had manipulated her into doing something she hadn't wanted to. The pained look on Jackson's face as he stared out the windshield made her want to die.

Willow pulled on a pair of latex gloves and took the book. "Take your time," she murmured at Jackson.

He gave her a half smile and slowly pulled away.

"Tell me about the girls," Matt said, leaning between the bucket seats.

"I'm reading," Willow snapped at him. "Do you mind?"

"Sorry," he said with a sarcastic whine. "Jesus, it was just a question."

Jackson slammed on the brakes, sending everyone lurching forward. "Get out!" he said over his shoulder. "Take your own car. I'm guessing you know the way, and, quite frankly, you're grating on my nerves. From what I've heard, you and Mason were best friends, and you're acting like this is some sort of game."

"Whoa, easy big fella," Matt said. "I haven't seen Willow for almost three years. I'm just making nice."

"Making nice? She's engaged, and she hates you. There is no room for you in her life. Get over it and get on with it."

Joy bubbled up inside Willow's belly. Both dogs snarled from their place at the back of the vehicle. Had there not been a steel mesh divider blocking them, they'd have likely attacked. At least, she hoped they would have.

"You're engaged to *him*?" Matt's head turned left and right, like he was watching a tennis match. "That's fucking rich. Give me the notebook. It needs to be logged into evidence. Your services are no longer required on this case."

"Seriously?" Willow nearly threw the book at him. "Did you invite us to help because you thought you and I would make up? You're a cheating fucking piece of shit, and you somehow thought in your twisted fucking mind that I would just forgive and forget?"

"What happened at the bachelor party wasn't my fault," Matt bellowed. "I was drunk, and I was set up. How many times do I have to say I'm sorry? I'll fucking have it written across the sky if you want. If you had just talked with me, we could have worked through it."

The rear driver's side door opened, and Jackson grabbed Matt by the shoulder. Before Willow could process the movement, he dragged Matt from the car and tossed him onto the curb. He leaned close, pointing his finger in Matt's face.

"I'm filing a report with your boss," Jackson said, his breath tight, his rage just barely controlled. "Then I'm taking it to the NCIS Inspector General. And if that doesn't stick, I'll go straight to the Office of Professional Responsibility. You got drummed out of the FBI, and I will make sure you never wear a badge again. Not here, not anywhere."

Jackson climbed into the car and slammed the door hard enough to rattle the cab. The dogs immediately went silent. He slammed the vehicle into drive but didn't take his foot off the brakes. His hands trembled as he gripped the steering wheel. He took a long breath. "I'm sorry. I know you don't need me to fight your battles for you, but I had had enough of his... bullshit." He barely whispered the last word.

"I love you," Willow said. Butterflies were erupting in her belly. "You're right, I didn't need you to do that for me, but I'm so glad you did. I'd have likely given him a beating."

"I wanted to," Jackson said. He was staring out the window at Matt who was still on his back on the sidewalk. "I'm not sure I'd have stopped at just a beating, though." He pulled out his cell phone, his thumbs tapping frantically.

"What are you doing?"

"I'm looking for SSA Vicky Davidson's phone number," he said. Ringing filled the cabin and the supervisory agent's name appeared on the SUV's video display. "Gotta love Google search."

"Supervisory Special Agent Davidson."

"Good morning," Jackson said. "This is Special Agent—"

"Jackson Brooks," she said. "What can I do for you?"

"I'm calling to give you a heads up that I'm going to be filing a formal complaint against SA…" Jackson's brow furrowed. "Matt… something. I can't remember his last name."

"Carver. Special Agent Matt Carver." A tired sigh came through the speaker. "What did he do this time?"

"Abuse of power, inappropriate behavior to my partner SA Banks, and…"

"Being a general dickwad?" The woman groaned. "Apologies. That was unprofessional and inappropriate."

"And completely accurate," Willow finished, trying to hold back a laugh.

Jackson's face was carved from granite. "Agent Carver invited the FBI to help NCIS with the Jane Gamble murder investigation. When SA Willow Banks refused his sexual advances, he threw us off the case."

Willow grimaced at the words. It wasn't entirely accurate. Technically, Matt hadn't made a sexual advance, but from Jackson's point of view, it likely had looked that way.

"Can you hold for a second?" She didn't wait for a reply. Elevator music replaced her voice.

From the sidewalk, Matt's phone rang. He jumped to his feet and pulled out his phone. "Vicky, how can I help?" He used his best seductive tones and smiled at Willow. The smile melted away, and he turned his back. He stopped speaking, his head slowly bobbing. His body language suggested he was being scolded, and he didn't like it. The conversation lasted a couple of minutes. Matt stuffed his phone in his pocket at glared at Jackson.

"Sorry about that," SSA Davidson said, cutting off the light jazz music. "I'd like to meet with you and Agent Banks."

"This is SA Banks," Willow said. "Agent Carver has critical evidence in his possession, the victim's notebook. I'd really like to have a chance to examine it."

SSA Davidson paused for several long seconds before responding. "Tell him I said to hand it over. Are you amenable to us meeting?"

"We can meet," Jackson said, "but I'm still filing my report. Where's your office?"

"I would expect nothing less, Agent Brooks. I'd like to meet off base…"

Willow looked toward Jackson for his opinion, who was busy unbuckling his seatbelt. He was out the door in seconds, catching Matt before he wandered off.

"We're heading to my brother Mason's home," Willow said to SSA Davidson, assuming Jackson would be okay with it. "Can we meet there? I need to check in on his girls. I'll send you the address."

"That would be fine. I have his address already." She hung up immediately after agreeing.

Jackson climbed back into the truck, flashed a smile, and the notebook. "I have the evidence," he said, speaking to the video screen.

"She already hung up," Willow said. "We're going to meet with her at Mason's house. Let's get going. I want to have a chance to talk to the girls before she gets there."

Chapter Sixteen

Jackson

Jackson hummed a random tune as he drove down Bay Street, through the heart of downtown Beaufort. Willow was quietly sitting beside him, reading through Jane's notes and not saying a word. He wanted to know what she was finding in its pages, but he knew to give her space, to let her process whatever emotions she was dealing with.

Small shops, restaurants, banks... the street was touristy, but functional. It reminded Jackson of Court Street, back home in Florence, Alabama. He needed to call his parents to let them know what was going on, and that he didn't expect they'd be coming home any time soon. He stole a glance at Willow, who continued to appear deeply engrossed by what she was reading.

Jackson rolled down the window and hung his elbow out the door. The putrid smell of lowcountry pluff mud filled the cabin. Its potency seemed to wax and wane over the course of the day. He assumed that, if it was coming off the saltwater marshes that covered a large percentage of Beaufort County, that it likely had something to do with the changing tides. He didn't know, and he didn't care. He also couldn't fathom how anyone could like the stink.

"The cool air feels good," Willow said, finally pulling her nose up from the notebook. She tilted her head back, stretched, and sucked in a long breath through her nose. "It's been too long since I've been home." She fixed her gaze on Jackson, her eyes glassy. "Please don't let me stay away for so long again. I was angry with Mason, but I took it out on everyone else too. In the end, I only hurt myself."

"Is that what you've been thinking about for the last twenty minutes?" Jackson asked. "I thought you were reading through Jane's notes."

The question made Willow smile.

"I've been reading," she said, tapping a finger on the cover, "and thinking about my family and how much I miss them." She slid the notebook back into the evidence bag and pulled off her latex gloves. She rolled down her window, sucked in another deep breath, and took a look over her shoulder. "Ruby seems fine. Do you think she could smell the cadavers from the street?"

"I do," Jackson said. He wasn't sure if she was avoiding the book's contents, or if she just needed a break from the case. "It looks like your scent training with Ranger is paying off. Giving him the lotion to scent was genius, although, I'm kind of surprised the forensic team didn't search the ashes."

"Why would they?" Willow said. "Jane wasn't a suspect and there was no connection to her killer and the fireplace. Everything else in the room was in plain sight. Then again, they'd have found that the room had been tossed…"

"I'd really like to have a chat with Caroline, the forensic tech lead," Jackson said. "I'd like to know if it was her team who'd tossed the room, and if they'd found any other prints in there." Even if it hadn't been the CSI team, it could have been Matt or someone from the Beaufort PD. But, like Willow said, there was no reason for law enforcement to tear Jane's room apart.

"Are you interested in knowing what I read?" Willow said. "I'm surprised you haven't asked yet."

Jackson shrugged and gave her a grin. "I assumed that you'd tell me in good time. Anything stand out?"

"I'd say everything stands out." Willow's eyes bulged. "It looks like Jane was on duty from around 6:00 PM until 6:00 AM every day, and all-day Saturday and Sunday. She logged the date and time of every entry."

"It sounds like she was living there," Jackson said. "I mean, she was either at her day job, or at the construction site. We should talk to her naval commander, that is, if we're still allowed to work the case."

"Vicky gave us the notebook," Willow said. "We're on the case." She got a pained look on her face. "Remember when we met with Matt the first time, he said that he was being told to wrap the investigation up ASAP? Does it feel like she's trying to wrap it up?"

A knot tightened in his gut as he remembered how quickly Davidson had ordered Matt to hand over key evidence. It didn't line up with what Matt had claimed that first day.

"No," Jackson said, raising an eyebrow. "But we've seen this before, people in charge gaslighting everyone around them. We best keep our wits about us when we talk with SSA Davidson. Until we get to know her, I don't trust Vicky one iota."

"I'm interested in hearing what the police chief has to say about the two bodies you discovered," Willow said. She had that predatory look she got when she had the upper hand. "They don't fall under NCIS jurisdiction, and if Jane is right, they will fall directly under ours."

"There's something in Jane's book to suggest federal jurisdiction?"

"How does a human trafficking ring sound?" Willow asked. "I'd say that falls squarely under the FBI's purview."

Human trafficking.

The words hit Jackson like a gut punch, unleashing a flood of memories he'd spent years trying to suppress. The late-night raids.

The hollow-eyed kids. The monsters they were pulled from. And the ones they couldn't save.

He stared straight ahead, saying nothing.

Beside him, Willow turned, her voice soft. "You okay?"

Jackson drew in a slow breath through his nose and forced himself to relax. "Yeah. It just caught me off guard."

That was the understatement of the year.

The nightmares still came—less often now, but no less vivid. The migraines had mostly faded, yet the weight of what he'd seen and done remained, buried just beneath the surface. The ghosts would never go away. All Jackson could do was learn to live with them.

Willow stared at him but didn't press. She never did when it came to that part of his past. She just sat quietly, steady and present. And somehow, that helped.

After a few moments, he cleared his throat. "Do you think Cooper could talk to his boss? Grease the wheels a little?"

"It's worth a shot," Willow said gently. "But we should start with NCIS. If Vicky's willing to let us assist..."

"And if Alice doesn't yank our leash," he said, cutting her off. His voice was still tight. "We're supposed to be building the Florence office, not chasing cases in another state."

"Jax..." She reached for his arm briefly. If you're not up for this and you'd rather sit this one out, I understand. But my brother's freedom is on the line, and if Jane was right about the human trafficking..."

"I'm okay, Will. Really," he said, more firmly this time. "I'll deal with it. I'm not letting you do this on your own."

She gave a small nod, accepting that. Not pushing. Just... there.

From the back seat, Ranger unleashed a series of high-pitched barks, with Ruby joining in immediately after. A moment later, Sarah and Pickle came into view, chasing each other in the front yard.

"Ruby and Ranger are home," she squealed as Jackson pulled into the laneway.

"It's good to know where her priorities are," Jackson said, sliding the SUV to the side of the driveway. "You didn't even get honorable mention."

"She shares your obsession with dogs," Willow said, patting his shoulder. "She'll likely have a better connection with you than with me."

"Hardly," Jackson said. "You two have history. I'm just a visitor here." He hopped out of the Suburban and released the dogs. Ranger bounded over Ruby to get out first. Her pregnancy was really slowing her down.

"Hi Jackson," Sarah said, giving him a shy wave. "May I please play with your dogs?"

"Not my dogs," Jackson said, motioning to Willow. "They're *our* dogs." He waggled his eyebrows at Willow. "I appreciate you asking, but you don't need to. You can play with them any time you want."

The little girl squealed with delight and raced off, calling all the dogs to her as she threw herself on the ground.

"Told you," Willow said. "You're already her favorite."

The comment made Jackson's ears burn. He didn't know how to be a child's favorite anything, and he didn't know if the child's fascination with him would upset Willow. "I'm shiny and new," he said, doing his best to deflect. "Tomorrow, I expect she'll be onto a new favorite, but you'll always be her Aunt Willow."

She lightly slapped her hand on the hood of the car. "You don't need to charm me, Mr. Brooks. You've already won my heart. I can't blame Sarah for her behavior. You're utterly loveable."

The heat in his ears spread to his cheeks, and his knees wobbled. He didn't know what he did in life to deserve such love, and he would never take it for granted. The thought made his chest tighten. Willow had once given her love to Matt, and the idiot had thrown it away. He was a moron. Jackson would walk across molten lava to be with Willow.

Chapter Seventeen

Willow

"I can't tell you much," Willow said to Ivy and Emma who were desperate to hear news about their father's case. "It's against the rules for federal agents to discuss active investigations."

Emma appeared somewhat mollified by the explanation, but Ivy wasn't having any of it.

"Fine," she said, a challenge in her tone. "Can you tell us if Daddy's okay? Where's the big lawyer who's supposed to take care of him? I mean, everyone knows that Uncle Hunter is a good lawyer, but he said he doesn't do criminal law."

"When did you hear that?" Willow asked. If Cooper had been sharing details, she was going to have strong words with her older brother.

Ivy looked away, unwilling to name her source. She had likely been eavesdropping last night, and Willow couldn't blame her for it, but they'd need to be more careful about what they said around the children.

"Well," Willow said, knowing that she needed to be as honest as possible, "we're having trouble finding a lawyer to take your dad's case. But I have complete faith in Uncle Hunter. When he sets his mind to something, he never fails."

"What's going to happen to us if Daddy goes to jail?" Emma asked, tears immediately welling up in her eyes. "Ginny says we're going to get stuck in a foster home or in an orphanage. Ginny says bad things happen to girls in orphanages."

"Ginny's a fucking cunt," Ivy said. "I told you to stop talking to her."

Willow's head snapped back at her niece's use of language. She was about to say something, to reprimand her, but stopped short when she realized the hypocrisy if she did.

"Well, she is," Ivy continued, seemingly confused by her aunt's lack of reaction to her vulgar outburst. "All my friends are calling Dad a murderer and a rapist. I got a thousand text messages today. Some even said I probably helped and our whole family will burn in hell."

Jesus Christ. As if these kids aren't going through enough.

Willow took a slow deep breath, trying not to unleash a string of expletives. "People," she said, shaking her head. "They're the worst."

She wanted to hug the girls and tell them everything would be okay, but she wouldn't lie to them. They'd see right through it, and they'd stop talking to her about anything meaningful.

"I haven't checked any of my personal mail or social accounts," Willow continued, her voice earnest, "but I'm sure I've gotten the same thing. I'd say to ignore them, but these are the people we have to live with and see every day. It's going to be bad, and until your father is cleared, it's going to get worse. I can say with certainty, when it's over, it will die down. People will find other things to fixate on."

"Ginny will stop being mean to me?" Emma asked.

"Probably not," Willow said, refusing to lie. "Some people are mean all the time. It's all they know. It's how they make themselves feel important. In my experience, people who are mean for no reason have problems of their own. Big problems. So, they lash out any place they can."

"Ginny's mom's a drunk," Ivy said to her younger sister, twisting a strand of hair around her finger. "Her father left them a year ago. Aunt Willow is right. She used to be nice before that all happened to her."

"Really?" Emma's eyebrows drew together. "But she told Cassie that I was going to end up in prison like Daddy and be someone's... *bitch.*" She winced as she whispered the last word, perhaps fearful she'd be punished for having used a bad word.

"Because she's jealous of what you have," Ivy insisted, her voice hardening. "Dad always shows up to your ballet recitals, and soccer, and anything else you do. Her mom doesn't even come to her volleyball games anymore, and she's the team's manager." She met Willow's eyes. "Ginny also got great big tits around the same time. It made her popular with the boys, if you know what I mean." She grinned, a flash of something too adult in her expression for Willow's liking.

Ivy's candor had caught Willow off guard. The casual cruelty of teenage girls wasn't surprising, she'd been one herself, but hearing it from her niece made her heart sink. She was going to say it wasn't good to perpetrate rumors, to remind Ivy that they of all people should understand how damaging gossip could be, but the boobs comment completely derailed her prepared speech. This was new territory. No FBI training had prepared her for navigating the murky waters of teenage girl dynamics while their father sat in jail accused of murder.

"Not everyone handles pain the same way," Willow finally managed, choosing her words carefully. "Some people turn it inward. Others, like Ginny it seems, turn it outward."

"I don't care why she's mean," Emma said quietly, her small hands balling into fists. "I just want her to stop."

Ruby and Ranger rushed through the living room to look out the window. Pickle wasn't far behind, barking her head off.

"We've got company," Willow called out to Jackson. He and Cooper were in the kitchen preparing food. She joined the girls who were already at the window. "I'm guessing it's SSA Davidson."

"Dinner's ready," Jackson said, carrying a tray laden with panini sandwiches, crispy nuggets, and a variety of dipping sauces.

The golden-brown bread had perfect grill marks crosshatching the surface, with strings of melted cheese escaping from the edges that stretched like delicate bridges between plate and sandwich. Steam rose from the freshly pressed meal, carrying the rich aroma of roasted meat, caramelized onions, and the acidic tang of mustard. Willow's mouth watered instantly, her stomach clenching with a hunger she'd been too distracted to notice until now.

"Girls," she said, corralling Emma and Ivy. "Can you take the dogs into the backyard with you to eat your dinner? We need to talk about things you're not allowed to hear. But I promise, if there is anything I can tell you afterwards, I will."

"There's fresh lemonade and a plate of fried chicken bites still in the kitchen," Jackson said, widening his eyes at Ivy and Emma. "I couldn't carry it and the sandwich platters. If you don't hurry, Sarah and Pickle are going to eat them all."

"You didn't make them too spicy, did you?" Willow asked, knowing Jackson's penchant for spicy food. "I don't think either of them should eat that."

Jackson smiled. "I made three batches. Mild, medium, and extra spicy. Just how you like them. I left the mild ones in the kitchen."

"I like the spicy too," Ivy said, eyeing the tray. She was so much like her aunt it made Willow's heart ache. Having chosen to stay away was the worst decision she'd ever made, and that included accepting Matt's marriage proposal.

"Grab a plate and load up on whatever you like," Jackson said. "Take some sandwiches too, if you want."

While Cooper answered the door, Ivy reluctantly made two plates of food and took Emma with her.

"Chief?" Cooper said, his posture immediately straightening.

"Sergeant," the woman said, sniffing the air. "I didn't mean to interrupt your meal. I received a call from NCIS Supervisory Special Agent Davidson. She asked me to meet her here to discuss the Gamble murder."

Cooper backed up, inviting the casually dressed woman into the foyer. "Chief Stevens, this is my sister, FBI Special Agent Willow Banks, and her partner, Special Agent Jackson Brooks." The two dogs moved beside their respective handlers. "And these are their K9s, Ranger and Ruby."

The chief moved forward, her hand extended. "Call me Janet," she said. After having introduced herself, she took a knee. "Can I say hi to your pups? They're gorgeous. I have an Irish Wolfhound at home." She looked up and smiled. "There is no bed in the world made big enough to accommodate him."

"Release," Willow said, letting Ranger choose if he wanted to visit the woman. Ruby was already on her, licking her neck and face. Ranger was less enthusiastic, but he let her pet him all the same. Dogs know dog people.

The sound of tires over gravel interrupted the conversation.

"It looks like SSA Davidson is here," Willow said, opening the front door to greet her before she had exited her car. The afternoon sun glinted off a candy apple red mustang, not the black government-issue sedan she had expected. The driver's door swung open, and a black shoe and navy-blue pantleg appeared. Matt had described Davidson as a bulldog, and Willow had pictured someone with a tenacious personality, perhaps a bit stern, but professional. She froze mid-step on the porch.

Vicky Davidson hauled herself from the driver's seat, her compact frame moving with surprising agility despite her stocky build. Her face was broad with pronounced jowls that quivered slightly as she scanned the street, her deep-set eyes narrowing against the sunlight. Her suit was impeccable but stretched tight across her shoulders, and her black hair was cropped close to her skull in a no-nonsense cut that required zero maintenance.

Willow did a double take when a man slipped out from the passenger side. Unlike Vicky, who embodied the bulldog comparison in the most literal sense, the man was tall and muscular, with shoulders that strained against his button-down shirt. The high-and-tight haircut and the way he immediately scanned the street, settling his gaze on the approaches to the house, screamed military training. The question was, why had Davidson brought backup?

As a black Dodge Charger neared, its tinted windows revealing nothing of the occupants inside, Willow's concerns ratcheted up several notches. The vehicle slowly crept along, like a predator stalking prey. Vicky's head whipped around when the driver revved the engine three times, her jowls quivering with the sudden movement.

A low rumble came from Ranger's chest, and the hair on the back of Willow's neck snapped to attention.

"Easy," she whispered, though her own muscles had tensed in response. The dog's ears pricked forward, his body coiled like a spring. She felt the slight tremor in his shoulder, the canine equivalent of her own adrenaline spike.

The vehicle slowly continued down the street before stopping three houses away.

A flash of naked fear crossed Vicky's face before being quickly masked by professional composure. She took two quick steps toward the porch, pausing when Ranger moved to intercept.

"Agent Willow Banks, I presume," the woman said. "I'm Vicky and this is my husband, Greg." Her eyes flashed of desperation. "I'm assuming this is Ranger? I've heard a lot about you both. Your SAC speaks very highly of you." She looked back at Greg, waving him forward. "I'm sorry for bringing this to your home," her voice dropping to just above a whisper. Her eyes darted back to the man standing guard by the car. He replied with a curt nod. She looked towards the Charger. "But can we please take this inside?"

Willow took the hint. She was trying to hustle the conversation along and get out of sight. Her husband continued to survey the area, like he was looking for threats.

"Ma'am," he said with a thick southern drawl. "We'd greatly appreciate some urgency to your hospitality, if you take my meaning."

Willow moved to the side. "Chief Stevens is already here."

The pair rushed past and disappeared in seconds.

"Pretty fucking strange, don't you think?" Willow said to her K9. The dog tilted his head to the side while holding her gaze, his intelligent brown eyes communicating a shared suspicion. Ranger had been through enough operations with her to recognize when something was off. His ears flicked forward, then back, as if to say he didn't like any of this either.

"Let's go see what this is all about," she murmured, resting her hand briefly on Ranger's head. "What's got a federal agent and a muscle-bound marine acting like scared rabbits?"

Chapter Eighteen

Jackson

Jackson threw open the kitchen door, startling Ivy and Emma. "Can you two help me carry iced tea and glasses?" Getting drinks had been a ruse. His true intent was to make sure the girls weren't eavesdropping, which they were. Sarah was outside with Pickle, but Ivy and Emma were parked at the kitchen table, easily within listening range. He considered sending them to their room but decided against it.

Not his house, not his kids.

"I get it." He took a seat next to the girls at the table. "You're worried about your dad, and you're curious about what's going on in the next room. I would be too." He looked over his shoulder to the door leading to the dining room, the murmur of tense voices barely audible. "But Aunt Willow told you to make yourselves scarce, and I don't know about you, but she scares the heck out of me when she's mad." He made a monstrous face and turned his hands into clawed weapons. Emma laughed, but Ivy... not so much.

Jackson looked directly into Ivy's eyes. "Aunt Willow said she'd tell you everything she could when we're done out there. She doesn't lie, and neither do I."

"What about when she abandoned us?" Ivy asked, fire in her eyes. "Our mom died, and she just disappeared. She said it was her work, but we all knew she was angry at Dad, and she took it out on us. My dad deserved a fucking medal for what he did, saving her from her dirtbag fiancé."

During his time working on the Violent Crimes Against Children task force, Jackson had witnessed plenty of kids dealing with loss at crime scenes, in interviews, and in the aftermath of every kind of violence imaginable. Some got quiet. Some lashed out. Ivy? She was a fighter.

Willow hadn't abandoned them, not really. But to a kid who'd lost her mom, who had to watch her dad pick up the pieces alone, it must have felt like that. It wasn't fair, and Jackson wasn't about to insult her by pretending it was.

"I would very much appreciate it if you could curb your colorful language," Jackson said. His voice was calm without a hint of scolding. He didn't know what else to say. "At least when you're talking with me."

"Aunt Willow swears all the time," Ivy shot back. She leaned back in her chair, a challenge flashing in her expression. "Do you tell her to stop?"

"Is that why you cuss?" Jackson asked. He rested his elbows on his knees and leaned forward. "Because you want to be like her?" The question made Ivy turn away. "Will wasn't angry at your dad. At least, I don't think so. She was hurt, and embarrassed, and she was furious with herself. She's the most amazing and perceptive person I've ever met, and yet she couldn't see past her fiancé's lies. Her world, her confidence, and her... everything blew up in her face." He thumped his fist over his chest. "Her heart was broken, and she needed to escape. Unfortunately, you girls got caught in the crossfire."

"She sure sounded angry at Daddy," Emma said. "We learned some new swear words that we'd never heard at school."

A list of Willow's favorite words ran through Jackson's mind, making him cringe internally. He went to the fridge and pulled out a pitcher of iced tea.

"Grab some glasses," he said. "There are six of us. Can you two manage that? You can bring them out with me, meet who's there, and then you need to skedaddle. These people are here to help your dad, and they won't talk if you're around. They're all very good at their jobs, and they'll know if you're listening in."

Emma nodded frantically while Ivy seemed suspicious. He probably should have sent them to their rooms, but pushing them out wouldn't do anything except make them more desperate to listen in. He hoped giving them something, even if it was insignificant, might help

"I promise," Jackson said. "Will and I will tell you everything that we can. For now, I'm asking you to trust us. Can you do that for us? Please?"

"Fine," Ivy said carrying a tray of six glasses. She moved through the door like a waitress, fully accustomed to the task. It seemed that, with her mother gone, she had taken on the role of caregiver to her two younger sisters.

The girls handed out their glasses and disappeared back into the kitchen. A moment later, the back door slammed shut. Jackson wasn't sure if they actually joined their little sister in the backyard, or if it was a con. He stepped to the kitchen door and called the dogs over.

"Guard," he whispered. Ranger and Ruby lay down by the kitchen door, calm but alert.

"I told them we'd tell them everything we could," he murmured to Willow as he sat next to her, earning him a quiet thank you. "What did I miss?" he asked the rest of the group.

"Not much," Vicky said. Her husband moved to the window and pulled back the curtains enough to peek outside. "We were waiting for you." He motioned to the sandwich in his hand. "Thank you for the food, it's much appreciated."

"I'd like to know why you called me in," Janet said to Vicky. She appeared annoyed but her body language suggested she was on edge.

Defiance radiated in Vicky's posture. "Because the bodies that were found in the walls at 400 Port Republic Street have no connection to the navy, and they don't fall under NCIS jurisdiction. But it's highly unlikely that they're not connected, so I figured an interdepartmental task force would make sense here."

"It's surprising you'd suggest that," Janet said with a harrumph. "I have never seen you voluntarily work with the BPD on anything. Why start now?"

Greg closed the curtain and looked over the assembled group. "Because Vicky and I are royally fucked, and we don't know who we can trust."

"Then why are you trusting us?" Willow asked. "You don't know us from Adam."

"That's not exactly true," Vicky said. "I've indirectly dealt with the chief for years. I believe she's a solid police officer with impeccable credentials. She's one of the few people willing to stick her neck out for what's right."

Judging by the confused look on Janet's face, the NCIS agent's respect was news to her.

"As for you and Agent Brooks..." Vicky continued, "Your boss, SAC Baldwin once told me you were a rising star and the best agent she'd ever worked with. It was because of her belief in you that I agreed to take Agent Carver. Alice didn't sugar coat it. She warned me what he was like, but she also said he was a solid investigator who wasn't afraid to get his hands dirty. I needed someone like that on my team, despite his... *ways.*"

"If you trust us, why do you have NCIS agent sitting in front of the house?" Willow asked.

"He's not a fed," Greg said, peeking outside at the edge of the curtain. "He's Military Police from the Provost Marshal's Office. Vicky and I are being watched." His broad shoulders sagged. "After you hear what we have to say, you might choose to arrest us."

"Major," Janet said. She stood and moved closer to the marine. "If the BPD takes you into custody, the provost marshal will be at my door in minutes, waving jurisdiction paperwork just like he's already done four times this year."

"Five times," Greg corrected. "One of them never even made it to your precinct. Lieutenant Colonel Pratt shut it down before the guy was even booked."

"Jesus Christ," Janet muttered. "I followed up on every single arrest. Every time you stepped on my case, I checked to see what happened to your marines."

Jackson's curiosity peaked as he took in the somewhat cryptic conversation. "Maybe you can fill the rest of us in on why you think you two would be arrested."

"We can worry about jurisdictional issues afterwards," Willow added.

"In the past year, on four separate occasions, my team caught marines carrying large quantities of drugs. Cocaine in particular," Janet said. "We wasted hundreds of hours working our CIs, doing surveillance, and gathering leads. Every time we pulled the trigger and arrested them, the provost marshal would swoop in, claim jurisdiction over marine personnel, and haul them away." Her eyes were locked on Greg. When she turned back to Willow, her expression filled with disbelief. "And these assholes never pressed charges. Never. From what I could tell, they confiscated the drugs and claimed insufficient evidence to convict."

While Vicky looked down at her hands, all eyes turned to Greg, waiting for his explanation. "You're not wrong," he said, looking somewhat ashamed. "But you're not fully right either."

The story was turning Jackson's stomach. It hadn't been so long ago that he had been forced to deal with dirty cops, and people in power using their position to bring drugs into the country. How could anyone make a dent in the drug trade if law enforcement aided in their success?

"How long has this been going on?" Willow asked.

"Too long," Vicky answered. She wiped her hands on her navy slacks and looked to her husband. "Five years ago, I was sent to MCAS Beaufort to work a homicide case, a gunnery sergeant had been beaten to death in a bar fight. Greg was an MP. He helped me gather the evidence and work the leads. It turned out, the base had more than its fair share of violence, and NCIS decided to temporarily post me there until things were under control. One thing led to another, a permanent installation was set up, and Greg and I fell in love."

"And that's when Lieutenant Colonel Pratt made his move," Greg said. "He waited until he had leverage over Vicky."

"I was making a case against him," Vicky said. "The violence was almost always drug related, and it all pointed directly at Pratt."

"I was coming into work one morning," Greg said, the muscles on his jaw clenching. "There were eight MPs waiting for me at the front gate. As soon as I was on the base, they stopped my car, yanked me out, and arrested me. They pressed my face against the hot asphalt while they supposedly searched my car. They conveniently found two kilos of coke in my trunk."

"Pratt came to see me minutes after the arrest," Vicky said. "He outright admitted they had planted the drugs and that there was no way I could prove it. He said, if I stop my investigations into him, he'd release Greg." She wrapped her arms around her belly and shuddered. "He was innocent. What was I supposed to do? Pratt said Greg would likely get shanked in prison. MPs don't survive long behind bars." There was a hitch in her voice as she spoke. "It's been five years since that happened, and I still haven't figured a way around it."

"Because you accepted the deal," Janet said, shaking her head. She strode across the room and sat next to Cooper. "And now he owns you."

"Not completely," Greg said.

"Look," Vicky jumped in, cutting her husband off. "Drugs are coming into the country with or without our help. We didn't help, not exactly..." She seemed hesitant to continue. "But I was told when to prosecute and when to stay clear."

"Fuck," Willow said. "The provost marshal told you who to arrest and who to let go. That way, you didn't look completely incompetent. Was Matt a part of this scheme?"

"No, at least not that I'm aware of," Vicky said. "I did what I was told, and Matt knew nothing about it. He's a sleazy piece of shit, but he's an excellent investigator. I put him on every other case and kept him away from Pratt. There are plenty of crimes involving navy and marine personnel that have nothing to do with the provost marshal."

Even if he didn't agree with it, Jackson understood why Vicky and Greg were doing what they were doing. But, given how it happened, he didn't know if he'd have done anything differently had it been Willow. If she was being railroaded, he'd move heaven and earth to protect her. Except, when the immediate threat had passed, he'd rain hellfire on whoever had tried to harm her.

"So, what changed?" Jackson asked, tension creeping up the back of his head.

"Murder," Vicky said, her voice dropping to a harsh whisper. "Consequences be damned. We refuse to cover up a murder."

"How do you feel about human trafficking?" Willow said, a challenge in her voice.

Chapter Nineteen

Willow

Willow carefully watched Vicky and Greg's reaction to the allegation that Jane's death may have involved human trafficking. Greg appeared confused, while Vicky's facial expression clearly showed doubt.

"According to Jane's notebook," Willow said, nodding her head, "she suspected Michael Fitzpatrick was trafficking the migrant workers he had brought in to work at the job site. She had no definitive proof, but it seemed that she was building a case against him."

"We've never had an inkling," Greg said. He shot his wife a questioning look. She shook her head in response.

"Never," she replied. "At no point did we ever suspect Pratt being involved in anything other than drugs."

"After Mr. Banks was arrested for Gamble's murder," Greg continued, "Pratt told me to make sure Vicky knew NCIS wasn't supposed to look beyond the obvious."

"Pratt asked you to cover up Jane's murder?" Willow asked. She'd never met the Lieutenant Colonel, but she was looking forward to slapping cuffs on him. "Is this why you told Matt to hurry up and close the case, because Pratt told you to?"

Vicky's head snapped back in indignation. "I never said any such thing. Where would you have heard such a thing?"

"From Matt," Jackson said. "It was practically the first thing he said to us when we met. Although, if you didn't tell him..."

"The colonel has something on him, too," Cooper said. Janet's eyebrows shot up, wordlessly asking if everyone agreed.

"Unlikely," Jackson said, offering Willow an apologetic look.

The idea that he'd defend the man she hated shocked Willow. "And why's that?" she challenged. "The man's a fucking sleazeball. I'm sure he's got all sorts of skeletons he doesn't want aired."

"Because of everything he's done since he called us in..." Jackson paused, seemingly trying to word his thoughts more delicately. "I don't know. Not exactly, but my gut tells me he wants to solve this murder as much as we do. I doubt his motivation is purely professional, but..."

"What am I missing?" Janet asked. "Y'all seem like you're dancing around a topic that none of you want to come out and talk about. Well, stop it right now. What the fuck is going on?"

"Willow and Agent Matt Carver used to be engaged," Cooper said.

"And Matt and the suspect used to be best friends when they were growing up," Vicky added. "But none of this explains why Matt would lie about me."

"Because he's a fucking manipulative prick." Willow rolled her eyes and sighed. "I'm guessing that his invitation into the investigation was a childish attempt to get me to give him another shot. His eyes bugged out of his head when he saw my engagement ring, and his warped little mind has been working overtime to find a way to win me back."

"Listen to me," Greg said. He took a seat next to Vicky and squeezed her hand. "I don't give a shit about your weird interpersonal drama situation. My wife and I are putting ourselves in significant danger being here and telling you what's going on. Can we muster enough self-control to keep this conversation on track?"

"I couldn't agree more," Willow said, thankful to steer away from her wreck of a history. "What I want to know is why Pratt told you to not get involved in the murder of one of his people. You think he'd be looking to deliver a world of hurt on whoever had brutally raped and stabbed Jane."

"Good god," Janet said. "The poor woman was raped as well?"

"I'm afraid so," Willow said. The thought of Jane's final minutes in life made her sick.

"The only thing that makes sense," Greg said, ignoring the outrage over Jane having been sexually assaulted, "is that Pratt is connected to the Fitzpatricks. I mean, everything about this case involves them. Liam owns the home the murder took place in. Sean owns the security firm that had hired Jane. Michael owns the placement agency supplying the workers."

"Do the Fitzpatricks have any ties to criminal activity?" Jackson asked. "The only thing I've heard is that Mrs. Hargrove thinks Liam Fitzpatrick pulled some strings to get a permit to renovate the home at 400 Republic. Getting the historical society to back him up might be shady, but I don't think it rises to the level of murder and human trafficking. Unless they're operating under the radar like their father did."

"What does their father have to do with this?" Willow asked.

"Nothing," Vicky quickly replied. "The man was killed a couple of years ago. He was supposed to have testified against some big fish after he was arrested for having nearly thirty kilos of coke on his boat. An ex-marine murdered him on the way to the State's Attorney's office."

"Did Fitzpatrick ever give a clue as to who the big fish were?" Willow asked. "He must have said something to warrant a meeting with the State's Attorney."

"Only that the US Coast Guard, and a senator were involved," Janet said. "There had been speculation that it was the Florida

State Senator, but there was no proof. Everything was circumstantial and speculative."

"What would the Coast Guard have to do with it?" Jackson asked.

"Maritime traffic intel," Greg said. "If someone had inside access to Coast Guard patrol schedules, they could move shipments through without ever getting spotted."

Willow's adrenaline was pumping as an idea took hold. "What if Fitzpatrick was providing the fishing boats to pick up drugs in international waters and then bringing them back with his fish-haul. Think about it. If whoever is bringing in the drugs knows where the Coast Guard are patrolling, they could easily avoid detection. They transfer the coke to Fitzpatrick, he brings it in, and then he passes it off to Pratt. With his military connections, he can easily ship it across the country completely undetected."

She turned to Janet and raised her eyebrows. "I'm guessing Pratt's using his own people to handle the distribution, and that's why you've been catching some every now and again. With his position, he can likely pull records of every person working on his base. He finds those with some sort of financial hardship, or those who already have a troubled past, and he recruits them."

"And now he's graduated from importing drugs to importing people?" Jackson asked. "And using the Fitzpatricks to bring them in, train them, and then sell them?" He looked ill.

"It seems that way," Willow said. "According to Jane's notebook, the workers at 400 Republic behaved like they were being constantly scrutinized. When their boss, Michael Fitzpatrick, showed up at the house, they all became visibly nervous. He pulled them aside one by one to speak with them. Jane was certain he was threatening them."

"Could it be they were afraid to lose their jobs?" Janet asked. "Maybe he was just very strict?"

"If that were the case," Jackson said, jumping into the conversation, "he'd have been interviewing their crew chief, or Mason, or the other workers. He wouldn't be grilling them individually."

"According to Jane," Willow said, "Michael Fitzpatrick also spoke with one of Mason's employees, Thomas Warner. Fitzpatrick had warned Thomas to stay away from one of the chefs, Anika Augustin. She wrote that Fitzpatrick threatened to have him removed from the premises if he didn't leave Anika alone. Jane had spoken to Anika about it, and the woman denied having had any contact with Thomas. But, after that day, she rarely left the kitchen."

"Someone snitched on Anika?" Cooper asked as he rubbed his temples. "It's the only way Fitzpatrick could know anything about their time together. That's why he spoke with each one individually. They were all spying on each other."

Willow glanced over at Jackson. The conversation was weighing on him, and she was about to make it much worse. She had read some other disturbing details in Jane's notebook but had chosen to keep them to herself until she knew if it meant something... more. Now, based on everything she was learning, it definitely meant something more.

"There are some other details in Jane's notebook," Willow said with a wince. "There were three provocatively dressed young teenage girls who spent all their time flirting with Mason and his crew. Despite their constant advances, none of Mason's guys took the bait. Mason had warned his entire renovation team, very loudly and very publicly, to do their job and leave the children alone. One of the house staff, a woman, pushed the girls to continue making advances. She told Mason that his men didn't need to interact with the girls, but that the girls needed to practice."

Willow felt Jackson go still beside her. Not just still. Rigid. His breathing slowed. His hands that had been resting on his knees, curled into tight fists.

Vicky kept talking, unaware. "None of this is definitive proof, but—"

"No." Jackson's said, speaking before she could finish. His voice was flat, menacing. "It's not proof."

Willow glanced at him. His jaw was clenched so tightly that she could see the muscles twitch.

Vicky hesitated. "I just mean—"

Jackson exhaled in frustration, cutting her off a second time. "Traffickers rarely leave trails. They keep their victims isolated. Afraid. Drugged. Beaten, if that's what it takes." His voice was low, vibrating with something Willow couldn't quite place. "These girls are being groomed to become sex slaves." His breathing became rapid and his face turned red while fury consumed him. "Matt had said that the Fitzpatricks have a fleet of fishing boats too. Think about it. They've got boats, a labor agency, a security firm, and buildings. That's not a coincidence. That's a supply chain."

Then his voice rose.

"If Anika Augustin knows something, we need to get it out of her. She's our best lead."

Willow's stomach twisted. "She's a victim," she reminded him.

Jackson shot to his feet. His chair scraped against the hardwood floor, a piercing sound in the quiet room.

"Yes, she's a victim, but she's not a child." His voice was razor-edged. "Children need protection. Adults... adults need to talk. Because if she won't, she's helping to turn them into sex workers or something much worse."

Willow barely recognized him. His expression was dark, his eyes flashing with something deeper than just anger. He was scaring her. Then, without another word, he turned and stormed into the kitchen, sending Ranger and Ruby scattering.

Silence hung heavy in his wake.

Janet exhaled. "Jesus. If that's the way he treats victims, he shouldn't be on this case."

Willow's head snapped toward her. Her voice was cold steel. "Shut your fucking mouth."

Janet blinked. "Excuse me?"

"Jackson worked VCAC for three years," Willow said, her voice tight. "Do you know what that means?"

Janet didn't answer but held Willow's gaze.

"It means he's seen things no one should see. Heard things no one should hear. It means he's pulled children out of places that make this look like a goddamn fairy tale." Willow leaned forward. "So before you judge him, maybe ask yourself, how many child traffickers have you taken down?"

Janet lowered her eyes. "None. It's not a problem here in Beaufort."

"Well, now it is." Willow exhaled. Her heart was still pounding. She pivoted toward the kitchen, to where Jackson had disappeared. He wasn't okay. And maybe... neither was she. She couldn't fully know what he had gone through, but she understood why this case was affecting him so deeply. She didn't care if the police chief took offense to his reaction. Jackson was kind and caring, and rock solid. She would support him, because she trusted him. Completely.

Willow was about to follow him when he returned, looking like a storm ready to be unleashed.

"This is not a suitable location for this conversation," he said. He motioned with his thumb back to the kitchen.

Chapter Twenty

Jackson

All eyes snapped to the doorway where Ivy stood, arms crossed and chin raised in defiance. Emma hovered just behind her big sister's shoulder, eyes wide with apprehension.

Jackson watched Willow's face fall as she spotted her nieces. She'd been trying so hard to shield them from the worst of this case.

"Girls, this isn't a conversation for you," Chief Stevens said, her tone authoritative but not harsh. "Cooper, why don't you take the girls upstairs while we finish our discussion down here?"

Ivy stepped fully into the living room. "No. This is about Dad, and we have a right to know."

Emma moved to stand beside her sister. "Is Dad in more trouble?" she asked softly.

Jackson caught Willow's eye, trying to convey support without words. He noticed Sarah appearing from behind her elder sisters, clutching onto a picture book. Pickle trotted in behind her.

"Sergeant Cooper, remove the children," Chief Stevens repeated, this time with less tact. "Take them to your house, if you must."

"This is their home," Willow snapped, surprising Jackson with her vehemence. He'd never heard that particular tone from her before. It was fiercely protective, almost maternal. "If you have a problem with the girls being here, *Chief*, then we can move this meeting to NCIS or BPD, but I'm not sending my nieces away from their own house."

Vicky was visibly tense. "I can't go to either of those places," she said, voice low. "I have no reason to meet with the FBI or the local police. Officially, I'm here to search for Jane's laptop." She glanced nervously at Greg, who reached for her hand. "If Pratt finds out I'm actively working with you..."

Jackson understood immediately. Vicky and Greg were risking not just their careers but potentially their safety. The tension in the room ratcheted up another notch.

"The girls stay," Willow said firmly, turning to her nieces. "But that doesn't mean you get to hear everything. Understand? Ask us whatever you want, and we'll do our best to answer all your questions."

Jackson pulled out two more dining room chairs, placing them beside where he and Willow had been sitting. Willow led Ivy and Emma and the three of them took a seat.

While Jackson moved to stand behind the girls, he watched Sarah wander over to Ruby, who had settled into the corner. The child nestled beside the pregnant dog, and Ruby shifted slightly, making room against her warm side. He felt a moment of concern for Ruby, she'd had an exhausting day, but the dog seemed content with Sarah's gentle attention.

"What's happening to Dad?" Ivy demanded as she took a seat. "And who are those girls you were talking about? The ones who are my age."

"And where's Anika?" Emma added, sitting beside her sister. "Is she okay? She makes the best cookies."

Jackson watched Willow with Ivy and Emma. Her movements were calm and subtle as she searched for a way to be honest with these girls, hopefully without terrifying them. Her empathy and intuition that made her an excellent dog handler appeared to translate directly into how she dealt with children.

She's going to be a great mom.

"Your dad is innocent," Willow said, gesturing to everyone in the room. "And we're going to prove it. All of us."

Relief washed over Emma's face, though Ivy remained tense, skeptical.

"Listen carefully," Willow continued. "It's going to take time for that to happen, and it might be a while before your dad comes home. The circumstances of this case are more complicated than we initially thought."

Ivy looked at Emma before turning back to Willow, widening her eyes. "Because Jane was *friends* with my dad."

"Yes, but there's more," Jackson said, wondering where Ivy had gotten that idea. "We've discovered that she might have been killed because she found out something serious was happening where your dad works."

"Something illegal?" Emma asked quietly.

Jackson was impressed by the child's perceptiveness. The quiet ones often saw more than people gave them credit for.

"Yes. We believe people were using the house where your dad worked to do bad things."

"Like hurting those girls?" Ivy pressed, her eyes keen and probing. "The young ones you were talking about?"

Willow took a deep breath and slowly let it go. Jackson could almost see her weighing each word in her head while she formulated an age-appropriate response. "We think some people might have been brought to this country against their will, or under false pretenses. Jane was trying to help them and it cost her life."

"You mean to save them from being used as sex slaves?" Ivy said bluntly. Her gaze raked every person in the room, challenging anyone to deny it. "I'm not stupid, Aunt Willow. It happens all the time on TV and in movies."

Jackson's knees buckled. The simple, matter-of-fact way Ivy said those words shocked him. A fourteen-year-old child shouldn't know that term and she certainly shouldn't know what it meant. His work with VCAC had shown him the worst side of people, but he never got used to the collision of childhood innocence with such extreme darkness.

"You're right," Willow acknowledged. "And no, you're not stupid. Far from it. But there are details of this case that aren't appropriate for anyone your age, and I won't apologize for trying to protect you from that. There are bad people in this world who do very bad things."

Emma's expression contorted with fear. "Is Dad in danger?" she asked, getting straight to what Jackson realized was her primary concern.

Willow took Emma's hand, her fingers trembling slightly. "We're taking every precaution to make sure everyone is safe. Your dad included."

"And us?" Ivy challenged, her eyes darting around the room at the assembled adults.

Jackson gently rested his hand on Ivy's shoulders, wanting to offer some additional reassurance. "Especially you," he said softly. The girl relaxed slightly under his touch, her expression softening. The smallest victories sometimes meant the most.

Ranger had moved to Willow's side, pressing against her leg. Jackson watched her absently stroke the dog's head, drawing strength from his presence. Ruby remained with Sarah, the two of them a quiet island of calm in the storm of tension.

"I need you to trust me," Willow said, looking between her nieces. "I know I haven't given you much reason to lately, but I'm here now. I know I'm repeating myself, but I promise I will tell you everything you need to know. That being said, there are some things related to this case that I can't share, not because you're kids, but because they're part of an active investigation."

Ivy studied Willow's face for several long seconds. Jackson held his breath, recognizing the importance of this moment. Finally, Ivy gave a single, reluctant nod.

"I understand the girls needed to hear some of this," Janet said. "But there's more that we can't discuss here. I'll set up a secure workspace at the precinct. We can continue this there. If SSA Davidson doesn't want to physically be there, we can connect with her remotely."

"She's not wrong," Cooper said, giving Ivy an apologetic look. "There are details we need to discuss and there is no possible way to filter the content." His face screwed up, like a revelation had slammed into him. "How do you know Anika makes the best cookies?" he asked Emma. "Have you met her?"

Sarah piped up from the corner. "Daddy took us to work last week."

"PD day," Ivy added. "I didn't want to go, but the old house was actually pretty cool. Too bad Dad doesn't spend as much time fixing up our house."

"When we got there," Emma chimed in. "Anika made us breakfast, and she baked muffins and cookies for us. Everyone was really nice, even though they didn't speak English very well."

"Of course they didn't speak our language very well," Ivy said. "They all come from Haiti."

Jackson sucked a quiet breath. Haiti was a country strangled by corruption, poverty, and lawlessness. It was a place where desperation made people easy prey. Smugglers didn't need to lie to recruit workers; they only had to promise food, a roof, and a chance for a better life.

Chapter Twenty-One

Willow

Willow sat cross-legged on the bed, surrounded by papers. The bedside lamp cast a warm glow across the scattered documents, creating islands of light in the otherwise shadowy room. Ranger was stretched out on the floor, his chin resting on his paws. His eyes were alert, following her every movement. Ruby lay beside him, her back pressed against his, snoring loudly.

The house had finally quieted. After the revelations of the evening, the girls had gone to bed reluctantly, each processing the information about their father in their own way. Ivy had retreated behind a wall of teenage anger, while Emma had asked a thousand questions that Willow couldn't fully answer. Sarah, thankfully oblivious to most of it, had simply wanted a bedtime story from her aunt, a request that had caught Willow completely off guard.

She had handed over Jane's notebook along with Mrs. Hargrove's to Chief Stevens to be logged as evidence. Barely an hour after the chief left, she had emailed Willow a digitized copy, which Willow had promptly printed. The pages of Jane's observations lay open in her lap, its pages filled with the dead woman's detailed notes.

Jackson emerged from the bathroom in a worn FBI Academy t-shirt and sweatpants, toweling his damp hair. Had the bed not been covered in paperwork, his still-damp body would have made for a wonderful distraction.

"You're still at it," Jackson observed, sitting on the edge of the bed. "Find anything else?"

Willow pointed at a passage in Jane's notebook. "Yeah, and it's not good." She pushed her hair back from her face, suddenly aware of how exhausted she was. "Listen to this. On December 6th, the Friday before she was killed, Jane wrote that Michael Fitzpatrick showed up at the worksite at 6:02 AM."

Jackson's eyebrows rose. "That's specific."

"Jane was meticulous." Willow turned the notebook so Jackson could see the neat timeline entries. "She noted that Fitzpatrick had harsh words with her about *minding her business about deliveries this weekend.* Later that same morning, he spoke with Mason."

She flipped to the next page. "Jane overheard him telling Mason that two new gardeners would be starting on Monday, and that Mason needed to manage them until Fitzpatrick could get a head gardener to properly train them." Willow tapped the page. "Jane had underlined three times that the Gardeners arrived on Saturday morning at 1:57 AM."

"That's the Saturday before the murder," Jackson said.

"Exactly." Willow reached for another stack of papers, Evelyn Hargrove's notes. "And look what our neighborhood watch captain recorded." She flipped to a dog-eared page. "On December 6th, she noted two black men arriving by boat after dark. She wrote, Two dark-skinned men arrived on a fishing boat. No luggage. Escorted inside by M. Fitzpatrick."

Jackson took the pages and studied the entry. "The dates don't line up. Jane said they arrived on the 7th and Evelyn said the 6th."

"They line up," Willow said, shaking her head. "Most people consider that the night belongs to the day before. We can follow up with Ms. Hargrove, but I'm sure it's what she meant."

"Do you think these were the men we found dead in the service corridor?"

"It fits," Willow said. "Two men arrive on the 7th. They're supposed to start work as gardeners, but they end up dying somehow. Then, on the 9th, Jane is murdered, and we find two bodies hidden in the wall."

Jackson flipped through Evelyn's notes. "Did you see this? Evelyn reported a white van showing up at 4:30 AM. Does the woman ever sleep?" He set the papers down, his expression grim. "We need to see the surveillance videos from the house. The exterior is covered with security cameras. I'm guessing that the white van was there to pick up the dead bodies."

"And Jane refused to ignore what was happening," Willow said quietly. "What if that's why she was killed? Because she wouldn't look the other way."

The room fell silent as Willow's theory settled over them. Ruby shifted in her sleep, a small whimper escaping her.

"We need to interview the workers." Jackson stood and began pacing the small guest room, as if trying to physically work through the problem. "Let's pay Michael Fitzpatrick a visit and find out where his staff stays when they're not on the job site."

"Starting with Anika," Willow added just before her face went slack in stunned disbelief. "According to Evelyn, a police car drove right past the house. A minute later, he came back, sat in his car, and waited."

"Drove past?" Jackson asked. "That makes no sense."

"Unless he saw the van and, for some reason, didn't want to investigate." Willow knew Officer Dade to be lazy and a coward. Based on her past experience with this officer, if he believed there was danger, he would do everything to avoid it.

"We can deal with that tomorrow, too. It's after eleven," Jackson said, glancing at the bedside clock. "We've got the meeting at the police station first thing."

Willow made no move to gather the scattered papers. "I don't think I can sleep." She looked up at Jackson, the fear she'd been holding back finally seeping into her voice. "I'm worried about Mason and the girls."

Jackson sat back down beside her, close enough that she could feel the warmth radiating from him.

"We'll deal with that as it happens," he said, his voice calm and steady. "Speculating is only going to drive you crazy."

"I know, but—"

"Mason's safe," Jackson interrupted gently. He reached out and took her hand, his thumb tracing circles on her palm. "He's under lock and key with security monitors on him 24/7. Greg has MPs he trusts keeping an eye on him. And tomorrow, we start pushing back against whatever the hell is going on here."

Willow let out a long breath, feeling some of the tension leave her body. She leaned into Jackson, allowing herself a moment of vulnerability that she rarely showed to anyone else. "When did you get so smart?"

"I've always been smart," he said with a small smile, wrapping his arm around her shoulders. "You've just been too stubborn to notice."

Despite everything, Willow found herself smiling back. "Bullshit."

Jackson's arm tightened around her, and he pressed a kiss to her temple. "We're going to figure this out, Will. All of it. I promise."

The certainty in his voice was reassuring, even if Willow knew it wasn't a promise either of them could guarantee. Even still, she allowed herself to believe it for now. "I know."

They sat in comfortable silence for a moment, listening to the soft breathing of the dogs and the distant hum of the house's heating system.

"You know what's funny?" Willow said after a while. "Yesterday, my biggest worry was that you'd be mad at me for not telling you about Matt sooner. And now..."

"And now we're unraveling a human trafficking operation in your hometown," Jackson finished. "Life comes at you fast."

Willow snorted. "That's one way of putting it."

Jackson stood and began helping her gather the scattered papers. "We should at least try to sleep. Tomorrow's going to be rough."

Willow knew he was right and reluctantly allowed him to take Jane's notes from her hands. As he placed them on the nightstand, she noticed the tension in his shoulders, the deliberate way he was moving. The revelations about the trafficking operation had hit him hard. She'd seen the haunted look in his eyes earlier when they discussed the young girls being coached to flirt with the workers.

"Are you okay?" she asked quietly. "Really okay? After everything we heard today about the girls..."

Jackson paused, his back to her. For a moment, she thought he might brush off the question, but then his shoulders sagged slightly. "No," he admitted. "But I will be."

He shifted to face her, and in the soft lamplight, she could see the weariness in his eyes. "I'm sorry about earlier. I shouldn't have snapped like that."

"You don't need to apologize," Willow said. "Not to me. Not ever."

A sad, grateful smile crossed his face. "I just... when I think about what those girls might have been going through, it brings everything back. All the cases. All the victims."

Willow rose from the bed and crossed to him, placing her hands on his chest. "I know. And I've got your back, just like you've got mine."

The simple truth of that statement seemed to steady him. Jackson covered her hands with his own, the contact grounding them both.

"Come on," he said after a moment. "Let's at least lie down and pretend we're going to sleep."

Willow smiled and led Jackson to bed. Before crawling in beside him, she switched off the lamp, plunging the room into darkness, save for the moonlight filtering through the curtains. As they settled into bed, Ranger repositioned himself at the door, maintaining his guard even as he rested. Ruby, still fast asleep, barely stirred.

In the darkness, Willow could feel the steady rise and fall of Jackson's chest beside her. Despite everything, the case, her brother, the danger, the uncertainty, there was a comfort in his presence that she'd never found anywhere else.

"Hey, Jackson?" she whispered.

"Hmm?"

"Thank you. For being here. For coming with me."

His arm tightened around her waist, pulling her closer. "Always, Will. Always."

As exhaustion finally began to claim her, Willow's last conscious thought was of Jane Gamble's final entry in her notebook, dated December 9th, just hours before her death.

Something big is happening tonight. M says to stay out of the way and that crossing the Fitzpatricks will lead to nothing good. Fuck that!

Not heeding those words had cost Jane her life.

Who's M? Michael Fitzpatrick? Mason? Oh Jesus, could it be Matt?

Chapter Twenty-Two

Jackson

Jackson felt the bite of cold morning air on his face as he and Willow crossed the parking lot of the Beaufort Police Station. The building was a bland, two-story structure of weathered brick and narrow windows. Utilitarian and unremarkable, much like most small-town police stations he'd visited over the years.

He missed the reassuring presence of Ruby padding along beside him. Both dogs had been left at Mason's house to keep the girls company. He'd worried about leaving Ruby behind given her pregnancy, but she'd seemed content enough curled up with Sarah, and Cooper had arranged for his wife to check in throughout the day.

Inside, Jackson took in the morning bustle of the station: officers changing shifts, the pungent aroma of over-brewed coffee, phones ringing in the background. The desk sergeant, a portly man with salt-and-pepper hair and reading glasses perched on the end of his nose, looked up as they approached.

"Morning," he said, his drawl thick even in that single word. "Y'all must be the FBI agents from Alabama." He reached for his phone. "Let me call Sergeant Banks. He's expecting you."

While they waited, Jackson studied the station's bulletin board, noting the mix of community notices and wanted posters. A sign advertising the department's annual Christmas toy drive hung slightly askew. Beneath it, a child's crayon drawing of a police officer holding hands with a little girl was pinned with care. Even in police stations, reminders of kindness persisted.

Cooper appeared moments later, looking more rested than Jackson had expected given yesterday's revelations. He carried a coffee mug emblazoned with the Beaufort PD logo.

"Morning," he said, nodding to them both. "Follow me."

Jackson stayed close behind Willow as Cooper led them through a maze of desks where detectives and patrol officers typed reports or spoke quietly on phones. The squad room had the controlled chaos typical of any police department, a place where the worst of humanity was processed with paperwork and procedure. He'd spent enough time in stations like this to know their rhythms, to recognize the particular blend of boredom and tension that defined police work.

Cooper stopped at a door marked "Conference Room 2" and pushed it open. The room was spartanly furnished, a large table surrounded by chairs, whiteboards and corkboards covered in notes and timeline data, and stacks of files arranged in meticulous order. Five thick binders were arranged at intervals around the table, each accompanied by a legal pad and pen.

"Chief was here all night," Cooper said, gesturing to the binders. "Put together everything we have so far: Mason's arrest record, Jane's autopsy and lab reports, and preliminary ME findings on our two John Does. We also received the full report from the NCIS crime scene team."

Jackson picked up the nearest binder and flipped it open. The familiar format of police reports and lab work created a strange comfort, an ordered approach to chaos.

"Anything conclusive on cause of death for the men in the wall?" he asked, focusing on what mattered most right now.

Cooper shook his head. "ME's initial assessment suggests carbon monoxide poisoning, based on visual indicators. Cherry-red lips, discoloration of the skin. Lab work will confirm, but he seems pretty confident."

"That tracks with what we saw when we found them," Jackson said, remembering the blue-tinged lips of the bodies and the way they'd been positioned, as if they'd simply fallen asleep.

"If they were poisoned," Willow said, flipping through the pages of her binder, "it was either on the Fitzpatrick's boat, or on whatever boat had brought them in from Haiti. Had the source been at the house, there would have been more people getting sick."

"It had to have been the Fitzpatrick's boat," Jackson said. "In my experience, traffickers will not accept sick or injured people. Had they arrived in bad condition, they'd have been killed and tossed overboard."

"What makes you think they were transferred," Cooper asked. "Couldn't the Fitzpatricks have brought them in themselves?"

"Unlikely," Jackson said as he took a seat. "The journey would require a boat of significant size, something the Fitzpatricks don't have. I checked their website last night. They primarily catch shrimp and near-shore species. Their biggest ship is only forty-two feet and they boast that their fish and seafood are locally sourced."

"When's Janet getting here?" he asked, wanting all players at the table before discussing thoughts and details. He looked up at the three whiteboards, noticing them for the first time. They were already covered with people's pictures, titles, and a tremendous number of sticky notes. The chief really had been busy.

"Soon," Cooper said, checking his watch. "She went home to shower and change. Been working since yesterday without a break." He moved to a small table in the corner where a coffee maker gurgled. "Coffee? It's not great, but it'll wake you up."

"Please," Willow said, moving to the window that overlooked the parking lot.

"Same for me," Jackson said, continuing to flip through the binder. "What about Agent Davidson? When will she be joining us?"

Cooper poured three cups of coffee. "She'll call in around nine."

Jackson accepted his cup with a nod of thanks, the bitter scent of burned coffee rising with the steam. He took a sip and winced internally. Police station coffee was universally terrible, a fact that transcended state lines and jurisdictions.

"Hunter stopped by the base this morning," Cooper said. "Mason seemed nervous, but more concerned about the girls than himself." He hesitated a moment before adding, "He also asked Hunter to help him prepare a will."

Jackson's attention sharpened, instantly alert to the implications. A will meant Mason was expecting the worst. It also meant he believed his life was in serious danger.

He watched Willow's reaction with concern, seeing her face pale, her body go rigid. "A will? Why would he..." Her voice cracked slightly. "He thinks he's in danger?"

"It's probably just a precaution," Cooper offered, but Jackson could hear the lack of conviction in his tone. "Given everything that's happened..."

"I need to see him. Today." Willow's tone left no room for argument, and Jackson recognized the determined set of her shoulders. It was the same expression she wore when working difficult cases, a blend of stubbornness and absolute commitment.

"Will," Cooper said, his voice low and measured. "That's not a good idea right now. We need to maintain a careful distance until..."

"Like hell we do," Willow interrupted, her posture stiffening. "He's drafting a fucking will. He thinks he's going to die."

Jackson stood, placing a hand gently on her shoulder, feeling the tension coiled beneath her skin.

"Willow," he said quietly, using his body to partially shield her from Cooper's view, creating a momentary bubble of privacy. "Right now, the best thing we can do for Mason is to focus on building this case. Greg assured us he's being protected." He caught her gaze, holding it, trying to convey both understanding and steadiness. "Trust that we're all doing our part."

He felt a flutter of relief when she reluctantly agreed. The tension in her shoulders didn't entirely disappear, but it diminished slightly beneath his touch.

"Fine," she conceded. "But I want regular updates on what's going on with him." She patted his chest and retook her seat.

Jackson returned to his binder, quickly scanning the index. "I don't see any mention of the security videos from the property," he said. "I spotted three cameras at the front of the house. There were likely many more around the entire property."

"There was nothing logged in the NCIS reports," Cooper said. "I noticed the same thing. My guess is that the hard drives got pulled by the killer. If the cameras have cloud storage, we can have those subpoenaed. Maybe NCIS has already done that."

"That's a fucking shame," Willow said, annoyance in her voice. "Because according to the neighbor, Mrs. Hargrove, a white van had shown up before she called 911, and then Dade showed up after her 911 call, and the lazy fat fuck drove right past the house. He came back a couple of minutes later and then sat in his car and waited."

"Fuck me," Cooper said. "I didn't see that. I can get IT to pull his GPS records for the night. If that's true, the chief is going to shit an actual alligator."

"I want to have another chat with Officer Dade," Jackson said. "The guy lied through his teeth the last time I talked with him, and I'm angry with myself for having been fooled by him."

Cooper pulled out his cell phone and made a call. "Hey, I want Officer Kent Dade called in. I need to have a—" He stopped mid-sentence, and a darkness twisted his expression. "I don't care if he called in sick last night. Send an ambulance over to pick him up if you have to. I want him in my office in thirty minutes, or you can tell him to start looking for a new job." He winked at Willow. "Also," Cooper added quickly, "I want his full GPS records for his vehicle starting from December 8th. Tell IT I want them before Officer Dade arrives." He jabbed his finger at his phone, disconnecting the call.

"How is he still a cop?" Willow asked. "The man is as useless as he is fat."

"Because he's friends with the city manager," Cooper said. "Back before Stevens took over, Dade and the previous chief were buddies. They used to play poker with the city manager and members of the city council. Firing him was impossible, at least not without significant blowback. If the neighbor's account of what happened is accurate, I don't think there is anyone who will be able to protect him from Stevens. I would be surprised if he wasn't brought up on formal charges."

"What if Dade pulled the tapes himself?" Jackson said. "He'd likely have had time between arresting Mason and the EMTs arriving."

"Jesus," Willow said. "Jane's laptop was missing when I searched her room. Do you think he took that, too?"

Cooper shook his head in disbelief. "Everything suggests Dade was either directly involved or had turned a blind eye."

"His timing doesn't make sense otherwise," Jackson agreed, recalling the officer's contemptuous demeanor during their interview. Dade's bluster was intended to throw them off, to make him appear annoyed because they were wasting his time. "His delay to arrive on scene, and the amount of time it took him to report the arrest... How had I not picked up on that?"

"Forget about that," Willow bellowed. A horrified expression contorted her face. "Mason knew the killer was still in the house. He had to. Why didn't he say anything to us or to Hunter?"

"He's afraid for his girls," Jackson said, a knot in his neck suddenly tightening. "It's also why he wants a will. He's been threatened, and he'll stop at nothing to protect his children."

The conference room door swung open abruptly, and Chief Janet Stevens walked in. Her hair was still wet, and she had deep dark circles under her eyes. Most concerning was her expression that looked uncomfortably like pity.

Jackson sprang to his feet, immediately recognizing the face of someone bearing bad news. "Chief?"

"We were just reviewing the evidence," Cooper said, gesturing to the white boards. "We found significant inconsistencies in Dade's behavior and—"

"That can wait," Janet interrupted, her voice taut. Her gaze swept across the room, landing nowhere in particular as if she couldn't quite decide how to deliver her news. "Coast Guard just pulled a candy-apple red Mustang out of the Beaufort River."

The air seemed to vanish from the room. Jackson's memory flashed back to the red Mustang that Vicky and Greg had arrived in yesterday.

"When?" Cooper asked, standing so quickly he slammed his chair against the wall. "Are we sure it's the Davidson's?"

"We're certain," Janet said. "Apparently it went off the Woods Memorial Bridge sometime after midnight. The car's registered to Gregory Davidson."

Willow's face went pale. "Did they find him in his car?"

"No," Janet confirmed, her voice dropping. "No bodies have been recovered yet. Divers are still searching."

Jackson felt a cold weight settle in his stomach. This was no accident. He'd seen the way Greg was constantly surveying their surroundings yesterday, and how he continuously looked out the window. The marine knew they were being watched. And now...

"Jesus Christ," Cooper muttered. "Have you contacted SSA Davidson?"

"Can't reach her," Janet replied, shaking her head. "She's not answering her cell, and NCIS says she hasn't reported in this morning. I've sent a cruiser to their home."

Concern for the Davidsons hung heavy in the room. If Vicky and Greg had been targeted, it meant Pratt or the Fitzpatricks knew they were cooperating with the investigation. The circle of people they could trust was shrinking rapidly.

Willow's phone rang, shattering the tense silence. She glanced at the screen and immediately answered. "Hunter?"

Jackson watched her face transform from shock about the Davidsons to something even more urgent as she listened.

"When?" she demanded, already moving toward the door. "How bad?" Another pause. "We're on our way."

She ended the call, her eyes finding Jackson's. "Mason's being rushed to Beaufort Memorial. Hunter says he started convulsing during their meeting."

"What happened?" Cooper asked, following his sister.

"They don't know," Willow said, her voice strained. "One minute they were reviewing documents for his defense, and the next..." She shook her head, unable to finish.

Jackson grabbed his jacket, exchanging a meaningful look with Cooper. The timing was too convenient to be coincidence. First the Davidsons, now Mason. It was clear someone was systematically removing threats. Mason had been holding back information, probably to protect his daughters. If he'd been poisoned, it meant the provost marshal or the Fitzpatricks were afraid he was finally ready to talk. There was no way to overtly harm him while in custody but poisoning his breakfast would be easy to do and even easier to hide who'd done it.

"I need to make some calls," Janet said as they headed out, though Jackson noted her hesitation. Working through official channels when they didn't know who to trust could make things worse.

But Jackson knew they wouldn't find Greg or Vicky alive. Not after what they'd revealed yesterday. As he followed Willow out, the gravity of their situation crystallized with terrifying clarity. This wasn't just about clearing Mason anymore. It wasn't even just about Jane's murder or human trafficking.

Now it was about keeping Willow's family alive and staying alive themselves.

Chapter Twenty-Three

Willow

Willow's fingers tightened around the steering wheel as she tore down Ribaut Road toward Beaufort Memorial. Jackson sat rigid beside her, his face set in tense lines. In her rearview mirror, she could see Cooper's police cruiser following close behind, its lights flashing, its siren silent.

"How the hell did this happen?" she muttered, swerving around a slow-moving sedan. "He was in military custody. How does someone just..." She couldn't finish the thought. The implications were too disturbing.

"Someone on the inside," Jackson said quietly. "It's not too surprising that Colonel Pratt would have people to do... whatever."

Willow yanked the wheel right, taking the turn into the hospital entrance too fast. The tires squealed in protest. She barely registered Jackson reaching for the SUV's *oh-shit* handle.

"The Fitzpatricks or Pratt," she said through clenched teeth. "Has to be."

The hospital loomed ahead, its emergency entrance glowing red in the morning light. Willow screeched to a halt in the ambulance bay, not caring that she wasn't supposed to park there. She was out of the car almost before it stopped moving, Jackson right behind her.

The automatic doors whispered open as they rushed into the emergency department. Cooper joined them seconds later, his badge already in hand.

Willow approached the front desk, her heart hammering. "Mason Banks," she said, struggling to keep her voice level. "He was just brought in. Possible poisoning."

The woman behind the desk, middle-aged with tired eyes, typed on her keyboard and frowned. "I'm sorry, we don't have anyone by that name registered here."

Willow felt the blood drain from her face. "What do you mean? He was being transported here. Military police escort." Her voice rose. "He should be here by now."

The desk attendant shook her head, looking genuinely apologetic. "I'm sorry, ma'am. We haven't admitted anyone by that name."

"Maybe there was a delay," Jackson suggested, placing a steadying hand on the small of her back. "Or they took him to a different hospital."

Willow shook her head violently. "No. Hunter specifically said Beaufort Memorial." A terrible thought struck her. "What if he died en route? What if..."

"Slow down," Jackson said, his voice low and steady. "We don't know anything yet."

Cooper stepped forward, badge extended. "I'm Sergeant Banks with Beaufort PD. The patient is my brother. He was in military custody at MCAS Beaufort, being transferred here after an on-base medical emergency. Can you check if an ambulance has radioed ahead?"

The attendant gave in and picked up a phone, speaking quietly into it. Willow paced, her mind racing through worst-case scenarios like Mason dying in the ambulance and his daughters becoming orphans.

"He has to be okay," she whispered to Jackson. "He has to be. I never..." She swallowed hard. "I never told him I understood why he did it. About Matt. I've been so angry for so long, and for what? He was trying to protect me."

Jackson squeezed her hand. "You'll get to tell him."

The desk attendant hung up the phone. "We have a possible poisoning victim arriving now."

Relief crashed through Willow so forcefully that her knees buckled. "That's him. That has to be him."

A commotion at the ambulance entrance caught their attention. Doors burst open as a gurney surrounded by medical personnel and two stone-faced MPs rushed through. Willow caught a glimpse of Mason's face, ashen and slack, an oxygen mask covering his nose and mouth. An EMT was straddling him on the gurney, performing chest compressions.

"Mason!" Willow lunged forward, but Jackson caught her arm.

"Let them work," he said, gently restraining her. "We can't help him right now."

A doctor in blue scrubs jogged alongside the gurney, barking orders. "Get me a tox panel STAT. Full cardiac workup. Oxygen saturation?"

"Seventy-eight and dropping," an EMT called back. "BP 80/40, heart rate 42 and bradycardic. Pupils fixed and dilated."

"Bay three!" the doctor shouted, directing the team through a set of double doors.

Willow trailed after them, badge out. "I'm his sister," she called. "FBI. Please, let me—"

A nurse intercepted her, palm raised. "Ma'am, you need to stay back. The team needs space to work."

Through the doors, Willow could see them transferring Mason to a hospital bed. His shirt had been cut open, and electrodes were being placed on his chest. The doctor leaned close to Mason's face, examining his eyes.

"Cherry-red mucous membranes," he announced. "Combined with rapid onset, decreased LOC, and metabolic acidosis. This looks like cyanide poisoning. Get me hydroxocobalamin, 5 grams IV push. Run it wide open."

Willow's breath caught. Cyanide. As she feared, someone had deliberately poisoned her brother. This wasn't an accident or a coincidence.

A movement to her left caught her attention. Matt Carver stood against the wall, his face pale with concern. For a split second, their eyes met, and then Jackson was moving.

Before Willow could react, Jackson had crossed the space and slammed Matt against the wall, forearm pressed against his throat. "What the fuck are you doing here?" he growled, his face inches from Matt's.

Willow lunged forward, grabbing Jackson's arm. "Jackson, stop!" Despite everything, she knew Matt was here for Mason. Regardless of what had passed between them, for years, they were as close as any brothers could be. "Let him go."

To her surprise, Matt made no move to defend himself. He kept his hands visible at his sides; his eyes locked on Jackson's. "I'm sorry," he said hoarsely. "I didn't know this would happen."

Jackson released him but remained close, muscles tense and ready. "Why are you here?"

Matt straightened his collar, taking a cautious step away from the wall. "I was looking for Vicky. We had an 8 AM meeting at the Provost Marshal's office, but she never showed." He glanced toward the trauma bay where doctors worked frantically on Mason. "She called me last night. Said she had initiated a joint task force and wanted me to retake the lead on Jane's murder."

Willow stared at him, her skepticism battling with her desperation for information. "Why would she do that? It looked to me like she had taken over as lead investigator."

Matt shook his head. "She said she needed someone she could trust. Said things were more complicated than she realized." He ran a hand through his hair. "I thought she was at the PM's office, but when I got there, they told me about Mason. That he'd collapsed during a meeting with Hunter."

"Cyanide doesn't just happen," Cooper said, stepping forward. "Someone did this deliberately."

"And they tried to kill Vicky and Greg too," Jackson added. "Their car was found in the Beaufort River."

Matt's eyes widened. "Jesus. They're dead?"

"We don't know yet," Willow said. "No bodies have been recovered. Dive crews are still searching for them."

"Shit," Matt whispered. "That explains why Charleston called me this morning. They said they couldn't reach Vicky and wanted to know if we needed a team sent down." He looked at Willow. "I told them I'd let them know."

The automatic doors swished open, and Hunter rushed in, looking harried. His suit was wrinkled, his tie askew. "How is he?" he asked breathlessly.

"They're working on him now," Cooper said. "Looks like cyanide poisoning."

"My God." Hunter's face paled. "It can't be a coincidence that he called me in to help draft his will."

A commotion from Mason's trauma bay drew their attention. A nurse rushed by with a crash cart. Inside, the doctor was applying defibrillator pads to Mason's chest.

"Charging to 200," he called out. "Clear!"

Mason's body jerked with the shock. On the monitor, his heartbeat remained flat.

"Again. Charging to 300. Clear!"

Willow pressed her hand to her mouth, terror climbing up her throat. For nearly three years, she'd held onto her anger, punishing Mason for shattering her illusions about Matt. She'd missed birthdays, holidays, and weekend visits with her nieces. All because she couldn't forgive him for showing her the truth.

And now, watching doctors fight to restart his heart, she saw with painful clarity what she'd been too stubborn to admit. Mason had not been controlling her or ruining her happiness out of spite. His own life was in a tailspin, and he had stepped up to protect her, to make sure she wouldn't suffer at the hands of man who didn't deserve her.

"Please," she whispered, not caring who heard. "Please don't die. I need to tell you I'm sorry. I need to thank you."

In the trauma bay, a nurse was administering medications through Mason's IV line. Another had taken over chest compressions, counting rhythmically as she pressed down on his sternum.

"Hydroxocobalamin's in," someone called out. "Pushing epinephrine now."

"Come on," the doctor urged, watching the monitor. "Come on, come back to us."

Willow felt Jackson's arm around her shoulders, pulling her close. She leaned into him, drawing strength from his solid presence.

"Rhythm!" a nurse called suddenly. "We've got sinus tach."

"Okay, we've got him back," the doctor said, his voice steadier now. "Keep that hydroxocobalamin going. I want cardiac enzymes every hour and continuous monitoring. Let's call up to the ICU. He'll need a bed."

Willow sagged against Jackson, her knees weak with relief. "He's alive," she whispered. "He's alive."

After what felt like an eternity, the doctor emerged from the trauma bay, pulling off his latex gloves. His forehead glistened with sweat, and dark circles shadowed his eyes. He looked toward the small group huddled in the hallway.

"Family of Mason Banks?" he asked.

Cooper stepped forward, Willow and Hunter flanking him. "We're his siblings. I'm Sergeant Cooper Banks, Beaufort PD. This is my brother and sister."

The doctor inclined his head, exhaustion evident in every line of his face. "I'm Dr. Purnell. Your brother presented with classic signs of cyanide poisoning. We've administered hydroxocobalamin, which is the antidote, and he's stabilized for now."

"For now?" Willow echoed, latching onto the qualifier.

"Cyanide causes cellular asphyxiation. Essentially, it prevents cells from using oxygen," Dr. Purnell explained. "The hydroxocobalamin binds with the cyanide molecules to create a harmless compound the body can eliminate. But there can be lingering effects, especially to the heart and brain. We'll need to monitor him closely for the next 48 hours."

"But he'll recover?" Hunter asked. "I mean, fully recover?"

Dr. Purnell's expression grew cautious. "The fact that he received treatment quickly is in his favor. The hydroxocobalamin is working. His oxygen levels are improving. But I don't want to overstate anything. He's still very ill."

"Can we see him?" Willow asked.

"Once we get him settled in the ICU. A nurse will come get you." The doctor glanced at his watch. "Should be about thirty minutes."

As he attempted to leave, Willow reached out and touched his arm. "Thank you," she said, her voice thick with emotion. "For saving my brother."

Dr. Purnell offered a tired smile. "I'm just doing my job, but you're welcome."

As the doctor walked away, Willow faced the others. The immediate crisis had passed, but the larger danger remained.

"Someone tried to kill Mason," she said, her voice hardening. "And they may have succeeded with Vicky and Greg. We need to figure out who did this."

Jackson's expression was grim. "And we need to make sure Mason's daughters are safe. If they're targeting him, the girls could be next."

"I posted a car outside the house on my way here," Cooper said. "But you're right, we need more."

"Do the girls know?" Willow asked. "Did you call your wife? Is she with the girls?"

"The girls don't know," Cooper said. He looked as worried as Willow felt. "I called Genevieve to let her know, but she said she didn't want to worry the girls, not until Mason's condition was certain.

Willow glanced back toward the trauma bay where nurses were preparing Mason for transfer to the ICU. Her brother was alive, but someone had nearly succeeded in silencing him permanently. First Jane, then Vicky and Greg, and now Mason. The circle of death surrounding Pratt and the Fitzpatricks spread wider with each passing hour.

"I'd like to tell the girls, if it's okay with you," Willow said. "I'm going to bring them here. I don't want them to think we're hiding things from them."

"Go," Cooper said. "Jackson and I will watch over Mason." He gave Matt a look of pure loathing. "We'll bring this asshat up to speed as well."

Chapter Twenty-Four

Jackson

Jackson leaned against the wall outside Mason's ICU room, phone pressed to his ear. Through the window, he could see Mason's still form on the bed, tubes and wires connecting him to an array of machines. The steady beep of the heart monitor provided a reassuring rhythm, though Mason remained unconscious. The doctors had stabilized him after his earlier cardiac arrest and revival, but Dr. Purnell had been clear to say that Mason was still in critical condition.

"Alice, I need your help," Jackson said, keeping his voice low. "This is bigger than we initially thought."

"Walk me through it again," Special Agent in Charge Alice Baldwin replied, her tone all business.

Jackson shifted, glancing down the hospital corridor where Cooper and Matt had moved several yards away to make their own calls. Cooper was updating Chief Stevens, while Matt was supposedly contacting NCIS in Charleston. Jackson still wasn't entirely convinced Matt was trustworthy, despite him showing up at the hospital. Trust was in short supply right now.

"We've got four people targeted in less than twenty-four hours," Jackson said. "Jane Gamble was murdered at the renovation site. Then SSA Victoria Davidson's car was pulled from the Beaufort River. Both her and her husband are still missing and presumed dead. Now Willow's brother, Mason, has been poisoned with cyanide while in military custody."

"Jesus!"

"I know, and it gets worse. Jane discovered evidence of a trafficking operation run through the renovation site. The migrant workers are brought in by boat, then 'placed' through Michael Fitzpatrick's agency. His brother Sean provides security through Maritime Defense Solutions, and the third brother, Liam, owns the properties. It's a perfect setup—transportation, housing, security, all controlled by the same family."

Alice's sigh carried over the phone. "Jurisdiction is going to be a nightmare. NCIS has claim on Jane's murder since she was Navy, Beaufort PD has the bodies in the wall, and now we've got attempted murder of a civilian in military custody."

"That's why we need FBI involvement," Jackson pressed. "The migrant workers are coming in by boat from Haiti, which means they're crossing international waters. That puts it firmly in federal territory."

A nurse passed by, smiling politely at Jackson. He smiled back, noting her ID badge—Olivia Zhao, RN. She entered Mason's room to check his vitals.

"Without formal approval," Alice said. "This is still NCIS jurisdiction. Just because you and Will have been invited, it doesn't give me the right to send in resources. Besides, they'd need to come from Charleston. What I can do is provide some remote support for you. I'll contact the Charleston field office and read them in. They can contact NCIS Charleston. We'll see what happens from there."

"I understand," Jackson said, trying to keep his anger and frustration at bay.

"Do you?" Alice asked with a tinge of sarcasm. "Because I know you both. Stay within bounds. Gather information, support local law enforcement, but don't go cowboy on this."

Jackson smiled grimly. "I hear you."

"That said…" Alice paused. "Prevention of loss of life is always authorized. Do what you have to do to keep everyone safe."

"Copy that."

"Where's Willow now?"

"She went to pick up Mason's daughters," Jackson said, glancing at his watch. "Cooper arranged a police escort. After the cyanide attempt, we're not taking any chances."

"Good. Keep me updated, as often as possible. I'll continue to do what I can from my end."

Jackson ended the call and immediately dialed his parents. With everything going on, he needed to let them know what was happening and that he and Willow wouldn't be home anytime soon. A pang of worry gripped him. He had left Ruby with Mason's daughters this morning, and he hoped Willow was bringing the dogs with the girls.

His mother answered on the second ring. "Jackson! How's everything going? Your father and I are watching the news, something about a car being pulled from the Beaufort River. Is that anywhere near you?"

"Momma, I can't really talk about the case right now," he said, softening his tone. "I just wanted to…"

"Say hi?" his mother replied, concern evident in her voice. "I'm glad you did. Dad and I have gotten used to having a full house."

"I love you, Momma." The words stuck in his throat. "Give Dad a hug for me, okay?"

"Oh, mercy. Jax, honey? What's wrong? Is everyone okay?"

"We're all safe, but it's been hard. Willow's brother is in the hospital. An assassination attempt was made on him this morning. I guess I just needed to hear your voice." His comment was met with a long silence. "Momma?"

"I just spoke with your father," she said. Her tone firm and absolute. "We're on our way. We'll call you from the road to get directions." In the background, Jackson heard the chime of his father's gun cabinet.

"I'm bringing my Saint Hubert medal," his father said. "I've got Jackson's as well."

Travis Brooks only carried the medal when he went hunting—a ritual he'd passed to Jackson as a boy. *"Saint Hubert's the patron saint of hunters," his father had told him. "We bring him with us, not for the kill, but to come home safe when the hunt is over."*

"Momma!" Jackson said, his pulse racing. "No. Absolutely not. It's not safe."

"We love you, Jax," she said, completely disregarding his words. "We'll talk soon."

His mother disconnected, leaving Jackson talking to a dead line. He tried calling her back, but the phone immediately went to voicemail. She was likely lining someone up to watch their kennels and care for the six dogs they were boarding.

Tension gripped Jackson's neck. He pocketed his phone and rolled his shoulders, trying to release the knot that had settled there. He hadn't slept well last night, and today's events were only adding to his exhaustion. His gaze drifted back to Mason's room, where Nurse Zhao was adjusting something on one of the machines.

A doctor approached from the direction of the nurses' station. He was wearing a pristine white coat with a stethoscope around his neck.

"Afternoon," Jackson said politely, noting the ID badge clipped to the doctor's coat pocket—Rodriguez Chavez, MD.

The doctor barely glanced at him, nodding curtly. "I need to check on my patient," he said, his accent thick Irish brogue rather than Hispanic like his name suggested.

Jackson's instincts flared. The accent didn't match the name, and something about the man's movements felt wrong. He shifted slightly to block the doorway.

"Dr. Chavez, hold up a minute," Jackson said. "I didn't know you were on Mason's case." He deliberately used the first name, watching for a reaction.

The man's eyes narrowed. "I'm certain the world is full of things you know nothing about. Now, step aside and let me do my job."

Jackson spotted the telltale bulge in the coat pocket, the fabric hanging heavier on that side.

"Hold," Jackson said, his voice hardening. "Step away from the door."

For a split second, they locked eyes. Then the man's hand plunged into his pocket.

Jackson reacted instantly, grabbing onto the man's arm as it emerged with a gun. He drove the assassin's wrist against the doorframe with all his strength. A sickening crack echoed through the corridor as the man howled in pain, the weapon clattering to the floor.

"Cooper!" Jackson shouted, maintaining his grip on the man's broken wrist. "Gun!"

The man drove his knee up, but Jackson twisted to take the blow on his thigh instead of his groin. Pain shot through his leg. He countered with a hard elbow to the man's solar plexus, driving the air from his lungs.

The assassin slammed his forehead into Jackson's face, snapping his head back and sending him reeling. Blood filled Jackson's mouth as his lip split, and his grip faltered just long enough for the man to break free.

Sprinting down the corridor, the assassin shoved past a startled Matt and barreled toward Cooper who was drawing his weapon.

"Stop! Police!" Cooper shouted as he moved to block the hallway.

The suspect sprinted forward and wove through the bystanders, easily avoiding Cooper's attempt to intercept him.

"Matt, guard Mason!" Jackson called as he took off in pursuit, blood dripping from his chin.

The corridor ahead bustled with activity. The assassin plowed through a nurse pushing a medication cart, sending supplies flying and the nurse tumbling to the floor. Cooper got tangled in the fallen equipment, cursing as he tried to regain his footing. Jackson vaulted over the entire mess without breaking stride.

The assassin yanked a fire alarm as he ran, filling the corridor with a piercing wail. He slammed through a door marked "Stairs."

Jackson followed through the door seconds later, weapon drawn and Cooper right behind him.

"Which way?" Cooper asked, his own weapon ready.

"I'll go up, you go down," Jackson decided quickly. "Radio for backup."

Cooper nodded and plunged downward. Jackson took the stairs upward two at a time, his weapon raised, and the fire alarm masking any footsteps above. He'd barely cleared the first landing when he caught movement one flight up. The assassin leaned over the railing, a gun in his left hand, firing aimlessly.

Jackson threw himself against the wall as two shots cracked through the stairwell. The bullets struck where he'd been standing a split second earlier. He returned fire immediately, squeezing off three rounds in rapid succession.

The assassin jerked backward, his weapon clattering across the concrete landing. He folded over the railing momentarily, then slumped to the floor, blood spreading across his white coat.

Jackson approached cautiously, weapon trained on the motionless figure. The man's eyes were open and fixed in a death stare. Jackson kicked the fallen weapon away and checked for a pulse out of procedure rather than necessity.

Cooper called up the stairs, "Jackson?"

"Clear," he replied. "He had a second gun. He's down."

Cooper holstered his weapon as he approached. "Dead?"

"I'm afraid so," Jackson said, motioning toward the blood-soaked lab coat. "I didn't have a choice."

"Would have been nice if we could have questioned him," Cooper said, searching the man's pockets. "No ID, no wallet, nothing."

A distant crack echoed from below—unmistakably a gunshot. Then another. And another.

"The ICU," Jackson said, already moving. "There's a second assassin!"

They thundered down the stairs, Jackson's heart pounding against his ribs. If they'd both been drawn away from Mason on purpose...

The ICU door burst open under Cooper's shoulder, and they rushed through. More gunshots echoed from down the hall. They sprinted past panicked staff taking cover behind counters and in doorways.

As they rounded the corner toward Mason's room, Jackson saw a body sprawled on the floor outside the door, blood pooling beneath it. A female nurse lay against the wall nearby, two staff members working frantically to stem the bleeding from a wound in her shoulder.

Jackson burst into Mason's room, weapon leading, and froze at the sight before him.

Matt stood beside Mason's bed, a hypodermic needle poised above the IV line. Blood spatter covered his face and shirt. Across the bed, the nurse Jackson had seen earlier stood wide-eyed, also spattered with blood.

"Don't move!" Jackson shouted, aiming directly at Matt. "Put it down. Now!"

Matt stared back, his brow furrowed. "What? Jackson, I—"

"Put. The. Needle. Down." Jackson's voice was ice, his aim unwavering.

Cooper appeared beside Jackson, his weapon drawn. "Do as he says, Carver."

Matt slowly placed the syringe on the tray beside him, raising his hands. "It's not what it looks like," he said carefully. "I swear to God, it's not."

The nurse spoke up, her voice shaking. "He saved Mr. Banks's life! There was a man—he came in right after you left—he was trying to inject something into the IV. Agent Carver shot him."

Jackson kept his weapon steady but shifted to see around the bed. Another body lay on the floor on the far side, two bullet holes visible in his chest. Another white coat. Another fake doctor.

"Three assassins," Matt said, hands still raised. "They sent three. I took out one in the east wing. He showed up right after the fire alarm sounded. When I got back here, this one was already inside." He glanced at Nurse Zhao. "She tried to stop him, but he threw her against the wall. I had to take the shot."

The nurse rubbed her shoulder. "He's telling the truth. If he hadn't been here..."

Jackson slowly lowered his weapon, though wariness remained. "Why were you holding the syringe?"

"It has Epinephrine," Matt said. "The nurse was about to administer it when the killer came in the room. Mason's blood pressure was crashing after all the commotion."

As if on cue, the monitors around Mason began beeping frantically. His oxygen levels were dropping, his heart rate spiking erratically.

"He's waking up," the nurse said, moving quickly to check the displays. "The stress response—his body's flooding with adrenaline." She pressed the call button. "We need a doctor in here. Now!"

Mason's eyes flew open, wild and disoriented. His hands clawed at the tubes in his throat, his body arching in panic.

"Mason, you're safe!" Cooper rushed to his brother's side, gently restraining his hands. "You're in the hospital. You're okay."

A medical team rushed in, a real doctor barking orders as they surrounded the bed. Jackson backed away to give them space, while his mind tried to process the last three or four minutes. Matt had killed two assassins and apparently saved Mason's life.

Outside in the hallway, Cooper joined Jackson as security personnel secured the scene. "Three assassins," Cooper said quietly. "Someone really wants Mason dead."

"And they almost succeeded," Jackson replied, watching as staff members covered a body with a sheet. "If Matt hadn't been here..." He trailed off, unwilling to complete the thought.

Matt approached them, wiping blood from his face with a towel, his clothes still spattered red.

"Thank you," Jackson said. "If you hadn't been here... thank you."

Matt shook his head. "I know he and Willow hate me, but I still care about both of them. I'm not going to let anything happen to either of them." He wiped blood from his neck. "A hit team? They weren't exactly skilled, but they were determined. The question is, why?"

Dr. Purnell emerged from Mason's room, looking grim. "He's awake but incoherent and extremely agitated. He keeps saying that someone threatened his daughters and that they're in danger. I had to sedate him lightly to keep him from pulling out his tubes, but he's insistent on speaking to his family."

Jackson felt his phone vibrate. Willow. He stepped away to answer. "Will?"

"We're ten minutes out," she said, voice tense. "The girls and Genevieve are with me. How's Mason?"

Jackson glanced through the window at Mason's form, now semi-conscious. "He's awake, but Will, there was an incident. There was another attempt on his life."

A sharp intake of breath. "But he's okay, right? You said he was awake."

"He's fine." Jackson hesitated, trying to decide what to say about Matt's involvement. "But the hospital's not secure yet. The girls shouldn't see this. There are multiple fatalities and blood everywhere."

"I can't turn around, Jackson," Willow said, her voice suddenly urgent.

"Why not?"

"Because it's not safe here either." Her voice dropped, clearly trying to keep the girls from hearing. "There's a black SUV that's been following us since we left the house. The officer escorting us is calling for backup, but—" She broke off. "Jackson, I think they're after the girls now."

Jackson's blood ran cold. "Where are you exactly?"

"Heading up Ribaut Road, just past the technical college."

"Get here as fast as you can," Jackson instructed, already moving toward Cooper. "Drive straight to the emergency entrance. We'll meet you there."

He ended the call and grabbed Cooper's arm. "The girls are in danger. Someone's following their car."

Cooper's face hardened. "Security is compromised. We need to move Mason."

"There's no time," Jackson said. "Willow's already on her way here. We need to secure this floor and prepare for their arrival."

Cooper was already calling for additional units.

"I need you to stay with Mason," Jackson said to Matt, the words feeling strange in his mouth. "Don't let anyone in that room who isn't Dr. Purnell or Nurse Zhao, understood?"

Matt motioned for him to leave, his expression earnest. "I've got him. Go help Willow."

Jackson and Cooper raced toward the emergency entrance, weapons ready. This was no longer just about finding Jane's killer or exposing a trafficking ring. This was about survival. And Jackson would do whatever it took to protect Willow and those girls.

The Fitzpatricks and their allies had just escalated this into a full-on war.

Chapter Twenty-Five

Willow

Willow ended the call, her eyes flicking to the rearview mirror. The black SUV maintained its distance, always three or four car lengths back. To an untrained eye it was never close enough to seem threatening, but it was clearly following them. It had been waiting outside Mason's house when they'd left, sliding into traffic behind them as soon as they pulled out of the laneway.

The police cruiser escorting them was two cars ahead, lights flashing but siren silent. Officer Miles had called for backup five minutes ago, but so far, no additional units had appeared.

"Aunt Willow?" Emma's voice came from the back seat. "Are we almost there?"

Willow forced a calm smile into the rearview mirror. "Almost, sweetie. Just a few more minutes."

In the third row of seats, Sarah sat quietly petting her dog, oblivious to the tension. Emma watched the passing scenery with anxious eyes, while Ivy stared directly back at Willow, her gaze piercing. The girl wasn't fooled by Willow's false calm.

"Is that car following us?" Ivy asked bluntly.

Willow hesitated, searching for the right words. Before she could answer, Genevieve, Cooper's wife, reached back from the passenger seat and squeezed her niece's knee.

"We've got a police escort, honey," she said smoothly. "Everything's fine."

In the cargo area behind the third row, Ruby and Ranger were both alert, ears perked and bodies tense. Ranger had been whining softly since they'd left Mason's house, picking up on Willow's anxiety. Ruby seemed equally unsettled.

Willow glanced at the girls in the mirror, their faces reflecting varying degrees of concern as they listened. She couldn't turn around now—not with that SUV following them, and not with the increasingly clear message that Mason's daughters were now targets.

She pressed harder on the accelerator, the speedometer climbing. She blew past her police escort and didn't let up until the hospital emergency entrance became visible.

"What's happening?" Ivy demanded, leaning forward between the front seats. "Why are we going faster?"

"Your father is awake," Willow said, offering the partial truth that would explain their urgency. "I just want to get there quickly."

As they approached the hospital, Willow saw two police cruisers screech to a halt at the emergency entrance, positioning themselves to block access. Jackson and Cooper stood outside the ambulance bay, weapons drawn but held low, scanning the approaching traffic.

Willow pulled into the covered entrance, with the police escort stopping alongside them. To her surprise, the black SUV made no attempt to follow. Instead, it smoothly continued past the hospital, disappearing down a side street as if it had never been following them at all.

To Willow, the message was clear: we know where the girls are, and we can find them anytime.

The two police cruisers that had been blocking the entrance immediately hit their lights and sirens, pulling out in pursuit of the SUV.

"Stay in the car," Willow ordered the girls as she put the vehicle in park. "All of you."

She stepped out just as Jackson reached her door, his face tense with concern. Cooper ran to the passenger side where Genevieve was already emerging.

"They followed us from Mason's house," Willow said quickly, keeping her voice low. She led Jackson away from the car. "Black Chevy Tahoe, tinted windows, with only a single occupant. He was waiting for us to come out."

"Did the driver approach you at all?" Jackson asked, scanning the area even as he spoke to her.

"No, just followed at a distance. Always keeping us in sight." She glanced back at the SUV where the girls were watching. "It looked like the driver wanted us to know we were being followed."

From inside the car came the sound of Ranger's barking. The rear door suddenly opened, and Ivy stepped out with both K9s at her heels. Ranger's barking only stopped when he got to Willow's side.

"Ivy, I told you to stay in the car," Willow snapped.

"I heard enough," Ivy replied, her chin jutting out defiantly. "Someone tried to hurt Dad again. And someone was following us." She slammed the car door before Emma or Sarah could follow. "Tell me what's happening. Now."

Jackson and Willow exchanged glances. Jackson sighed quietly, acknowledging the futility of trying to shield Ivy from the situation.

"Your father was poisoned this morning," Jackson explained, keeping his voice calm but direct. "Then, while he was in the hospital, there was another attempt on his life. Three men disguised as doctors tried to get to him."

Ivy's face paled, but her expression remained resolute. "Did they hurt him?"

"No," Jackson assured her. "We stopped them."

Willow noticed he didn't mention the deaths, the blood, or any of the violence that had unfolded upstairs. Those were details Ivy didn't need right now.

"And now someone's following us," Ivy said, putting the pieces together. "Because they want to hurt us too."

Ruby immediately moved next to Ivy while Ranger pressed against Willow's leg. She reached down absently to stroke his head, her mind racing. The coordination of these attacks was terrifying. When poisoning Mason failed, they sent assassins to finish the job while simultaneously targeting his daughters. This wasn't just about silencing witnesses anymore. This was the systematic elimination of anyone who might cause problems.

"We're not going to let that happen," Willow promised, meeting Ivy's eyes. "But I need you to help me keep Emma and Sarah calm. Can you do that?"

"Of course," Ivy said, her expression eerily adult for a four-teen-year-old. "I've been doing that since mom died and you abandoned us."

The harsh truth of that statement hit Willow, making her wince. While she'd been nursing her anger at Mason, this child had been stepping into the role of surrogate mother to her sisters.

Cooper approached, phone in hand. "Got word from the pur-suit units. They caught the SUV. The driver's in custody, and they're taking him to the station right now."

"Did he say anything?" Jackson asked.

"Only that Major Davidson sent him, and he needed to talk to us," Cooper replied. "He's military police."

"An MP," Willow said, the realization settling coldly in her stomach. "What if it was Pratt who sent him. Jesus fucking Christ." Her gaze flashed to Ivy who was taking it all in, nothing showing in her facial expression.

Cooper thumbed toward the door. "I'll head to the station as soon as we get you all settled. We need to find out who he's working for."

"Let's get inside," Jackson said, glancing around the ambulance bay. "We're too exposed out here."

While Willow and Ivy moved toward the emergency entrance, Jackson and Cooper returned to the car for the two younger girls. Emma emerged looking nervous, while Sarah had her face buried in Pickle's neck. The dog dangled in the small girl's grasp, content as ever. As Willow waited and watched from inside, her hands trembled. Now that the immediate danger had passed, the adrenaline crash left her shaky.

As he approached, the concerned look on Jackson's face said that she was doing a shit-poor job of masking her emotions.

"Are you okay?" he asked quietly, falling into step beside her while Cooper led the group through the emergency ward.

"No," she admitted, keeping her voice low so the girls wouldn't hear. "I'm terrified, Jackson. For the girls, for Mason. If anything happened to them..." She couldn't finish the thought.

Jackson's hand found hers briefly, squeezing once before letting go. "I know. But we're going to keep them safe."

Inside the emergency department, a security guard approached. He looked at the name on Cooper's vest and held out his hand in greeting.

"Sergeant Banks," he said. His body language suggested he was beyond frazzled. "Detective Phillips called down. There was too much... *evidence* to clean up. They've moved your brother to the VIP wing on the seventh floor." The guard's eyes flickered toward the children. "He said to give them about ten more minutes to finish securing the ward."

"Thank you," Cooper replied. "Can you escort us up when it's ready?"

The guard agreed and stepped away, speaking quietly into his radio.

Emma tugged at Willow's sleeve. "What evidence?" she asked, her voice small but perceptive. "Did something bad happen to Daddy?"

Willow knelt to Emma's eye level, aware that Sarah was now listening too. She had to make a quick decision about how much truth to share.

"Some bad people tried to hurt your father today," she said carefully. "But he's okay. He's in the hospital, and the doctors are taking good care of him."

"Why would anyone want to hurt Daddy?" Sarah asked, clutching her chubby dachshund to her body.

Before Willow could formulate an answer, Ivy stepped in. "Because Daddy saw something he wasn't supposed to see. And these bad people don't want him telling anyone about it."

Willow was surprised by Ivy's accurate assessment, but even more by her calm delivery of the information. She spoke to her sisters without condescension, but also without unnecessary detail.

"Will you be staying with them?" Cooper asked Jackson as they waited, slightly apart from the others.

Jackson shook his head. "I think I should go with you to help question the driver. We need answers fast."

"I agree," Willow said, joining their conversation. "Go. We'll be fine here, and I'll call you after we've seen Mason."

"Matt's watching over Mason," Jackson said, his eyes searching hers. "Your brother wouldn't be alive if not for him."

The thought that she was in her ex's debt made Willow nauseous. She closed her eyes and took a slow, deep breath.

"I can stay," Jackson said.

"Go," she repeated firmly. "Find out who's behind this. That's what we need most. My personal issues don't matter right now."

"Okay. I'll take the dogs with me." Jackson glanced at Ranger, who hadn't left Willow's side. "Though I might have to drag this one away."

"Take Ruby," Willow said. "I'm going to keep Ranger and Pickle with me. I'll feel better if they're both here."

Jackson didn't argue the point. He called Ruby to his side and left with Cooper.

Ten minutes later, the security guard returned. "Detective Phillips says it's clear now. I can take you up, but the dogs can't come. There is a strict no-pet policy."

"Neither of these dogs are pets," Willow said, brooking no argument. "One is a federal agent and the other is an emotional support animal. The girl's father has had multiple attempts on his life. Do you really want to make this a hill to die on?"

"As you wish," the guard said. "But if anyone says anything, you can tell them I had told you about the policy."

Willow gathered the girls, grateful that Jackson and Cooper had already left. She didn't want them to see her hands shaking as she ushered Genevieve and the children to the elevator.

"Are you ready to see your dad?" Willow asked as the elevator doors opened on the VIP floor.

Sarah bobbed her head eagerly, while Emma gave a hesitant "Yes." Ivy simply stepped forward, leading the way.

Detective Phillips, a slim man with a no-nonsense demeanor, met them outside Mason's room. His expression was impassive as he introduced himself. He gave a nod of recognition to Genevieve before quietly addressing Willow. "We've increased security on this floor. No one gets in without proper ID and clearance."

"Thank you," Willow said. She appreciated the precautions, even as she wondered if they would be enough against the professionals who had already penetrated hospital security.

"He's sedated, but conscious," Phillips added. "The doctor said short visits only."

Willow understood. She addressed the girls, preparing them for the possible shock. "Remember, your dad is still very sick. There will be tubes and wires, and it might look scary, but it's all to help him get better."

She ordered Ranger to guard the hallway and pushed open the door to Mason's room, her heart clenching at the sight of her brother. Mason lay propped slightly upright, an oxygen mask over his face, IVs in both arms, and monitors beeping steadily around him. His skin was ashen, with dark circles beneath his eyes.

Each girl reacted differently to the sight of their father. Sarah, with a child's lack of fear, immediately ran to the bed, tossed Pickle onto her father's lap, and tried to climb up. "Daddy!" she cried.

Mason's eyes fluttered open at the commotion. They were unfocused at first, then sharpened as he saw Sarah beside him. He reached up with an unsteady hand to remove the oxygen mask.

"Don't," Nurse Zhao said quickly. "You need that, Mr. Banks."

Mason ignored her, pulling the mask aside. "My girls," he croaked, his voice a painful rasp. "You're safe."

"Daddy, you look awful," Sarah said with a child's brutal honesty, patting his arm.

A ghost of a smile crossed Mason's dry lips. "Feel awful too, squirt."

Emma froze in the doorway, her eyes wide and suddenly filling with tears. Willow gently placed a hand on her shoulder.

Ivy walked to the opposite side of the bed, trying to hide her distress. "Is he getting better?" she asked the nurse who stood checking Mason's vitals.

"Yes," Olivia Zhao, according to her badge, answered with a gentle smile. "His condition is improving."

Willow moved to help Sarah, who was struggling to climb onto the bed without disturbing any of Mason's equipment. "Careful, sweetheart," she murmured, lifting the child onto a small space beside Mason. She snatched Pickle away, who was actively giving her brother a facewash.

Emma finally moved from the doorway, approaching the bed with cautious steps. "Does it hurt?" she asked softly.

"Not anymore," Mason assured her, though Willow could see the lie in his eyes. He was in pain but hiding it for his daughters.

Mason's gaze found Willow across the bed, and he extended his hand to her. She took it, concerned by the weakness of his grip.

"I'm sorry," he whispered, so low that only she could hear. "Should have told you sooner. About them. About everything."

Willow wanted to ask for details, but Mason's attention had already shifted back to his daughters.

He looked at each of them in turn—Sarah, Emma, and finally Ivy—before his gaze returned to Willow. His grip on her hand tightened fractionally.

"Guard them with your life," he said, voice suddenly clearer, more urgent. "They'll never stop coming."

The monitors beside him began beeping more rapidly as his heart rate accelerated. Nurse Zhao stepped forward quickly.

"That's enough for now," she said firmly. "He needs to rest."

"No," Mason rasped, fighting to stay conscious as the nurse replaced his oxygen mask. "Not safe... anywhere..."

His eyes fluttered closed again as the sedation reasserted itself, and his grip on Willow's hand went slack.

"Daddy?" Sarah called, patting his arm with increasing urgency. "Daddy, wake up!"

"Is he dying?" Emma whispered, panic edging into her voice.

"No," Nurse Zhao assured them. "He's just sleeping. The medicine makes him very tired."

Ivy was already backing away from the bed, her face pale. "What did he mean?" she demanded, looking directly at Willow. "Dad said they'll never stop coming. Who are *they*?"

Willow felt the weight of three pairs of eyes on her, all expecting answers she wasn't sure she had. The Fitzpatricks, obviously. Lieutenant Colonel Pratt, most likely. But beyond that? How deep did this go?

"I think we should let your father rest now," she said, carefully helping Sarah from the bed. "We'll come back later when he's feeling stronger."

Outside in the hallway, Willow spotted Matt Carver standing by the nurses' station, deep in conversation with Detective Phillips. Her initial instinct was to steer the girls in the opposite direction, but Matt had already seen them.

"Genevieve," Willow said quietly, "could you take the girls to the vending machine in the waiting room we passed? I need to speak with Agent Carver."

"Come on, girls," Genevive said. "Let's go see what they've got to eat. I'm starving!"

"Ranger, stay with the girls," Willow commanded, reinforcing the order with a hand signal. The Belgian Malinois immediately complied, choosing to stand closest to Sarah.

As they walked away, Willow saw Ivy glance back suspiciously, clearly aware she was being removed so the adults could talk freely. She looked at Matt, sneered, and gave him the middle finger.

She is so much like me.

Matt approached as soon as the girls were out of earshot. Despite everything, Willow had to acknowledge he looked professional and composed, a far cry from his obnoxious self the last time she'd seen him.

"How is he?" Matt asked, nodding toward Mason's room.

"Sedated," Willow replied, keeping her tone neutral. "He woke up briefly, when we went in. He's terrified for his children."

"Fuck," he said, shifting his weight, seeming uncomfortable. "I'm sorry for what I did, for everything that I did. I know there is nothing I can do to make it right, but..."

"Thank you for saving Mason's life," Willow said. In part because she meant it, but mostly because she wanted to change the subject. "What happened, exactly?"

Her stomach flopped as Matt recounted the multiple attacks on her brother. The assassins' attempts were beyond brazen. They were suicidal. Who could possibly wield so much power as to have men willingly lay down their lives for a kill?

"I don't know what to do," Willow blurted. The last thing she wanted to do was sound like she was asking for Matt's help, but she was drowning in her fear for Mason and his daughters.

"Call in reinforcements," Matt said. "NCIS won't help with this. Your brother is the prime suspect and there is no way they're going to protect someone who they believe killed one of their own. I think Mason is safe here, for now at least. Very few people know he's been moved to this floor and security has been tripled. There are also two police officers outside his door and at every entry point. There are also extra guards in the security office to man the video feeds."

The precautions would help keep Mason safe, but the girls couldn't stay there forever. "I'm going to take the girls to the police station until I can find an FBI safehouse for them. Are you able to stay here with Mason?"

"I have no place else to be," he replied with a casual grin. "It would look terrible if my prime suspect was to suffer harm on my watch. Go get the girls and get them someplace safe. I've got this covered here."

Willow looked at him, really looked at him for the first time since their relationship had imploded. The man she'd once planned to marry had saved her brother's life today. It didn't erase the past, but it did complicate things.

"Thank you," she said simply, unable to formulate a response that wouldn't open old wounds. "Call me if there's any change in his condition."

"I will," Matt promised. "You know, he's going to be pissed when he finds out I saved his life. Twice."

"Yes, he will," she said. "But hopefully he's big enough to thank you for it, too."

As she walked away to find the girls, Willow couldn't help thinking that maybe she could set aside her hatred. The idea made her feel a little lighter, like a burden she had been carrying had suddenly become lighter. She glanced back over her shoulder at the man who had once promised her everything and had delivered none of it.

She gave her head a shake. She'd never forgive him. Not completely.

Chapter Twenty-Six

Jackson

Jackson stood at the entrance of the Beaufort Police Station, scanning the parking lot for any signs of Willow's SUV. She had called to say they were heading out and should be at the station in twenty minutes. The late afternoon sun cast long shadows across the asphalt as a cool breeze ruffled his hair. His body ached from the confrontation at the hospital, and a scrape on his knuckles had dried to a rust-colored crust, and his split lip throbbed with a dull, persistent pain.

At the sound of tires on pavement, Ruby's tail began wagging in lazy circles as Willow's SUV pulled into the lot followed by a police cruiser. He watched as they parked, tension easing slightly at the sight of the passengers, all safe and accounted for.

Willow emerged first, her movements tense with exhaustion and stress. Genevieve helped the girls out of the vehicle, Sarah clutching Pickle in her arm, while holding Ivy's hand. Her small face was drawn with confusion and fear that she was too young to fully process. After Emma got out, Ranger followed and rushed to Willow's side.

"Go on," Jackson said to Ruby. "Go say hi."

The children's expressions softened as the Golden Retriever nuzzled against them, her maternal instincts seeming to heighten with her pregnancy. Cooper met his wife halfway and gave her a hug, speaking words too soft for Jackson to hear.

"Everything okay?" Jackson asked as Willow approached.

She gave a slight nod before quickly checking to ensure the girls couldn't hear. "For now. Any word on the driver they brought in?"

"Chief Stevens is waiting for us in the JTF room," Jackson said, placing a gentle hand on her lower back as they walked toward the entrance.

"I was thinking," Cooper said, as he guided his wife and nieces through the station's double doors. His voice pitched for the girls' benefit, "how would you three like to meet Zeus? He's one of our K9 officers."

The desk sergeant stepped out to greet them. "He's in the break room," he said. "And the pizza should be arriving shortly."

Sarah's face brightened immediately. "A police dog? Like Ruby and Ranger?"

Cooper smiled, the expression warming his tired face. "Exactly like them. And I bet Officer Reeves will let you pet him if you ask nicely."

Jackson caught Willow's eye, surprise flashing between them at the mention of Reeves. He was the same Officer Reeves whom they had evaluated back in Alabama, who had ignored his K9 partner's alerts during their evaluation session.

"Looks like Reeve's getting a second chance," Jackson said. "Either that, or the chief hasn't decided what to do with him yet."

"Let's hope he learned to trust his partner," Willow replied, her tone revealing her doubt. "God knows we could use all the competent officers we can get right now."

"This way," Jackson said, leading Willow toward the conference room Chief Stevens had designated for their joint task force. Ranger fell into step beside Willow, his training keeping him alert even in the safe environment of a police station. "Let's see what the chief has to say about our mysterious driver. Cooper's going to join us after he gets everyone settled."

Chief Janet Stevens stood reviewing documents, her posture rigid with exhaustion. "How's Mason?" she asked without looking up as they entered.

"Stable and awake," Willow answered, dropping into a chair. While Ruby curled up in the farthest corner from the door, Ranger settled at her feet, his body positioned to face the door—a protective posture Jackson had noticed the dog often took in unfamiliar settings. "He's been moved to the VIP wing and extra security measures have been implemented." She leaned forward, hands flat on the table. "I want to know about the MP who was following us. Where is he?"

Janet finally looked up from her documentation, her expression carefully neutral. "We've already interviewed him and let him go."

"You did what?" Willow's voice rose sharply as she pushed back from the table. Ranger's head snapped up, instantly alert to his handler's distress. "That man was stalking us! He was following my nieces!"

"Willow—" Jackson started, but she cut him off with a slashing motion of her hand.

"No, Jackson. Three assassins just tried to kill my brother, someone's targeting his daughters, and they just let a suspect walk?" She turned her fury back to Janet. "What the hell were you thinking?"

Chief Stevens held up a hand, unfazed by the outburst. "If you'd let me explain before flying off the handle." She paused until the outrage in Willow's expression lessened. Keeping her voice calm and even, she continued. "The suspect's name was Captain John Romalis, an MP at MCAS Beaufort. He was trying to deliver a burner phone given to him by Major Davidson."

Jackson took a seat next to Willow, confused by the revelation.

"He apologized if his presence caused problems," Janet continued, "but he needed to make sure you weren't being followed by anyone else. Had the police not cut him off, he'd have delivered the phone himself at the hospital."

"Greg Davidson," Jackson said, struggling to comprehend the implication. "He's alive?"

"He is," Janet said. "We let Romalis go as quickly as possible. If Pratt gets suspicious about why we detained him, it could compromise whatever operation Major Davidson is running. Both he and Vicky are alive and well."

Willow sank back into her chair, the fight visibly draining from her. "How did you find out?"

"When I called the pre-programmed number in the phone, Major Davidson answered," Janet said with a small shrug.

The door opened, and Cooper slipped in, taking a seat across from Willow. "The girls are with Genevieve in the break room. Reeves is showing them how Zeus finds hidden objects." He glanced between their faces, reading the mood. "Did I miss something important?"

"Vicky and Greg are alive," Jackson filled him in. "The guy following Willow was trying to deliver a burner phone from them."

Cooper's eyebrows rose. "Well, I'll be damned. Where are they?"

"The NCIS field office in Norfolk, Virginia," Janet said. "They've spent the last six hours briefing the Assistant Deputy Director on what's happening in Beaufort." She picked up a folder and passed it across the table. "And there's more. They said that Jane Gamble was working with NCIS."

"Working with them how?" Jackson asked, leaning forward to examine the folder's contents.

"Jane was an NCIS agent. Vicky had no idea until this morning. She was deep cover, and her presence was need to know. She was helping uncover what they believed to be a drug ring involving Mikhail Sokolov, a Russian oligarch living in Miami," Janet explained. "NCIS Norfolk had been working with the DEA and Coast Guard to uncover their method of bringing drugs into the country. Two years ago, they were certain that naval bases in Florida were involved, but as they closed in, the drug shipments disappeared."

"Let me guess," Willow said. "They assumed the operation had moved up the eastern seaboard?"

"It coincides with when Jane Gamble was transferred to Beaufort," Janet said. "NCIS wanted someone on the inside. They had already suspected Pratt's involvement in drug smuggling, so they installed her as an MP."

"Wasn't this also around the same time that Fitzpatrick Sr. was killed?" Jackson asked. The timing of the two events was too obvious to be coincidental. "Maybe Sokolov wanted to horn in on Fitzpatrick's operation, and when he wouldn't comply, they set him up to get arrested and took him out. The fact the shooter was also from Miami can't be overlooked."

"You've got a keen eye, Brooks," Janet said. "NCIS had come to the exact same conclusion, and that's what prompted them to send in a deep-cover agent. The trouble was, Jane never uncovered a connection to Sokolov. The oligarch left the country a few months after she arrived in Beaufort, and Norfolk nearly pulled her out, but the drugs coming into the port never slowed. What was most interesting was that Sean Fitzpatrick had made multiple visits to Lt. Colonel Pratt in the weeks that followed. At that time, Jane reported that Fitzpatrick was hiring marines to work part-time for his security agency. Norfolk dug into their records and found they all had money issues, which made them all susceptible to external influences. NCIS wanted Jane to find out more, so they set her up to have a mountain of student-loan debts."

"And after Fitzpatrick hired her, she literally stumbled upon the human trafficking ring," Jackson said, scrubbing his heavily stubbled chin.

"That's what Norfolk thinks," Janet agreed. "At no point did they find evidence the Fitzpatricks were involved in any of the drug operations."

Jackson tapped his fingers against the table, trying to piece it all together.,. "What if the Fitzpatricks got out of the drug game when their father was killed? Maybe having the oligarch's operation moving north pushed them out. If they couldn't move drugs…"

The others staired at him, waiting for him to continue his thoughts.

"The Fitzpatricks had everything they needed to move into trafficking people," Jackson suggested. "The boats, the security company, the placement agency."

"Or maybe they took the opportunity to expand their operation," Cooper said, picking up the thread. "If these guys are dirty, it's doubtful they'd simply walk away from a lucrative revenue stream."

"Either way, we've got multiple players with reason to want Jane silenced," Willow said. "And Mason, too, since he was at the scene."

The door burst open, banging against the wall with such force that they all jumped. Officer Dade stumbled in, his uniform disheveled and his face pale beneath a sheen of sweat. Ranger immediately leapt to his feet, a low growl building in his chest.

"I need protection," Dade gasped, his eyes wide with panic. "My squad car's been shot to hell. I barely made it here alive."

Chapter Twenty-Seven

Willow

Ranger shadowed Willow as she moved toward the door, scanning the hallway beyond. Her hand brushed her weapon, instinct kicking in. Ranger was calm—no growling, no tension in his posture. He was waiting for her to act.

Willow took in the entire precinct. Outside of a few curious individuals, the place was calm, normal. No gunshots. No sirens. No shouting from patrol. Just Dade, loud and breathless, sucking the air out of the room. She didn't trust him. Not on his best day. And something in Dade's story didn't sit right with Willow. If he had come under fire, he'd have called it in and requested immediate backup. He wouldn't have driven to the police station, and he wouldn't have come looking for the chief to say what had happened to him.

"Where? Who fired at you?"

"Black SUV," Dade panted. "Followed me from the gas station on Ribaut Road. Started shooting when I turned onto Harrington. I gunned it, lost them somewhere around the high school, but they could be right behind me."

Jackson glanced at Cooper, who was already on the radio calling for patrols to search the area.

"Why are you eyeballing me like that?" Dade asked Willow, his expression indignant. "You should be doing something about this, not standing around gawking at me. I need protection."

You need protection? Where were you when Marissa Wilson needed protection?

Willow's throat tightened. A burning, acidic lump had formed somewhere behind her sternum, pressing against her vocal cords. She forced herself to take a step back, trying to find her professional voice. "Officer Dade, we need to verify your report and coordinate with—"

"I don't have time for your bureaucratic bullshit!" Dade snapped. "People are trying to kill me! Do your damn job and find them!"

Dade's voice. That entitled tone. The smug fucking look on his face. It yanked her back to high school, to that ghost of Christmas past that she could never shake.

"Well?" Dade demanded, spreading his hands. "Are you people going to help me or what?"

She tried to breathe through it, to remember she was an agent, not a teenager with blood on her hands. But it was no use. Rage clawed its way out of her chest before she could stop it.

"You want protection?" Willow growled at Dade, struggling to keep a professional demeanor. "Where was Marissa Wilson's protection when she was being harassed every day at school? You were supposed to be our Resource Officer, but you couldn't be bothered to get off your ass when she begged for help!"

"That was over fifteen years ago," Dade shot back, his eyes fixed on Willow with arrogant defiance. His mouth twisted into the same dismissive smirk she remembered from high school. "Let it go already."

He remembers. He remembers Marissa, remembers her pleas for help, remembers choosing to do nothing—and he still doesn't give a shit.

"She swallowed a bottle of pills because of what those girls did to her!" The words tore out of her throat, and suddenly she could hear the whispered cruelty echoing off locker doors. You were too busy napping in your patrol car or stuffing your face at Dairy Queen to do your goddamn job!" Willow's voice cracked. "And now you want us to risk our lives protecting yours? Fuck that! Fuck you!"

Willow's hands curled into tight fists to keep them from shaking. She hadn't even noticed she'd stepped toward him until Ranger braced at her heel, tense and ready. Her vision blurred, and not from fear. The fury was so raw, it scared her. She wanted to scream, tear out his heart, and ram it down his throat. Instead, she stood there, vibrating.

"Agent Banks," Chief Stevens interjected firmly, "control yourself. What has gotten into you?"

Willow's spine snapped straight, her rage barely contained. "Fine," she said, her voice ice-cold as she straightened her jacket. "But don't expect me to shed any tears if your protection detail fails to do their job." With a quick hand signal to Ranger, whose growling ceased immediately, Willow turned and stalked out.

Willow leaned into the wall, sucking in air like it might calm her pounding heart. Ranger pressed against her legs, silent but alert. She hadn't meant to snap. Or maybe she had. Dade's face had dragged it all back: Marissa's shy smile, the last empty desk after winter break, and the gut-deep certainty that no one would ever be held accountable.

She told herself her behavior had been unprofessional, and that losing her temper in front of Jackson and the chief had been a mistake. But beneath the guilt and the self-recrimination, there was a seed of satisfaction she couldn't quite quell. Someone needed to say it and hold that bastard accountable.

And if she was being honest with herself, it had felt good to see him flinch. To see a crack in that smug, untouchable mask he always wore. It was wrong. She knew it was wrong. But she was tired of carrying that memory like a corpse slung across her back.

Marissa's mother still lived in town. Willow had seen her once, years ago, outside the grocery store. The woman hadn't even looked at her. That absence of recognition, or deliberate dismissal, had haunted her for weeks.

Maybe she deserved that.

Behind her, she could hear the voices, the posturing, the bullshit. She didn't care. She needed out. But first, she needed to hold it together. For the girls. For Mason.

"Who was Marissa Wilson?" Jackson asked quietly.

Willow's eyes opened, the pain and guilt in them fresh despite the years. "A girl who sat next to me in biology. Sophomore year. Sweet kid. Shy. The popular girls decided to make her life hell." She ran a shaky hand through her hair. "She reported it over and over. Dade was our School Resource Officer, and he never did a damn thing."

Understanding dawned. "And she took her own life?"

Willow closed her eyes and sighed. "Her mother found her. Two days before Christmas break." Tightness squeezed her chest until she found it difficult to draw breath. She hesitated, her mouth dry. "I wasn't just a bystander, Jackson. I wasn't just someone who saw it happening."

He looked at her, confusion flickering.

"In my freshman year of high school, I was five-foot-ten and the target of every lame-ass joke the girls could hurl at me. They were merciless and relentless, and I hated it. The next year, after Marissa moved to Beaufort, she became their new whipping girl, and I joined in. I laughed. I passed notes. I spread rumors. Not because I had anything against her, but because it was easier. Because if they were after her, they weren't after me. I was a fucking coward who took the easy way out, and Marrisa paid the ultimate price because I wouldn't stand by her."

Jackson's expression didn't shift, not in judgment or in sympathy. He just listened.

"I didn't know what I was doing until it was too late," Willow added, quieter now. "And I've been trying to make up for it ever since."

Jackson stepped closer, close enough to offer comfort without crowding her. "I'm sorry, Will."

"It was a long time ago," she said. The waver in her voice betrayed the lie. Some wounds never fully healed. They just scabbed over enough to function around them.

"I want to check on the girls," Willow said, desperate to escape her shame.

Jackson hesitated. "Will... I understand that Dade failed to do his job, but, right now, you sound more upset with yourself than with him. There had to be something more. I've never seen you like this before."

She didn't answer right away. Her eyes slid to the far wall, unfocused. Then she nodded. "It was my senior year. February 12, 2011. A date I'll never forget, the very day I decided I wanted to go into law enforcement."

Jackson waited, giving her the space she needed.

"There was a school shooting. Two rival gang members settling a score. One of them, Damian Ellis, burst into my AP English class looking for the other, Justin Wright. They'd been fighting over money, drugs, and a girl. You know, typical gang bullshit."

The memories flooded back in bitter, painful fragments: the door crashing open, students screaming, and Mrs. Hartwell raising her hands.

"Damian had a gun. Started waving it around, threatening everyone. Mrs. Hartwell tried to talk him down. He fired two shots into the ceiling. I was sitting by the window... and I could see the parking lot. I could see Dade. Just sitting there. In his cruiser."

"I'm guessing he chose to ignore the situation?" Jackson asked incredulously.

Willow scoffed. "Oh, the motherfucker heard the gunshots. The bastard hunkered down and tried to hide. Damian pointed his gun at Mrs. Hartwell until she backed away. And then... Damian shot Justin. Three times. And then three more. Right there in front of us."

Her voice cracked. She didn't blink.

"As soon as Damian stepped out into the hallway, Coach Smyth shot him with a shotgun. Coach saved us. Not Dade." She paused. "When I looked back out the window, Dade had moved his cruiser to the far side of the lot behind a school bus."

Jackson's jaw tightened. "Unbelievable."

"He never even got out," she said bitterly. "We sat in that room with two dead bodies for twelve minutes until backup arrived. Dade claimed he was *assessing the situation*. That he didn't want to make it worse."

Jackson asked, carefully, "Was he disciplined?"

Her lip curled in disgust. "They demoted him from Corporal to beat cop, and only because there had been a public outcry." A grim smile crossed her face. "I might have had something to do with telling the press about it."

"That took courage," Jackson said softly. "You couldn't have been more than seventeen."

"Eighteen. And it didn't take courage. It took rage. I knew how to use a computer, and I knew how to find email addresses for newspaper editors. And I knew the truth." She looked down the hallway towards the break room. "Not that it mattered. Dade kept his badge, and he's still fat, still useless, and he's still a fucking coward."

For a long moment, they stood in silence. The guilt of her actions still weighed on her. She needed to be somewhere that she could do good. Someplace where she wasn't the villain in someone's story. Right now, that meant being with the girls. It was the only thing keeping her upright.

"I want to check on the girls." She took Jackson's hand and gave it a squeeze.

"I'll be there in a minute," Jackson said, squeezing her hand back. "I want to talk to Dade before they take him away. I have questions for him, and I want to make things as difficult for him as possible."

Willow groaned, pushed off the wall, and composed herself before heading to the break room. Ranger followed, silent and loyal.

"If you feel the need," Willow said, looking back over her shoulder, "feel free to tear out his heart and ram it down his throat."

Jackson's smile and thumbs-up gesture made her happy.

Chapter Twenty-Eight

Jackson

Jackson returned to the conference room, where Cooper was putting cuffs on an incredulous Officer Dade. "We're arresting him on an obstruction charge," he said. "He'll be safe in holding until we decide what to do with him."

A police badge and gun sat on the conference room table. Maybe Dade's protective custody wasn't exactly what he had hoped for when he had come rushing into the room.

"I want to talk to him," Jackson said. "I want to know what happened to the video tapes and Jane's laptop. They were both missing from the murder scene."

"Lock him in Interrogation Room 2," Janet said. "The handcuffs stay on."

"I'm a victim," Dade shouted, his head swiveling to everyone in the room, desperately seeking a friendly face. "They tried to kill me."

"You probably shot up your own shop," Janet said. "I wonder if the bullets in your ride are going to match with your gun. Unlike you, ballistics don't lie."

Dade paled, his eyes darting as he scrambled for an angle. "I can show you who killed Jane," he blurted out. "I have the security footage from the house. I can give you everything, but I want full immunity and witness protection. And I want it all in writing, otherwise I'm not saying shit."

"Take off his cuffs," the chief said. "Escort him out the front door. We'll see how long he stays alive after I tell Michael Fitzpatrick that he fingered him as the murderer."

"You lying cunt," Dade bellowed, fighting against his restraints. "You do that and I'm as good as dead. I doubt he had nothing to do with it, but..." His chest heaved as he fought for words. The way his eyes were darting about, whatever he said next would likely be a lie. "Fitzpatrick pays me to not look too closely at who comes and goes from his houses. I have no idea what he's doing, but he knows that my patrol takes me past his places on the regular. I got gambling debts, and I wasn't doing anything wrong."

"Allowing criminals to be criminals is the exact opposite of what we do," Janet snarled. "And after I book you on conspiracy and bribery, I'll make damn sure you're charged as an accessory to every crime we can tie to the Fitzpatricks. Including the murder of Petty Officer Jane Gamble."

"I want a lawyer," Dade said, now in full panic mode. "I'm not saying another word without counsel."

"That is your right," Chief Steven's said. "But you've already voluntarily confessed in front of two police officers and an FBI agent. Even the best criminal lawyer in the country is not going to keep you from going to prison for a very long time."

Everyone waited until Dade realized that his only way out was to cooperate. He had already unwittingly confessed to multiple crimes, and his leverage was all but gone. He hung his head and cursed under his breath. "I don't know where the laptop is, but I have the security footage. I took it after I cuffed Jane's killer. I was afraid..."

It bothered Jackson that Dade still believed Mason was the killer. Had the murderer been in the house? The officer didn't seem to know anything about him.

The chief moved close enough that Dade was forced to back away. "That we'd have seen you drive past the house and then sitting in your fucking cruiser for three minutes before making entry?"

Dade turned his head and nodded.

"Where's the video?" Jackson asked.

"The SSD card is at my house, inside the curtain rod of my bedroom." Dade now looked completely defeated. "I'll get it for you," he added, hope in his eyes.

"How's about you give us your house keys and permission to search the premises?" Jackson said. "That is, if you want to show us that you're fully cooperating."

Dade had the look of a trapped animal. Jackson had no idea what else might be in his house, but there were clearly things that the cop didn't want anyone to find.

"No," he finally said after weighing his options. "You can enter my home to get the video, and nothing more. If you want to do a full search, get a fucking warrant."

"Mirandize him and lock him up," Chief Stevens said. "And put him on suicide watch. I don't want anything happening to our star witness. If he still wants a lawyer, make sure that happens. I'll call the magistrate and get that warrant." She gave Dade a pitiful look. "It's a shame you don't want to cooperate more fully. It might have actually helped your cause."

As Cooper pulled him from the conference room, Dade finally relented. "Search my house. I don't care. My keys are in my front-right pocket. All you'll find is my shoebox in my bedroom closet. It's got the money Fitzpatrick has paid me. I had planned on opening an offshore account to hide it, but I never got around to it."

"Thank you," Chief Stevens said while Cooper retrieved his keyring. He tossed it to her, and she motioned for him to take Dade away. "I'll be sure to let the DA know you cooperated, for whatever good that might do."

***

It hadn't taken long to find the memory card and the box of cash in his home. By the time Jackson and the chief had returned, Willow was back in the conference room, looking sheepish. Cooper was sitting beside her; a laptop open in front of him.

"Make a copy of this and upload it to our secure server," Janet said as she handed the SSD card to her sergeant.

Cooper plugged the drive into a card reader. "It looks like there are three months of recordings here," he said. "They're arranged by date."

"Bring up the tape from the ninth," Jackson said. "Right now, that's the only date we're interested in."

After a bit of typing and a few mouse clicks, Cooper pointed to the largest of the wall-mounted monitors. "Here's the ninth."

A grainy black-and-white video appeared on the wall-mounted flatscreen. The timestamp in the corner read December 9, 4:33 AM. The camera angle showed the front entrance of the antebellum house, its architectural details barely discernible in the night vision recording. A man was standing on the front porch looking away from the house.

Jackson moved closer for a better look. Video evidence rarely lied, though interpreting it correctly was often the challenge. He positioned himself where he could watch both the screen and Willow, still concerned about her emotional state.

"This looks like it's from the camera over the front door," Jackson said, remembering having seen one there. He had noticed two other cameras as well, one on each side of the home. "Are there separate files for each camera?"

"And why is the time only starting at 4:33?" Willow added.

"There's only one file per day," Cooper said. "I'm guessing that the cameras are motion activated, and this is the first time someone came into view that day. I'm also guessing that all the cameras' videos are appended together into a single file."

"We can figure that out later," Janet said. "Run the video so we can actually see what's happening."

"It looks like Mason," Jackson said. Even with the grainy night-vision footage, he could make out the man's build and general features. "I'm assuming this is when he's leaving after his tryst with Jane Gamble."

Willow confirmed it with a nod. "That's him." The figure paused to lock the door behind him, then walked briskly out of frame, shoulders hunched against the pre-dawn chill.

The group waited impatiently while the video of the front door continued for a minute before cutting out and restarting with a timestamp of 4:37 AM. This time, a different camera had sprung to life, triggered when a white panel van with no visible markings pulled into the laneway. As the van pulled up along the side of the house, it triggered security lights which instantly blinded the camera. A man emerged from the vehicle, looking like a ghost on the screen.

"We can't see shit anymore," Willow said. "Is it just me, or is the camera and flood light placement more than a little suspicious?"

The ghostly visage disappeared around the side of the house.

"Well," Jackson replied, "if it's intentional, it explains why they do late-night deliveries. It's the only way they can come and go without being identified."

"According to the BPD log, this is six minutes before dispatch reported Evelyn Hargrove's 911 call reporting screams," Cooper said, displaying the information on a smaller wall-mounted monitor. "Assuming it was Jane that the woman heard scream, she was alive and well when Mason left."

The group watched in silence as a minute passed, and the time-stamp jumped to 5:14 AM when Mason reappeared at the front door.

"What happened to the video of the van?" Willow said, anger in her voice. "Shouldn't the cameras have turned on when it left?"

"We're all seeing this for the first time, Sis," Cooper said. "But I'd bet we didn't see the van leave because it was still there when Mason showed up."

"He returned for his wallet over thirty minutes after the 911 call," Jackson murmured, mentally tracking the timeline they were building. He checked the next few entries on the call log. "Another 911 call was placed from inside the house about two minutes after Mason entered."

"There's no way he killed Jane," Willow said. "Unless he called 911 and then attacked her. And where the fuck was Dade when this was going on? According to the dispatch log, he gave a ten-minute ETA at 4:43. Over thirty minutes later, the fat fuck still isn't there. No doubt he was cowering in a corner somewhere."

Based on Willow's stories, Jackson had no doubt that Dade avoided the house. He was being paid to see nothing, and if the van was in the laneway, then he'd have turned a blind eye.

"Well," Cooper said. "I've got Officer Dade's GPS data. I can pull up his route for the night and see where he spent his time." The dispatch log disappeared and was replaced by a spreadsheet containing date, time, longitude and latitude coordinates, all broken down into one-minute segments. "One second," he said. "Let's put this into something more readable." He tapped away on his laptop and the spreadsheet was replaced with a map of Beaufort, and the GPS data displayed on the left-hand side. He scrolled through the log until he got to 4:43 AM. He clicked on the row and a marker appeared on the map.

"It looks like he was at Taco Bell when dispatch called him," Cooper said.

"That tracks," Willow said. "If the Dairy Queen was open 24/7, he'd likely have been there."

Cooper clicked the next row on the spreadsheet and the marker moved a block up the street to a gas station. He clicked the next row, and then the next. For ten minutes, the car never moved.

"He was relieving himself at the gas station," Jackson said. "He'd mentioned it when I interviewed him with Matt."

"The coordinates don't change for ten minutes," Cooper said as he clicked through the rows of data. He picked random rows to see where the cruiser's location would show up. At 5:15 AM, the GPS showed him in front of the house where Jane had been killed. At 5:16 AM, he was up the street and around the corner. Everyone sat in stunned silence. The officer had intentionally left the scene of a 911 call. At 5:19 AM he had returned, and for the next two-plus hours, his cruiser didn't move.

"Holy fuck," Willow said, splaying her fingers on the board-room table. "The sonofabitch waited thirty minutes before showing up. How is this fat fuck still on the force?"

"Continue the video," Janet said. "Let's see what it shows."

The camera at the side of the house came to life at 5:21 AM showing a grainy image of a portly man standing near the rear of the van. A moment later, the flood lights activated and the image of Dade all but disappeared. It was difficult to tell for certain, but it looked like he was now cowering beside the van. After a long delay, he finally moved toward the side entrance and disappeared from view. Sixty seconds after he disappeared, the timestamp jumped to 5:27 AM. The flood lights were on and the same ghostly figure moved to the driver's side of the van. Seconds later, the van backed out of the laneway.

"He went to the side entrance," Willow said, her breathing shallow and rapid. "He triggered the same floodlight. Look! Right there. The fucking van is still in the driveway. He was in the house a full six minutes before the driver of that van left. He never said anything about it in his report. The motherfucker was covering it up."

"And now we know why Mason was being targeted," Jackson said. "He was there with Jane's murderer. He likely saw him and could testify against him. My guess is, the killer threatened to harm his children if he talked."

"We need to get Mason and the girls to a safe house," Willow said. "I'll call Alice to see if she can arrange one for us."

"That's going to take time," Janet said. "In the meantime, I've got a plan. It's not perfect, but it will do until the FBI can give him a better place to lay low."

Jackson's eyebrows shot up, prompting the police chief to continue.

"Sergeant Cooper and three more squad cars are going to escort you back to the hospital," she said. "We're going to make a big show of police presence. We're going to dissuade anyone from making an unwanted visit to Mr. Banks and his family at the hospital."

"I'm sorry, Chief, but that's not much of a plan," Willow said, cocking an eyebrow. "There is already a pretty strong police presence at the hospital."

"Trust me," the chief said with a nervous smile. "It's going to work."

Chapter Twenty-Nine

Willow

Willow slowed and pulled over, letting an ambulance pass in front of her. Its lights flashed and sirens wailed as it sped toward Beaufort Memorial Hospital. Anxiety gripped her as she watched it disappear down the street.

It wasn't the ambulance carrying Mason. That one had left twenty minutes earlier, taking a different route entirely—the long way around to Highway 21, then south toward Fripp Island. No lights, no sirens. Nothing to draw attention.

"You think anyone's watching the hospital?" she asked Jackson, who sat in the passenger seat beside her.

"Someone probably is," he replied, scanning the rearview mirror. "But between all the commotion at the hospital and the police escort we arranged, they won't know which vehicle to follow."

Willow wanted to believe it was true. She pressed the gas when the light turned green. She hadn't been convinced Chief Stevens' plan would work, but it seemed to have gone off without a hitch. The entire seventh floor at Beaufort Memorial had been sealed off with access restricted to allow only fully vetted staff to enter. By all appearances, Mason Banks remained there under heavy guard. Meanwhile, Mason and his family were actually heading to a secluded house on a private island, accompanied by a paramedic friend of Cooper's. With any luck, the Fitzpatricks, and whoever else was involved in this mess, would continue to waste their time and resources watching the hospital.

"It's extremely low season on Fripp right now," Willow explained as she navigated through Beaufort's quiet streets. "From December through February, it's practically deserted except for the full-time residents. Christmas week will bring some tourists, but that's still two weeks away."

"And nobody would connect Janet to the place," Jackson added. He, too, had been skeptical of the idea but after a brief discussion with their SAC, they agreed that it was the best course of action until a longer-term safe house could be arranged. "The reservation was made months ago, before any of this started. If the house is as secluded as she says, it should work out well."

"You think Ruby will be okay with Mason and the girls?" Willow asked, though she already knew the answer. She needed the reassurance of saying it aloud.

"Yes," Jackson confirmed. "She wouldn't leave Sarah's side anyway. And I talked to my parents—they're already on their way. They'll meet them on the island in about two hours."

Willow raised an eyebrow. "They made good time."

"Dad drove like hell once I told him what was happening," Jackson said with a small smile. "Mom said they barely stopped except for gas and comfort breaks."

They rode in silence for a few minutes, the only sound the soft hum of the engine and the occasional crackle of the police radio Cooper had loaned them. As she turned into the parking lot of the Beaufort Police Station parking lot, Willow could feel Jackson's eyes on her, studying her profile in the dim light. She had unloaded some of her darkest and innermost secrets on him in the past three days, and she wondered if he still felt the same way about her.

They pulled into a parking spot and Willow shifted the truck into park. "I'm not what you bargained for, am I?" she said. A lump formed in her throat as she waited for a reply. Her pulse quickened as Jackson stared at her for several long heartbeats, his expression devoid of any emotion.

"I knew you were a hot mess from the first second I laid eyes on you," he replied, his voice calm and annoyingly monotone. "But I also saw how you cared for Ranger, even though you had zero connection with him. You humiliated yourself in front of a restaurant full of strangers, just so that he could have a chance of survival. You verbally eviscerated an elderly busybody, and you did it in such a way that she thought you would be perfect for me. Even though I hadn't been looking for a relationship, I found myself agreeing with her."

Willow's mouth opened to speak but no words came out. She wasn't exactly sure what she was going to say, and she wasn't exactly sure if she had just been insulted.

"I'm not finished," Jackson said. "I was dealing with my own personal demons at the time. I was in therapy for having shot and killed a fourteen-year-old boy. I was suffering from night terrors and constant migraines. In all that time, you never judged me or questioned who I was as a person. You loved me for who I was, and when I proposed, you accepted without hesitation. Life comes at you hard and fast sometimes, and the split-second decisions we make can have a profound impact on us and the world around us. Do you really think that my learning about a few small slices of your past life would change how much I love you?"

The earnestness in his eyes made the lump in Willow's throat double in size. "You are the best person I've ever met..." A tear tumbled down her cheek which she quickly swiped with her fingertip. "I'm broken in more ways than I can count, and yet you continue to stand by me. Whenever my heart aches, you can heal it with a single touch. I can't believe how lucky I was to have stumbled into your life."

The circumstances that led Willow to seek out Jackson crashed into her. She had needed help with Ranger because his handler,

Kate, had died in the line of duty, and she had been killed because Willow had acted brashly. She had thrown herself headlong into a dangerous situation without thinking how it might affect her partner or her K9. More tears tumbled down her cheeks, too quickly to wipe them all away.

"What's all this for?" Jackson asked, tucking loose strands of Willow's long blonde hair behind her ear. He cupped her chin and gently turned her face toward him.

"Because I'm a hot mess with a long history of colossal screwups, and I don't deserve you," she said. A smile managed to find its way to her lips. "But I'm so fucking happy that you accept me anyway, warts and all."

Cooper's squad car pulled in beside them, the headlights briefly illuminating their faces before he cut the engine. Willow composed herself, pushing the old memories back into their box. This wasn't the time to dwell on the past, not with her family's lives still in danger.

"Do you need a minute?" Jackson asked. He held up a finger to Cooper to say they'd be right out.

"Nah," Willow said with a snort-laugh as she opened her door, filling the cab with cool December air. "My brother's seen me have an emotional meltdown plenty of times. One more isn't going to change anything. Let's get this shit show moving."

Ranger immediately jumped down beside her, and Jackson came around the truck to meet them just as Cooper approached from his squad car.

"Everything okay?" he asked, noting his sister's slightly red-rimmed eyes.

"Just the usual emotional clusterfuck," Willow said with a shaky laugh.

Cooper stepped closer with his arms open. "That's my sister," he said, giving Willow a hug. "She's got a soft heart and a filthy mouth, like a Hallmark Christmas card written by Samuel L. Jackson."

"What meme did you scrape that from?" Willow said, giving her older brother a punch in the gut. She quickly checked Ranger to make sure he understood it was all in fun. He was looking the other way, like he was giving her time to do what needed doing, or he was scanning for actual threats. Outside of his playtime with her nieces, Willow never saw him switch off from doing his job.

Cooper let out a grunt and buckled over. He moaned for a few seconds before breaking into a belly laugh. He looked up and rubbed his stomach. "But you still can't punch worth shit. I thought the FBI might have trained you better." He took a feigned fighting stance before holding his arms wide, inviting his sister in for a hug.

She opened her arms, stepped close, and unleashed a full-force punch into his belly. This time, Cooper buckled over and toppled onto his face. "I'll step into the ring with you any time, Big Brother, and we can go at like we did when we were kids."

When Cooper didn't get up, Willow dropped by his side, concern flooding her. Ranger, too, quickly moved in and nuzzled Cooper's neck, perhaps trying to rouse him, or to keep the game going.

"You know," he said with considerable effort, "I was in a good mood until you stepped out of your truck." He gave Ranger a quick pat on the back, stood straight, and sucked in a deep breath. "And now," he said, smiling broadly. "And now I'm in a terrific mood. It's so good to have my sister home, and after we get Mason and the kids home safe and sound, I'm going to accept your boxing match challenge. We have an excellent ring here at the precinct." He turned to face Jackson and grinned some more. "As long as that's okay with you, big fella."

Cooper, at six-one, was a big man. But Jackson's muscular six-foot-three frame made him look small. Willow and her brothers were all tall and lean, just like their father had been. At five-foot-eleven, she was the shortest in the family—except for her mother who was barely five-nine.

"You've met your sister, right?" Jackson flashed Willow his own charming smile, the sort of smile that said she was the luckiest girl on the planet. "She does what she wants, when she wants, and I'll be right behind her while she does it."

The truth of that statement stung more than she'd have liked to admit, but she appreciated the sentiment. Was she really that obstinate? Was it really her way or the highway?

The smile on Jackson's lips never faded. If he meant it, it wasn't in a bad way, but most likely, he was just joining in on the sparring match—choosing to use words over physicality.

"You two are too much for me," Cooper said, raising his hands in surrender. "I only came out here to share some exciting news. Our good ol' friend Officer Dade has been spilling his guts ever since we put him in holding."

Willow felt a surge of satisfaction that Dade was about to get his just desserts. "What did he say?"

"He knew there was someone else in the house when he entered," Cooper replied as they walked toward the station doors. "Said he was surprised to see Mason there—that he was expecting it to be someone else."

"He saw the killer?" Jackson said. "Who was it? Did he identify him?"

"Dade's still convinced that it was Mason who killed Jane," Cooper said. "But he also said there were two other people in the house. The one he saw was Caucasian, about six feet, short sandy-brown hair, and maybe two hundred pounds. Dade never saw the other person. He was upstairs, ransacking Jane's bedroom."

"Did he say why they were there?" Willow asked. It bothered her deeply that Dade still believed Mason was the killer. She knew her brother. Despite what he had done to her, he was a good man and he'd never, under any circumstances, kill someone.

"To retrieve the corpses," Cooper said, holding the door open for them. "The guy Dade saw tried to get him to help put the bodies in the van, but Dade said there was no time. Backup and the EMTs would be there in a few minutes. So the guy told Dade to secure the video tapes and he'd come for them later."

"What about the van?" Willow continued, thinking she'd rather be asking these questions directly to Dade.

"Nothing of interest, other than that it was a plain white panel van with South Carolina plates." Cooper waved to the desk sergeant as they continued into the squad room. "He didn't take down the plate number. When I pressed him, he admitted that *looking not too closely* was part of his duty to Fitzpatrick."

They stepped into a small conference room where Chief Stevens was waiting with a stack of files.

"We've got Dade on conspiracy to commit murder, obstruction of justice, tampering with evidence, accessory after the fact, and the list goes on," she said, looking up as they entered. "The U.S. Attorney's Office is already involved because Jane was a federal agent."

"He could get the death penalty for this," Willow said, the realization settling coldly in her stomach.

"Possibly," Janet said. "Though the U.S. Attorney might agree to life in prison depending on how much useful information Dade can provide about the operation. He's waived all rights to an attorney and is willing to comply completely. The Deputy USA is coming here along with federal marshals to take him into custody."

Willow had never believed in the death penalty and had argued against it many times during her criminology classes at the academy. The justice system was too flawed, too prone to error. Too many innocent people had been executed over the years.

But as she thought about Dade—about his cowardice, about Marissa, about his willing participation in a conspiracy that included child trafficking—she couldn't find it in herself to care what happened to him.

"I don't agree with the death penalty," she said finally. "But I won't shed a tear for that man if that's the sentence he gets."

Janet's expression was grim but understanding. "Well, we've got a long way to go before that decision is made. In the meantime, we need to figure out what to do about the Fitzpatricks. Dade's statements confirmed they're behind the trafficking, but we don't have nearly enough evidence to bring them in."

Cooper's phone buzzed. He checked it and showed the text to Willow. "Ambulance just arrived at the location. Everyone's safe."

Willow exhaled a slow, deliberate breath. Mason and the girls were safe for now. It was a small victory, but she'd take it. She'd have liked to be with them, but she had a job to do. "How do you think Michael Fitzpatrick is going to react when three federal agents come knocking?"

Jackson got a perplexed look on his face. "You want Matt to meet us there?"

"Fuck no," Willow said, thumbing toward Ranger. "NCIS has no reason to talk with him, but we do." She offered Jackson a crooked smile. "I plan on making this as uncomfortable as possible for Fitzpatrick."

For the first time since this case had started, they were on the offensive. And Willow intended to keep it that way.

Chapter Thirty

Jackson

Anxiety bubbled in Jackson's stomach when they rolled into the parking lot. Michael Fitzpatrick's placement agency, Maritime Workforce Solutions, maintained an office space in a strip mall just outside Beaufort's city limits. It was a tidy little storefront flanked by two larger operations, a mini-mart and a dry cleaner.

The night before, Willow had called Mason to question him about people being at the house when he'd found Jane. He was adamant that he didn't know anyone else was in the house with him but he was far more forthcoming with information about the Fitzpatricks and their operation. He'd said that, over the months that he'd worked on the house, the staff had turned over at least four times. All except for one woman, who seemed to be in charge when Michael Fitzpatrick wasn't there. She was a tall Caucasian woman whose name he never learned. She was only there on occasion, but she was the only constant when it came to personnel.

Mason had also said that one of his workers, Thomas Warner, had grown close to Anika Augustin, one of the chefs who worked at the house.

For Jackson, the most disturbing tale that Mason had shared was that during the week leading up to Jane's murder, men had come to the house, and had taken turns going upstairs, dragging two of the young girls along with them. When they returned, the girls had been red-faced with tear-streaked cheeks and swollen eyes. Mason and his staff had been taken aside and told, in no uncertain terms, that they saw nothing and that there was a huge Christmas bonus in it for them if they kept it that way. Michael had told Mason that, if he didn't comply, Ivy would make a nice addition to his *stable.*

That single sentence had twisted Jackson's stomach into a knot that had yet to release. He would bide his time and when the opportunity presented itself, he would, to use Willow's colorful phrasing, *fuck that man up*. And when Michael Fitzpatrick got thrown in federal prison, Jackson would make sure that everyone there knew he was a child trafficker and pedophile.

Jackson blinked, unaware that he'd zoned out. Ranger and Willow were standing outside their SUV staring at him. "You coming? We can go in without you if you'd prefer." She had a wicked smile on her face. Willow understood completely that there was no force on earth that would stop him from going in.

"Me first," Jackson said as they approached. He stopped long enough to read the words etched into the storefront glass. *Maritime Workforce Solutions. Est. 1999.* His pulse thrummed in his ears as he wondered if they'd been trafficking humans for twenty-five years unchecked. He pulled open the door and quickly assessed the office space.

The twenty-by-twenty room was smaller than Jackson had expected. Three desks arranged side by side, effectively blocking anyone from going to the single door at the back of the room. Three burly men occupied the desks, each wearing camo-patterned T-shirts with the company logo silk-screened over the heart. As one, they stopped typing on their computers and glared at the new arrivals.

"How can I be of assistance?" asked the man in the center. He stood from behind his small utilitarian desk, showing his camo-colored pants and the holstered handgun at his hip.

Ranger immediately went into high alert. Willow gave him a quick hand signal and flashed her badge. "I'm FBI Special Agent Willow Banks, and this is my partner, Special Agent Jackson Brooks. We're here to speak with Michael Fitzpatrick."

Jackson gritted his teeth, hoping that that he could take the lead when they got their chance to speak with Michael.

"He's not hiring," the greeter said. "We've got all the people we need. If you have a card, leave it. If something comes up, I'll be sure to contact you."

A low growl erupted from Ranger's chest, a precursor to Willow's reaction. The two other men also stood, flexing their muscles in a pathetic show of physical strength. All three looked like they spent most of their day at the gym pumping iron.

"Maybe you meatheads should consider your next words carefully," Willow said, stepping past Jackson. "Otherwise, I won't put a good word in for you at the food bank when we put you out of your jobs."

"Gentlemen," Jackson said, taking a step forward to put himself beside Willow. "I'm uncertain as to why you feel a need to be antagonistic. We're not looking for trouble. We're just here to speak with your boss."

"Show me your warrant," the greeter said. "Or you can turn your skinny asses around and harass someone else."

"Or you can make an appointment," the man on Willow's side of the room said, looking her up and down like she was a piece of meat. "Mr. Fitzpatrick might have an opening in the new year for someone as tasty as you."

Willow laughed at the joke. "Tell you what," she said, still laughing. "How's about if I can have you down and restrained in less than ten seconds, you let us pass."

"And if you fail?" the gym rat retorted. "Maybe we put you in handcuffs and skin your mutt."

Ranger snarled, his tongue licking between his impressive set of canines. He leaned forward, waiting for a command.

"My dog thinks you're threatening me," Willow said in her own threatening tone. "Do you think you can pull your handgun before he rips out your throat?"

The idiot's hand dropped to his side arm and Willow ordered her K9, "Ranger, hold!" The dog sprung forward, leapt over the desk, and grabbed the fool by the wrist as he drew his weapon. Ranger used his momentum to throw his target off balance and drag him to the floor. While his captive screamed, Jackson and Willow drew their guns and leveled them on the remaining two men.

"Enough of this!" A red-headed man in his early forties emerged from behind the lone door. His tailored suit stood in stark contrast to his employees' mercenary-style clothing. "I've already called the sheriff's office. They should be here shortly." Jackson caught the slight upturn of the man's mouth, suggesting he wasn't particularly concerned about their presence.

"Ranger, release," Willow said, calling her dog back to her. Without hesitation, he unclamped his jaws from the man's wrist and slowly backed away. When he was out of arm's reach, he turned and padded back to Willow's side.

Jackson had retrained his aim at the newest arrival. From the pictures he'd seen pinned on Chief Stevens' murder board, this was Michael Fitzpatrick. "Your men made threats toward my partner," he said with a matter-of-fact tone. "He went for his gun, and our K9 subdued him."

"My brother doesn't hire my protection team based on their intellect," Michael said. "But they are extremely well trained and don't act unless provoked. I watched the entire thing on my security cameras." He pointed to the three cameras positioned around the perimeter of the room. "I have more than enough proof that you two were the aggressors in this encounter, and I have no doubt the sheriff will see things my way."

Rich, powerful, and connected. The Fitzpatricks didn't have the BPD in their pocket, at least not entirely, but the county sheriff's office might be a different story. The man was overly confident and fully accustomed to getting his way.

It might be a weakness to be exploited.

"I'm not sure why you feel the need to create a security wall while you cower behind locked doors," Jackson said. "Perhaps you and your brothers are not the men I believed you to be. I hear Scots wear nothing under their kilts, but I suspect you wear a diaper."

"I'm Irish, you imbecile," Michael said. "It makes me think the FBI hire new recruits from fashion magazines. It appears you have more in common with my associates here than I realized."

"Then man up and let us talk to you," Willow said, throwing her long, blonde ponytail over her shoulder.

Her comment made Michael chuckle. His three bodyguards followed suit, laughing more than they should have. "Ask me your questions. I'm an open book."

"I'd like to speak with your workers assigned to 400 Port Republic Street," Jackson said, sliding his sidearm back into its holster. He pulled out his notepad and pen. "Can you tell me where they are staying? I'd also like to see their H-2B visas and work permits."

"I don't know where you can find my employees," Michael said with the smooth ease of a public figure trained in media relations. "Once they are off the clock, their time is their own. As to their documentation, leave me your business card and I'll have my executive assistant email them to you."

"Are you suggesting that you don't provide lodging for your workers?" Willow asked. "You leave it to non-English speaking people, who've never stepped foot in our country, to find their own housing?"

"I didn't say that I don't," Michael said, annoyance simmering in his bright blue eyes. He didn't like being challenged, especially by a woman. "I said I don't know where to find them. My executive assistant handles all those details. I look after my employees and their performance at their place of work. I take great pride in the services I provide, and I personally guarantee client satisfaction. If my people deliver anything less, I immediately correct the issue. It's why I keep such a small office space. I'm rarely ever here."

"What is your EA's name and where might we find her?" Jackson asked.

Michael rolled his eyes and shook his head. "How gauche that you would infer that my assistant is a woman." He grinned at Jackson. "I mean, Alicia is *definitely* a woman, but I find it insulting that you immediately assumed she was one."

"Can you give us *Alicia's* full name and where we can find her?" Willow said, making it very clear that Michael's games were grating on her nerves. "Does she share an office with you in the back?"

"She does," Michael said with a lecherous tone. "But I'm afraid you've just missed her. She left on Christmas vacation yesterday. She's gone to Ireland and won't be back until the middle of January."

Jackson scrubbed the back of his neck, trying to loosen the knot twisting at his muscles. The man was toying with them, intentionally wasting their time.

Ranger's head snapped around at the sound of three vehicles pulling up to the front of the building. The Sheriff's department had wasted no time in answering Michael Fitzpatrick's summons.

"We'll come back with a warrant," Willow said, eyes locked on Michael. "It's funny, we didn't think you were involved in Jane Gamble's murder, but your stonewalling has made it perfectly clear that you are, at the very least, a conspirator to the crime."

"Show me your hands," the sheriff's deputy said as he stepped inside, his gun raised and leveled at Jackson's chest.

"Responsive as always, Jake," Michael said in a jovial, familiar tone. These men were definitely in his pocket, and he didn't care that he was flaunting it. "These federal agents were just leaving. Sorry to have bothered you."

"No bother at all, Mr. Fitzpatrick," Jake said. "The sheriff couldn't make it himself, but he sent best wishes to you and Alicia, and he said to enjoy your vacation in Ireland."

He's about to run. He's not as self-confident as he's trying to appear.

Chapter Thirty-One

Willow

"What did you see?" Willow asked when Jackson shut the car door. He handed her a soda and a bag of pretzels. "Why did you need to visit the minimart and the drycleaners?"

Jackson screwed off the top of his drink and took a swig. "When we drove into the parking lot, I was able to see how deep the building was. It has to be at least one-hundred feet. What we could see of Fitzpatrick's office space inside was twenty feet deep, at most. Fitzpatrick's office might be eighty feet, or there might be multiple offices, but I doubt it. I wanted to see how big the operations were on either side." He grinned. "So, I picked us up some snacks. The cashier looked like he was carved from the same redwood as the three in Fitzpatrick's office. The minimart is, at most, forty feet deep. The storefront of the drycleaners is even smaller, and it had another gorilla working at the front desk. I asked him if they had 24-hour turnaround, and how much it would be to get three suits cleaned. The clerk told me they were having mechanical difficulties and that I should visit an alternate cleaner."

"Fuck me," Willow said, her eyes narrowing as she processed the information.

"Exactly," Jackson responded. "And look behind us. There are three all-white panel vans and two cube vans on the far side of the lot."

Willow's sucked a slow breath through her nose. "We need to get inside that building, but we'll need a warrant first. And we need someone watching this place until we get it." She reached for her phone and activated the SUV's hands-free system. "I'm calling Cooper. You okay being on speaker?"

Jackson offered a thumbs-up.

"Hey, Cooper," Willow said into the system. "Jackson's with me, and you're on speaker. We need officers to sit on Marine Workforce Solutions on Robert Smalls Parkway near the Savannah Highway intersection. Can you make that happen?"

"I know where it is, Sis," Cooper replied, disappointment evident in his voice. "And I'd like to help, but it's outside BPD jurisdiction. The Beaufort County Sheriff doesn't take kindly to us stepping on their toes."

Jackson leaned forward. "I don't have proof, but I've got a bad feeling Fitzpatrick is holding his victims there. I'm guessing he owns the minimart and the dry cleaners on either side. I went into both, and based on the strip mall's footprint, they're much smaller than they should be."

"Give me a sec," Cooper said. "I need to talk with the chief."

"I can try to draft the affidavit for a no-knock warrant on my phone," Willow offered, "but it'll be a pain in the ass to do that. If I had my laptop, it'd be a lot easier."

"Can't we get Hunter to write it up?" Jackson asked. "Surely he knows how."

Willow let out a slow breath. "I'm sure he does, but he doesn't know Judge O'Hara. She'll give us the warrant if I ask, but if it's not worded just right, Fitzpatrick's defense attorney will rip it to shreds. Anything we find would be inadmissible."

Jackson shot her a curious glance. "How can you be sure she'll help?"

Willow grimaced. "She's a religious fanatic—thinks she's the right hand of God and that it's her duty to smite the wicked." She threw in a theatrical gesture. "Because of that, she's been the target of more death threats and assassination attempts than I can count. I worked two of those cases, and after sitting in a hotel room with her for a few days, we built a rapport. I've leaned on her a few times since, when I needed her particular brand of judicial assistance."

Jackson's eyebrow arched. "A handy card to play, but I don't want to leave here without a replacement. We need eyes on the place. If we're right about Fitzpatrick, he'll evacuate the victims, and we'll have nothing when we breach."

"I'm back," Cooper said. "The chief gave a detective and few officers some extra *time off*. They should be there in a half hour or so. They'll be in their personal vehicles, so no official BPD presence."

"Give Janet our thanks," Willow said. "We're going to head back to the station when they get here. In the meantime, do you think you can get the blueprints for the mall from public records? It's unlikely they'll be current, but I'll take what you can get."

"Can you also get the corporate details on the minimart and laundromat?" Jackson added. "I'd like to be sure I've got this right."

Cooper disconnected and Willow gripped the steering wheel, twisting its leather wrapping in her hands. "If the county sheriff's office is cozy with Fitzpatrick, we're going to need more firepower."

Jackson leaned back against the headrest. "Agreed. But if BPD can't step in because it's outside their jurisdiction, we'll need to get creative."

"Alice," Willow said. "She can coordinate with the Charleston field office since this would technically fall under their jurisdiction. Would you mind calling her? I'm going to start getting my thoughts together for the affidavit."

Jackson dialed Alice's number and put it on speaker. Their supervisor answered on the second ring.

"Agent Baldwin."

"Hey Alice, it's Jackson. I'm here with Willow. We're outside Marine Workforce Solutions, and we've got a situation."

"I'm listening." Alice's voice was crisp, focused.

"We have strong reason to believe Fitzpatrick is holding trafficking victims at this location," Jackson explained, running down the details and his suspicions.

"Jesus," Alice said. "Do you have a warrant?"

"I'm working on getting one," Willow chimed in. "We've arranged for some off-duty BPD officers to keep eyes on the place, but they can't officially assist since it's outside their jurisdiction. The Beaufort County Sheriff's Department appears to be in Fitzpatrick's pocket."

"I see." They could hear Alice tapping on her keyboard. "I'll coordinate with the Charleston field office. They should have primary, but if they can't mobilize quickly enough, I'll reach out to the State Police. I still have several contacts there from my time in Charleston."

"Thank you," Willow said. "We need to move quickly. If Fitzpatrick suspects we're onto him—"

"He'll evacuate the victims," Alice finished. "I understand. Keep your distance for now. Don't engage unless absolutely necessary."

"Yes, ma'am," Jackson responded.

"How are your parents doing, by the way?" Alice asked, her tone softening slightly. "I've been meaning to call them."

Jackson smiled despite the tension. "They're fine. Last I heard, they were enjoying their time with Mason's girls. Mom's already asking when Willow and I are having kids."

"Before you're even married?" Alice chuckled and then drew a ragged breath. "Is her cancer back?"

"No, no," Jackson said, waving his hands for extra effect, even if Alice couldn't see. "She's still in full remission."

"Thank God," Alice said. "How's Travis? Is he having fun playing bodyguard for Willow's brother? It's got to be a nice change for him."

The comment made Jackson laugh. "I'd say so. I spoke with him a while ago, and he mentioned the safe house they're staying in is *highly defensible*. Said they'd have plenty of notice if anyone decided to pay an unwanted visit."

"That sounds like Travis," Alice said. "Good to know Mason's daughters are in capable hands. I'll make those calls right away and get back to you within an hour. Stay safe, both of you."

"Will do," Jackson said before ending the call.

Willow had been paying attention to the conversation while she tapped out her notes on her phone. "Your dad's right. Based on his description, the vacation rental is perfect with a single access road, a gated community, and excellent sight lines."

"I'm sure they're fine," Jackson said, though his expression remained serious. "I just hope we can shut this operation down quickly. The longer this goes on..."

"I know," Willow said softly. "As soon as the BPD get here, we'll head back to the station and start working on that affidavit for Judge O'Hara. Alice will come through for us. She always does."

Just as Jackson motioned toward the old Honda that pulled into the parking lot, Willow's phone buzzed with a text from Cooper: *Officers in place. Blue Civic and gray F-150 at opposite ends of the lot. Will alert if there is movement.*

Willow pulled out of the parking lot and made her way to the precinct. They drove in silence for several minutes, both processing what they'd just discovered. The scale of the Fitzpatricks' operation was larger than they'd initially thought, and with law enforcement compromised at multiple levels, they would need all the help they could get.

At least they had eyes on the building. Now they just needed the firepower to do something about it.

Chapter Thirty-Two

Jackson

Frustration coiled in Jackson's gut as he watched Willow check her phone for the third time in ten minutes. Her tension was palpable as she paced the length of the small BPD conference room. Every passing minute without that warrant increased the risk that Fitzpatrick would move the trafficking victims.

"Anything?" Jackson asked, looking up from the desk where he'd spread out architectural drawings of the strip mall.

Willow shook her head. "Judge is taking her sweet time. It's not like her, but her clerk assured me that Judge O'Hara was working on it, and that she'd get back to me as soon as possible." She stuffed her phone into her back pocket and took a seat at the table. Ranger immediately laid down at her feet. "That was four hours ago."

Jackson surveyed the room, taking measure of their expanded makeshift task force. Chief Janet Stevens stood by the whiteboard, arms crossed and looking deep in thought. Sergeant Cooper Banks sat beside Officer Mike Reeves, who was stroking his K9 partner Zeus's head. Matt, whose presence SSA Davidson had insisted on, leaned against the wall in the corner, somehow managing to look both bored and intensely focused, at the same time.

Jackson's gaze lingered on Reeves and Zeus. The K9 handler's nature to rely solely on himself concerned Jackson. He wondered if Reeves had learned anything from his failure back in Alabama, or if he'd continue to ignore his partner's instincts when it mattered most. But they needed all available K9 units, and this was a chance for Reeves to prove himself in the field.

At least Zeus knows what he's doing, even if his handler doesn't always listen.

The large wall-mounted monitor flickered with SSA Vicky Davidson's face, the video occasionally freezing before stabilizing.

"These floor plans," Jackson said, moving to stand beside Willow, "they're the originals filed with the county when the mall was built, but based on what I saw while I was at the three businesses, there have been significant renovations."

"And none of those changes were filed with the city," Willow added.

"Shocking," Chief Stevens said dryly. "And no one in the city or county planning committees would have blocked the Fitzpatricks, with or without permits."

Jackson watched as Willow's expression darkened when Matt pushed off the wall and stepped closer to the table. Her annoyance at his presence was obvious, even though she was clearly trying to mask it. Jackson understood her reluctance to have Matt involved, but they needed all the help they could get. This operation was simply too big.

Jackson turned his attention back to the video call. "Vicky, any thoughts on the connection between the drug busts BPD has been making and the Russian oligarch's operations moving north?"

"There's too much of a coincidence," Vicky replied, her voice crackling through the speakers. "The timing of Mikhail Sokolov deciding to move his operations north aligns perfectly with the rise in drug busts that Beaufort PD has made in the county. He may have fled the country, but he could still be running the operation remotely."

Matt shook his head. "I think the oligarch's a red herring. According to DEA intel, Sokolov was moving massive quantities of product from both the Mexican and Colombian cartels—tens of millions of dollars' worth. Compared to that, Fitzpatrick was nothing more than a pimple on the guy's ass. What *isn't* a red herring, in my opinion, is Pratt's role in the local trade. My guess? He was working with Fitzpatrick Sr. right up until Sr. got pinched. When he decided to start naming names, Pratt had him killed and then cut a new deal with one or more of the Fitzpatrick boys."

"Greg's been thinking the same thing," Vicky added. "He suspects Pratt has ties inside the Coast Guard and has someone feeding him intel on patrol routes. Pratt passes that info to the suppliers and the Fitzpatricks, and they run the drugs in around enforcement. Greg doesn't think that Pratt is involved in the human trafficking side at all. He believes the Fitzpatricks expanded into that on their own."

The door swung open, drawing everyone's attention, as a tall, broad-shouldered man in tactical gear stepped into the room, his posture radiating authority. The SWAT patch on his chest identified him immediately.

"Lieutenant Bill Boivin, South Carolina State Police," he announced without preamble. His gaze swept the room, assessing each person before landing on Chief Stevens. "I understand you're planning a raid on a suspected human trafficking location."

"We are," Chief Stevens confirmed. "Thank you for joining us, Lieutenant."

Boivin strode into the room with the confidence of someone accustomed to taking charge. "I'll be leading this operation," he stated rather than asked, his tone leaving no room for discussion.

Jackson felt his eyebrows rise. Here we go.

"Actually," Willow said, straightening her spine, "this is a *joint* task force, but the case is ultimately under FBI authority."

Boivin faced her, his expression hard. "And you are?"

"Special Agent Willow Banks, FBI," she replied, matching his intensity. "This is my partner, Special Agent Jackson Brooks."

Jackson bobbed his head in greeting, but remained silent, measuring the lieutenant. Boivin had the bearing of someone who'd seen plenty of action.

"With all due respect, Agent Banks," Boivin said, his formality doing little to mask his feeling of superiority, "SWAT has the expertise for this kind of operation. My team has conducted dozens of raids on similar targets."

"The organization of the raid itself should be under your leadership," Willow conceded, surprising Jackson slightly. "But the overall operation falls under our jurisdiction."

Sensing an opportunity to defuse the tension, Jackson stepped forward. "Lieutenant, I should take the lead on entry team assignment," he said.

Boivin tilted his head toward Jackson, a challenge in his eyes. "And why is that, Agent Brooks?"

"Because unless I'm wrong, I'm the only member in this room who has significant experience in human trafficking operations," Jackson replied evenly. "I've led multiple raids with the Violent Crimes Against Children task force, and I know what to look for and how traffickers typically respond during raids."

The room fell silent as Jackson and Boivin locked eyes. Jackson could see the lieutenant processing this information, weighing his options.

"I've run plenty of drug house takedowns," Boivin countered. "Dirt-bags are dirt-bags."

"Except, this isn't a drug house," Jackson said quietly. "These are people being held against their will. Terrified people who might bolt at the first sign of trouble, or worse, be used as human shields by their captors. The tactics and the rules of engagement are completely different."

After a tense moment, Boivin grunted his approval, though his expression remained tight. "Fair enough. You and I can plan out how we're going to breach and which teams will go where."

Jackson turned back to the table, where Willow had spread out the floor plans. "Here's what we know from what I observed yesterday," he said, tracing his finger along the strip mall blueprint. "The MWS office space is much smaller than it should be based on these plans. Same with the minimart and the dry cleaners."

He pointed to the back wall. "These walls have been moved inward, creating hidden spaces behind them. I'd bet good money that's where they're holding the victims."

"Because of Beaufort's high-water table," Willow added, "it would be near impossible for there to be any underground tunnels. If the victims are being held there, they'd be in those hidden rooms."

Everyone appeared to be in agreement.

"Other than the three you mentioned, did you check out any of the other businesses in the mall?" Boivin asked. "Could their spaces have been modified too?"

Jackson shook his head. "We didn't want to tip off our suspicions. We couldn't risk alerting Fitzpatrick."

"The chief's off-duty officers checked out three of the business spaces," Willow added. "They all appeared to be the correct size."

Jackson studied the floor plan, his mind racing through tactical scenarios. "Here's what I'm thinking," he said finally. "SWAT makes entry directly into the MWS offices. That's where we'll likely meet the heaviest resistance. The off-duty officers watch the rear of the mall in case anyone tries to squirt out the back."

He looked at Willow and then at Officer Reeves. "Willow and Reeves will take their K9s into the minimart."

A flicker of doubt crossed Willow's eyes as she glanced at Reeves, sharing Jackson's concern for the young handler.

"And," Jackson continued, "I'll take Matt and enter through the dry-cleaning company."

Chief Stevens and Sergeant Cooper immediately protested.

"And what are we supposed to do—just sit this one out?" Cooper demanded.

"You've had a long day," Willow said, feigning extreme sympathy, following it up with a wink. "You should probably clock out before the teams head to the mall."

Before he could respond, Cooper's phone rang. "It's Detective Phillips."

Jackson remembered him from the hospital.

He quickly accepted the call. "You're on speaker. The chief is with me along with the JTF team. Any news from MWG?"

"Sir, Michael Fitzpatrick is leaving the building. Do you want us to follow him? If we do, we're going to lose eyes on the location."

Jackson locked eyes with Willow, a silent communication passing between them. Following Fitzpatrick might tip him off but letting him go meant potentially missing an opportunity.

"No," Jackson said after a moment of consideration. "Leave him alone. Following him might alert him that something's up."

There were no objections, though Jackson could tell not everyone was convinced it was the right call.

As if on cue, Willow's phone buzzed. She checked it, her expression shifting from tension to determination. "It's here," she announced. "We've got no-knock warrants for all three businesses. Unlimited access to search the premises for people, computers, and files for any information related to the human trafficking operation and human rights violations."

Jackson felt a surge of adrenaline. After all the waiting, it was finally happening.

"Alright," Boivin said, turning to the group. "Let's finalize the entry plan. My team can be geared up in thirty minutes."

"Actually," Jackson interjected, "I think we should wait until after 8:00 PM."

Boivin's head snapped toward him. "Why the delay? We have the warrant now."

Jackson moved to the window, subtly gesturing outside. "Remember those panel vans and cube trucks in the parking lot yesterday? I'm thinking they might be what's used to shuttle the victims. If we move too early, we might miss critical evidence about their transportation network."

Willow caught on immediately. "You think they're moving people during the day?"

"It's possible," Jackson replied. "Hiding in plain sight by moving them during business hours when there's natural traffic would make sense. Traffickers often transport victims during normal business operations to avoid suspicion." He looked over at Chief Stevens. "Those vans should be watched. If they leave, they might lead us to where the victims are being kept during the day."

A thoughtful look crossed the chief's face. "Agent Banks is right. Sergeant Cooper and I have had a very long day, and we're going to knock off early. Maybe we'll take a drive, get some fresh air."

Cooper grinned and nodded knowingly. "Right. Just two off-duty cops spending some time together outside the city limits. Nothing official."

Jackson appreciated their quick understanding. They couldn't officially conduct surveillance outside their jurisdiction, but as private citizens on their own time, they could certainly keep an eye on those vehicles.

"If anything interesting happens during our... leisure time," Chief Stevens continued, "we might just call some friends about it."

Boivin looked like he wanted to argue, but after a moment's consideration, he relented. "Eight o'clock gives my team time for more thorough prep anyway." The lieutenant jabbed his finger at the street map. "There is only one access road to the mall. It's going to be pitch dark by 6:00 PM. I suggest I split my team and post them ahead of time, a quarter mile away in either direction. If anyone tries to come or go, we can deal with them, if necessary."

Jackson glanced at Willow, who gave him a slight nod of approval. They were going to shut down Fitzpatrick's operation and, hopefully, rescue the victims before any lives were lost.

And maybe, Jackson thought, we'll find evidence that links back to Jane's murder and the other victims.

The raid was on, but patience might just give them an even bigger payoff.

Chapter Thirty-Three

Willow

Willow adjusted her bulletproof vest for the third time in as many minutes, tugging at the Velcro straps until they sat flush against her torso. Her fingers traced the ceramic plate covering her vital organs, a ritual she'd performed before every high-risk operation since her first year with the Bureau. The vest felt heavier tonight. Everything did.

They were minutes away from raiding Maritime Workforce Solutions and the two adjoining businesses. Minutes away from potentially rescuing trafficking victims, or walking into a trap, or worst of all, finding an empty building stripped of evidence. Her mind cycled through these possibilities as she waited inside her SUV, parked two blocks from the strip mall. From their position, they had a clear view of the front of the building.

Shortly before 6:00 PM, ten Haitian workers were paraded across the parking lot and into the largest of the nondescript trucks parked in front of the MWS office space. There had been no attempt to hide them. For the most part, the migrants looked like typical day workers heading to their jobs.

After Willow had passed on the information, Cooper and the chief followed the truck at a discreet distance as it traveled to various B&Bs and hotels owned by Liam Fitzpatrick. At each location, people unloaded and entered the back of each building. Moments later, different people returned to the truck and got on board. After visiting three locations, the truck returned to the strip mall, where the people climbed out and entered the MWS building.

Cooper reported that the truck driver had seen him watching, but he didn't seem to care. He acted like he was either untouchable or doing nothing wrong.

Either option was troubling.

At 7:55 PM, with everyone in position, Jackson performed a quick mic check. "Brooks, checking comms. Repeat, Brooks checking comms."

"Loud and clear, Agent Brooks," Lieutenant Boivin's voice replied through Willow's earpiece.

"I got you," Will replied into her mic, keeping her voice low despite the privacy of her vehicle. "Good hunting."

She glanced across the street to where Jackson and Matt were getting out of Matt's vehicle, making their way toward the dry cleaner's entrance. Four SWAT team members followed behind them, their assault weapons at the ready but pointed down. Even at this distance, Jackson's tall frame was unmistakable as he adjusted his earpiece. There was a subtle nervousness in his posture and movements. Her heart tightened—not with fear, exactly, but with concern for the emotional state he was trying so hard to hide, and the acute awareness that came with sending someone you loved into danger.

"Officer Reeves, you ready?" she asked, turning her attention to the man beside her.

"Yes, ma'am," Reeves said, his jaw set with determination. "We won't let you down."

Willow studied him for a moment. He was anxious—she could see it in the slight twitch at the corner of his mouth and the rigidity of his posture. But his eyes were clear, focused. Since their training exercise in Alabama, something had shifted in him. There was a new humility there, a readiness to learn. She'd observed him with Zeus during their brief prep time, noticing how he watched his partner more closely and responded more readily to the dog's subtle cues.

"Remember," she said, "trust Zeus. He knows what he's doing."

"Yes, ma'am. I've been working on that. It's my new mantra."

"You shouldn't need to convince yourself of the truth in that statement. It needs to become second nature, like your dog is an extension of you." She opened her door and stepped out into the cool December air, then opened the rear door. "Ranger, come." Maybe seeing her and Ranger in action will help him see what it looks like. Sometimes people needed to see it to believe it.

The Belgian Malinois emerged with silent efficiency, alert and ready. His dark eyes scanned their surroundings, ears perked forward attentively. Officer Reeves did the same, inviting Zeus out. The two K9s had been sitting calmly in the back seat, pretty much ignoring each other, which pleased Willow greatly. During high-stress operations, the last thing they needed was canine temperament issues.

Lieutenant Boivin approached on foot, his SWAT gear making him look twice his normal size. He had a naturally formidable and intimidating presence. "Agent Banks," he said with a curt nod. "We're in position. The other teams are ready."

"Status on the subjects inside?"

"Thermal imaging shows three heat signatures in the MWS office, five in the minimart—the four customers who had entered, plus the clerk. Nobody appears to be in the dry cleaners. I'm concerned that the interior wall composition is interfering with the readings. The cleaners are open for business, so we should have identified at least one person present."

It was odd that the cleaners appeared empty, and having four customers in the minimart was concerning. She'd hoped for fewer civilians, but they'd prepared for this contingency. "Can I get four of your team members to enter the mini-mart with us? I know I turned them down before..."

"Done," Boivin said. He gestured to four operatives who quickly moved into position behind Willow and Reeves.

The K9s were going to be able to alert them quickly if any of the customers were carrying concealed weapons, but if things got ugly, having the extra firepower would be welcome. She hoped it wouldn't come to that.

Willow caught Jackson's eye across the street. He gave her a single nod indicating everything was in place on his end. She returned the gesture.

"All teams, this is Brooks," Willow heard through her comms. "Radio silence until breach at 8:00 PM sharp."

The digital readout on Willow's watch showed 7:59 PM. Sixty seconds until they moved.

Ranger pressed against her leg, sensing the shift in her energy. She placed her hand briefly on his head, the contact grounding her. His ears twitched forward, muscles coiled in readiness beneath her palm.

"Remember," she said to Reeves, keeping her voice low, "the primary objective is to secure any victims and identify any threats. Once we're in the minimart, the K9s will lead on threat assessment. Keep Zeus close until we've identified suspects and cleared the civilians."

"Understood."

The seconds ticked down. Willow drew her weapon, holding it at the low ready position. Her heartbeat slowed, the familiar calm of operational focus settling over her.

"Execute," Lt. Boivin said at precisely 8:00 PM.

The three groups immediately made entry into their respective assigned places of business. Willow was at the lead of her team. They moved as a unit, flowing into the minimart in a single file. The fluorescent lights inside flickered slightly with a high-pitched hum. A faint smell of burnt oil and overripe produce hung in the air. The narrow aisles were cluttered with poorly stocked shelves, their tight angles offering potential cover for threats.

"FBI! Hands where I can see them!" Willow shouted as she and her team stormed into the minimart.

The clerk behind the counter froze—broad-shouldered, shaved head, his right wrist bandaged and stiff.

Ranger's growl identified the man before Willow's mind had a chance to place him. He was the same bastard Ranger had brought down ten hours earlier at Maritime Workforce Solutions. The one who'd reached for his gun and nearly got his throat ripped out for it.

Beneath his too-tight T-shirt, his ballistic vest was clearly visible.

Her weapon locked on him. "Step away from the counter. Hands behind your head."

The clerk didn't flinch. His eyes found Ranger and narrowed, jaw clenching in rage. Willow knew that look—humiliation, resentment, and something close to fear. But not enough of it.

Ranger's growl deepened, low and guttural.

The clerk didn't comply.

Willow didn't repeat herself. Instead, she motioned to the nearest SWAT officer. "Secure him."

The SWAT operator approached cautiously, weapon raised. "Step away now. Last warning."

But the man moved fast, dropping behind the counter.

"Hands! Show me your hands!" the SWAT officer barked.

Ranger exploded forward, barking furiously. He cleared the counter and landed out of sight. Snarls and screams followed. Like her dog, Willow vaulted over the counter, finding Ranger's mouth clamped on the man's bandaged arm, shaking it like a pull-toy.

"Ranger, off!" Willow bellowed, her weapon trained on the downed suspect. The dog immediately complied but stayed close, flashing his teeth with each high-pitched bark.

Two SWAT operators converged, dragging the man out from behind the counter and forcing him to the floor. One shouted, "Weapon on the floor!" The other kicked it aside and cuffed the man, keeping a knee pressed between his shoulder blades.

Willow turned her attention to the four customers. Three of them appeared terrified, cowering against the wall. The fourth, a woman near the drink cooler, was standing rigid, her gaze locked on Zeus.

He didn't bark. He stared. Tail high, hackles bristling.

Reeves moved quickly. "Ma'am, step away from the cooler. Hands in the air."

The woman hesitated for too long.

Reeves stepped forward, his weapon raised. Calmly but firmly, he issued his command. "Do it now."

She obeyed, but Willow caught the way her sleeve shifted, and Reeves clearly did too. A second later, he was behind her, securing her left wrist. "Zeus, hold!"

The dog barely moved, but his demeanor changed dramatically. His body tensed, his head lowered, and he put his teeth on display.

Still holding her wrist, Reeves pulled up the woman's sleeve. A knife. Concealed in a wrist sheath, cleverly disguised under layers of knit and denim. With his left foot, he kicked her behind the knee, causing her legs to buckle. He followed her to the floor, twisting her arm behind her back.

"Clear," he said.

Willow exchanged a quick look with him as he relieved the woman of her blade and cuffed her. She offered no smile, no praise—but approval. Quiet and unmistakable.

The remaining customers were found to be clean and herded outside, visibly shaken but unharmed. Willow made sure that the state police had taken down all their information and informed them that they may be called upon as witnesses, should the need arise.

Willow returned to the still-prone clerk with Ranger at her side, head high and eyes alert.

"You remember me?" Willow asked coolly. "You should, because my K9 definitely remembers you." She leaned in close enough to smell his breath. "You know that you're fucked, right? Maybe if you tell me what's going on here, I can do something to help you out."

The clerk didn't respond, his expression remaining neutral.

"Fine," Willow said. "Sit tight."

If the minimart clerk had been armed and ready for them, what were Jackson and Boivin facing next door? And if this woman had been planted here to intercept responders, then who was still hiding behind those unscanned walls?

She needed to go out the back exit, which she was certain would lead to a holding room, or a passage to a holding room. They had discussed various options for how the space might be organized, but it was all guesswork. Lt. Boivin hadn't liked that they would be stepping through doors without knowing what they were heading into, but it didn't stop him from wanting to do it. Each member of his team had felt the same way. Taking down human traffickers outweighed all their concerns for personal safety.

With guns at the ready, they exited out the rear emergency door, Willow and Ranger at the lead. Reeves and Zeus were directly behind her. They'd send the dogs first if the situation called for it.

The rear door opened onto a long, narrow brick corridor with a single door at the end of it. From its placement, there was no doubt the far door led directly to the back parking lot. The SWAT team had already entered through the MWS front door, so Willow decided her team would breach through the back.

After exiting the convenience store, Willow's team moved up the back alley to the MWS rear exit. At the far end of the alley, Cooper and Chief Stevens were waiting in the car. Just as Willow was about to breach, Jackson and his team emerged from the rear door of the dry-cleaning business.

Relief flickered for a heartbeat—he was safe. But it did nothing to settle the unease rising in her throat. They were only two-thirds done. He shook his head to indicate he had found nothing. Willow did the same, despite the altercations her team had experienced. She resisted the urge to radio Boivin.

In perfect tandem, Zeus and Ranger's ears suddenly pricked forward, their attention focused on the MWS rear exit.

"They've got something," Reeves whispered. "Behind the door."

"Both dogs alerted," Willow whispered to her team. "Proceeding with caution." She motioned for Jackson to hurry.

"What do you think they're picking up?" Reeves asked quietly.

"Not enough to go on," Willow replied. "If I were to guess, I suspect they're hearing people beyond the door."

Jackson and his team arrived, moving silently into position. He met Willow's eyes, his quick glance conveying volumes. She gave him a slight nod, but her heart lurched at the tension in his frame. For a breathless second, the operation fell away, and all she saw was the man she loved walking into his own private hell.

She reached for the door handle, hoping beyond reason that it was unlocked. Just as her thumb pressed on the latch, the door swung outwards. Outside of their bodies stiffening, neither Ranger nor Zeus reacted to the oversized man filling the doorway.

"The location is secured," Lt. Boivin said, shaking his head. "But you're going to want to see this. It's like a fucking hippy commune in here."

Chapter Thirty-Four

Jackson

Jackson stepped through the doorway behind Lt. Boivin, the rich aroma of food immediately assaulting his senses. The space resembled a college dorm sterilized for inspection day. Every cot was perfectly made, every plate washed and shelved. But the silence was oppressive. These weren't comforts—they were camouflage.

The large common area held at least thirty Haitian migrants standing in rigid lines, their eyes downcast with a quietness that spoke of deep-seated fear. Neat rows of cots lined the far wall, with a thin curtain that presumably separated the men from the women at night. Security cameras were perched in every corner, their red lights blinking steadily, providing constant surveillance. In the kitchen area, four Haitian women cooked at industrial-sized stoves, their faces tight with worry.

Jackson glanced at Willow, who stood beside Ranger near the entrance, her expression mirroring his surprise. He moved toward the kitchen, drawn by the cooks' submissive demeanor, hoping it might reveal something about their captivity. He left the team behind and approached the women.

"You can keep cooking," he told them gently, "but I need to ask you some questions."

The women continued their work mechanically, moving quickly and never making eye contact with him or each other. The silence was unnerving. Jackson focused on the eldest, a woman with deep lines etched into her face and graying hair pulled back in a tight bun.

"How long have you been working for Michael Fitzpatrick?" he asked.

She didn't respond, continuing to stir a pot of what smelled like a heavenly stew. Jackson pressed gently, "It's okay. You can talk to me. We're here to help."

Across the room, a tall, hawkish Caucasian woman in handcuffs called out, "They don't speak English." There was smug satisfaction in her voice that made Jackson's jaw clench.

The youngest cook, a Haitian woman in her twenties with quick, darting eyes, made a soft harrumph sound, earning herself harsh glares from the other three women. Jackson noted her reaction immediately. She understood more than they wanted him to know.

He turned back to the room, taking in the full scene. Willow stood near the rear entrance, calm and focused, her hand resting lightly on Ranger's head. The dog was alert but steady, scanning the room the same way she was. The SWAT team, heavily armed and in full tactical gear, seemed out of place in the dormitory setting. They were watching over the prisoners while Matt leaned against a wall, quietly observing, while Officer Reeves and Zeus stood at attention beside him.

"What's your name?" Jackson asked the Caucasian woman. "What is your position here?"

"Am I under arrest?" she replied. "If so, under what charges? You and your team are traumatizing these poor people." A smug smile crossed her lips as her gaze shifted to the cameras that surrounded the room. "I see four different logos on four different jackets. That's four ways your little stunt here can be torn apart in court. Warrant or no warrant to search these premises, you have no right to terrorize us. Surveillance is running. Every second of your armed invasion has been captured—facial recognition, audio, timestamps. Our attorneys will eat you alive, and we'll be out before midnight."

"You must be Alicia," Jackson said, remembering how Michael Fitzpatrick had said she was his executive assistant. The flash of concern on her face suggested she was exactly who he thought she was. "According to your boss, you are in Ireland on vacation."

Alicia's expression remained stoic, and her posture never changed. She was cool under pressure, and something about her demeanor made Jackson's skin crawl. If anyone knew where the children were, it was this woman.

"Lieutenant Boivin," Jackson said, his eyes locked on Alicia's. "Arrest the MWS staff on suspicion of trafficking, false imprisonment, and anything else you think the prosecutor can make stick. You will treat each one of them respectfully. I don't want any of these people getting off on a technicality."

"My pleasure," Boivin said, taking the woman by her upper arm. "I've already called for transport vehicles. They should be here in thirty minutes."

"Excellent," Jackson said. "Get them out of here along with the rest of your team. Matt and Reeves, go with them, and bring Zeus with you. I want all of you out of here." He needed to clear the room of intimidating presences if he was to have any hope of getting the migrants to speak freely. "And can someone please disable these cameras, or, at least, cover them up."

Lieutenant Boivin motioned for members of his team to cover the cameras. Without waiting, he stepped forward, his posture stiffening. "Covering the cameras is a smart move, Agent Brooks, but make no mistake. I determine who stays and who goes."

Jackson met his gaze with an icy stare. "These people are terrified. They won't talk with your team looming over them. They especially won't talk with Fitzpatrick's people watching. If you want any useful intelligence from this raid, give me the room."

Boivin held his gaze for a moment before shrugging. "Fine by me. We'll toss the office space while we're waiting for transport. Our warrant is pretty fucking broad, and I plan to make full use of it." He gestured to his team and the MWS employees. "Let's go, people. Move to the office space."

As Alicia passed him, her eyes locked with his, cool and unreadable. Jackson stared back.

You know exactly where those kids are. And I'm coming for them.

After they had filed out, Willow approached Jackson. "What are you doing?" she asked quietly.

"The MWS staff are scaring them into silence," he explained. "These people won't talk with them in the room."

Willow leaned closer. "Jackson, some of the migrants may report back to the Fitzpatricks."

Jackson cursed under his breath. His VCAC instincts were tuned to children, not trafficking operations involving adults. "You're right. I wasn't thinking."

He scanned the migrants, looking for signs of comprehension as he announced, "I need to speak with each of you individually." About half stared blankly, while the rest showed the subtle tells of shifting eyes, shuffling feet, or tiny nervous hand movements. Not one stepped forward as a leader, which spoke volumes about how they'd been controlled.

"Let's separate those who understand English," Jackson said to Willow. He raised his voice. "Who here can cook?" Several hands rose tentatively. "Good. Go help in the kitchen, please." Once they moved away, Jackson called out, "Who here is on a valid work visa?" This question created a commotion, with the workers quickly chatting amongst each other, with the English-speaking lot explaining the question to the others. One woman in particular moved through the group, motioning for the others to raise their hands.

Jackson beckoned the woman to him, then did the same with the young cook who had made the harrumph sound, and the older one who had glared at her.

"Let's make something perfectly clear," he said to the three. "These people are trafficking children. Do you understand what I'm saying? So, I don't care if you're frightened. If you lie to me, you're protecting child traffickers, and I *will* come after you next." Then, lowering his voice, he added: "But if you tell me the truth, I'll do everything I can to keep you safe."

He led the trio behind the curtain that separated the sleeping areas, instructing Willow to watch the others with Ranger and look for any signs of distress or overt anxiety. Using the sleeping area and the curtain to create some private space, Jackson spoke with each woman individually. The first two interviews yielded nothing but rehearsed lines: "Mr. Fitzpatrick is a good boss. He treats us respectfully. Free housing lets us send money home." Their flat tones and empty expressions made it clear they'd been either coached or threatened into compliance.

The third interviewee, the young cook, sat reluctantly across from Jackson on a cot, her lowered head and rounded shoulders suggested she expected a scolding. Folded on her lap, the chef's hands were rough and calloused from kitchen work, her fingernails cut short and clean.

"I'm Jackson Brooks, FBI," he said gently. "I'm here to help. What's your name?"

"Antoinette," she murmured, her French accent thick, her eyes fixed on her lap.

"Would you like me to find someone who speaks French?" he offered.

She shrugged. "English... ça va." The casual French phrase slipped out naturally.

"The woman in handcuffs claimed you don't speak English," Jackson said. "But that's not true, is it?"

Antoinette's mouth twisted slightly. "She say, 'Nou pa pale'—we don't talk. We are servants, yes? Nou koute, nou travay—we listen, we work." Bitterness colored her tone.

Jackson leaned forward, sensing an opening. "What about the young girls? I've heard they're told to speak, to get close to clients."

Antoinette flinched, her hands fidgeting in her lap. The reaction told Jackson everything he needed to know, but he needed her to say it.

He softened his approach. "What were you running from in Haiti, Antoinette?"

The question broke through something in her. "Gangs take everything… my house burn, my brother fight them, and they kill him. No food, no safety." Her voice grew more passionate as she continued. "They say come here, work, save my mama, and my little ones. I came here because Haiti kill us slow, and I want them to live."

Her voice broke as she added, "They are children—les petits. The masters give them to fat men, cruel men. They force them… to do terrible things." Her hands clenched into fists. "If they fail, they gone—ti sè mwen, my little sister, taken. Mr. Michael laugh—he say, 'More money for me.'"

Rage flooded through Jackson. Haiti's collapse had left these people desperate, and the Fitzpatricks had turned that desperation into a prison. Jackson could see Antoinette's fear of retaliation in her darting eyes and hunched shoulders.

"I'll protect you," he whispered. "What you said stays with me. I'm going to yell when I come out, to make them think you gave me nothing. It's for your safety. Trust me."

"I have already trusted you," Antoinette jutted her chin out. "I, too, will disappear because I spoke to you. I will be sent away, and nobody will ever hear from me again. I don't care if they got me papers to work here, and I don't care if I ever pay back what I owe, but I won't let another child be ruined because I was too afraid to speak up. I have nothing left but my life for them to threaten me with, and this is no life."

"You've got nothing useful to say. Get out!" Jackson roared, loud enough for everyone to hear. He threw open the curtain and pointed to where the other migrants were standing. "Why the hell won't any of you help yourselves? Why won't you help *les petits*?" he continued, his arms flailing, his gaze raking across every person in the room. "I'm begging for answers, and all I get is 'Mr. Fitzpatrick's a good boss. He treats us respectfully.' The same damn lies, over and over! You're either scared—and I get that—or you've become the same kind of monsters you ran from. Which is it? You came to America to escape the violence, and here you are helping people who would commit violence against children."

He kicked a nearby cot, sending it crashing onto its side. His voice echoed in the room as the migrants shrank back.

Retreating behind the curtain, Jackson slumped onto a cot, face in his hands. The performance had been mixed with genuine anger at what these people had endured, and it had drained him.

"You're not alone anymore, Antoinette," he whispered, too softly for anyone to hear. "We'll stop this. I swear to you."

"Are you okay?" Willow asked, her voice soft and caring.

"I will be," Jackson said, not looking up. The growing tension in his neck gripped him like a vice. "We've got a witness who will talk, and if we can find Anika, I'm certain she can help us as well."

Chapter Thirty-Five

Willow

Willow stifled a yawn as she pored over the documents they'd seized during the raid on Maritime Workforce Solutions. The fluorescent fixtures in the conference room buzzed quietly overhead, casting harsh light across the scattered papers and making her eyes burn with fatigue.

"These records are too good and too clean," she said, pushing a folder toward Jackson. "I've never seen any business this thorough."

Jackson looked up from his own stack of documents, dark circles under his eyes. "What have you found?"

"Michael Fitzpatrick keeps impeccable, highly detailed records," Willow replied, gesturing at the documentation spread before them. "Photos of every person working for the firm. According to his documentation, he has forty-eight migrants working for him, and they all have valid H-2B Visas."

She tapped her pen against a thick, heavy binder. "What we didn't find were visas for Anika and the two deceased males at the murder site, nor any records of children."

Lieutenant Boivin entered the room carrying a cup of coffee that smelled strong enough to strip paint. His combat gear was gone, replaced by a rumpled dress shirt with the sleeves rolled up to his elbows.

"Any news from the other teams?" Willow asked.

"State police and BPD detectives checked every location where MWS has workers assigned," Boivin said. "Every single person is exactly where they're supposed to be according to these records." He tapped a binder with his index finger. "Working hours match up too."

Willow felt a growing frustration as she continued reviewing the documents. Everything looked legitimate on paper, which made her even more suspicious. No business was this perfect.

"We know there were multiple accounts of children being at the murder scene, but no one will admit to it," Jackson said, rubbing the back of his neck.

"We can't push Antoinette on the matter," Willow said. "We need her to stay on the inside until her testimony can be leveraged. If Fitzpatrick suspects she talked to us..." She didn't finish the thought. She'd seen what happened to people who crossed the Fitzpatricks.

Officer Reeves appeared in the doorway, Zeus at his side. The K9 handler looked exhausted but determined.

"Before we left, Zeus and I did another sweep of the dormitory area," he reported. "We found nothing. No hidden rooms, no secret passages, no additional spaces that weren't already accounted for."

Willow offered her thanks. She was impressed with how seriously Reeves was taking his role, and how he seemed to be trusting Zeus's instincts completely now.

"What about the computers we seized?" Jackson asked, running a hand through his hair. "Could there be inconsistencies between these flawless paper records and what's in their system?"

"That's what I'm hoping," Willow replied, her expression darkening slightly. "If our tech team can crack the encryption. Fitzpatrick's lawyers claimed they're under no obligation to provide passwords without a specific warrant."

"If there are two sets of books, that's where we'll find them," Jackson agreed. "The digital tracks are always harder to cover completely."

"Speaking of lawyers," Boivin said, his expression darkening. "Fitzpatrick's legal team came and went about two hours ago. They left explicit instructions that none of the MWS employees in our custody were to be questioned without representation."

"So we've got a half dozen people downstairs we can't talk to," Willow said, frustration evident in her voice.

"And we can't relocate the migrants either," Boivin added. "The lawyers argued it's their home, and there's nowhere else to put them while we figure this mess out. I've got four men stationed at the strip mall to ensure their safety and keep the scene secure. Until we finish processing the scene, only the residents are allowed inside."

Jackson frowned thoughtfully. "Michael Fitzpatrick might expect to be raided, and as such, makes sure that he has all his I's dotted and T's crossed for just this reason."

A sudden thought made Willow sit up straighter, dread tightening in her chest. "Mason had several people working on the house restoration, but Thomas Warner stands out. He was friendly with Anika, and now she's missing—and there's no record of her ever working for MWS. I'm worried his life might be in danger."

Jackson's expression shifted immediately to concern. "You think Fitzpatrick would go after him?"

"After what happened to Mason? Absolutely," Willow said, already reaching for her vest. "If Thomas is involved with Anika, they might think he will corroborate Mason's testimony."

She whistled for Ranger, who had been resting in the corner of the room. The Malinois immediately rose and came to her side, alert and ready for action.

"I'll have some of my people meet you there," Boivin offered. "I can have them ready to roll in thirty minutes."

"No time," Willow said, tying her wavy blonde hair into a quick ponytail. "You stay here and coordinate. Reeves, you and Zeus are with us."

Reeves straightened, immediately alert despite his exhaustion. "Yes, ma'am."

"We're not taking any chances," Willow said as she strapped on her vest. Jackson quickly followed suit, grabbing his own tactical gear.

"According to Google, his house is eight blocks from here," she said, holding out her phone. "Cooper texted me Thomas's address earlier when we were looking into Mason's crew."

As they hurried out the door, Boivin called after them, "I'm sending backup anyway. Be careful, these bastards don't play around."

Willow drove while Jackson rode shotgun, with Reeves and the two K9s in the back seat. The tires squealed as she pulled out of the parking lot and onto the empty street.

"Do we know if Thomas has any family?" Jackson asked, checking his weapon.

"None that I'm aware of," Willow replied with a grimace.

"That means Thomas would be alone at the house," Jackson said, his expression grim. "It makes him an easy target."

Willow took a sharp turn, sending everyone shifting in their seats. "If we're right about Michael Fitzpatrick, he's been operating this trafficking ring for years without detection. He's not going to let a construction worker bring him down."

The residential street where Thomas lived was quiet, with most houses dark at this late hour. As they approached his address, Willow slowed the SUV, scanning for any signs of suspicious activity.

"Fuck me," Willow said, pointing at the house. "The lights are on and the front door is open."

Chapter Thirty-Six

Jackson

"There's no vehicle in the driveway," Jackson whispered as he and Willow approached Thomas Warner's small two-story home. Their breath fogged in the cold December air, the beam from his flashlight sweeping across the empty driveway where Thomas's blue F-150 should have been. The front door stood ajar, creaking softly with each gust of wind. Both agents immediately reached for their weapons.

"Reeves, check the garage," Jackson said, nodding toward the side of the house. "See if his truck's in there."

Reeves peeled off with Zeus while Jackson and Willow approached the entrance, Ranger pressed tight to her leg.

Jackson gave a silent count with his fingers—three, two, one—then stepped inside, Glock raised. "FBI! Thomas Warner?" he called.

No answer. The interior was dark, too still. The air smelled of garbage, something sour and rotting. The silence was oppressive. Ranger's hackles were raised, an uncharacteristic behavior for him. Jackson couldn't tell if he was reacting to the situation or Willow's emotional state.

The two agents swept the first floor, following standard room-clearing protocol. The living room, dining room, half bath, and a small office all proved to be empty. As they headed toward the kitchen, Ranger's agitation increased dramatically.

Just as they reached the entryway, a crash of metal erupted from within, followed by a second, louder bang, and what sounded like something tipping over.

Jackson flinched, his weapon snapping up. Willow stepped back and motioned to Ranger to stay close.

"Kitchen," Jackson whispered.

Willow gave a tight nod.

Another loud thump was followed by the unmistakable sound of glass breaking.

Jackson took point as they edged forward, clearing the doorframe in a two-man stack. He pivoted into the room, weapon drawn.

And froze.

A raccoon, paws deep in a torn trash bag, looked up at them from the middle of the kitchen floor. Two more were already halfway inside the fridge, which hung wide open and spilling leftovers onto the linoleum. One of them had its head stuck in a yogurt container.

Willow lowered her weapon, exhaling hard. "Jesus Christ."

The raccoons looked up at the intruders, chittered and scampered for the open back door. A particularly fat one paused long enough to glare at them, snatched an open yogurt container off the floor, and waddled through the open back door like he owned the place.

Jackson let out a breath that was half laugh, half exasperation. "Furry little home invaders."

"I thought we were about to find a body," Willow muttered. Ranger gave a single bark as if offended by the intrusion.

"We still might," Jackson said, eyes narrowing. "We still need to clear the second floor."

They continued up the stairs, each step deliberate and silent. Jackson took the lead, with Willow and Ranger following close behind. At the top of the stairs, Willow and Jackson went in opposite directions. Jackson quickly cleared the bathroom before continuing on to the guest bedroom beyond.

"Clear," Willow announced after checking the master bedroom, her voice barely above a whisper.

"Clear," Jackson echoed moments later from the guest room.

Willow pointed to a closed door opposite the master suite. She let Ranger sniff it, letting him tell her if there was anyone behind. When he didn't react, she pulled open the door. "Storage," she said with a huff. "Thomas is a packrat." Ranger moved into the room, continuing to sniff for anyone who might be hiding.

Reeves rejoined them, ascending the stairs with Zeus. "Garage is empty. No sign of the truck. The backyard is completely empty too. I waited a few minutes in case there was a squirter. When I saw the family of raccoons take off, I figured it was safe to come inside."

"They caught us off guard," Willow said. "I'm glad they didn't argue. Those little fuckers can be ornery when they decide to be. I swear to Jesus, they have no fear of humans."

"Now that we've chased off the immediate threat," Jackson laughed as he flicked on the hallway light. "Let's see if we can find any clues about where Thomas might've gone. Willow, why don't you take the master bedroom, and I'll check out the main bath and the guest room."

"Zeus and I will take the main floor," Reeves said. "I'd like to give him a chance to do a full sweep, if that's okay."

Jackson gave the officer a nod of approval. "Have at it. We'll want a full report when we come down."

As Reeves and his K9 headed down, Willow flashed Jackson a thumbs up. The officer had conducted himself well thus far. It hadn't been a high-pressure op like his training session had been, but sometimes it was doing the simple things well that provided the most information.

"He had a guest," Jackson said as he returned to the master suite. Willow and Ranger were searching the bedroom far more carefully than he had. A Ruby-sized pain gripped his heart. He missed his dog terribly, and a sudden wave of worry ripped through him. He shook it off and refocused his mind to the task at hand. "The bed was impeccably made, and the room was beyond tidy."

Willow flashed Jackson a curious look.

"No bachelor keeps a guest room that spotless," he said with a smile, "but it was the toiletries arranged neatly on the nightstand that were the giveaway."

"Well," Willow said with a laugh, sweeping her arm in a wide arc. "Judging by the disaster that is his bedroom, I would agree with your assessment. There are clothes everywhere and the ensuite bathroom looks like a hurricane swept through it. My guess is, he packed in a hurry."

"I'm willing to bet a month's pay that Anita was his guest," Jackson said. "There were no personal belongings of any kind in the guest room, and I think it's in her nature to leave a space cleaner than she found it."

"I would agree," Willow said as she pulled out a business card. "Found this tucked in Thomas's end table. *Cynthia Burke, Immigration Attorney.* Could be that he was trying to help Anika emigrate from Haiti."

"Makes sense," Jackson agreed. "We found no documentation for her, so it could be she's an illegal and he wanted to help her fix that."

"Agent Jackson," Reeves called from downstairs. "You might want to see this."

They joined the K9 officer in the small kitchen. Two coffee mugs sat unwashed in the sink. A half-empty bottle of milk stood on the counter, its cap nowhere to be seen.

"That milk's gone rancid." Reeves sniffed the air with a grimace. "I also found this," he added, holding up Thomas's smartphone in a gloved hand. "Found it plugged in behind the toaster. Who leaves without their phone these days?"

"Someone who knows cell phones can be tracked," Jackson replied grimly.

"Anything else?" Willow asked, prompting the officer to give his full report.

"Not much, ma'am," he said. "I found no keys to his truck or home, the interior garage door was unlocked, and there were no shoes in the boot tray by the front door." His brow knitted together while he tried to remember what he had seen. "Oh," he said triumphantly. "He likes mystery novels. There's a stack of them by the recliner in the living room... and Zeus didn't turn up anything. Is that okay? Should he have?"

"It's all good," Jackson said. "Ranger came up empty as well. Sometimes there's nothing for them to find. Kind of like mentioning how mystery novels might tell us where he is." He gave Reeve's a crooked smile telling him he was giving him a hard time, but all in fun.

"Okay," Willow said, her head swiveling around while she continued to take in the kitchen. "Thomas has taken off, and he's likely got Anika with him. The question is, where would they go?"

"Shit," Reeves bolted from the room, returning with a framed photo a few moments later. "I forgot to mention this. I found a picture of Mason with Thomas." The picture was of the two men with their arms over each other's shoulder while they each held up a stringer of fish. Behind them was a rustic cabin painted a shockingly bright blue.

"Reeves, call it in," Jackson said. "We need this place secured until we can get a warrant to properly process the property. We don't want to have evidence tossed because we didn't follow protocol."

While Reeves and Zeus stepped out of the kitchen to call it in, Jackson massaged the back of his neck. He gestured toward the small dining table. The weary pair took a seat, while Ranger curled up beneath the table and closed his eyes.

"How many different directions can one case pull us?" Jackson asked. "We can't seem to get traction on anything."

"Except raccoons. We definitely scared the shit out of some raccoons." Willow said, rubbing her eyes. "I feel like a thousand-piece jigsaw puzzle has been dumped in front of us. We've got a shit-ton of leads, but nothing concrete to work from."

"Two units should be here shortly," Reeves said. "They're going to pick up my cruiser before heading over." He leaned against the pantry cabinet like it was the only thing keeping him upright. Zeus took a spot beside Ranger and immediately fell asleep.

"Let's review the day, while we wait," Jackson said. He needed the conversation to stay awake. "We know that MWS keeps impeccable records of their staff, and we found a worker who has issues with the company."

"And she's willing to help us," Willow said. "We just need to find a way to make that happen without tipping off Fitzpatrick that we have someone on the inside."

"And we know that Thomas Warner is missing, and he might have another of Fitzpatrick's workers with him," Reeves added. "And based on the smell of the open bottle of milk, he's been gone for a while."

"Maybe he bolted the morning of the murder?" Willow said. "If Anika was still at the house when Jane was murdered...she might have called Thomas for help."

"Once we get a warrant, we'll send his phone to IT to get his call log downloaded," Jackson said. Cracking it wasn't going to happen overnight.

"No need," Willow said, waggling Thomas's phone. "There's no security code. I have full access."

Jackson's heart rate stepped up a notch while he waited for Willow's response. "He hasn't made a single call, and there's been only one incoming call in the last four days—an unknown number at 5:11 AM, on December 9th, the same morning Mason was arrested."

Jackson's stomach churned. He didn't want to believe it was possible, but the timing was suspicious. "What if Anika and Thomas were working for the Fitzpatricks' trafficking ring?"

"It's incredibly unlikely," Willow said. "But we can't discount it either."

"Maybe Thomas's exit was staged," Reeves said. "The house doesn't show signs of a struggle. No blood, nothing broken. The doors weren't forced. It looks like he left in a rush, but who leaves without closing and locking the front door?"

Jackson frowned. The pieces didn't add up. "Thomas might have accidentally forgotten his phone, but the most likely reason for leaving it behind was to avoid it being tracked."

"Guilty or not," Willow said, "where did they go?"

Jackson shook his head. "That's the million-dollar question. If Thomas is protecting Anika from the Fitzpatricks, he'd take her somewhere they couldn't find her. If he's working with them... they'd help him relocate."

"If Thomas is hiding, Mason might have an idea where he'd go," Willow said. She checked her watch and groaned. "Damn it. It's nearly 3:00 AM. I'll call him in the morning, but I hate waiting on this."

"We all need to get some sleep. We'll reconvene at the station in the morning. In the meantime, we need to put out a BOLO on Thomas's truck."

"I already did that," Reeves said, shifting slightly. "While I was waiting in the backyard, I called it in. Figured the sooner, the better, but I probably should've cleared it with you first."

"You did everything right," Jackson said. He was starting to have hope for this young officer. Perhaps his failure had shaken loose the one thing that had been holding him back. Time would tell.

Chapter Thirty-Seven

Willow

Morning arrived with the harsh buzz of Willow's alarm. With a groan, she silenced it quickly, not wanting to wake Jackson, who was still asleep beside her. The guest room at Mason's house wasn't large, but it was comfortable. Morning light filtered through the blinds, giving the space an almost magical quality.

One that wouldn't last.

"Morning," Jackson growled with a stretch and a yawn. "I hope you slept better than I did."

"I doubt it," Willow said, her voice still rough with sleep. She reached for her phone, wanting to check for any updates that might have come in through the night. "I'm torn, and I can't let it go. It's creeping into my dreams."

"You're torn between searching for Thomas and helping Antoinette?" Jackson asked. He slipped out of bed and padded to the bathroom. He waited by the door while Willow's foggy brain tried to come up with an answer.

"Yes." It was the best answer she could muster, splitting her attention between Jackson and the phone in her hand. A fragmented memory of a dream intruded her thoughts. "And I'd like to know where the underage girls are. They're being held someplace else, away from the rest of the workers." In her dream, they were being held in the belly of a great beast… but she wasn't about to say that out loud.

"I had nightmares about them, too," Jackson admitted, crossing his arms over his bare chest. A shadow crossed his face, one that Willow hadn't seen since the days they first met. His time working in the VCAC had nearly killed him.

"Hey," Willow said. An email from Chief Stevens gave her the perfect excuse to change the conversation before Jackson got swallowed by his old demons. "I've got an email from Janet. I guess she's not getting much sleep either." She opened the email and quickly scanned the contents. "It looks like IT cracked the encryption on two of Fitzpatrick's laptops, but they haven't found anything significant in either one. They're going to keep at it. They have a few more to get through."

"They won't find anything," Jackson said. "Remember? Fitzpatrick left early. If he had anything incriminating, he wouldn't have left it behind. We'd need a much broader warrant to search his home, his car, and anywhere else he might stash evidence."

"And that's not going to happen," Willow said. She closed her eyes and wished this case had never happened. "I can't see Judge O'Hara granting me another warrant after this one went tits up."

Jackson had a pensive look, like he was hoping to figure it out on his own. "I'm going to take a shower. I'll make us some breakfast when I'm done, and we can meet up with the others at the precinct."

The sound of running water might've lulled Willow back to sleep if she'd let it. She kicked off the sheets, hoping the cool air would wake her up, but all it did was raise goosebumps on her skin. She quickly pulled the covers up to her chin and waited for the shivers to stop.

"I had a thought," Jackson said while scrubbing his hair with a towel.

Fuck. I fell asleep.

Willow's eyes snapped open in an effort to look alert, but Jackson's sly grin told her he wasn't fooled. But, like the true southern gentleman he was, he didn't mention it.

"What if Fitzpatrick runs a fully legit business, and uses it as a cover for his trafficking? This would allow him to use illegals in plain sight."

"Maybe," Willow said with a stretch and a yawn. "I'm not sure how that helps us though."

"I'm not sure either." Jackson slipped into his dress shirt while he considered his words. "Think about it though. His records were too perfect. So much so that it would make an investigator not want to bother checking more closely. But there are a lot of hoops to jump through to apply for H-2B visas, and those hoops leave a digital trail. All we've seen are hard-copy documents, and documents can be forged."

"Damn it!" Willow muttered. "I know you don't want to, but we need to get ICE involved. No one cuts through immigration red tape faster."

"And," Jackson said, "nobody will deport these poor souls faster than them either. Look at where these people are coming from. They've been treated like cattle since they got here, and they're going to get treated even worse if they get sent back home."

"I understand," Willow said. She slipped out of bed and wrapped her arms around the man she loved, the man with a heart as big as Texas. "You can't save everyone, but we can save some from a fate worse than death." She looked up into his soulful brown eyes. "You know that more than anyone. We need to put these monsters in prison."

"I know," Jackson murmured, pulling Willow close, holding on like she was the only thing keeping him afloat. "But these are decent people looking to live a better life. I feel like a monster turning them in when they've done nothing wrong."

"I love you, Jackson Brooks." Willow pressed her cheek against his. "Don't ever change."

"I love you, too," he said, drawing her chin up to give her a kiss that lingered until Willow's knees buckled. "We didn't say what time we were meeting the others..."

"No, we didn't," Willow said, tugging him toward the bathroom with a wicked grin. "I need a shower... and an extra set of hands."

***

While Jackson made breakfast, Willow called his father. Mason intentionally had no phone with him, and nobody knew Jackson's father was in South Carolina.

"Good morning, Will," Travis said when he answered. "I've got you on speaker. Are you calling with information or are you looking for updates on what's going on here?"

Willow loved her future in-laws. "A little of both," she said. "Jackson wanted to know how Ruby is doing, and I wanted to speak to Mason."

"Have you no interest in how *I'm* doing?" Maybelle, Jackson's mother, said from a distance. Her voice was filled with playful sarcasm, which made Willow smile. "The girls are fine, too. Thanks for asking."

"Good morning, Momma," Willow said. "I thought I'd get business out of the way first."

"Hey, Will," Mason said. "Tell Jackson his parents are some of the nicest people. The girls are having a blast."

"And tell him that Ruby's doing fine," Travis said, lowering his voice. "Momma's keeping a close eye on her. She's full of life and joy, but she tires quickly. We're making sure that little Sarah isn't running her ragged. That child's got more energy than a lightning storm in July."

"And the others?" Willow asked. She couldn't believe how much she missed them after having been absent for so long.

"Emma's been clingy with her father and hardly lets him out of sight. Ivy has been asking a million questions. She wants to know why we're staying here, what dangers to expect, and the whole nine yards." Travis chuckled. "That girl's got a good head on her shoulders. Been picking my brain about my police background. Reminds me a bit of Jackson at that age."

"How's security looking?" Jackson called out.

"Tight as a drum," Travis replied, his tone shifting to a more professional register. "The bridge is the island's only land access point, and the gate attendants have our list of approved visitors. House sits about 50 yards back from the road with clear sight lines in all directions."

"Are the girls around?" Willow asked. "I need to ask Mason some sensitive questions."

"No, they're taking the dogs for a walk," Mason replied. "And I told them to steer clear of any water. We don't need Pickle turning into a gator snack."

"Great," Willow said. "I'm going to be blunt because there is no easy way to say this. We think Thomas is on the run, and that he's got Anika with him."

Her brother sucked in a breath. "And you need to know where he might go?" He paused for a few moments before continuing. "He'd have likely gone to one of two places. He either caught a bus to his folks' place in California, or he's hiding out at his cabin on Lake Marion. My money's on the cabin, though. Almost no one knows about it, and it's damn near impossible to find."

"Is that the bright blue one I saw in the picture at his house?" Willow asked.

"Nah. That was a place we rented in Port Royal. His cabin is a one-room building the size of an outhouse and there is no real road to it. You need a four-wheeler, or a truck with high clearance. If you don't know where to look, you'll never find it. That's why I think he might have gone there."

"Jesus Christ," Willow said, throwing her head back in frustration. "Are you saying we can't find it without you?" She immediately regretted swearing, knowing how Maybelle felt about taking the lord's name in vain. "Sorry about that, Momma."

"Don't you worry about me, child," Maybelle said. "You be you, and I'll be me."

"I can send you a map with GPS coordinates," Mason said. "Be careful near the water's edge. The lake is teeming with gators and snakes."

Willow hung up, heart thudding. One thing was clear: they were going to need backup—and boots thick enough to walk through hell.

Chapter Thirty-Eight

Jackson

"You ever been to Lake Marion before?" Reeves asked, his eyes fixed on the winding county road ahead. They'd been driving for nearly forty minutes since leaving Beaufort, the scenery gradually shifting from developed suburbs to stretches of pine forests interrupted by the occasional gas station or bait shop.

"Can't say that I have," Jackson replied, adjusting his earpiece while checking the signal strength on his phone. Two bars—not great, but enough to maintain their connection to the JTF meeting. "You?"

"A few times. Good fishing, if you're into that sort of thing." Reeves glanced in the rearview mirror at Zeus, who sat alert in the back seat, ears perked forward as if already on duty. "My dad used to take me when I was a kid."

The Jeep Cherokee they were traveling in wasn't a police vehicle, which was intentional. If Thomas was as skittish as they suspected, the sight of anything official might send him deeper into hiding. Reeves's personal vehicle, though weathered, was perfect for the terrain they'd be navigating.

"I appreciate the ride," Jackson said. "And your willingness to come out here on short notice."

A flicker of something, determination perhaps, or the lingering shadow of his past failure, crossed Reeves's face. "Seemed like the right call. Zeus is better at tracking in wooded areas than most K9s." His nostrils flared. "Besides, I owe you both. After that training exercise in Alabama..."

Jackson waved off the comment. "That's in the past. You're proving yourself now, that's what matters."

The radio crackled to life, Chief Stevens's voice filtering through, slightly distorted but understandable. "—forensics has completed their preliminary analysis on the bodies found at Port Republic Street. Dr. Patel confirms both died from carbon monoxide poisoning."

Jackson adjusted his earpiece again, pressing it further into his ear to catch every word. "This is Brooks, I'm here with Reeves. We're patched in."

"Good timing," Willow's voice came through, the familiar cadence immediately centering him despite the miles between them. "Janet was just going over the ME's findings."

"As I was saying," Chief Stevens continued, "cause of death was carbon monoxide poisoning, but Dr. Patel noted some unusual findings. The concentration was extremely high, suggesting deliberate exposure rather than accidental. Both victims showed signs of having been restrained—ligature marks on wrists and ankles."

"So they were tied up and deliberately exposed to engine exhaust," Matt's voice interjected. "That's cold."

"That's not all," Chief Stevens added. "Lab found diesel residue, fish scales, and chitin on their clothing. The chitin likely comes from shrimp shells, and the fish scales match Atlantic menhaden, a commercial fishing staple in the area."

"Evelyn Hargrove mentioned seeing men arriving by boat the night before Jane was killed," Jackson said.

"Exactly," Willow confirmed. "We think they were transported on one of the Fitzpatricks' fishing vessels, probably kept in the hold with the engines running. Whether it was intentional murder or just callous disregard for their safety..."

"Either way, it's manslaughter at minimum," Lieutenant Boivin's voice cut in. "Maybe second-degree murder if we can prove knowledge of the danger."

Jackson watched the landscape change as Reeves turned off the main highway onto a narrower county road. Pine trees pressed closer to the roadside, the sunlight filtering through the branches in dappled patterns across the dashboard.

"We need to get on those boats," Cooper said through the connection. "If they're using them to transport victims, we might find evidence—or worse, more victims."

"I'll contact Coast Guard Station at Tybee Island in Georgia," Vicky Davidson's voice came through, the connection slightly distorted. "They can board and inspect without a warrant under maritime law. I have contacts there who can expedite it."

"Good," Chief Stevens replied. "We need to move quickly before—"

The signal wavered, Chief Stevens's voice cutting in and out as they descended into a valley. "—Fitzpatrick might—" More static. "—another shipment—"

"We're losing the signal," Jackson said, switching his phone to speaker mode and holding it up. "Chief, can you repeat that last part?"

"If that's true," Willow added, her voice barely audible, "we need to—"

The connection dropped entirely, the call ending with a soft beep. Jackson checked his phone—no service.

"Lost the signal," he muttered, tucking the device back into his jacket pocket. "Hopefully we'll pick it up again further ahead."

Reeves turned the Jeep onto an even narrower road, this one unmarked and barely maintained. Gravel popped beneath the tires as they bumped along. "Not likely. We're heading into one of the most remote sections of the lake. Cell coverage gets spotty out here even on a good day."

Zeus whined softly from the back seat, perhaps sensing the change in atmosphere as they ventured further from civilization.

"Alright," Jackson said, mentally shifting gears. "Let's talk strategy. According to Mason, this cabin is deliberately hard to find. If Thomas is hiding there with Anika, he's going to be on high alert."

"Armed too, if Mason's right about him being a skilled hunter," Reeves added. The road narrowed further, branches occasionally scraping against the sides of the Jeep. "How do you want to play it?"

Jackson considered the question. "We need to identify ourselves clearly but not spook him. Mason's our best angle. We need to let Thomas know he sent us to help."

"Think that'll work?"

"It's our best shot," Jackson replied. "The alternative is he thinks we're Fitzpatrick's men coming to silence him and Anika. That scenario doesn't end well for anyone."

The road curved sharply before opening into a small clearing that served as a makeshift parking area. Reeves slowed the Jeep to a stop, and both men immediately tensed at the sight before them.

"We've got company," Reeves said quietly, nodding toward the far side of the clearing.

Three vehicles were parked in the small space: a blue Ford F-150 that matched the description of Thomas Warner's truck, and two black Chevy Silverados with mud-splattered exteriors and reinforced bumpers. Each of the trucks had a trailer hitched to the back.

"Fitzpatrick's men," Jackson murmured, taking in the scene. "Looks like they found Thomas first."

Reeves killed the engine and they sat for a moment, assessing. "Two trucks. So we're dealing with at least two hostiles, maybe more."

Jackson agreed, studying the ground around the vehicles. "There are ATV tracks everywhere. They've definitely unloaded and headed deeper in." He pointed to where multiple tire tracks led from the trailers onto a narrow trail disappearing into the woods. "The ground's too hard here for footprints, so we can't tell how many people we're dealing with."

"Or if Anika is with Thomas," Reeves added grimly.

Zeus had gone alert in the back seat, his posture rigid and focused. Reeves glanced at his partner, then back to Jackson. "How do you want to play this? Call for backup?"

"No cell service," Jackson reminded him, checking his phone again to confirm. He placed his hand on the hood of a truck. "Still a bit warm. They beat us by maybe a half hour. By the time we drive back to get a signal, it could be too late for Thomas and Anika."

Reeves hesitated, his fingers drumming on the hood of his jeep. "So we're going in blind. Two of us against at least two of them, on their terms, in terrain they've had time to scout."

"We have one advantage they don't," Jackson said, looking at Zeus. "Your partner. If they're on ATVs, we can track them."

"But we still don't know how many we're up against," Reeves pointed out.

Jackson weighed their options and scanned the clearing one more time. "What we know is that there are two trucks and two trailers. We can assume at least two hostiles, but there may be more. We stick to the plan: identify ourselves as FBI, and make it clear we're here to help Thomas, not hurt him." He double-checked his weapon, then added, "Just remember, what we know and what we think we know are two very different things."

Reeves nodded, but the grimace betrayed his memory of the training exercise where he'd made exactly that mistake—trusting intel over his instincts. "Zeus and I will lead. He'll alert if he picks up on anyone before we see them."

"Good," Jackson agreed. "Let's gear up and move out. Thomas and Anika's lives could depend on how quickly we find them."

They exited the vehicle and moved to the back, where they methodically equipped themselves with the gear they'd brought. Jackson strapped on his vest, checked the ceramic plates, and secured additional ammunition in the vest's pouches. He checked the scope and magazine on his rifle before shouldering the weapon. Reeves did the same, then helped Zeus into his own protective K9 vest, running his hands along the material to ensure a proper fit.

The forest settled around them in silence, no traffic noise, no hum of civilization, just the distant call of birds and the whisper of wind through the pines.

"How do you plan to use your K9?" Jackson asked. It wasn't time for a training session, but he needed to know that the officer had the right mindset.

"He might not have a specific scent to work with, but he can still detect human presence. From there, we'll have to evaluate the situation as it unfolds." He called Zeus to his side and patted his head. "Ready to work, boy?"

Zeus's ears perked forward, his posture shifting subtly. The transformation from dog to working K9 nearly instantaneous.

The officer's response was exactly what Jackson had hoped for.

"Let's head out," he said, eyeing the ATV tracks that led into the woods. "Follow the trail but stay alert. We don't know who else might be out there."

They set off along the ATV trail, Zeus taking point a few feet ahead. The forest floor was covered in a thick carpet of fallen pine needles that muffled their footsteps. The air was cool and damp, carrying the scent of decaying vegetation and the musty tang of lake water. Gnats clustered in the still pockets between trees, and the occasional buzz of a mosquito broke the quiet. Somewhere distant, a woodpecker tapped rhythmically, the only sound that wasn't theirs.

A sudden flutter of wings burst from a thicket off to the left, causing Jackson tighten his grip on his rifle. Neither Reeves nor Zeus even seemed to react.

Jackson was wound too tightly. He sucked in a breath through his nose and slowly blew it out his mouth. He ducked under a low-hanging branch and swiped away the spiderwebs that clung to his face.

"I'll give Thomas credit," Jackson muttered. "He picked a hell of a hiding spot."

"Not bad for someone who wasn't planning an escape," Reeves agreed. "Mason said almost nobody knows about this place?"

"According to him, just a handful of people. Thomas apparently likes his privacy."

They continued through the woods for nearly twenty minutes, moving at a steady jog as they navigated around thickets and fallen trees. Zeus moved ahead, occasionally pausing to investigate something before continuing on.

"Wait," Reeves suddenly said, his voice low. He pointed to the ground. "Look."

Jackson followed his gesture to what looked like a game trail—a narrow path worn through the undergrowth. He checked his phone's GPS and groaned. Despite having no phone signal, GPS continued to work, operating under different technology and offline maps. "It heads in the wrong direction, but maybe it circles back toward the lake."

"Should make our approach easier," Reeves said, "even if it takes us on a longer path."

"Which way?" Jackson asked. "Easier path, or straight in?" He watched Reeves weigh the options, hoping the officer trusted his instincts.

"We follow Zeus," he said. "Trust my partner. That's what you told me, right?"

"Trust your partner," Jackson agreed, trying his best not to smile.

"Zeus, seek!" Reeves said. The dog took off into the underbrush and Reeves gave chase.

There's hope for you yet.

Through brush and bramble, over rock and stump, the trio hurried along. Jackson recognized the dog's behavior. He had picked up a scent on the wind and was no longer following the ATV trail. Instead, he was picking the fastest path to his target. At this rate, Jackson expected to be at their destination in no time.

Zeus had raced ahead and disappeared past a stand of pines and cypress. Jackson could only hope that he wouldn't engage on his own. Reeves stopped dead, and Jackson nearly slammed into him. Zeus was lying down, his eyes and ears trained on the ramshackle cabin up ahead. Two side-by-side ATVs were parked nearby.

Calling this a cabin is generous.

Exactly as Mason described it, the structure was barely more than a shack—a single-room building with weather-beaten wooden siding and a small, covered porch. A narrow dock extended from the shore into the lake, but no boat was visible.

"No smoke from the chimney," Reeves observed. "No movement at the window."

Zeus remained calm, showing none of the alertness or tension that he would have if he had detected human presence nearby.

"We need to know if anyone's inside," Jackson said. "We can't breach unless we know what we're walking into."

"Zeus can tell us if someone's inside," Reeves said. "He signals someone is behind a door. I'm confident he can do the same for this small cabin."

Jackson wanted this to be a teaching moment, but there wasn't time. "Definitely," he said. "Give him the exact same command. He'll figure it out."

Reeves crouched next to his K9. "Check!" he whispered and pointed at the cabin. The dog leapt forward and moved directly to the building. Rather than heading to the front door like Jackson expected, Zeus first sniffed around the perimeter, his nose close to the ground. When he got to the front door, he snuffled along the bottom edge and sat down. He looked back at Reeves, his ears erect and his body relaxed.

"All clear," Reeves said, heading forward. "Wherever Thomas or the Fitzpatrick men are, it's not here."

With his Glock at the ready, Jackson stepped past Reeves and took point at the doorway. He checked to make sure his cohorts were ready before turning the knob and throwing the door open. Heart racing, he stepped inside and swept the room with his gaze.

"Clear," he said. It was redundant with Reeves at his side. The room was eight by eight, at best. A double bed was stuffed in the corner and a small table with two chairs took up most of the center space. A propane fridge and stove filled one corner of the room. Counters and cabinets wrapped every other exposed inch of wall space.

Two rifle cracks rang out—close.

Jackson and Reeves dropped into a crouch, and Zeus moved to the door.

"Zeus, come!" Reeves shouted. "Zeus!"

A third gunshot echoed through the trees.

Chapter Thirty-Nine

Willow

"This is such bullshit," Willow muttered, pacing the length of the dock as she awaited Matt's arrival. The morning sun beat down on the weathered planks, making the air shimmer with heat despite the December chill. Ranger sat at attention nearby, his ever-vigilant eyes tracking her movement.

Three fishing vessels were docked in a neat row—two smaller boats and one larger trawler. According to the dock manager, they'd returned about an hour ago with their morning catch. The heavy scent of fish and salt water hung thick in the air.

"Can you believe this?" she muttered to Ranger, not caring if the dock workers thought she was nuts for talking to her dog like he understood every word. "After everything that's happened, I'm still forced to work with that lying piece of shit."

Ranger's ears twitched forward, his head tilting slightly as if considering her words.

"Yeah, I know what you're thinking," she continued, stopping to scratch behind his ears. "Be professional. Focus on the case." She sighed heavily. "But Jesus Christ, I can't stand the way he looks at me. Like we have unfinished business or something."

The call from Alice had come through twenty minutes ago. With the Coast Guard's involvement, the operation fell under multiple jurisdictions. NCIS had to be involved, which meant

Matt needed to be there. Willow had pushed back hard, but the decision was non-negotiable. NCIS, FBI, and Coast Guard would work together. End of discussion.

Five men walked from the small processing facility over to the docks. From a dockside storage shed, they pulled out mops, buckets, and an assortment of other random equipment. As two of the men boarded the largest of the boats Willow looked to the parking lot, and then upriver. Nobody else was there yet, and these men looked like they were going to start destroying potential evidence.

"Come on, boy," she said, heading for the cluster of workers scrubbing down the deck. "We've got work to do."

Ranger fell in beside her, matching her stride as they approached the group. "FBI," Willow called out, badge held high. "I need everyone to stop what you're doing and step away from the boats."

The workers exchanged wary glances but continued their tasks.

"Did you not hear me?" she approached the nearest man, a weathered fisherman in his fifties. "Federal agent. Step away from the boat."

"We're just cleaning up," he replied, not looking up from the net he was mending. "Captain says it needs to be done right after we dock, and we're already behind schedule."

"I don't care what your captain said," Willow replied, her patience wearing thin. "This is now a federal investigation. Either you step away willingly, or my partner here will help convince you." She gestured to Ranger, who stood at perfect attention, alert and imposing.

The man's eyes flicked to the dog, then back to Willow. Something in her expression must have convinced him she wasn't bluffing. He sighed, set down his work, and stepped back.

"All of you," she called louder. "Off the boat. Now. Line up over there." She pointed to a spot away from the vessels.

Slowly, reluctantly, the workers complied. One younger man looked ready to bolt, but a quick command to Ranger had the dog reposition himself, effectively blocking any escape route. The workers lined up as directed, their expressions ranging from annoyed to nervous.

"This is bullshit," one of them muttered. "We're just doing our jobs."

"And I'm doing mine," Willow replied. "Ranger, guard."

The command was clear. Ranger would hold the workers in place while she conducted her search. The Belgian Malinois positioned himself in front of the line of men, his posture alert but not threatening. Unless someone tried to leave, he would remain passive.

Willow approached the first vessel, the largest of the three. A commercial shrimp trawler, about sixty feet long with a weathered hull and rust-caked equipment that spoke of years on the water. She climbed aboard, her thick-soled boots finding purchase on the slick deck.

The overpowering stench of fish, brine, and diesel fuel combined into a nauseating miasma. Now she understood why the crews cleaned their vessels so promptly after returning to port. The odor would quickly become unbearable otherwise.

She moved methodically through the boat, starting on the upper deck. The wheelhouse was cramped but orderly, navigation equipment neatly arranged, logbooks stacked on a small shelf. She flipped through them quickly, noting dates, times, and locations of fishing expeditions. To her untrained eye, everything appeared legitimate and thorough.

Moving below deck, Willow had to hunch over to navigate the narrow passageway. The fish hold had been recently emptied but still reeked of its former contents. Tiny fish scales glittered on the floor, catching the beam of her flashlight. The space was large enough to hold several tons of catch—or, potentially, dozens of human beings.

She ran her fingers along the walls, looking for hidden compartments or false panels. If this vessel was being used to transport people, there would need to be some way to conceal them during Coast Guard inspections.

"Shit," she muttered, wiping fish slime from her hands onto her pants. The smell was making her slightly dizzy, and the gentle rocking of the boat against the dock wasn't helping.

Moving further aft, she found the engine compartment. It was as tight and cramped as she'd expected, barely room for one person to work on the massive diesel engine that powered the trawler. Carbon monoxide would build up quickly in such a confined space, and if the ventilation system failed, exhaust fumes could be diverted into the fish hold or other spaces where people might be hidden.

That had to be it. The ME had found diesel residue on the victims' clothing, along with chitin and fish scales. If they had been kept in the hold while the engine ran with the ventilation system malfunctioning...it would explain the carbon monoxide poisoning.

She moved back to the fish hold, examining it with fresh eyes. Along the forward bulkhead, she noticed a series of small cracks along the upper edge of the metal sheathing—barely noticeable unless you were looking for them. She lacked the equipment to test it, but it was entirely possible that the engine room was being inadvertently vented into the hold.

"Morons," she whispered, pulling out her phone to take photos.

Finding nothing else of immediate interest below deck, Willow made her way topside, planning to move on to the next vessel. She emerged into the sunlight, blinking as her eyes adjusted after the darkness below.

Her phone buzzed in her pocket. Matt, according to the caller ID. She considered letting it go to voicemail but decided against it. Better to get this over with.

"Banks," she answered curtly.

"Where are you?" Matt asked. His normally smooth voice was frazzled.

"I'm at the Fitzpatrick's fishing boats," Willow snapped back. She couldn't give two shits about why he sounded nervous. "Same place you're supposed to be, and where the hell is the coast guard? They were supposed to be here by now."

"Fuck!" he shouted. "I see you. Get off the boats, Will. Get away from them right now! I received a credible tip that the boats are rigged to explode."

Willow looked to the parking lot where Matt was racing towards her, his arms flailing. She had just finished inspecting the boat. There were no explosives present, at least none that she could see. Her gaze swept over to Ranger who was still guarding the dockhands. He had some training in bomb detection...

"Get the fuck off the boat!" Matt screamed. "Everyone, get away from the boats!"

Willow stepped off the trawler and onto the docks. Matt never slowed. He continued running until he was at her side. "I'm serious, Willow." He grabbed her arm hard. "We have to get off this dock. Immediately."

She yanked free. "What the hell's your problem? I just finished inspecting this boat. I saw no signs of explosives. Why do you think—"

"Will, you're not safe here," Matt said, voice raw with urgency. "Please, for once in your life, don't argue. I've already called the state police. The bomb squad's en route."

That stopped her cold. Willow's instincts flared. Matt looked pale. His hands were shaking. This wasn't ego or jurisdiction.

It was fear. Real, visceral fear.

She fell in beside him, scanning the dock. "What the hell is going on?"

"Not here." He kept his voice low, angling his body between her and the boats as they backed away. "My contact—she overheard two MPs talking about 'sinking the evidence.' I didn't know what it meant until just now. The coast guard should have been here over forty minutes ago. If they're not here, it's because somebody diverted them."

"You have a source?" Willow asked, pulse spiking. "Since when?"

"A while. She's junior, not part of any official investigation. But I trust her. And if she's right... these trawlers are wired to blow. Do you remember Greg Davidson saying that he thought there was a coast guard connection of some sort?"

Ranger's frantic barks interrupted the conversation. Willow turned to see one of the workers holding a cell phone. As he looked up, a deafening roar split the air. The shock wave hit her a split second later, knocking her backwards as a ball of orange flame erupted from the largest trawler. Her back slammed against the wooden dock, the air driven from her lungs.

Though stunned, she saw the second boat explode, then the third. The sequence of destruction seemed to happen in slow motion. Pain wracked her body as debris rained down around her.

She tried to call for Ranger but couldn't force air through her throat. Dark spots swam across her vision as a piece of burning lumber struck the dock nearby, sending up splinters and sparks.

Her final coherent thought as consciousness slipped away was of her fiancé, Jackson, miles away searching for Thomas, unaware of what was happening—and Ranger, who she'd commanded to stay guarding the workers.

The world faded to black as the dock collapsed, sending Willow into the frigid water below.

Chapter Forty

Reeves

Officer Mike Reeves crept through the thick underbrush, working his way north of the cabin. A rifle shot cracked through the forest silence like a whip, making him instinctively drop into a crouch. Zeus froze beside him, ears alert, body tensing. Two more shots followed in quick succession.

"That's coming from beyond that ridge," Mike whispered to Jackson, who had taken cover behind a fallen tree trunk.

"That sounds like a single shooter," Jackson said. "Let's move up carefully."

Mike's hand automatically found Zeus's fur, an unconscious gesture of reassurance that steadied his own nerves as much as it did the dog's. The black German Shepherd remained perfectly still, focused intensely on the direction of the gunfire.

"Zeus, find," he commanded softly. The dog immediately surged forward, leading them through the thick undergrowth at a rapid but controlled pace. Mike and Jackson sprinted after him, moving swiftly but silently through the forest.

More gunfire erupted ahead. As they approached, Zeus slowed, his posture changing to a predatory crouch.

Jackson knelt beside Mike, rifle at the ready. "What's he telling you?"

Mike hesitated, not wanting to guess. Zeus was alert, intense, but the specifics were unclear. "He's detected someone, but I'm not sure who." He'd rather be honest than wrong.

Zeus had his attention fixed forward, then suddenly snapped his head to the right, ears pricked and body rigid.

Mike's stomach tightened. "Brooks, Zeus is picking up threats from multiple directions."

Jackson slunk forward, not saying a word. Mike couldn't tell if he was happy or displeased with how he was reading Zeus's behavior.

They edged forward cautiously until they reached the perimeter of a small natural clearing. From their position, partially concealed by thick underbrush, Mike could see two men crouched behind separate trees about twenty yards apart. Both wore tactical gear, pointing handguns toward an elevated position across the clearing.

Through his scope, Mike spotted what appeared to be a hunting blind. It was a sturdy structure of weathered logs built against a massive cypress, positioned atop a slight rise that commanded views in all directions. Rifle fire erupted from a narrow window slit in the blind, forcing one of the men to duck back behind his tree.

"I'm guessing Thomas is in the blind," Jackson whispered.

One of the men leaned out and fired several shots toward the blind. His suppressed weapon made little more than soft pops.

"They've got Thomas pinned in there," Mike said. "I'm guessing these two are keeping him busy while their pals take him from the rear."

Jackson motioned to the men's positions, sketching a quick plan in the dirt. "I'll circle around to approach the furthest target. You and Zeus take the closest one. They're focused on the blind, so we have the element of surprise."

Mike was prepared to agree when Zeus's muscles tensed, a low growl building in his throat. He was fixated on something to their left.

"Wait," Mike said, studying Zeus carefully. "There are more than these two. Zeus is picking up on someone to our left as well."

Jackson scanned the area, then scratched the back of his head. "New plan. We split up. I'll secure these two, you follow Zeus."

As they prepared to move, the nearest gunman stepped partially from cover, firing several more suppressed shots at the hunting blind. Then he called out, his voice loud and clear.

"Warner! We don't care about you! Just give up the black bitch and forget what happened! Do that, and you can live out the rest of your life in luxury!"

The response was another rifle shot from the blind, the man's head exploding in a pink mist.

Mike's stomach lurched. He'd seen corpses—overdoses, traffic fatalities, suicides—but this was different. Raw, immediate, intimate. The spray still floated in the cold air.

Zeus remained fixated on the direction of the third man, his posture conveying an urgency Mike hadn't seen before.

He traced the dog's line of sight and caught movement. Another camouflaged figure was moving through the trees, circling toward the blind.

"Brooks," Mike whispered urgently, pointing. "I spotted the third hostile. He's flanking the blind."

The dog kept glancing back at Mike, then toward a different section of the forest.

"Wait," Mike said, studying Zeus carefully. "I think there are more than three. Zeus is alerting to multiple positions."

"Go," Jackson whispered, raising his rifle towards the obvious targets. "I'll shoot when you do."

"Zeus, easy!" Mike commanded, as the German Shepherd crept to the left, tracking an invisible trail. Mike kept pace with his partner, rifle ready.

Thirty yards through the dense foliage, Zeus froze. His gaze locked onto a shadowy figure crouched behind a fallen log. The man was aiming a rifle toward the blind, so focused on his target that he remained oblivious to their approach.

Mike took careful aim and fired twice. The man jerked backward and collapsed, weapon falling from lifeless hands. Two more rifle shots reported immediately afterwards from Jackson's position.

Three down.

Mike hoped that was all of them, but Zeus wasn't satisfied. Without command, he pivoted and dashed in another direction. Mike followed, his pulse pounding out of control.

After another twenty yards, Zeus stopped, laid down, and growled. Peering through dense undergrowth, Mike discovered what had triggered his partner's alert—a fourth man was at the base of the blind, preparing to climb its ladder.

Taking a breath, Mike steadied himself, lined up the shot, and squeezed off a pair of rounds. The fourth attacker fell from the ladder, his legs tangling in the rungs.

More gunfire echoed from the clearing where he'd left Jackson. The rapid exchange told Mike that his partner was facing significant resistance.

Jesus, how many men did Fitzpatrick send?

"Zeus, come." The German Shepherd returned instantly, alert but no longer signaling danger. "Find Jackson," Mike commanded, trusting his partner knew best.

Zeus took off immediately, choosing a path through dense underbrush that Mike hadn't anticipated. Arms pumping hard, he struggled to match the dog's pace. Sweat poured down his back while his heart hammered against his ribs.

The K9 raced past Jackson, who had taken cover behind a wide oak. The dog was in takedown mode, locked onto a threat. Jackson didn't hesitate—he burst from his position and followed close behind.

A scream of agony tore through the trees, followed by a sharp canine yelp.

By the time Mike caught up, Jackson was kneeling beside Zeus. The man the dog had brought down lay sprawled in the dirt, throat torn open, a bloodied knife still clenched in his lifeless hand.

"Fucking hell," Mike breathed, dropping beside his partner. His hands shook as he tried to staunch the wound on his dog's side. "It looks bad. It looks fucking bad."

Zeus had done exactly what he was trained to do. In the eyes of the department, K9s were tools—disposable assets. But not to Mike.

Seeing his dog motionless, his fur drenched in blood, gutted him. A broken sob ripped out of his throat. He didn't care if it made him look weak. It felt like a piece of his soul was being torn from his body.

"The wound looks superficial, but he's bleeding badly," Jackson said. "If we can't get a clotting agent on this..."

The Jeep they'd left behind was a twenty-minute sprint away—longer if there were still hostiles nearby. Worry gnawed at him. He'd let Zeus take point without thinking it through—

"Focus," Jackson said, his hand resting on Zeus's rapid-breathing chest. The glassiness of the agent's eyes told Mike he understood the pain he was feeling. "We need to finish this. Don't let his sacrifice be for nothing."

"Motherfuckers," an overly muscled man said, his handgun raised and poised to shoot. "Ben was my best friend, and your fucking dog ripped him apart. I'm going to let you watch your dog die, and then I'm going to shoot you both in the head."

"Kill us," Mike said, standing up to face their attacker, "and you'll receive the death penalty. Killing a police officer and an FBI agent..." He let it hang there, letting the concept work through the gunman's head.

"Like I'm worried," he said. It wasn't false bravado. "The people I work for are untouchable. Once we get rid of this last witness, they can pick up right where they left off." He pressed his thumb against a button on his collar. "Our guests have been neutralized. Return to target."

"I recognize you," Jackson said. He stood straight, towering over the muscle-bound man. "I'm afraid your cohorts have all been dealt with, and backup will be here before you can make it to your truck." He pulled out his phone and waggled it. "Sat phone. Works everywhere."

Jackson's claim was a bluff. No sat phone. No backup. Indecision flashed across the man's face. It was a gamble that he didn't appear ready to call.

"Boss?" the gunman said tentatively into his comms. "Gonzales? Flores? Anyone there?"

"They're all dead," Mike said. "Right now, you're looking at prison time but if you don't lower your weapon—"

The gunman's head exploded, spraying blood and grey matter. Confusion flashed across his face in the brief moment before he crumpled to the ground. Mike looked to Jackson who had the same bewildered expression, along with a copious amount of gore covering him from head to toe.

The forest fell eerily silent for three long seconds.

From behind a nearby stand of palmetto palms, another man called out, "Who are you? Identify yourselves!"

Jackson raised his hand, turning toward the voice. "Thomas Warner, I'm Special Agent Jackson Brooks, FBI. This is Officer Mike Reeves with Beaufort PD. Your friend, Mason Banks sent us to find you. He gave us coordinates to your cabin."

The pause grew long while Thomas considered his next move.

"How do I know you're really from Mason?" His voice was wary. "Lie to me, and it will be the last words you ever speak."

"Mason said you two have been fishing here every year since you started working for him seven years ago. And he says you still owe him a beer because he out-fished you this past summer."

Thomas emerged cautiously, rifle held ready but pointed down. He walked with a pronounced limp. Behind him, a young Haitian woman peered out, fear and exhaustion etched on her face. "I beat him fair and square," Thomas said. "He never landed his final fish. A gator took it before he could get it in the boat."

The story made Mike laugh despite the situation. "I'm Officer Mike Reeves, and we're here to get you and Anika somewhere safe, somewhere nobody knows about."

"Goddamn, I thought we were dead," Thomas muttered. "They've been coming after us for two days. The pair that showed up yesterday didn't fare so well either. I figured that if we survived the day, we were going to get carpet bombed next."

"Thank you," Anika added, her Haitian accent thick with emotion.

Zeus whined, contorting himself while trying to lick his wound.

"Do you have clotting agent in your cabin?" Jackson asked. "We have a badly injured K9 here."

"I have an extensive first aid kit," Thomas responded. He came closer, warily looking at the dog. "Let's get him to my cabin. I was a field medic with the marines before I got the bottom half of my leg blown off." He crouched with a grunt and hiked up his pant leg, revealing a carbon-fiber prosthetic. "I'll do what I can to stop the bleeding, but he's going to need a proper surgeon to fix that wound."

Mike scooped Zeus into his arms. The dog thrashed weakly, whimpering, his blood soaking through Mike's shirt like warm ink.

"I know, boy," he whispered into his K9's ear, voice cracking as he used the dog's ruff to wipe away the tears freely streaming down his face. "We'll get you patched up." He could only hope that Thomas could treat him before he died of blood loss.

"Go," Jackson said. "Anika and I will meet you there. We need to talk."

Hoping that Thomas could keep up, Mike ran headlong into the trees, desperate to get Zeus to the cabin. His footfalls matched the speed of his heartbeat. Close behind, he could hear the steady thud of Thomas's boots against the ground.

"You've got to be okay," he said to Zeus, his voice breaking on the words. "Please fight. I can't lose you."

The plea was part prayer, part promise—and all he could offer.

Chapter Forty-One

Willow

Beeping.

Steady, rhythmic, insistent beeping was the first thing Willow became aware of as consciousness slowly returned. The sound tethered her to reality, pulling her back from the darkness.

Her eyelids felt impossibly heavy as she struggled to open them. When she finally managed, harsh fluorescent light sent daggers of pain through her skull, forcing them closed again.

"Ranger?" Her voice emerged as a croak, barely audible even to herself.

A warm weight shifted against her side in response, and she felt the gentle press of fur against her arm. She forced her eyes open again, squinting against the light until a familiar silhouette came into focus—Ranger's alert face watching her intently, his dark eyes reflecting a mixture of concern and relief. He was lying on the bed beside her; his body pressed protectively against hers.

"Hey, buddy," she whispered, trying to lift her hand to touch him. The movement sent pain radiating from her shoulder down her arm, pulling a gasp from her lips.

Ranger whined softly, his ears flattening in sympathy. He inched closer, careful not to disturb the tubes and wires connecting her to various machines.

"Jackson?" she said. Willow wanted to lift her head to look around, but the throbbing pain made any movement unbearable.

Willow took inventory of her surroundings as her vision cleared. Hospital room. Private. The walls were a bland shade of beige, the windows covered with half-drawn blinds that filtered the late afternoon sunlight into diffused columns across the linoleum floor. Machines blinked and hummed beside her bed, monitoring vitals she couldn't interpret.

"Jackson?" she called, stronger this time. The effort made her throat ache. "You there?"

No answer came. The room contained only her and Ranger.

A nurse appeared in the doorway, her expression brightening when she noticed Willow was awake. "Good to see you're with us again. How are you feeling?"

"Like I went ten rounds with a freight train," Willow muttered. "Where's Jackson, my partner?"

The nurse shrugged. "I'm sorry, dearie, but I don't know who that is."

Willow nodded, immediately regretting the movement as pain lanced through her skull. "How bad is it?" she asked, gesturing vaguely at herself.

"Mild burns on your right arm and back, minor lacerations, moderate concussion, and some water in your lungs," the nurse recited, adjusting Willow's IV. "Nothing major broken, though your right shoulder was dislocated. You were beyond lucky."

Lucky wasn't exactly the word Willow would have chosen. She closed her eyes as a wave of nausea swept over her.

"I'll let the doctor know you're awake," the nurse said. "He'll want to check on you."

As the nurse left, Willow sank back into the pillows. The effort to stay conscious was exhausting, but she fought against the pull of darkness. She needed to remember what had happened, needed to make sense of it.

Ranger nudged her hand gently with his nose, his warmth a comfort against the sterile chill of the hospital room. She focused on his presence, letting it anchor her.

"Good boy," she whispered. "Best boy."

The words seemed to trigger something in her mind, a flash of memory breaking through. Ranger was in the water, swimming toward her with powerful strokes as debris rained down around them.

Darkness threatened to claim her again, and this time she didn't fight it, allowing herself to slip back into unconsciousness, back into her disjointed memories...

Water. Cold and murky, closing over her head.

The explosion had hurled her off the dock into the freezing water. Disoriented and breathless, she thrashed blindly, unable to tell which way was up. Burning debris pierced the murky water, catching the dim surface light in flickers of orange and gold.

Something large, a part of the dock, perhaps, drifted over her, momentarily trapping her beneath its weight. Panic surged as she pushed against it, her movements sluggish and weak. Her lungs screamed for air, the pressure building until spots danced across her vision.

Then movement in the water—a dark shape cutting through the murk. Ranger's teeth clamped around her forearm, tugging insistently. She allowed him to guide her, trusting him to lead her to the surface when her own sense of direction had failed.

When they broke into the air, the sound hit her first—sirens, shouting, the crackle of flames. She gasped, drawing in a ragged breath that brought both sweet relief and a stabbing pain in her chest. Ranger pulled her toward the shore, surging through the water with surprising speed despite dragging her weight.

Her feet barely found purchase on the slick muddy shoreline, and she stumbled forward, collapsing onto her hands and knees.

Salt water poured from her mouth as she retched, each heave sending fresh pain through her battered body.

Through blurred vision, she saw Matt lying on the grass reeds yards away, surrounded by first responders. The right side of his face was an angry red, blistered and raw from burns. He wasn't moving, but she could see the slow rise and fall of his chest as paramedics worked on him.

"Agent Banks?" A Coast Guard officer knelt beside her. "Can you hear me?"

She tried to respond, but another coughing fit overtook her, bringing up more salty marsh water.

"We need another medic over here!" the officer shouted over his shoulder. "Agent down!"

"Rang—" she tried to say, reaching for her partner who stood dripping and vigilant beside her.

"Your dog's okay," the officer assured her. "He's right beside you. I can't believe he pulled you from beneath the dock. It's the most heroic thing I've ever seen."

More uniforms surrounded her now—Coast Guard, paramedics, police. Hands gently lifted her onto a backboard, voices calling out medical terminology she couldn't focus on. Pain blossomed across her back and shoulder as they secured her, drawing a moan from her lips.

"BP dropping," someone called. "Possible internal injuries."

"Get her stabilized for transport!"

The world tilted and spun around her as they carried her toward a waiting ambulance. The wail of sirens and the bark of shouted commands were more than she could endure. Willow squeezed her eyes shut, hoping beyond reason that it might ease her agony.

While being loaded into the ambulance, she caught glimpses of the destruction—the dock reduced to burning timbers, thick black smoke billowing from where the boats had been, debris scattered across the water's surface. Nothing remained of the vessels that might have contained evidence.

"Ranger," she managed to whisper as they slid her stretcher inside. She couldn't leave without him.

"The dog comes too," someone said. "He doesn't leave her side."

Relief washed over her as she felt Ranger jump into the ambulance, his wet fur brushing against her hand. As the doors closed and the vehicle lurched into motion, darkness claimed her once more.

***

Willow gasped awake, the memory so vivid she could almost taste the salt water in her throat again. The sudden movement sent pain shooting through her injured shoulder, drawing a hiss from between clenched teeth.

Ranger raised his head, concern in his eyes.

"I'm okay," she murmured, trying to slow her racing heart. "It was just a dream."

The door opened, and Chief Janet Stevens stepped in, her usually composed face showing signs of strain. Dark circles shadowed her eyes, and her clothes looked slept in.

"Banks," she said by way of greeting. "Good to see you awake."

"Chief," Willow acknowledged, trying to sit up straighter but failing as white-hot pain shot through her shoulder. "What happened to the workers who were at the docks? Someone had a cell phone..." The image was foggy, but she was certain one of the dock workers had triggered the explosion.

Janet's expression tightened. "They're okay... but Matt Carver's down the hall with second and third-degree burns. They're prepping him for transfer to the burn unit in Charleston."

Willow absorbed the news, trying to piece her fragmented memories together. She remembered seeing Matt's face and feeling him shove her onto her back.

Had Matt shielded me from the explosion? Should that have been her heading to the burn unit?

"I know this isn't the best time," Janet said, taking Willow's hand, "but I need to ask you some questions."

"What about the guy with the cell phone?", Willow started. "I think he detonated the bombs."

"That's our theory too," Janet said, sounding a little too much like a mother appeasing her child. "I need to know what you remember from the docks. Every detail."

Willow closed her eyes, organizing her thoughts despite the pounding in her skull. "I arrived at the docks around 11:00 AM. Workers were cleaning the boats. I used Ranger to secure them while I searched the first vessel..."

As she recounted the events leading to the explosion, something nagged at the back of her mind—a detail she was missing, something important she'd seen but hadn't fully registered in the chaos. It hovered just beyond her grasp, frustratingly elusive.

"Matt showed up and told me to get away from the boats, and then I saw the guy with the cellphone—and then I felt the shock wave," she said. The details in her mind were foggy at best. "I think Matt had tried to shield me or push me away."

Janet paused from her note taking. "And how did Matt know there were bombs on the boats? Did he tell you?"

"I think he said he had a CI. Someone on Pratt's payroll maybe?"

"Had he ever mentioned this person before?" Janet pressed. "You'd think he'd have mentioned it earlier if he had someone inside the provost marshal's office."

Had Matt explained this to her? It seemed the police chief believed Matt was a suspect. He was a womanizing dirtbag, but Willow didn't believe he was corrupt.

"We know that Vicky and Greg had both been compromised," Janet said grimly. "Which raises the question of which side he's on."

A thought suddenly struck Willow. "Where's Jackson?"

"We haven't heard back from him since he lost cell signal, but I'm sure he's fine. I need you to focus on what happened to you. Tell me more about what Matt said. Try to remember."

"I'm trying to fucking remember," Willow snapped, grabbing her head to try and stem the pain. "I fucking hate the guy. Don't you think that if he did or said something suspicious, I'd have remembered that?"

The police chief pursed her lip, and her expression softened. "I'm sorry for pressing, but this is fucked up. I've checked with the coast guard. The boat they were sending to search the fishing boats had been called away on an emergency, and it turned out to be a wild fucking goose chase. The call was from a burner phone, but the coast guard has been able to track its source. It came from inside the marine base. After our meeting, Matt went directly there. We couldn't ignore the coincidence."

"I get it," Willow said, concerned by her lack of memory. "I'd do the same. But that's all I remember. What did Matt say when you questioned him?"

"He's in a medically induced coma..." Janet let the comment hang there.

Willow didn't want to think about how badly injured Matt was. If he had been injured trying to protect her... "What about the guy with the cell phone..." she asked, quickly changing the subject. "Did I already ask you about him?"

"You did," Janet said. "I'm going to let you get some sleep. I'll check in on you later." Her expression brightened. "I forgot to mention, we've got a warrant for the arrest of Michael Fitzpatrick. We found his fingerprints at the scene of Jane's murder. They were on her wrist and all over the house. Apparently, her skin cream provided near-perfect impressions. We've got him, Willow."

"Do you have him in custody?" Excitement coursed through her body.

"Not yet. We haven't seen him since he left his offices. But we've got an APB on him and both the FBI and NCIS have dedicated a shit-ton of resources to locate him. Get some sleep. I'll let you know if there are any new developments."

"Keep me updated on Jackson," Willow said. "Tell me the moment you hear from him."

"I will." Janet moved toward the door, then paused. "You do the same, okay? I'm going to hang out here for a while. I've got some officers coming, and I want to make sure Matt's transfer is handled properly."

"I will." She closed her eyes for a moment to ease her eye strain. When she opened them back up, Janet was gone and Willow found herself alone with Ranger once more, the quiet beeping of the monitors the only sound in the room. She stroked her partner's fur.

"Just you and me for now, boy," she murmured.

The Belgian Malinois rested his head on her chest, his dark eyes watching her with unwavering loyalty. She was sidelined for the moment, but far from defeated.

That nagging feeling returned—the sense that she'd seen something important at the docks, if only she could remember what it was. As exhaustion pulled at her once more, Willow clung to that feeling, determined to unravel the mystery when she awoke.

Her eyes drifted closed as the medication in her IV pulled her back under. Her last coherent thought was of Jackson, out there somewhere chasing down Thomas Warner, unaware of how close she'd come to death today.

Be careful, Jax. Come back to me.

Chapter Forty-Two

Jackson

"I'm sorry," Jackson said to Anika, trying to spare her the discomfort of looking at dead bodies while he photographed them. He wanted to preserve as much evidence as he could. It might be hours before someone got there, and the local wildlife would likely decimate the corpses. "If you want to move back..."

"No," she said, her voice a mix of anger and resentment. "I will not look away. I know death. I live with it. All my life, I see people die. These are bad men. They deserved their punishment."

Jackson stared down at the man Thomas had killed. Blood had pooled beneath him, slowly seeping into the forest floor. The side of his head was gone, but his face remained.

"I do not know these people," Anika said, her mouth twisted with disdain. "But I know who they work for. Michael Fitzpatrick is... a cruel man."

After taking the photos of the two dead men, Jackson searched them, hoping to find IDs. One had nothing, and the other had a set of keys in his pocket, the only items connecting either of them to the outside world.

"Were you there the night Jane Gamble was murdered?" Jackson asked. "Is that why these men were hunting you?"

Anika's lip twitched. "I was there to say final prayers over my father and brother. Michael Fitzpatrick wanted to throw them away, like they were trash. When they arrived from Haiti, they were both very sick. I tried to help them, but I was told to do my work and that they would be okay. The bastard put them to work the next morning, even though they could barely stand."

"I'm very sorry for your loss," Jackson said, knowing the words were barely more than a platitude. "But can you tell me how they were transported to America?"

"We paid a man in Haiti," she said, her chest heaving as she tried to suppress her grief. "He took us to a ship in Port-au-Prince, where we were locked in shipping containers. We were given food and water, but for days and days, we never saw the sky. If people got sick, they were sliced open and thrown overboard. The captain would let the sharks deal with the bodies. When it was time for us to leave, the moon was high in the sky, and we were in the middle of the ocean. We were transferred to a smaller fishing boat. It was two hours, maybe more, before we were on land again. The whole time, Michael Fitzpatrick told us his rules, and he explained that we owed him one hundred thousand dollars. When we paid off the debt, we would be free to do as we please. From the minute we stepped foot in America, I knew we'd never be free. Michael said he would pay us twenty American dollars for each hour we work, but he made us pay him for our food and for our beds, and at the end of the day, we had no money to save for our freedom."

"How many children did Michael bring?" Jackson asked. While Anika was talking, he had been searching for the men he and Reeves had killed. If Ruby had been there, they'd have found them all by now. As it was, he was trying to look for tracks through the forest while trying to remember where he'd heard Reeves' gunshots.

"On my journey," Anika said, "Michael brought three girls. The youngest, Roseline, was only twelve. I was an English teacher in Haiti, and I was supposed to teach the new arrivals to speak the language. Michael said that if anyone couldn't learn to speak

English, he would feed them to the alligators, and he'd let his men rape me every night for a month."

A familiar tightness climbed the back of Jackson's neck. He fought to keep his expression neutral, but inside, he was boiling. Rape threats. Children trafficked. If he let himself feel it fully… It had been months since his last migraine, and he feared another was about to take hold. He closed his eyes, slowly inhaled through his nose, pictured Willow's smiling face, and exhaled. The tension hadn't eased, but it helped calm his mind.

"Over there," he said, pointing to a fallen body. It was strange to him that a dead body had no effect on him. Likely because Jackson knew the criminal deserved what he got. He took photos from multiple angles before using his boot to roll the man onto his back. From there, he took several more shots and moved on to the next.

The pair moved through the forest in relative silence as Jackson located and photographed each suspect. When they arrived at the final one, the first man that Jackson had shot, Anika spat on the ground and unleashed a series of curses that Jackson didn't understand.

"Red hair," she said. "Fitzpatrick hair."

The man was slumped on the ground, his face against the trunk of a palmetto tree. He had tight wavy red hair, just like Michael Fitzpatrick's. Anika strode forward and spat on him. "Langet torma," she said.

Again, Jackson had no idea what it meant, but he could infer. After helping Anika move away from the body, he took his photos and laid the man on his back. It wasn't Michael. It was his younger brother, Sean.

***

When Jackson returned to the cabin, Reeves was holding Zeus in his arms, a thick layer of compression bandages around his torso. The officer's shirt and pants were stained crimson.

"Thomas was able to slow the bleeding," Reeves said, "but he's going to need stitches and a transfusion. He's lost a lot of blood."

"Get him in the Jeep," Jackson said. It's not what he wanted to do, but the animal's life was a time-sensitive priority and until the dog was cared for, Reeves would be useless. "I'll take you to the vet, but you're going to have to tell me where to go."

"Thomas is going to take me in his truck," he replied, shaking his head. "That way if Zeus takes a turn, he'll be able to help." Reeves saw the doubtful look on Jackson's face. "I'll protect Thomas with my life."

"And we'll both protect Anika," Thomas said as he stepped out from his cabin carrying a shotgun in one hand and his hunting rifle in the other. He was wearing a backpack that was likely filled with medical supplies and ammunition.

"Take the Jeep," Reeves said to Jackson as he made his way to Thomas's truck. "The keys are in the ignition. Head east on the forestry road about three miles. You should get bars there. Call the chief and let her know I'm heading for the Animal Medical Center on Shorts Landing. She'll know where it is."

"Drop the dog off and get Thomas and Anika to the safe house where we're keeping Mason and the girls," Jackson said. He didn't like the idea of widening his circle of trust, but these were desperate times... "My parents are with Mason and the girls. My dad is an ex-police captain. I'll call ahead to let them know you're coming. He'll meet you at the gatehouse."

Seconds later, Thomas's truck tore down the road, kicking up a cloud of dust behind him. Jackson had tried to catch up, but Thomas had already vanished down the forest track, a road he had driven a hundred times before.

The forestry road was barely more than a dirt track, rutted and overgrown in places. Jackson pushed the Jeep as fast as he dared, his mind racing faster than the vehicle. They'd just killed five men, including Sean Fitzpatrick. When the information got out, the remaining brothers would likely react in one of two ways—they'd go to ground, or they'd go on the offensive. For Jackson, the choice was obvious.

They're going to go scorched earth.

When he finally saw the signal bars appear on his phone, Jackson called Willow. He needed to hear her voice, to tell her what had happened and figure out their next steps.

The phone rang three times before someone answered.

"Agent Banks's phone."

Jackson's stomach dropped. Not Willow's voice. "Chief Stevens? Why do you have Willow's phone?"

A beat of silence, then: "Brooks. Where are you?"

"What's happened? Where's Willow?" The sick feeling in his gut intensified.

"There was an explosion," Janet said, her voice carefully calm. "I'm at the hospital with Willow. She's sleeping right now."

The world seemed to tilt around Jackson. His grip tightened on the steering wheel while he struggled to draw a breath. "How bad?"

"She's alive," Janet quickly assured him.

He gulped a lungful of air. She was alive, but not fine.

"She suffered minor burns, a concussion, a dislocated shoulder, and water in her lungs. She fell into the river when the dock collapsed."

"Water? Wait—what exploded?"

"The boats. All three of Fitzpatrick's fishing vessels that Willow was investigating. They were rigged to blow."

"Is she conscious? Can I speak to her?"

"She's been slipping in and out," Janet replied. "They've sedated her for now, but she was asking for you earlier."

He closed his eyes briefly and muttered a thank you to the universe. "What did she say before they sedated her?"

Another pause, longer this time. "She said Matt knew about the bombs."

Jackson slammed the brakes, sending the Jeep into a four-wheel skid. The vehicle came to a precarious stop at the edge of a deep ravine. He looked over the edge, his mind too clouded by fury to make sense of what he'd heard.

"Brooks? You still there?"

"Did she explain?" he asked, his voice unnaturally calm. He stepped lightly on the gas pedal and eased the Jeep back onto the road.

"No. She was barely coherent. She said that Matt was told about the bombs by a CI." Janet paused a moment. "I have my doubts."

"Where is Matt now?"

"Down the hall from Willow. Second and third-degree burns on his face and arms. They're prepping him for transfer to Charleston's burn unit."

Jackson's mind raced. If Matt was involved, who else might be compromised? Greg and Vicky had already helped Colonel Pratt smuggle drugs into the country. It wasn't much of a stretch to think that Matt had been complicit too.

It didn't fit. Matt was a sub-human piece of dogshit, but he was helping solve Jane's murder. His motivations might have been suspect, but finding the murderer was clearly a priority for him.

"I need to make another call," he said abruptly. "Keep me updated on Willow."

"Will do. And Brooks? Whatever you're thinking of doing right now... remember we need evidence."

"I've got evidence," Jackson said as he pulled the Jeep onto the shoulder of the road. "I'm going to send you some photos. Five men attacked Reeves and me at Thomas Warner's cabin. It didn't go well for them. I'm certain Sean Fitzpatrick was one of the fatalities, but I need identification on the other four. You should call the local authorities and send them out. I suggest using a float plane, because getting to Thomas's cabin by car is a pill." Jackson selected the clearest photos and sent them. "Reeves, Thomas, and Anika are all doing well and on their way to the safe house. I wasn't sure what else to do with them."

"Fuck me," Janet said after an extended silence. "That's definitely Sean Fitzpatrick. Look, I'm going to contact Vicky. They need to search Matt's house and his office, and any place else I can think of. We're going to need NCIS's help to make this happen. Beaufort PD has no standing on the marine base."

"Coordinate with Vicky," Jackson said, pulling the car back onto the road. He slammed his foot on the accelerator. "I'm going to contact the FBI to see how quickly they can send backup."

Chapter Forty-Three

Reeves

When Mike explained the situation to the clinic's receptionist, she led him to a room and promptly returned with the veterinarian in tow. The vet gave the dog a quick but thorough examination and said that, with a blood transfusion, clean stitches, and plenty of rest, he'd be ready for duty again. Two vet techs placed the now-sedated dog on a stretcher and quietly wheeled him away.

Mike's legs buckled, dropping him hard to the floor. Cross-legged and shaking, he buried his face in his hands and sobbed. The guilt he'd carried all the way from the cabin finally broke through.

He was too emotionally attached—that much was clear to him now. He didn't know how he'd react next time he was forced to send his dog into danger, fearing his hesitation would get his dog or a fellow cop killed in action.

"I can't do this," he said, wiping the snot off his lip.

"I know," the vet said as she sat beside him on the examination room floor and handed him a box of tissues. "I work with dogs every day. Even if I don't know them, it breaks my heart if they cross the rainbow bridge. I know what they mean to their owners and the dreadful loss they feel." She thumped her chest. "I feel it too. It makes me a better doctor. It gives me empathy, and it keeps me focused. I think the same is true for you. Your bond with Zeus makes you a better handler. It means you won't send him blindly into danger—and that makes both of you safer. I've known you for most of your life, Mike Reeves. You'd put yourself in harm's way to protect anyone, and Zeus will gladly do the same for you."

The piercing crack of a gunshot shattered the moment. The shotgun blast that followed sent the vet face first to the floor; her hands wrapped over her head. Mike unholstered his side arm and went out the clinic's front door five seconds later.

A Sheriff's cruiser was in the parking lot with the deputy lying on the ground beside it, blood oozing from the massive hole in his chest.

Thomas had his arms wrapped around Anika, a shotgun hanging limp in her hand.

"He was going to shoot me," Thomas said. "He opened the door and dragged me out by my hair. He had his gun pressed against my cheek. When Anika told him to drop the gun, he turned it on her and fired. He missed."

"Get in the truck," Mike yelled. "I... I've got to go inside and let them know what happened."

The door to the clinic was locked. The staff had already gone into active shooter protocol. He pounded on the glass window.

"Call 911," Mike yelled. "Tell them to send Beaufort PD. Do you hear me? Beaufort PD and nobody else."

Thomas honked his horn. "Get in the fucking truck," he yelled. "You told them, and we need to get the fuck out of here."

Mike glanced into the back seat as he opened the passenger side door. He grimaced at the blood-stained upholstery. Anika sat there, a shotgun resting across her lap and a hunting rifle propped beside her. Thomas held a handgun in his lap, his expression drawn and serious. After Mike settled into the passenger seat and closed the door, Anika pressed the shotgun's barrel against his shoulder.

"If you've played us," Thomas growled, raising his handgun to Mike's face. "I will bleed you for a week and then gut you like a fucking deer."

Mike held his gaze, not speaking a word. Thomas and Anika had been hunted for two days and were freaked out. He didn't need to defend his position. He only needed to give them time to think it through.

Anika was the first to take her gun away. "Put your gun away, Thomas. If they wanted us dead, Mr. Brooks would have killed me when we were alone."

"Why did that deputy try to kill me then?" Thomas asked. He slipped his finger onto the trigger.

"The Fitzpatricks have bought the county sheriff," Mike said. "I'm guessing there was an APB on you and your truck. Maybe the deputy spotted it in the parking lot. All I know is Jackson gave you the location of Mason and his girls. His folks are there, too. Do you really think he'd have done that if he didn't trust you?"

Thomas put the gun on his lap, slipped the truck into drive, and pulled out of the parking lot. Police sirens could be heard approaching.

Mike pulled out his phone and called Cooper to let him know what had happened. He wanted to ask him for a police escort, but drawing attention to themselves was the last thing they needed.

***

Mike's headlights raked across the home's white and grey stucco exterior. He drove directly into the garage beneath the house and killed the engine. Like most houses in Beaufort County, this one sat atop concrete pillars. Good for hurricanes and floods, bad if you didn't like stairs. Unlike the typical lattice skirting around the base, this home had a fully finished ground floor.

Less good for hurricanes and floods.

He sat there for a second, hands still on the wheel. The porch light was on upstairs, and there were two small lights by the garage entrance. That was it. Everything else was black. Trees surrounded the house, and, supposedly, there was a golf course behind the house.

Footsteps echoed down the stairs leading to the house. Two elderly people stepped into the garage. Mike recognized them immediately from Jackson's description—Maybelle and Travis, his parents. Maybelle walked directly to Anika while Travis stood by the door, his arms crossed over his chest. He looked to be in his early sixties, yet he was tall and lean, and it was obvious who Jackson got his size and looks from.

"Come on up, honey," Maybelle said to Anika, handing her what smelled like a delicious, steaming mug of coffee. "Let's get you inside."

"You must be Officer Reeves and Thomas Warner," Travis said. He extended his hand in greeting, but his gaze never left the driveway.

"Call me Mike." He gave Travis a solid handshake. He looked so much like Jackson that it was uncanny. "I'm going to close the garage door."

When he turned back, Mike found Mason and his three girls standing next to Thomas. The smallest child was carrying a fat Dachshund like it was sack of potatoes. A large golden retriever ignored everyone else and went directly to Mike.

"Hello, Ruby," he said, taking a knee beside the dog, giving her head and ears a good scratching. "I hear congratulations are in order." He looked up to see Mason and Thomas exchanging a heart-felt hug while they whispered into each other's ears. From the look on their faces, it wasn't a pleasant conversation.

"I'm glad you got here safely," Mason said as he pulled away from his hug. He closed the distance between himself and Mike, his hand extended in greeting. "I understand I have you to thank for rescuing my friend. I'm really sorry to hear about your dog though. Will he be okay?"

"Zeus got hurt?" Sarah asked, panic in her voice. "How'd it happen?"

"He got a cut," Mike replied. He gestured to his own side where the cut had been. The memory of Zeus laying on the forest floor bleeding sent a sharp pain lancing through his heart. "But he's being well looked after." Mike turned back to Mason. "He's at the vet clinic. He was being treated when I left, but the vet expects Zeus will make a full recovery. She's supposed to call me in a while with an update."

Thomas's jaw tightened as he glared at Mason. "I told you that we should have said something earlier about what was... going on. If we would have, maybe none of this would have happened."

The eldest of Mason's daughters stepped forward. "Dad did what he could. He kept us safe."

"He's a good dad," the younger girl said, taking her sister's hand.

"Ivy, Emma," Travis said. His voice was firm, but not harsh. "That will be quite enough. Take your little sister upstairs and help Momma with dinner and be sure to wash your hands first. Those seashells you've been playing with are filthy. When we have some time, I'll show you how to clean and polish them."

"Yes, sir—I mean, Travis," Ivy said with a small nod, "Come on, Sarah. Ruby needs to be fed. You and Pickle can help with that." The small child squealed, hoisted up her wriggling dog, and bolted for the stairs.

"I'll help you with your gear," Mason said to Thomas. "I'll show you where you'll be sleeping."

"Do you think you can give us a quick tour of the property?" Mike asked. "I'd like to have a sense of our surroundings."

"The home is reasonably defensible." Travis pointed to the pillars and the cinderblock walls. "But don't be fooled by the concrete. Most of the exterior walls are two-by-four construction with a shiplap veneer. It provides good cover, but you could smash right through it, if you wanted. These posts, though, are reinforced concrete. This whole area creates something of a hunting blind, if we need to defend against unwanted visitors." He lowered his voice as he spoke the last words.

"On the second floor, there are small balconies off two of the bedrooms. They overlook the golf course at the rear of the home. The backyard is well lit, and anyone who comes from that direction will be a sitting duck. They're going to have to cross about fifty yards of open grass. We could get off a few shots before we become exposed."

"What about the main floor?" Mike asked. "You skipped over it."

"Because it's a fishbowl," Travis said, worry lines appearing on his forehead. "The entire rear of the main floor is glass walls. It makes for a good view, but it creates a weak point."

Maybelle called down the stairs for everyone to come up for dinner. Her tone conveyed that it wasn't a suggestion.

"We best not dawdle," Travis said, but the humor in his voice didn't quite match the seriousness in his eyes. "Momma gets ornery if we're not at the table when dinner is served."

Mike took a breath, but it caught in his throat. The lighthearted moment clashed with the weight in his chest. He hadn't expected the whiplash—the sudden switch from survival mode to normalcy. It felt wrong. Unnatural.

"I killed two people today," he said, his voice low, nearly swallowed by the whir of the ceiling fan. "I've never done that before."

The room fell quiet. Travis's eyes flicked to Thomas. Mason shifted uncomfortably.

The adrenaline that had carried him through the last few hours was wearing off. It left Mike feeling shaky, and the memory of his battle in the woods struck him hard. He was carrying a burden that he didn't know how to cope with. Dealing with shootings was covered in the academy, but it had only been theory back then. Now, it was very real, and it left him unsettled. A profound worry crept into his mind. "I thought it would mess me up more than it has."

"Mike," Travis said, his law-enforcement persona instantly replaced with a fatherly one. "Don't try to make sense of how you feel just yet. You're likely still in combat mode and, until you've had a chance to reflect, I expect you won't feel much, except numbness. At least, that's the way it was for me my first time."

Thomas agreed. "Until yesterday, I hadn't raised my gun to another human being. But I know I did the right thing and that there was no other choice. They were trying to kill Anika. Looking at it that way helps, but knowing I did the right thing didn't stop me from seeing their faces every time I closed my eyes last night."

Mike appreciated their support, but the words didn't help. Not yet. His mind was looping the sound of his own gunshots like a bad recording.

He needed to move. To do something physical.

"I'll grab our gear," he said, his voice firmer now, pushing past the knot in his chest. He didn't want to think about the men he'd killed. Not yet. What he needed was a task—something simple. Something that didn't involve blood or memory. "We've got quite a few guns to unload."

"We've already gotten most of it," Mason said. He had multiple guns slung over his shoulder and three shotguns cradled in his arms.

"I'm going to check on Anika," Thomas said, carrying multiple weapons of his own. He walked over and gave Mason an awkward hug, clapping him hard on the back. "I'm glad you're okay, my friend. When I heard what happened to you..." He pulled back and stared Mason in the eye.

"Same," Mason said. "You were right, I should have spoken up sooner, but I was afraid to."

Mike's phone buzzed, and he turned away to check it. It was a message from the vet:

Zeus's surgery went smoothly. He's resting. Vitals stable. Prognosis good.

He read it again, just to be sure. The vet hadn't mentioned anything about the shooting or the dead deputy. Maybe that was for the best.

"Vet says Zeus is doing well," Mike said. Unexpected emotions bubbled up, making his knees weak.

Travis clapped his hands together. "That's some good news, at least."

A high-pitched whine buzzed from somewhere outside. "Do you hear that? It sounds like a drone."

They all moved to the garage door, trying to get a view out of the row of small windows along its top.

"It's over the house," Travis said, racing for the stairs. "Grab your gear and get upstairs. I'll meet you there."

"They found us too fast," Thomas said. "That sheriff's deputy… he wasn't at the vet clinic by accident. He knew exactly where we were."

"Tracker on the truck," Travis said. "Has to be."

Mike thought about it. "When would they have put it on? We've been moving since this morning."

"Could have been on there for weeks," Mason said. "Depending on how long they've been watching you."

The drone buzz faded, then got louder again.

"It's mapping the area," Mike said. "Getting the layout."

"Which means they're coming," Thomas said, shouldering his rifle. He opened his truck's cargo box and pulled out another. And another. "Mason, grab the ammo containers and the handguns."

"How many weapons do you have?" Mike asked. "These aren't from the cabin."

"Do you mean with me?" Thomas said as he checked each of his three rifles. "Or in total?"

"My friend is something of a *collector*," Mason said. "He's got another large cabinet in his pig-pen of a bedroom." He hefted the steel ammo case. "It looks like he's got most of his munitions with him."

"It's cute that you think that," Thomas said, taking the box from Mason. "What I brought tonight?" He flashed a wide grin. "That's just my travel kit."

Chapter Forty-Four

Jackson

Jackson pushed past the two police officers standing outside Willow's room. His heart jumped when he saw her sitting up, eating a bowl of red Jello. She dropped her bowl and spoon onto her overbed table and wiped the back of her hand across her lips.

"How's Zeus?" she asked, clutching onto Ranger who was lying on the bed beside her. "Janet said he'd been wounded."

The question made Jackson laugh. Eight months ago, Willow had no real connection with dogs, and now it was the first thought on her mind.

Dogs will do that to you.

"He's at the animal hospital, but Reeves said he'll be just fine." Jackson noticed the gauze bandage on Willow's neck for the first time. "How are you?"

She touched her bandage and winced. "The burn stings like a bitch, but everything else feels fine now." She rolled her shoulder to show it was okay. "I think I got a small taste of what it's like to be a migraine sufferer. I thought the front of my head was going to pop off, but now I barely feel it at all. The boats—Matt got the worst of it. I think he shielded me." Her eyes narrowed. "Are you okay? Where's Ruby?"

"They've got you on really good pain meds," Jackson said with a smile. He stepped closer and took Willow's hand. Her pupils were tiny pinpricks. Now was not the time to question her about the explosion.

"The doctor said I can be released tomorrow," she said, throwing off the covers. She swung her legs over the side of the bed. "But I'm ready to go now. I feel great."

Ranger bounded to the floor. Like Willow, he was more than ready to leave.

"You get back in bed," Jackson said. He helped her lie down and pulled the sheet over her bare legs. "You're not leaving this room until the doctor says so."

Willow crossed her arms over her chest and pouted. She was incredibly adorable, and so unbelievably high right now. Her eyes suddenly went wide and her lips parted. "I got blown up! Ranger saved my life."

Hearing his name, Ranger bounded up and laid himself on Willow's lap.

She wound her fingers into the dog's neck ruff. "I remember the water," she whispered. "It was dark and cold. I couldn't breathe. I thought..."

Jackson squeezed her hand. "But you did breathe. You made it."

She nodded slowly, her moment of sobriety already slipping away. Her brow furrowed and she got a pained expression. "You went to find Thomas. Did you find him? How is he?"

As Jackson told his tale, including the incident at the vet clinic, Willow's eyes became more focused, like the events had a sobering effect on her. When he said that Reeves was taking Thomas and Anika to Fripp Island, she once again threw her legs over the side of the bed.

"We're going there," she said. She took a shaky step before regaining her balance. "Everyone who matters to the Fitzpatricks is at that house. They found Thomas once, and I don't think it was by accident." She rummaged through the cabinets in her room, yanking them open one by one. "Where the fuck are my clothes?"

she bellowed. "Jesus Christ, Jax. Did nobody think that maybe there's a tracker on Thomas's truck?"

"What in the world?" a rotund nurse with a headful of dirty-blonde curls said as she burst into the room. "You need to get yourself back in bed, little lady."

Jackson instinctively stepped back. This was about to get loud—and with Willow high and half-dressed, it would probably get weird, too.

"Little lady?" Willow said as she moved nearer, easily towering six inches over the nurse. "Where are my clothes? I'm leaving, right now."

"You'll do no such thing," the nurse replied, craning her neck up at Willow. "You're under my charge, and you aren't going anywhere without the doctor releasing you."

"Ma'am," Jackson said. He needed to intervene before Willow did something she'd later regret once the narcotic fog wore off. "She'll sign whatever forms need to be signed to get her out of here. I suggest you get her clothes and start processing her."

As the nurse stormed into the room's private bathroom, Willow swayed and flashed Jackson a goofy grin. He really hoped he wasn't making a mistake helping her leave.

"Here," the nurse said, practically throwing the clothes at Willow. "I'll have your paperwork ready at the nurses' station. Quite frankly, I'll be glad to be rid of you. Ever since you and your brother came here, this hospital has been in chaos. Complete and utter chaos." With a huff, she stomped out the door, pulling it closed hard behind her.

"I don't think she likes me," a wide-eyed Willow said. She pointed at Ranger, who was standing on the bed, looking as concerned as Jackson felt. "Not a dog lover." She blew a raspberry at the door and stripped off her gown. It puddled on the floor at her feet, leaving her buck naked. She struck a triumphant pose and shouted, "Ta-da!"

This was definitely a mistake.

***

"Where's Thomas' truck?" Jackson yelled, trying to be heard over the Jeep's squealing tires. "It's got a GPS tracker on it."

"There's nothing that can be done about that now," Jackson's father said. "It's been parked here for over twenty minutes. Even if we move it, they're going to come looking here first. I think now might be a good time to call for backup. This house is defensible, but we've got women and children here to think about."

"We're fifteen minutes away," Jackson said. "I'll see if I can get the state police there, but I have no clue where they're coming from. They could be an hour away."

"Don't call the sheriff," Willow said, sucking in a deep breath. "They tried to kill... Thomas. Ya, Thomas and... Jesus fucking Christ, just don't call them. They're on the Fitzpatricks' payroll."

Jackson glanced at Willow. She couldn't remember names, but she wasn't completely out of it either.

"I doubt NCIS or the FBI can be here quickly enough, but I'll call Alice," Jackson said. "She already knows we're in the middle of a shitstorm..."

Willow's eyes bugged out of her head, and she gasped. "You swore."

"Son," Jackson's dad said. "I've got to let you go. I'll call the front gate to let them know you're coming. I've already had a long conversation with the island's head of security. He seemed competent enough, but I didn't tell him anything about our situation. I did ask him about the protocols and the safety of the people staying here. He's got a staff of eighteen, and they've all got carry permits."

"Stay safe, Dad," Jackson said. "Give mom a hug for me."

"Love you, Son." The line went dead.

Jackson ended the call and stared straight ahead, a vice-like grip on the wheel. For a second, the enormity of it all—the kids, his parents, the wounded dog, Willow's fragile state—they threatened to paralyze him. Willow muttered a curse under her breath and started ranting about strategy, and somehow... that was enough to keep him going.

Jackson wished he had a siren as he pulled into a bidirectional center lane and pushed hard on the accelerator. He turned on his high beams, doing his best to be visible and warn potential oncoming traffic.

The next five minutes were nerve wracking. He needed to focus on the road, and Willow was trying to talk strategy. It seemed that the drugs coursing through her system gave her a unique, unorthodox approach on how to handle the Fitzpatricks, and that *motherfucker* Pratt, if he showed his ugly face on the island. Outside of his picture being placed on the murder board, neither of them had actually met the man.

When they exited the city limits, the Sea Island Parkway turned into a two-lane highway. The Jeep quickly caught up to someone driving well under the speed limit, forcing Jackson to pass him on a double yellow line through a blind turn.

"Don't get us killed, sweetie," Willow said, "but don't you fucking slow down either."

Ranger barked his agreement.

"Can you call Janet?" Jackson said. "We need to tell her what's happening."

Had he not been entirely focused on getting to Fripp safely, Jackson might have listened in on Willow's conversation. She was over-the-top animated in both words and gestures. The only thing he caught for certain was, *That's too long. We need them now.*

She hung up the phone and threw it on the floor. "The SWAT guy, Lieutenant Boivin, he's not coming. They're stuck at the marine base," Willow said, throwing her arms wide. "Vicky... she got a warrant to arrest Pratt. He's going to get his ass handed to him, I'll bet you."

Well, that was something, at least. Jackson took stock of who was at the house and what they had by way of weapons and ammunition. "Does Mason know how to use a gun?" he asked.

"Not even a little," she said in disgust. "Dad didn't like guns—at all—and Mason was Dad's little yes-man. If Dad didn't like something, Mason didn't like it either. Oooo... my dad flipped out when Cooper and I joined law enforcement, but Mom put him in his place. She could be *really intense* when she wanted."

And you take after your mother, no doubt.

"That gives us four shooters and two K9s," Jackson said. "You're going to find a safe place for Momma, Mason, and the girls."

Willow's brows formed a tight V, split by a vertical wrinkle in her forehead. She was counting on her fingers. "We have five... me, you, Travis, and... Reeves and Thomas."

"You are not shooting a gun," Jackson said, grabbing her hand. "You are way too high to be using a firearm."

"Fuck you, Jax," she said, turning to the window and firing invisible bullets from her finger gun. "Pew. Pew. Pew. I can shoot just fine. I can outshoot you, too. I won a long-range rifle competition, you know. I have the medal and trophy to prove it. You say you shoot good, but you don't have no trophies."

There was no sense in arguing with her. Even in her drug-addled state, he couldn't win. His mother, Maybelle, on the other hand, could convince Willow of anything. They had made an immediate connection from the first time they'd met. Maybelle had been instrumental in Willow becoming a respected K9 handler after only a few months. When they arrived at the house, Jackson would ask his mother to talk some sense into her.

They make an indomitable pair.

Chapter Forty-Five

Willow

Willow blinked hard, trying to sharpen the blurry edges of the world outside her window. Her head was still foggy from whatever they'd pumped into her at the hospital, but the open-air ride in the Jeep had helped.

The tires squealed as Jackson turned into the long, paved driveway. Willow leaned forward, eyes narrowing as the house came into view—a tall coastal structure framed by lush ferns and towering trees. The blue front door sat at the top of a wide, elegant staircase, and was framed by twin plate-glass windows that reflected the Jeep's headlights in fractured stripes. They pulled up at the base of the steps beside the garage, porch lights blazing above like spotlights on a stage. It was beautiful in the kind of way that made you feel like you didn't belong unless you were barefoot and holding a drink. But tonight, it looked like a fortress begging for siege.

Jackson parked in front of the garage entrance and slammed the gearshift into park. The porch lights cast long shadows across the front yard and the up lighting illuminated the palm and pine trees that separated the property from the neighbors.

"The chief has good taste in rental properties," Willow said, marveling at the location. Under better circumstances, she'd have thought this an ideal location to relax and recover. Her opinion changed as Travis appeared at the top of the stairs, silhouetted in the portico's glow. With a rifle slung over one shoulder, he looked like he'd stepped out of a different century. He took the steps two at a time and wrapped Willow in a fierce hug before she could speak.

"Don't you ever scare us like that again," he said, tightening his grip. When Travis finally released her, he gave Jackson a hard look. "We're in it deep, son. We best get everyone inside." He tossed a medallion to Jackson. "We're going to need St. Hubert's help if we're going to get out of this one."

"The patron saint of hunters has always ensured our safe return," Jackson said. His expression was grim as he slipped the pendant over his head. "What's the situation like? I'm guessing not good."

"Unclear at this time," Travis said, "but drones have been buzzing overhead on and off for the last ten minutes."

Willow's phone rang in her pocket. She yanked it out, her pulse jumping when she saw Cooper's name on the screen.

"Coop, what's—"

"They didn't find him," Cooper said, breathless. "The MCAS raid came up empty. Pratt's not there. His whole place was scrubbed, except for the dead body in his office… a young private, with a single shot to the head. I'm thinking she might have been Matt's informant."

Willow's stomach flipped. She staggered back a step and leaned against the Jeep's front fender.

"Coop—"

"We're coming to Fripp. Chief Stevens and I—we're on the road now. But listen to me, Willow. If Pratt's not on base and he left a dead witness behind, he might be—"

The line cut off.

She pulled the phone back and looked at the screen. No signal.

"Dammit."

Jackson glanced at her. "Lost the call?"

"Dead signal. Nothing. Cooper thinks Pratt might be headed here."

Travis swore under his breath, then turned and pointed toward the house. "We need to get inside. Now!"

Before Willow could answer, Ranger went stiff. He let out a deep threatening growl, then leapt from the back of the Jeep. His head swiveled about before unleashing a series of frantic, high-pitched barks.

A blur of golden fur shot down the steps. Ruby. She quickly acknowledged Jackson before charging past Ranger, doubled back, and began circling in place. Ranger joined her, his tail rigid, nose high, body vibrating.

"We're not alone," Jackson said. "Dad's right. We need to get inside."

The wail of multiple sirens drowned out his words.

"Cooper's coming," Willow said, relief burbling up in her chest. "And it sounds like he's not alone." She called Ranger to her side while she waited for her brother to arrive.

"They're not Beaufort PD," her future father-in-law said. He was up on the front porch with his rifle raised. "They're from the Sheriff's department."

It took a moment for Willow to put the pieces together. She knew the sheriff was deep in Fitzpatrick's pocket, but having them arrest everyone couldn't lead anywhere useful.

"Get inside," Jackson said. He grabbed Willow by the arm and dragged her toward the staircase. "Ranger, Ruby, come!"

"They're not going to arrest us," Willow said, struggling against his grip. She couldn't fathom why he'd be handling her so roughly. "We're FBI agents."

"They're not here to make arrests, Will," he said, pulling harder on her arm.

Red and blue flashing lights lit up the surrounding trees as the two cruisers came to a screeching halt in front of the house's long laneway.

Four men in uniform came out from the two cars, each of them drawing their weapons. "Sheriff's department," one of them yelled. "Drop your weapons and show me your hands."

They started shooting before anyone had a chance to react. Bullets whizzed past Willow's face, exploding against the concrete steps behind her.

From behind one of the large pillars flanking the staircase, Travis laid down suppressing fire as Willow and Jackson followed the dogs up the stairs. "Get inside, I'm right behind you."

"I'm staying," Jackson said as he dragged Willow behind the other pillar. He had his sidearm raised while he took a few deep breaths.

"I need a gun," Willow said as she peaked for a quick look from their elevated position.

"Will—" Jackson said, shaking his head.

"Are you shitting me?" Willow yelled. "I'm fine, Jax. Give me a fucking gun."

Travis fired off multiple shots in quick succession while he yelled for everyone to get inside. Ranger and Ruby's frantic barks said they were desperate to be released but now was not the time.

The front door flew open, and Reeves stepped out into the frame, shotgun booming across the porch. "Get inside! I'll cover you!" he shouted. He switched to his pistol as Willow ran past, Ranger at her side.

Willow ducked through the open doorway with Ranger tight at her side, heart hammering as she scanned the unfamiliar space. Adrenaline and fury burned away the last of the hospital fog. Her head was clearing, but she struggled to focus. Everything was happening too quickly for her brain to process.

She scanned the open space, trying to orient herself. The foyer was larger than she expected—airy and pristine, with pale walls and a wide rug that looked like it belonged in a beachside Airbnb, not a war zone. Flanking the blue double doors were tall plate-glass windows, both of them bright with moonlight and porch glare. She had no idea where Mason and the girls were. Or Maybelle. Or Anika. She ducked low beside the stairs and forced her breathing to steady. Gunpowder stung her nose. Her fingers itched for a weapon. If someone was coming for her family, they were going to meet her fury first.

Glass shattered with a deafening crack as bullets ripped through one of the tall windows, sending glass shards skittering across the foyer tile like glittering shrapnel. Ranger lunged forward, snarling.

"They're shooting through the damn windows!" she shouted. "We need cover now!"

"I'm out of ammo," Travis said as he came running into the house. "Two of them are down, but Jackson and Ruby are pinned."

"We're in," Jackson yelled, slamming the front door. "Dad, where's Momma?"

"She's safe," Travis said. "Focus on the task at hand. Momma bear can look after herself and the cubs."

"There are more guns and ammo in the living room," Reeves said, slamming the front door and rushing towards the back of the home. "Thomas brought an arsenal with him."

More sirens approached the house, and another salvo of gunfire erupted out front.

"Who are they shooting at?" Travis said, squinting out the window. He popped a fresh magazine into his rifle. "They're not shooting at the house."

"It might have been Cooper and the chief," Willow said. She grabbed a Beretta and stuffed it into the back of her waistband. There was a huge assortment of long guns arranged across the dining room table. Either Thomas was a firearms aficionado, or he was a complete nutjob. Either way, she was just happy to have access to that many weapons. She grabbed a Browning rifle, checked the clip, and bolted for the front door.

Jackson was peering around the corner, a concerned look on his face. The shooting had stopped out front, and Willow's immediate reaction was that her brother and the chief had been shot.

"It's not Cooper," Jackson said, catching her before she made it down the hallway. "It's the island patrol, and I don't think it went well for them. From what I can see, there are two deputies still up, and they're focused on the house. I can't be sure, but it looked like they were radioing for backup."

"That's it?" Travis said. He was wearing his Florence PD tactical vest. "Why'd they send drones for a four-man frontal assault?"

Ruby and Ranger started barking from the rear of the house. The sheriff's deputies out front had stopped shooting.

"They were a distraction," Willow said, racing towards her dog. "They're coming from the back."

Chapter Forty-Six

Jackson

Ruby stood at Jackson's side, tail high, muscles tight, her eyes fixed toward the back of the house. A low growl rumbled in her throat—barely audible, but enough to raise every hair on Jackson's arms. He dropped to one knee beside Ruby, and rested a hand on her shoulder. He could feel the vibration of her readiness. It heightened Jackson's nerves and drove up his anxiety.

"What's the plan for us?" he asked, deferring the situation to his father. He'd been at the house for several days, and he'd likely considered every possible contingency for such an event. "Where's Momma and the kids?"

"We're right here," Maybelle said, racking a shell into a shotgun. "Come on, girls. You know the drill. Anika, you're with me."

Jackson's gaze ping ponged between his parents. "Where are you going?" he asked his mother. He wanted to mention the weapon she was carrying but thought better of it. Anika hesitated for only a second before picking up a handgun from the dining table. Her grip was awkward, but steady. She didn't look afraid. Just resolved.

"There is a room downstairs," Maybelle said. "It's the owners' private storeroom. Your father picked the lock. That's where we're going."

"It's got a steel door and cinderblock walls," Travis said. "Closest thing to a panic room. And it's stocked with food and water."

"Take Mason with you," Willow said. "I don't want him anywhere near the guns. He's still recovering, and he's never handled a firearm in his life. The last thing I need is for my big brother to try to play the hero."

Maybelle grabbed a handgun. "I'll show him how to use it."

Willow didn't argue. She just nodded once and turned away. That was all Jackson needed to see. She was letting it go, at least for now.

"Thomas and I are going to take the second-floor balconies," Travis said. "We'll stay there until our position is compromised or someone tries to enter on the main floor."

"Willow and Ranger can take the main floor," Jackson said. "Ruby and I will cover the downstairs."

"No," Travis said. "Both of you will go downstairs with the dogs. It's the most likely entry point. Trust me, son."

"Ranger, come!" Willow was already descending the stairs, her K9 hurrying at her side.

"Everyone else," Jackson said, waving his mother and the rest towards the door. "I'll follow you down."

As the group herded past, Jackson caught his father's eye. "Holler if you need help."

"Same to you." His dad gave him a brusque nod. "Don't forget—the children come first. Above anyone else."

The children come first. It had been Jackson's mantra back when he was with the VCAC. It had been the only way he could cope with the unspeakable horrors he had witnessed. He clung to the idea that saving one child made everything else worth it. Until it didn't. Until the burden had threatened to drag him so deep that he could never return.

"The children come first," he echoed, following Willow to the ground floor. This time the words felt like a reminder not just to act, but to endure.

The patter of Ruby's footsteps down the staircase matched the pounding rhythm of Jackson's heart. All had been quiet for the past few minutes, but it did nothing to ease his building anxiety. By the time he hit the bottom of the stairs, the heavy door to the panic room was swinging shut. He caught a brief glimpse of Sarah clutching Pickle in one arm, Ivy guiding her and Emma from behind. Maybelle stood at the threshold, her weapon at the ready. The steel door swung shut with a solid, echoing thud.

"They'll be safe," Willow said, perhaps trying to convince them both. "Nothing short of explosives is going to get past the door." Her face paled. The use of explosives wasn't out of the realm of possibility.

"Ruby, seek," Jackson said. It was a general command used in search and rescue to find anything out of place, anything that didn't belong. Ruby immediately started sniffing around the perimeter.

"Ranger, seek!" Willow said. Her dog had been trained in the same manner, but his skills were no match for Ruby's. Then again, when it came to speed and ferocity, nobody matched the Belgian Malinois' level of sheer aggression.

"There are two entrances at the back of the house," Jackson said. "I can't see them trying to come through the garage doors, but I think we should split up."

"You go left, and I'll go right," Willow replied. "I want to stay close to the panic room. I'm not letting anyone get near my nieces. The children come first, and nobody's going to get past me. Not while I'm still breathing."

"It also puts you closest to the stairway to the main floor," Jackson said. "You could get boxed in."

"Then you best make sure that doesn't fucking happen. Okay?" She nodded towards Ruby. "Now get, and you best take care of our momma-to-be."

Jackson resisted the urge to give his fiancé a kiss and a hug. Instead, he shrugged his rifle off his shoulder and gave her a wink. "Love you."

"Prove it and stay alive."

Chapter Forty-Seven

Mason

The steel door sealed behind them with a heavy clunk.

Mason stood frozen in the center of the panic room, heart pounding. The room felt cold and dead, heavy with the kind of silence that pressed on the chest. He could hear the dogs barking, faint and muffled through the cinderblock walls. Then nothing. The silence was worse.

Sarah clung to Pickle in the far corner, her legs tucked under her. Ivy sat between her and Emma, her arms around her sisters, trying to look calm. She wasn't doing a bad job of it either, her chin was high and defiant.

If only he could be that brave. He looked at the gun in his hand. It was heavier than he'd expected, and it only deepened his sense of uselessness.

"Let me help you with that," Maybelle said, holding out her hand. "We need to check that the safety is on, and that you know how to turn it off, if the need arises."

He handed over the weapon, shocked by how comfortable the bone-thin woman looked with it. She pulled back the slide, checked the chamber, then popped the clip and shoved it back in—quick and confident, like she'd done it a thousand times before. "Fully loaded and ready to go. See this lever here?" she said, pointing to a tiny switch below the barrel. "It means the safety is on. If you pull the trigger, nothing will happen. Flip it down to disengage it. When you do, the weapon is hot." She flipped the safety back on. "If the time comes, flip off the safety, look at where you want the bullet to go and pull the trigger." She flipped the gun in her hand and offered it back to him.

Mason's father had hated guns. It was a trait he passed down to all his children, except for Cooper and Willow.

With a heavy sigh, Mason turned in place, taking in the supplies stacked against the far wall. The owner's storage room was built for utility, not comfort. It was stocked with linens shoved in plastic bins, crates of hurricane supplies, lanterns, battery packs, tarps, and bug-out bags stacked like they'd expected the world to end.

Travis had insisted this was the safest spot in the house, and he was probably right. But it didn't feel safe to Mason. It felt like a tomb. He rubbed his hands together and sat on an overturned crate. His palms were slick with sweat. His mouth tasted like copper.

There was a soft click, followed by a mechanical whirr, and then everything went black.

Sarah let out a terrified squeal.

"It's okay," Mason said, forcing calm into his voice. "It's just the power."

"But the lights—" Sarah began.

"I know, sweetheart. But we're safe. They'll come back on."

They didn't.

Mason reached blindly for the lantern he'd seen earlier, knocking it over before finding the switch. A dull orange glow filled the room. He moved it closer to the girls, placing it between them.

Ivy's eyes were wide but dry. She wasn't crying. She was planning.

"I think it's the bad guys," she said.

Mason swallowed. "It might be. But Aunt Willow and Ranger are right outside with Jackson and Ruby. They won't let anything happen to you."

"They're outnumbered," Ivy said quietly. "You heard them earlier—four up front, more out back."

"Are they going to get us?" Emma asked. Her gaze moved to each person, waiting for someone to say everything would be okay.

Mason didn't answer. He didn't want to lie, and he sure as hell couldn't tell the truth.

Ivy leaned her head against the wall, while Sarah climbed onto her lap.

"Everything's going to be okay," Ivy said. "We've got the police and the FBI protecting us." The lantern light flickered across her face. She looked older somehow, more mature, like she'd become a mother to her sisters. She stroked her baby sister's hair as she spoke. "We just need to be brave, like Aunt Willow. If she was here, what would she do?"

The words hit him like a punch.

What would Willow do?

She'd fight. That's what. She always fought and never backed down. Every day, she risked her life to save people she didn't even know. And Mason—he'd spent most of this nightmare waiting for someone else to fix it. While everyone else faced danger, he hid like a coward.

He looked down at his trembling hands. He made fists until the shaking stopped.

"I don't know," he said finally. "But I think she'd do whatever it took."

There was another long moment of silence before Maybelle reached for the lantern and turned it toward the door. "Maybe we should get ready."

Mason stared at the steel slab. Something moved in him—a hard, jagged thing that had been asleep his entire life but was waking up fast.

If it came to it, he wouldn't cower. He'd protect his family, no matter the cost.

Chapter Forty-Eight

Reeves

Mike had agreed to watch the rear of the main floor while Travis took the front and Thomas posted himself on a second-floor balcony. He wouldn't get off more than a few shots each before his position was compromised. The balconies offered little protection, but their vantage point was ideal.

Most of the lights on the main floor had already been turned off, but when the power was cut, the house went pitch black. The hum of appliances vanished, leaving behind a hollow silence. Even the air felt heavier, like it was waiting for something to happen.

Mike's pulse pounded in his ears. A light sheen of sweat slicked his skin. He stepped toward the patio doors and drew a slow breath in through his nose. He raised his rifle and peered through the scope. He had to force himself to loosen his grip.

Zeus would have already caught their scent by now.

The thought made his heart ache. His partner should have been there beside him, ears pricked, muscles coiled, sensing dangers Mike couldn't yet see. Instead, Zeus was lying sedated in some sterile veterinary ward, recovering from the knife wound that had nearly killed him.

The moon hung low and full, its light dulled by a thin veil of cloud. The world outside had gone pale and gray, drained of color, as if it too was holding its breath. Mike found himself trying to scan the shadows the way Zeus used to, knowing it was futile. A dog's nose could catch fear-sweat from fifty yards. Its ears could pinpoint a single footstep in tall grass. Mike had only his human senses, leaving him feeling exposed.

Movement caught his eye. A figure approached through the yard, cautious but swift, rifle raised and ready.

Mike sighted in, finger resting lightly on the trigger. His breathing slowed. His eyes had adjusted to the moon's dim glow, and the intruder was silhouetted in severe contrast. He should wait. That was the plan. Wait for Thomas and Travis to start shooting.

But his mind wouldn't settle. The crosshairs steadied on the approaching figure, and Mike found himself analyzing his own reactions with detached curiosity.

This might be the third person I kill today.

The thought should have disturbed him. In his five years as a K9 officer, he'd drawn his weapon only twice. Both times during standoffs, without ever firing a shot.

Until today.

Mere minutes ago, he'd put bullets into two men without hesitation. He had watched them drop and felt... nothing. No guilt. No relief. Just the cold, mechanical completion of a necessary act.

Thomas had warned him about this—how the emotional reckoning could hit later, in the quiet moments when sleep wouldn't come.

Zeus would growl right now, Mike thought, watching the figure advance. Low and steady. The kind of warning that meant real danger, not just territory marking. His chest tightened with the absence of that familiar rumble. They'd been partners for only four months, and Mike was still learning to read Zeus's alerts. He was still learning to trust his partner's instincts. Now he was alone. He felt somehow diminished, incomplete.

The first crack of gunfire startled him. Three more shots followed in rapid succession. Mike squeezed the trigger. The gunman in his sights staggered, and Mike fired again. The man dropped, swallowed by the tall grass.

He looked at the body, half hidden in the reeds.

Three. Three men I've killed today.

He waited for the guilt to hit, for his hands to shake, for something human to surface. Nothing came. Just the same cold assessment: Threat neutralized. Moving to the next target.

He panned left, searching for movement.

Why is no one shooting back?

"At least six made it to the house," Travis shouted, storming down the stairs. He charged past without waiting, vanishing out the patio door.

Mike hesitated. That wasn't part of the plan. Zeus would have given him a clear signal—stay or go—based on scents and sounds Mike couldn't interpret. Without that guidance, he felt like he was making critical decisions with half his senses shut down.

More shots echoed from above—short, controlled bursts.

Glass shattered in the living room behind him. Mike spun just in time to see a metal canister tumbling through the broken window. It hit the hardwood with a dull clink and rolled to a stop.

The flashbang exploded.

A blinding burst of white light filled the space, burning through his retinas like a welding torch. His ears filled with static, a shrill screech that pierced the center of his skull. His balance gave out. He dropped hard, the floor cold and unforgiving against his shoulder. The rifle slipped from his hands and skidded away.

Mike tried to get up, but the room spun sideways. His vision pulsed with dark spots, his thoughts scrambled and out of reach. Somewhere in the back of his mind, he knew he needed to move. To act. But his body refused to cooperate. He sought out Zeus, fearing what had happened to him. The K9's absence felt like a phantom limb. He kept expecting to feel warm fur against his body, to hear protective snarling, to know that someone had his back.

You're alone, he realized. Completely alone.

A second window broke.

The next grenade landed closer—near his feet.

This time, he had just enough clarity to cover his head with both arms, shielding his eyes and ears before it detonated. As the blast struck like a sledgehammer, jolting his whole body. Pain flared behind his eyes, and the ringing in his ears deepened into a low, pulsing roar. He couldn't hear anything over the ringing. He couldn't see more than shapes and shadows swimming in the dark. He clung to the floor, trying to remember where he was, what he was supposed to be doing.

For a moment, all that remained was panicked realization that the breach had begun.

And he was already down—and about to die.

Chapter Forty-Nine

Willow

The lights blinked out, and, from the panic room, one of the girls screamed.

They cut the power. It's starting.

A moment later, the backup generator kicked in with a low mechanical hum, and a faint red exit sign flickered on above the rear door. It didn't offer much illumination, but enough to mark the most likely point of entry.

Willow called Ranger to her side and positioned herself at the threshold leading to the stairs. The door frame offered partial cover, but little more.

Beside her, Ranger growled low in his throat. He was crouched in a tense position, weight forward, ears pricked toward the entrance. Willow raised her rifle and settled into a low firing stance. Every inch of her skin prickled. The waiting was worse than the attack itself. She tried to calm her breathing and slow her jack-hammering pulse, but not knowing what was happening outside drove her ever-increasing anxiety.

Jackson's twenty feet away, covering the opposite side. Reeves is watching the rear patio. Travis and Thomas are up top. The panic room's sealed, and everyone is safe inside.

But it didn't calm her. It made her heart race harder.

How many attackers? How coordinated are they? How much time do we have before they breach?

Never had she ever been on the receiving end of a raid.

Think, Willow. Calm your fucking mind. If you were leading this assault, what would you do? Where would you send your team? Would you split up your forces or keep them together?

The tactics she would follow solidified in her mind. There are established patterns used to crack a well-defended, fortified position, and she was confident that these people were well trained and that they'd follow standard procedure.

They'll hit with multiple teams, at multiple points of entry. They'll attack simultaneously, hoping to sow chaos and confusion while they make a systematic and coordinated entry.

Her thoughts drifted to Jackson, wondering if he had gone through the same thought process. She wished he was beside her so they could talk it through, they could face the threat together, and she could protect him.

She lowered her Browning long enough to run her hand over Ranger's head. His body twitched beneath her touch, but his focus never left the door.

Upstairs, gunfire had erupted, followed by the unmistakable sound of flash bang grenades. Ranger whined each time a bomb detonated but refused to retreat from the ear-piercing noise.

"Steady, boy. You stay beside me, okay? Do you understand?" Of course he didn't know what she just said, but if what she learned about canine behavior was accurate, Ranger would pick up on her tone and body language, and he'd parse out the words he didn't know and keep the ones he did. In this case, it was the command to *stay*. She had no doubt that, no matter the circumstances, her dog would not break from her unless told to.

She trained her rifle on the back door, waiting for someone to appear in its glass window. She took a slow, deliberate breath and moved her finger to the trigger, letting it rest gently upon it.

The window shattered as two cannisters flew into the small space. She grabbed Ranger's collar, pulled him out of the room and slammed the door shut. The concussive force shook the walls, but the door had blocked the bright light and deadened some of the sound. A crash, like the sound of wood slamming against the floor, came from Jackson's side of the house.

Ranger's barks sounded distant, like Willow was hearing them underwater. He moved to the closed door, snarling and lunging against it.

"Ranger, back!" she yelled. As soon as the K9 backed up, Willow fired three shots into the door. She rushed forward and booted it open, revealing a woman wearing military camo gear.

The intruder's eyes widened as Willow pointed her gun and put two quick shots into her chest, knocking her prone.

"Ranger, attack!"

He dashed past and pounced, sinking his teeth into her throat.

Again, Willow took up position behind the doorframe and focused her attention on the now open door leading outside. She didn't need to see her dog in action, the snarls and strangled cries were more than enough to tell her what was happening.

A second attacker stepped into the doorway and strafed the room in a hail of bullets. There hadn't been time to even duck for cover. Using the muzzle flashes as her target, Willow returned fire, putting three rounds into the man's chest. He landed hard on his back and writhed on the ground.

They're wearing full body armor.

Quickly, Willow drew her side arm and raced forward. Under the light of the exit sign, she could make out that the gunman was one of the three men she'd seen at Maritime Workforce Solutions. She was certain of it. He tried to raise his gun, and Willow put two rounds into his head.

"Ranger, heel," Willow called out. The woman was long since dead, but her dog hadn't stopped tearing her open. Another flashbang shattered the brief silence—then another, and another. The first had come from her left, where Jackson was. The last two had come from directly above her.

Gunfire followed. Multiple shooters, multiple locations.

Willow hesitated. Jackson was closest, but most of the shots were coming from upstairs.

The children come first.

How many times had that thought gone through her mind in the past few minutes? She looked over her shoulder, past the eviscerated woman, to the steel door and the panic room behind it.

They'll be okay.

At least, she hoped they would.

Willow poked her head out the door leading to the backyard. Moonlight illuminated the yard, making any movement easy to spot. Thirty feet away, where Jackson guarded the second entrance, gunshots echoed, each muzzle flash briefly illuminating the doorway.

She raised her rifle into shooting position and bolted forward. "Ranger, attack!"

Chapter Fifty

Jackson

Jackson moved into the side room just off the main hallway. The space was a recreational holdover from the house's more peaceful days—ping pong table in the middle, couch pushed up against one wall, and a massive flat-screen TV dominating the other. Two doors waited at the back: one to an extra bedroom, and the other to the stairwell that led up to the second floor.

Ruby pressed her nose to the base of the exit door, her tail stiff. She was assessing whether someone was on the other side of the door.

When she didn't signal an immediate threat, Jackson dragged the ping pong table to the back wall and flipped it on its side, forming a makeshift barricade. It wasn't ideal cover, but it might buy him a few seconds of concealment if someone burst through the door.

Jackson opened the bedroom door, creating a possible fallback position.

"Ruby, come!" he said, calling his dog away from the door. She was a capable protector, but no match for Willow's Malinois—*the mali-gator,* as Thomas had named him. Getting Ruby clear gave him peace of mind, letting him focus on shooting without fear of hitting her by mistake.

Ruby whined and moved to his side.

"Sit," Jackson said, and the dog immediately complied. He unslung his rifle and crouched behind the ping pong table, resting the barrel on its edge and taking aim at the door. He was concerned that Willow had little cover in the room next door and that she and Ranger would be exposed.

The power cut out, plunging the room into pitch blackness.

For a beat, there was only the sound of Ruby's nails tapping anxiously on the floor and Jackson's breath catching in his throat.

Then the backup generator kicked in, humming to life somewhere outside the house. A red exit sign flickered above the exterior door, bathing the room in dim, eerie light. Shadows stretched in every direction.

Welcome to hell.

Jackson glanced over his shoulder to the open bedroom door behind him. The frame was barely visible in the crimson glow. He returned his focus to the exit.

Gunfire erupted upstairs—definitely coming from inside the house. Thomas was likely engaging from his overwatch position. He wouldn't be able to stay there long before he started taking return fire. It was an excellent vantage point, but he'd be fully exposed once his position was compromised.

Loud bangs reverberated through the room. Concussion grenades were the harbinger of an imminent breach attempt. Either his dad or Reeves was going to be directly in the line of fire.

I should've taken the stairwell. I could've backed them up.

But now it was too dark. Too risky. He had to trust they could take care of themselves, and that Reeves and his dad could protect the main floor.

A crash of glass from the other side of the ground floor—Willow's side—was followed by two more ear-splitting blasts. Even through the walls, the sound was deafening. With each explosion, Ruby had flinched but never moved.

Glass shattered.

He turned his head just in time to see two metal canisters bounce across the concrete floor.

"Ruby, down!" he barked, lunging to cover her with his body. He wrapped his arms around her head, shielding her from the blinding light and thunderous bangs that were about to follow.

The blasts detonated before Jackson could shield his ears. The shockwaves slammed through his head, like they'd ignited inside his skull. His hearing collapsed into a high-pitched screech. His balance evaporated. Muscles locked. He fell hard on top of Ruby, unable to move, unable to speak, unable to think.

Gunfire followed, muffled and distant, like it was echoing through a long tunnel. Splinters exploded from the ping pong table as bullets shredded the wood. Shards bit into his exposed skin—forearms, cheeks, and neck. His vision swam. The world was tumbling and spinning at the same time. He fought back an intense wave of nausea.

Ruby tore out from under him.

The flash of movement barely registered before she launched herself at the gunman who stepped around the edge of the table. She grabbed his arm and shook it like a rag doll, driving the man back.

More gunfire echoed in the room, reverberating through his brain like a jackhammer. Jackson covered his ears and suppressed a scream that had found its way to his throat.

Another blur of fur and muscle struck the attacker from the side—Ranger, jaws locking around the man's face, ripping flesh from bone.

Jackson's brain struggled to keep up while the entire world tilted around him. He blinked hard, trying to clear his vision and his mind.

Willow appeared, eyes blazing, rifle up. She shouted something, but Jackson couldn't make it out. Her lips moved, her expression twisted in fury, but all he heard was the shrill whine of damaged hearing. She stepped past him, shouted again, then put a bullet into the man the dogs had brought down.

She turned to face Jackson, blood splatter covering her from the waist down. She held out her hand, offering to help him to his feet. She was saying something, but he couldn't make out the words. Even though the haze, just seeing her there... it steadied something in him. He raised his arm to grab her hand, stopping when Ruby stumbled over him.

She was pawing frantically at her muzzle, rubbing her eyes against Jackson's leg. With her eyes closed tight, Ruby staggered into the adjacent bedroom, sneezing and violently shaking her head. Ranger followed, coughing and snapping his jaws like something was burning him from the inside out.

Willow lowered her rifle and doubled over, coughing violently into the crook of her arm.

A moment later, the smell hit Jackson. A scorching, chemical tang that burned down his throat and clawed its way up his sinuses. His eyes flooded, then burned. His lungs seized like they'd been sprayed with acid.

Tear gas.

He gagged, fighting for breath. His limbs still wouldn't work right. The exit sign flickered through the rising haze, casting the gas in red, hellish light.

Willow reached for him, yanking on his shoulder. Her lips moved again, her expression urgent.

He still couldn't hear her, but the message was clear.

Get up. Move. Now.

Faint popping sounds registered in Jackson's ears, and Willow's head snapped to the left. Her expression shifted from urgent to pleading.

Chapter Fifty-One

Mason

Mason paced the length of the panic room like a caged animal. The walls, which once offered a sense of security, now felt like a coffin. With every distant gunshot, every low thump of an explosion, the concrete seemed to close in around him.

Sarah clung to Ivy's arm, wailing uncontrollably. Emma sat beside them, eyes wide, tears carving silent trails down her cheeks. Only Ivy seemed unshaken—her voice calm, her hands steady, as she held Sarah and spoke to her in low, reassuring tones.

It was Ivy's unwavering calm that broke Mason. Not the gunfire. Not his child's unrelenting wails. Ivy.

His fourteen-year-old daughter was sitting cross-legged on the floor, cradling her younger sister like a soldier comforting a wounded comrade. She was so fierce and composed, it made Mason's chest ache. Ivy shared Willow's strength and composure under fire—the kind of bravery that shouldn't have to exist in someone so young.

They were all out there—Willow, Jackson, Travis, Mike, even Thomas—risking their lives to defend this house. To protect his family. And where was he? Tucked in here with the women and children. Useless. Trapped.

Maybelle and Anika had taken positions by the door, weapons drawn. Neither spoke. They just stood there, breathing hard, waiting for whatever came next. Maybelle glanced over at Anika, a silent understanding passed between them—grim, resigned. These weren't warriors. Just women who refused to die cowering.

Anika coughed first—one sharp, dry bark that doubled her over. She pressed her hand to her mouth and winced. Maybelle followed a second later, her breath hitching before violent hacks overtook her.

Mason's eyes stung. He winced and blinked, trying to alleviate the pain. He took a breath—and immediately regretted it. Acute pain knifed through his lungs. He wheezed and choked uncontrollably. Through the burning tears, he saw smoke curling beneath the door.

Sarah shrieked and clawed at her eyes. "It hurts! My eyes—Daddy, it hurts!"

Ivy was already moving. She grabbed a bottle of water and soaked a towel from the stack of linens on the shelf. "Close your eyes," she told Sarah, "and hold this over your mouth." She pressed the dripping cloth gently to her sister's face.

Sarah cried harder but clutched the towel like it was a lifeline.

Ivy didn't stop. She handed a bottle of water to Emma, then tossed one to everyone else. Anika was pulling off towels and passing them around as well.

Ivy's eyes were bloodshot and watering, her cheeks streaked with sweat and smoke. She helped Emma wet her towel before she took care of herself.

Meanwhile, Mason watched. Dumbfounded. Mesmerized by his daughter's actions. He glanced at the door, seeing the smoke continue to fill the room.

Anika dropped to her knees and shoved a towel under the door. Maybelle did the same. It helped. Barely.

"We can't stay here," Maybelle said hoarsely, gagging. "This gas'll kill us."

Mason didn't hesitate. Not this time.

"Everyone get back," he yelled. He shoved his handgun into the back of his waistband and used both hands to press the towel tighter against his mouth and nose. "Now. Back away from the door."

Maybelle turned to him. "Don't do this."

"I'm going to find us a way out," he said, reaching for the doorknob.

Anika reached for his arm. "You'll get killed out there."

He ignored them. He didn't wait for Ivy's cry or Sarah's scream or Emma's begging voice. He couldn't. He wouldn't let his kids die in here choking on gas while he cowered behind a locked door. It was better to die trying than to wait for death to claim him and his family.

Mason took the lantern from Maybelle. Its soft glow barely pushed back the thick smoke curling beneath the door, but it was better than nothing.

He unlocked the handle and yanked the door open.

Smoke surged into the room like a living thing, curling around his legs, filling his lungs with fire. He coughed violently, eyes streaming. A shape emerged through the fog—a man, dressed in black, face hidden behind a gas mask, rifle sweeping the room.

Instincts took over. Mason raised the handgun and squeezed the trigger. The weapon bucked and the man jerked as the round hit. He pivoted toward Mason, raising his weapon.

Mason fired again. And again. Each pull of the trigger shook his arm to the bone. The masked man crumpled, swallowed by the smoke that hung close to the floor. Mason blinked through his tears, his lungs screaming. It was like trying to breathe through fire.

His hand trembled as he stepped forward, past the body, into the haze. The lantern slipped from his grip and clattered to the floor, its pale light casting flickering shadows across the concrete.

Another flash, dim and far. Pain exploded in his gut. A hot, crushing punch to his belly that dropped him to one knee. He couldn't even scream—just a raw gasp as warmth spread from inside his shirt. He saw the source of the shot and raised his weapon again, pulling the trigger. He surged to his feet and fired blindly until he'd emptied his gun.

Ripping pain exploded in his shoulder, spinning him around. Mason hit the wall, staggered, and went down hard. His head bounced off the floor, the impact rattled his skull. The concrete felt surprisingly cool and soothing against his cheek. He welcomed it.

More gunfire echoed in the distance, but it was quieter now. Less immediate. He couldn't feel the wounds anymore. Not really. Even the coughing had stopped. Had his lungs given up, or had he?

"Daddy!" A hand gripped his wrist. Strong. Trembling. Familiar. "Daddy, get up. Please get up."

Ivy.

His mind swam. He tried to stand, but his body refused to move. His limbs felt disconnected. Like they belonged to someone else.

"Dad's been shot!" she screamed. "Somebody help! He's bleeding badly!"

More shots rang out in the distance, but Ivy didn't budge. She lowered herself beside him and pressed her forehead to his.

"Don't die," she whispered, staring at him like she was looking directly into his soul. Ivy had green eyes. He wasn't sure if he'd noticed that before—he'd thought they were blue. They were so beautiful. She was so beautiful. "Please don't die. I can't lose you too."

Mason stared at her. The world was dimming, but her face was still bright—so much like Willow's. Ivy's strength, too, was so much like his sister's. Same fury. Same love. Same fire. He'd seen it in her earlier when she calmed Sarah, soaked the towels, saved them all. He saw it now in the tears she wouldn't let fall.

He thought of how he'd amended his will, certain he'd done the right thing. Ivy would be okay. They all would.

He blinked once and everything went still.

Chapter Fifty-Two

Willow

Ivy's blood-curdling scream cut through the chaos.

Willow flinched, coughing as the sting of tear gas clawed her eyes and throat. She blinked against the blur and bolted toward the sound, Jackson beside her. Boots slammed the concrete as they rounded the corner toward the panic room, to where Willow should have been guarding the children.

Two men in gas masks stood in the fog-filled room. One was helping the other from the ground, pulling him up by his jet-black military-style vest. When they caught sight of Jackson, one sprinted for the back door, with the other stumbling after him. Jackson raised his weapon, ready to give chase.

"Leave them!" Willow shouted.

Jackson hesitated, eyes flicking to her, then back to the men disappearing into the dark. He didn't fire.

Willow didn't watch them flee. Her gaze was locked on the scene outside the panic room.

Mason lay on the floor, sprawled on his side, a flickering lantern resting just beside him. Its pale, uneven glow illuminated his blood-soaked shirt—dark patches spreading across his stomach and shoulder. Sobbing, Ivy knelt beside him, both hands pressed against his belly. "Stay with me, Daddy. Please stay with me."

Willow dropped to her knees beside them. Her cough wrenched her chest, but she barely noticed. She reached out, hands shaking.

"Smoke was coming in the room," Ivy wailed. "He ran out of the room and started shooting."

The dead man sprawled six feet away was proof that Mason had taken down at least one attacker. "Mason... we're here. We're right here."

His eyes fluttered, his face pale beneath the sweat and blood splatter. His lips moved, but no sound came.

Willow's vision blurred again. All the words she'd spat at him—the anger, the blame—crashed into her, pushing the air from her lungs. He'd tried to protect her from making the worst mistake of her life. From Matt. From herself. She'd shoved him away. Mason couldn't die. Not without hearing her say she was sorry. Not after everything she'd done to him, to his family. He needed to be there for his children. They couldn't lose another parent. Willow pressed a hand to his shoulder, right over the wound, and whispered, "I'm sorry, Mason... I'm so goddamned sorry... You didn't deserve that. I know you were trying to protect me..."

He stared into Willow's eyes but said nothing. Ivy dropped over her father's chest and sobbed.

Heavy footsteps thundered in. Travis skidded to a stop beside them, rifle slung across his chest. His face was red, streaked with sweat and blood.

"Reinforcements are on site," he said, breathless. "The bastards are bugging out."

Jackson knelt beside Willow, a look of helplessness in his eyes.

"The hospital's too far," she said. She forced the words out through clenched teeth. "He won't make it."

Jackson looked to his father. "Where's Thomas?"

"He's not enough," Travis said. "There's a fire station not far from here. They've got EMTs and proper equipment. We need to move. Now!"

Willow wondered if there may be more attackers outside. The sheriff's men... if anyone tried to stop them, she'd fucking kill them all. "The Jeep's out front."

Jackson bent, slipped his arms under Mason, and hauled him up. Blood smeared across Jackson's shirt as Mason groaned, head lolling.

Willow stumbled after them, wiping her burning eyes. Ivy sprang up, yanked her shirt free of her pants, and pulled it low over her hips. She sprinted ahead to the garage door and hit the controls. Nothing happened.

"Move," Willow ordered, pushing past Ivy. "Are you trying get shot? We don't know who's outside." As Ivy backed away, Willow reached up and released the latch. She then heaved on the heavy metal door. The hinges groaned as the door slowly rose.

Red and blue lights strobed across the ground. The Jeep was right where it should be. Police cruisers lined the street and filled the home's driveway. Officers in tactical gear raised their weapons and leveled them at Willow and the others.

"Down on the ground," an officer bellowed, using his M4 carbine to point. "I said down!"

They didn't have time for this. Mason was bleeding out and desperately needed medical attention. The SWAT member didn't know that. He'd been called into a war zone, and he couldn't trust anyone.

"My dad is going to die," Ivy screamed. "Get the fuck out of our way!"

With Mason laying limp in his arms, Jackson moved forward at a steady pace, refusing to back down. "I'm FBI Special Agent Jackson Brooks, and this man needs immediate medical attention."

"Stand down, Officer," Cooper yelled, racing up laneway. "Peterson! Stand the fuck down!"

Willow intercepted her brother. "We need to get Mason out of here."

"Daddy!" Sarah's unmistakable screech came from inside the house. Ranger and Ruby were in the lead with Emma following close behind, her little sister's hand clutched in hers. Maybelle followed, her hand over her mouth. Further back, Thomas stood next to Anika, his arm wrapped tightly around her.

Travis strode forward and got into the Jeep. "Let's go, let's go!" he yelled.

"Go," Cooper said, motioning Jackson forward. He turned to the officers swarming the area. "Give them room."

Ivy darted past Willow and grabbed the Jeep's passenger door. "I'm coming!"

"No—" Willow started, but Ivy shot her a look that cut like glass.

"I'm coming."

"Get the back seat down," Jackson said to Ivy. "I need to lay your dad down."

Ivy clambered over the front seat, fumbling at buttons and latches until the seat backs finally dropped. She moved to the corner, giving Jackson as much room as possible. "Put him here," she said. "Rest his head on my lap. I've got him."

While Jackson lowered Mason into Ivy's care, Willow got into the front passenger seat. Ranger stood beside the vehicle, his eyes silently pleading to be invited along. "Get in," Willow said. The dog sprung from his spot, jumping over the closed door and into the back of the Jeep.

Ruby barked, insisting on her own invitation. Jackson opened the door, and she climbed in, much slower than her puppy-daddy had. Unlike Ranger, who had parked himself as close to Willow as possible, Ruby laid down beside Mason, resting her head across his legs. They had seemingly formed a close bond in their short time together. She was the most intuitive creature Willow had ever known: loyal, gentle, and impossibly brave.

"Get in, son," Travis yelled. "We gotta go!"

"Go," Jackson yelled. "Cooper and I will meet you there." He locked onto Willow's gaze, wordlessly saying everything would be okay.

Jackson was such a bad liar. Things were definitely not going to be okay. Even if Mason pulled through, their lives would be irreparably changed.

The Jeep lurched forward.

"Hold onto your daddy," Travis said. "It's going to get bumpy."

The only way past the police cars and SWAT vans clogging the exit was to cut across the property and through the neighbor's yard. Mason moaned as he jostled around while Ivy did her best to hold him still. They cleared the police vehicles and Travis hit the accelerator. He raced down the street before turning onto a gravel side street.

"This road's bumpy," he said while swerving around potholes.

Willow clutched onto the oh-shit handle while she watched her niece trying to keep her father steady. Ivy's expression was filled with resolve. She wasn't shedding tears. She was doing what needed to be done to keep her father safe.

Travis jerked the wheel hard, skidding around a corner. He flew across the intersecting road, never slowing. The Jeep lurched as it caught a curb and rumbled into the fire station lot. The bay doors were all open, the emergency vehicles visible within. Bright lights flooded the area, casting an ominous glow on the ambulance that was parked out front. Firemen and EMTs waited outside, a stretcher prepped between them.

Travis slammed the brakes beside the open bay door.

The EMTs rushed forward. Ruby refused to move, standing guard at Mason's side. One of the EMTs hesitated, glancing at Willow.

"Ruby, off," Willow ordered, voice tight.

The dog gave a low whine, but obeyed, hopping down just as they slid the stretcher into place.

They wheeled Mason toward the open bay, past stacks of hoses and gleaming fire trucks. The lighting inside was harsh, highlighting the ominous amount of blood.

The EMTs worked fast—cutting Mason's shirt open, exposing the wounds. One applied direct pressure to the abdominal bleeding while the other checked his vitals. "Pulse is weak but present," the first EMT called out. "Respiration's shallow. Let's get him on oxygen."

A firefighter darted in with an equipment bag. Another hauled over a portable monitor. They worked in rhythm—IV line started, oxygen mask over Mason's face, monitor leads attached to his chest. The machine began its steady beeping, displaying his vital signs in harsh green numbers.

"Blood pressure's dropping," one EMT said, adjusting the IV drip. "Eighty over fifty and falling."

Ivy moved close to Willow, slipping an arm around her waist. "He'll be okay, right?" The brave teenager was gone, replaced by a terrified daughter too young to be forced into this reality.

Willow wrapped her arm around Ivy's shoulder and pulled her close. "He'll be fine," she said softly, though she wasn't sure she believed it. She hated lying to her niece, but she needed to maintain hope.

"What are we going to do?" Ivy said, her red-rimmed eyes staring up at Willow. "Will we end up in an orphanage?" Tears slipped down her cheeks. "Aunt Willow, I'm frightened."

"I'm here," Willow whispered, voice hoarse. She pulled Ivy tighter. "I'm not going anywhere, and that would never happen. That I can promise you."

"I missed you." Her voice cracked. "But I'm glad you're here now."

Willow swallowed hard, heart splitting in two. "Me too."

Ruby pressed up against Ivy, her head bowed and tail low.

Willow raised her head, searching for Ranger. She loosened her grip on Ivy enough to scan the area. Her K9 was standing near the corner of the fire station, focused intently on the palmetto trees that bordered the property about twenty feet away, providing cover between the station and the street.

The monitor's steady beeping suddenly became erratic, then flatlined with a long, continuous tone. "He's coding," one EMT shouted. "Starting compressions! Grab the crash cart."

The air froze. Willow felt it—the moment everything ground to a halt.

"Don't do that," a man said. He stepped out from behind the palm trees, his gun leveled on Ranger. "Call off your dog, or I'll shoot him dead."

The defibrillator whined as it charged, rising in pitch.

Willow's lungs locked. She squeezed Ivy's hand.

"Ranger, come!"

The dog took two slow steps away from the armed gunman before returning to Willow.

The sound of the defibrillator discharging echoed in the quiet and Mason's body bounced on the gurney.

"I said, don't do that!" The gunman's weapon swiveled towards the two EMTs who never stopped working.

"Still no pulse," one said, "charge to three hundred." The machine whined as it recharged, and the gunman fired a shot into the air.

"Do you think I care if I kill every single one of you?" the gunman said. "Get away from him..." He leveled the gun at the EMT nearest Mason. "I can't let him talk. He's seen too much." The gunman's voice wavered. "But I need help getting us off this fucking island, and you want your brother alive. Cut me a deal."

Willow finally placed the vaguely familiar face. "Colonel Pratt," she said, stepping towards him. His photo had been displayed prominently on their murder board.

He was risking his own life to make sure Mason died on the slab. Whatever testimony her brother might give, it was damning.

"There are dozens of police here. You can't get away. Let them work on my brother and I'll put in a good word with the US Attorney. Maybe you'll spend life in prison instead of getting the needle."

"Clear," an EMT said. The sound of the defibrillator discharge followed.

Willow couldn't see what was happening. She was focused on Pratt and only Pratt. She needed to give the paramedics time to work on Mason. Ranger's growl rumbled in his chest. Pratt was nearly thirty feet away, more than enough time to shoot her dog before he got to him.

"Charge to three-sixty!"

Ranger sprang forward, nearly taking Willow's legs out from underneath her. As the Malinois dashed forward, Pratt's aim swiveled toward him. He never saw Ruby's attack coming from the side. The Golden Retriever's jaws clutched onto the man's wrist and dragged him to the ground. Ranger followed, latching onto his target's leg, ripping open his calf.

A police cruiser raced into the parking lot, Cooper at the wheel. Jackson was in the passenger seat beside him. A gunshot cracked and the passenger side window exploded in a shower of fragments.

Jackson!

"Call off your dogs." Another man stepped from behind the trees, rifle raised, face set in a snarl. "Call them off or I keep shooting."

Michael Fucking Fitzpatrick.

Willow's eyes fixed on his black vest, recognition hitting like ice water in her veins. Pratt and Fitzpatrick were the two men who'd escaped from the house. The ones Jackson had wanted to kill.

I should have let him.

Her hand unconsciously moved toward her holster. "Fuck you, Fitzpatrick." The words came out steady despite the sweat blooming under her arms. Her fingers gripped the Glock's handle just as a gun cracked.

Willow flinched, her body bracing for the impact that never came. Her weapon cleared the holster, and she spun toward Fitzpatrick.

Michael's gun clattered to the ground as crimson blossomed across the side of his body. A second gunshot made Willow jump. Michael stumbled to the side before falling in a twist.

To his right, Ivy stood resolute, unblinking. Her mouth contorted into a hate-filled scowl. In her hands she gripped a Beretta, smoke curling up from the barrel. "I wasn't going to let him take my dad too."

Willow's heart seized. There was no coming back from this.

The defibrillator discharged a third time.

Chapter Fifty-Three

Jackson

The gunshots still echoed in Jackson's ears as he sprinted toward the fire station, Cooper beside him. Glass crunched under their boots from the shattered passenger window. Across from the bay doors, the chaos unfolded—Ivy standing with the smoking Beretta, two men down near the palm trees, and the EMTs still working frantically over Mason.

"Go to Willow," Jackson said, breathing hard. "I'll secure the suspects."

Cooper darted toward his sister, who was pulling Ivy into her arms. Jackson drew his weapon and approached the fallen men, moving cautiously.

Michael Fitzpatrick lay twisted on his side, blood pooling beneath him. Jackson crouched and checked for a carotid pulse. Nothing. The man's eyes stared sightlessly at the night sky. Ivy's shots had been accurate and deadly.

Twenty feet away, Colonel Pratt was still breathing, though barely. Ruby had done significant damage to his wrist, and Ranger's attack had shredded his calf. Blood seeped through his torn pants, and his face was pale with shock.

"You're under arrest," Jackson said, though he doubted Pratt could hear him. As he slapped cuffs onto the man's wrists, Pratt's eyes rolled back, consciousness fading.

Jackson pulled out his phone and called for another ambulance, then turned his attention back to the scene unfolding in the fire station. The heart monitor's flatline tone gave way to erratic beeping. The EMTs kept working, but their movements had slowed, becoming less urgent and more methodical. The kind of movements that meant they were going through the motions because they had to, not because they believed it would help.

Mason was dying. Maybe already dead.

Jackson's chest tightened as he watched Willow holding Ivy, both of them staring at the gurney where Mason lay motionless. Cooper stood beside them, his hand on Willow's shoulder. Even from this distance, Jackson could see the defeat in their postures.

Red and blue lights flashed across the parking lot as two more squad cars pulled up. Jackson's parents climbed out of the first vehicle, followed by Emma and Sarah from the second. Pickle bounded out after them, tail wagging as if this were any other night.

"Daddy!" Emma screamed, her young voice cutting through the night. She ran toward the fire station, Sarah close behind her.

Jackson's parents intercepted the girls before they could reach the medical scene. Maybelle knelt down, gathering both children into her arms while Travis stood protectively over them. Sarah fought against the woman's embrace, trying to get to her father.

"Let me go!" Sarah screeched, wriggling to free herself. "I want my daddy!"

Jackson holstered his weapon and walked toward his family. The EMTs had stopped working now. One of them was speaking quietly to Willow, shaking his head. Cooper's shoulders sagged.

Mason was gone.

Travis looked up as Jackson approached. "Son, how bad is it?"

Jackson glanced back at the fire station, where Willow was crying openly now, Ivy still in her arms. "Mason didn't make it."

Maybelle's eyes filled with tears. She held the girls tighter. "Oh, those poor babies."

Sarah broke free from Maybelle's arms and ran toward the fire station. "Daddy! Daddy, wake up!"

Emma followed, tears streaming down her face. Jackson watched helplessly as the two girls reached their father's still form. Willow immediately pulled them close, her own grief momentarily set aside to comfort the children.

"What about the men who did this?" Travis asked, his jaw tight with anger.

"Fitzpatrick's dead. Pratt's alive, but barely." Jackson ran a hand through his hair. "Another ambulance is on the way, along with every available ambulance in Beaufort County."

Jackson looked back at the fire station where Willow was crouched between Emma and Sarah, holding them as they cried over their father's body. Ivy stood beside them, her face streaked with tears but her posture still strong.

Emma climbed onto the gurney beside her father, curling up against his still chest. Sarah stood beside them, her small hand resting on Mason's arm. Willow hadn't moved, hadn't tried to pull the girls away. She understood they needed this moment.

"We'll figure it out," Jackson said quietly. "Willow's not going through this alone."

Another ambulance arrived, its lights flashing but sirens quiet. Two paramedics got out, looking for instruction. Jackson pointed Pratt out to them. The two officers who'd driven his parents and the girls flanked the EMTs, ready to provide escort and guard duty at the hospital.

"I should check on them," Jackson said, nodding toward the fire station.

"We'll be right here if you need anything," Maybelle replied, giving his arm a squeeze.

Jackson walked slowly toward the group gathered around Mason's body. Cooper saw him coming and stepped back, making room. Willow looked up as he approached, her eyes red and swollen.

"I'm so sorry," Jackson said, his voice barely above a whisper.

Willow swallowed, unable to speak. Ivy looked up at him, her face hard despite the tears.

"I killed him," Ivy said matter-of-factly. "Fitzpatrick. I shot him."

"You protected your family," Jackson replied. "You did what you had to do."

"He was trying to make a deal, but he was going to kill Dad anyway," Ivy continued. "I could tell."

Sarah finally lifted her head from Mason's chest. "Is Daddy in heaven now?"

Willow smoothed the girl's hair. "Yes, sweetheart. I'm sure he is."

"He saved us," Emma said quietly. "We couldn't breathe, and he saved us from the bad men."

"Yes," Willow said, her voice breaking. "He did. Your daddy was a hero."

Jackson stood silently, watching this family mourn their loss. Behind him, he could hear the paramedics loading Pratt into the ambulance. The investigation would continue, but for now, this moment belonged to grief.

The EMTs began their own quiet work, respectfully preparing Mason's body for transport. Jackson knew they'd need to move soon, but for now, he let them have this time.

Sarah looked up at Willow. "What's going to happen to us now?"

Willow pulled the girls close. "I'm going to go home with you, and we're going to take care of each other."

"Promise?" Emma asked.

"I promise," Willow said firmly. "I'm not going anywhere."

In the distance, the ambulance carrying Pratt pulled away, its police escort leading the way. The immediate crisis was over, but Jackson knew the real work was just beginning. A family had been shattered, and somehow, they'd have to put the pieces back together.

As he watched Willow holding Mason's daughters, seeing the determination in her grief-stricken face, Jackson knew she'd find a way. *They* would find a way. Together.

Chapter Fifty-Four

Willow

The hospital waiting room smelled like disinfectant and stale coffee. Willow sat on a hard vinyl couch that was too small for her frame. Ivy was curled against her side, while Emma and Sarah flanked them like bookends. The girls hadn't spoken since the ambulance ride. Even Sarah's tears had dried up, leaving her with a hollow, thousand-yard stare that belonged on a war veteran, not an eight-year-old.

Sarah clutched Pickle tight against her chest, her small fingers gripping the beagle's fur. One of the nurses had tried to remove the dog, citing infection control, but Willow wasn't having any of it. They had nearly come to blows before a hospital social worker—a no-nonsense woman named Judith—had intervened, telling the staff to leave Pickle alone. "That dog's doing more good than we are right now," Judith had said, forcing the nurse to back off.

Ivy's fingers trembled against Willow's lap, and every few minutes she'd flex them, as if testing that they were still working. After forensics had taken pictures and bagged Ivy's clothes, the nurses had scrubbed away Michael Fitzpatrick's blood and given her a clean hospital gown

"Ivy?" Willow's voice came out as a whisper. "You okay?" It was a stupid, useless question but she didn't know what else to say.

Ivy didn't look up. "I killed him."

Emma shifted closer to her sister but said nothing. Sarah continued staring at the vending machine across the room.

"You protected your family," Willow said, using the same words Jackson had offered. She swallowed the hard knot in her throat. It shouldn't have been Ivy's responsibility to protect her family. Willow had failed her, forced her into an unthinkable situation. "I'm sorry that I put you in that position."

"I'm not," Ivy said. "He killed Dad, and he got what he deserved. It's just that—" She paused and stared into Willow's eyes, her fingers curling into the fabric of the hospital gown. "I don't feel anything. I thought it would make me happy... or guilty maybe." She lifted a shoulder. "But I just feel empty."

That hollow, frozen numbness—Willow remembered it too well. The first time she'd taken a life, she'd felt that same terrifying void. Not relief. Not guilt. Just... nothing. The academy had trained her for this, preparing her for the psychological aftermath, but it had been woefully inadequate. Either that or she hadn't believed what they were saying and had dismissed it out of hand.

And afterward? She'd buried it. Pushed through it. Because that was what the job demanded. What *she* demanded of herself.

But Ivy wasn't trained. She was a fourteen-year-old girl who'd just killed a man and watched her father die.

Willow squeezed her tighter.

"That's shock," Willow said softly. "Your brain's trying to protect you from everything that it can't process yet. It doesn't mean you're heartless... or broken. It just means you're human."

"Is Dad really dead?" Emma's voice cracked on the question.

Willow closed her eyes. She'd been hoping to avoid this conversation until they were home, until she'd had time to figure out how to explain the inexplicable. But children deserved truth, even when it destroyed them.

"Yes, sweetheart. Your daddy is gone. His heart stopped, and the doctors couldn't get it started again."

"They didn't try hard enough," Sarah said, her voice rising. "They should have tried harder!"

"They tried everything they could," Willow said. "Your daddy was hurt very badly. The doctors did everything possible."

Sarah launched herself into Willow's arms, sobbing with the raw intensity that only children could summon. "I want my daddy back! I want him back!"

Willow held Sarah tight, rocking gently while her own tears finally broke free. "I know, baby. I know."

Emma joined them, wrapping her arms around both Willow and Sarah. Ivy had stepped away, staring at her hands.

"Ivy," Willow said. "Come here."

"I can't." Ivy's voice was mechanical. "If I start crying, I won't be able to stop."

"That's okay."

"No, it's not. Someone has to be strong. Someone has to—"

"Not you," Willow said firmly. "Not anymore. That's my job now."

Ivy looked up, her green eyes wide and frightened. "What do you mean?"

Willow took a shaky breath. But she knew what she had to do. Until this very moment, she hadn't even considered what the future held. She was too busy trying to get through the present.

"I mean I'm staying. I'm going to take care of you. All of you."

"You can't," Ivy said. "You live in Alabama. You have a job. You have Jackson."

"Jackson and I will figure it out," Willow said. "But I'm not leaving you girls. Not ever again."

Sarah pulled back, her face streaked with tears. "Promise?"

"I promise."

Ivy finally broke. Her chin slipped down to her chest, and with each sob, her shoulders bounced. "I'm scared, Aunt Willow. I'm so scared."

Willow moved from the couch and wrapped the devastated child in her arms. "I know," she whispered, trying desperately to maintain control of her own emotions. She drew Ivy down to the couch, never letting go. "Me too. Me too."

They sat there in the harsh hospital lighting, four broken people clinging to each other. Willow's phone buzzed with multiple texts. She ignored them all. The outside world could wait. These girls needed her now, in this moment, as their entire world collapsed around them.

A nurse appeared at the edge of her vision. "Ms. Banks? The doctor would like to speak with you."

Willow looked at Ivy. "Can you stay with your sisters for a minute?"

Ivy slid into Willow's position. She pulled Emma and Sarah close. Even in her grief, she was still trying to be the protector.

Willow followed the nurse down a sterile hallway to a small consultation room. Dr. Campbell was waiting, his expression grave. Judith, the social worker who had helped Sarah keep Pickle, was with him.

"I'm sorry for your loss," he said. "Mr. Banks fought hard, but the damage was too extensive."

Willow nodded, not trusting her voice.

"There will need to be an autopsy," he continued. "Given the circumstances. But we can release the body to the funeral home afterward."

"Okay."

"The girls... they're going to need counseling. What they've been through tonight..." Judith shook her head. "Especially Ivy. I understand she was involved in the incident?"

"She defended herself and her family," Willow said. "She did what she had to do."

"I'm sure she did. But killing someone, even in self-defense, especially at her age... it's going to have lasting effects. I can recommend some excellent therapists who specialize in trauma."

Willow took the business cards she offered. Another responsibility. Another tool to help her nieces heal.

"There's something else," Judith said. "Child Protective Services will need to be notified. With their father deceased and no mother in the picture..."

"I'm their aunt," Willow said. "I'll be taking care of them."

"You'll need to file for guardianship. In the meantime, CPS will need to do a welfare check to make sure the children are in a safe environment."

Willow's jaw tightened. The idea of bureaucrats poking around, evaluating whether she was fit to care for her brother's children, made her want to punch something. Someone.

"How long do I have?"

"They'll probably contact you tomorrow," the doctor said. "But given the circumstances, and the fact that you're family, it shouldn't be complicated." He looked to Judith who gave a non-committal nod. She seemed far less confident than the doctor in how this would play out.

Willow hoped he was right. She thanked them both and made her way back to the waiting room. The girls were exactly where she'd left them, huddled together like survivors of a shipwreck.

"Ready to go home?" she asked.

"Is it still home without Dad?" Emma asked quietly.

Willow's heart broke a little more. "Yes, sweetheart. It's still home. Nothing can ever change that."

Ivy stood up, her movements wooden. "What about school? And my job at the marina?"

"We'll figure it out as we go," Willow said. She didn't know that Ivy had a job. "One day at a time."

Cooper appeared in the hallway, his face etched with exhaustion and grief. Sarah and Emma raced toward him, Pickle giving chase.

As they walked toward the exit, Ivy fell into step beside her. "Aunt Willow? When I shot that man... I wasn't thinking about protecting Dad. I was thinking about making that motherfucker pay for what he did."

Willow stopped. "Ivy—"

"I wanted him to die," Ivy said quietly, but with a razor-sharp edge. "I wanted him to suffer. Does that make me a bad person?"

It wasn't the violence in the statement that unsettled Willow — it was the way Ivy kept staring at the floor, jaw tight, like she was afraid to meet anyone's eyes for fear they'd see what she was thinking.

She rested a hand on Ivy's shoulder, steadying them both. "No. Never. It makes you human."

"Will I ever stop seeing it? When I close my eyes, I see him falling. I see the blood."

"I don't know," Willow said honestly. "But I'll help you deal with it. Whatever it takes."

Ivy wrapped her arm around Willow's waist, and they continued walking. Outside, the first hints of dawn were beginning to show on the horizon. A new day was coming, whether they were ready for it or not.

Cooper was loading the two girls and Pickle into his patrol car. He waited, leaving the back door open for Ivy. Once she'd joined her sisters, he closed the door and spread his arms wide. Willow fell into them, finally letting herself lean on someone else.

"Let's go home," he said quietly.

Home. The word felt foreign now, like a language she'd forgotten how to speak. But as she looked at the three girls who now depended on her, Willow knew she'd have to learn it again. They all would.

Together, they'd learn how to make it home again.

Chapter Fifty-Five

Jackson

Once the ambulances had cleared out, Jackson returned to the scene. Swarms of NCIS, FBI, Coast Guard, and State Police had descended.

He texted Willow twice. No reply.

He wanted to let her know that he'd be another hour or two, and that Ruby and Ranger were at the animal hospital. They'd be released shortly, along with Zeus. He'd slept through the night, and the big Shepherd was awake, alert, and on the road to recovery. He'd need rest while his stitches healed, and knowing Zeus, that wouldn't be easy. Still, he was going to make it.

Jackson was kept apart from his parents while the cops took their statements. Forensics arrived and bagged all their clothing as evidence, but at least his parents had been allowed to grab clean clothes from the house for themselves and for Jackson. Travis was an inch shorter and twenty pounds lighter, making the shirt and pants he'd lent Jackson uncomfortably tight in all the wrong places.

The FBI Deputy Director grilled Jackson himself, seemingly furious that he and Willow had arranged an unauthorized safe house in a residential neighborhood owned by powerful and influential people. Disciplinary action was threatened—until Alice arrived. She quickly took over, citing that she had given her agents full authority to act as they had, and if the Deputy Director had a problem with that, he could take it up with her. They were still locked in a heated argument when Jackson's parents came to join him.

"We've been cleared to leave," Travis said, wrapping his arm around Maybelle's shoulder. "What about you?"

Jackson raised his chin toward Alice and the Deputy Director, who stood nose to nose. The yelling had stopped, but the intensity lingered. "I guess so, unless my boss wants to rip another strip off my back."

"Forget him," Travis said. "He'll know where to find you if he wants to take another run at you. You need to get home to your family."

"Speaking of which, have you spoken to Willow?" Maybelle asked. "How are the girls holding up?"

"I've texted her, but she hasn't responded." Jackson stuffed his hands into his pockets. "I can only imagine what they're going through." A worried look crossed his face. "How are you, Momma? I've been so wrapped up in myself..."

"I can still taste the tear gas," she said, smacking her lips and making a sour face. "But I'll survive." She wrapped her arm around Travis and squeezed. "I wasn't in the line of fire, and I wasn't forced to take a life."

"I always hope that any life I take will be my last," Travis said. "But I won't lose sleep over them. They brought it on themselves."

"Speaking of sleep," Jackson said. "There is an extra bed at Mason's house." The words caught in his throat—Mason's house. His brain hadn't caught up yet, and his heart couldn't bear the thought.

His parents were already shaking their heads. "I'm sure we can find a hotel," Travis said. "It's a tourist town. There's got to be a hundred within a stone's throw from here."

"You and your family need time alone," Maybelle added. "We'll just be in the way."

"Never," Jackson said. "And, if I'm being honest, I could use your help. I have no idea what I'm doing with the children, even under the best of circumstances."

Travis gave him a long, searching look—then nodded once, solid as bedrock. "There's something I should tell you."

"Mason told us… things," Maybelle finished. "He said he'd known about what was going on at the house for some time, but—"

"The Fitzpatricks had threatened the lives of his children if he said a word," Travis finished. "He knew they were bringing in illegals and giving them fake documents. He also said that, even if life was hard here in the US, it was still better than what they had experienced back home. If they did their jobs, they were safe."

"Safe?" Jackson struggled to keep his voice down. "They were trafficking children! How could he have thought that these people were *safe*?"

Maybelle's face blanched. She looked to her husband who mirrored her look of shock. A jolt of tension clawed up Jackson's spine. How could he have forgotten? They hadn't found the teenagers from the house. They hadn't even started looking yet.

"If that is true," Travis said. "Mason knew nothing about it. He had been completely forthcoming with everything. He wanted, no…, he needed to get it off his chest. He even told us that he'd changed his will to name Willow as the children's guardian if something happened to him."

"He did what?" Jackson asked. Emotions overwhelmed him while his exhausted brain tried to absorb the news. How would they care for three children? Their jobs were demanding. They worked long hours. They lived three states away. "He never told Will. She'd have said something to me if he had."

"They didn't have time to talk about it," Maybelle said. "Mason was certain she'd make the perfect role model, and I couldn't agree more. Willow is exactly who they need in their lives right now. She's fierce and protective and won't take any guff. But I've also seen your fiancée's other side—kind, caring, and incredibly intuitive. She'll make an excellent momma bear."

While his head swam with implications, Jackson struggled to breathe. He knew nothing about raising children, and even less about dealing with young girls. Even the prospect of Ruby having puppies had overwhelmed him. He huffed. He was so far out of his depth. How would the girls cope with leaving South Carolina and moving to Alabama?

"Can they stay with us?" Jackson asked. His parent's place was plenty big enough, and the idea of having help... His mother slowly shook her head, crushing Jackson's spirits. The idea had been ridiculous. They'd already raised their family. Helping to raise three more wasn't what they had signed up for. "You're right. I understand. Willow and I can buy a place of our own. We can figure it out."

"Those girls can't be uprooted from their home," Maybelle said firmly, but in a way that told Jackson he wasn't thinking things through. "Their whole world just fell apart. The last thing they need is more upheaval."

Realization slowly set in. He swallowed hard. His life—*their* life—wasn't going back to the way it had been. Not ever. "So... we need to move to Beaufort?"

"Looks that way," Travis said. "Question is whether Alice will let you work from there."

"Men!" Maybelle said, her gaze moving between her husband and her son. "Those girls are going to need stability. Someone who will be there when they leave for school in the morning and when they come home at the end of the day. FBI work... It's not compatible with raising children. The hours you keep..."

"We can't quit our jobs," Jackson said. He knew his mother meant well, but this wasn't a simple fix. "We've got to support ourselves and the girls, and training dogs isn't going to cut it."

"You're going to need to do *something*," Maybelle said. "The children come first, remember? They *always* come first."

Maybelle's words landed hard. The truth of them pressed on Jackson's shoulders like a burden he couldn't shake. He opened his mouth to answer, but a quiet voice cut in.

"She's right," Alice said, joining the group. Excitement flashed in her eyes. "They do come first, and we've got a lead on where the trafficked children are being held."

The sudden shift knocked Jackson mentally off balance. He barely had time to consider her words before Alice pressed on.

"Do you have enough in the tank for another raid? Based on everything that's happened, I figured you'd want to be there." Alice thumbed toward a waiting SUV. "If you're in, we need to leave now. There's no time to plan. We're going in hot and blind."

Adrenaline spiked, making Jackson's hands shake. "I don't have Ruby, and Willow is unavailable."

"I understand if you'd rather sit this one out." Alice said, disbelief in her tone.

"I have no gear." He held his hands wide, showing off his undersized clothing.

"We're meeting SWAT at the house," she said with a grin. "They'll have plenty of gear, some that might even fit your oversized frame."

Jackson looked to his parents, wondering what they were going to do. He'd promised to take them to Mason's house.

"We've got this," Travis said, his hand firm on Jackson's shoulder. "Go do what you have to do."

***

"I need to tell you something," Jackson said as Alice put pulled into street-side parking spot. "According to my folks, Mason named Willow legal guardian over the children. That was the change in his will that he asked Hunter to draw up."

Alice blew out a low whistle. "Does Willow know?"

"She doesn't have a clue," Jackson said. "But I think she has already made the decision to look after them anyway."

"What about you?" Alice asked. "When you asked her to marry you... you didn't sign up for this."

"I'm not going anywhere," Jackson said. He had wanted a family, but not like this. "When I asked Will to marry me, I swore I'd never leave her side, that she could count on me until my dying breath." He gave a crooked smile. "It didn't sound as corny when I said it on one knee."

Alice snort-laughed and wiped a tear from his cheek. "You're a good man, Jackson Brooks. Let's bag these sons of bitches, so that you can get back to your new family."

"We need to move to Beaufort," Jackson said, unable to stop the words from leaving his mouth.

"Understandable," Alice said. She made it sound as if there wasn't any other option. "Can you put that aside for now? I need your head here with me. Can you do that?"

"Of course." Energy coursed through Jackson's body as he stepped into a set of camo fatigues. A SWAT command center had already been set up two blocks away to avoid tipping off whoever was holding the children. Child traffickers were predictable in these situations. They knew what it meant to be imprisoned alongside violent criminals who didn't tolerate their crimes, and for that reason, rarely went quietly.

"My team has surveilled the residence," the SWAT commander said. He was dressed in full body armor, his countenance matching his grim appearance. "We've got heat signatures for at least eleven people, maybe more. Some of the children are tightly clustered on the second floor, making their numbers difficult to ascertain. The good news is, there is only one dirtbag guarding them."

"How many hostiles on the first floor?" Jackson asked as he pulled on a Kevlar vest. "How many entry points? Can you get snipers in place?"

"I like this guy," the commander said to Alice. "I don't know where he's working now, but he'd fit on my team perfectly."

"Snipers?" Jackson said, ignoring the compliment. They were short on time, and the small talk was wasting what little they had.

"Two," the commander said. "On the north and west sides of the home. The blinds are drawn, but the thermal scopes don't care. They both have eyes on the dirtbag guarding the children. There are three doors on the main floor, one on the east, one on the west, and one on the south. There are five more identified dirtbags on the main floor. Based on my most recent intel, four are in the kitchen eating and the fifth is taking a dump."

"The snipers should take out the man on the second floor just before we breach," Jackson said. "If he hears gunfire, he might start shooting the children."

The commander gave an appreciative nod. "Not my first rodeo, son. But I'm glad you see things my way. We're going to make entry at all three points, using a detonator on the kitchen door. We want them to scramble, and we'll pick them off one by one in the chaos. These motherfuckers won't surrender. They never do."

It definitely wasn't his first rodeo. The commander understood the situation perfectly.

"Tell me where you want me," Jackson said. He took an M4 off the rack and systematically went through his prep-list. "Just make sure I'm at the front."

"We've got shield bearers up front," the commander said. "They lead the way and then we mop up. You're going to come with me through the south entrance. It's the nearest exit to their vehicles, and the most likely direction everyone will run."

In minutes, the teams were in position. The commander clicked his mic three times, the signal for the snipers to take their shot. Two loud pops sounded, followed by an explosion from the kitchen entrance.

A battering ram made short work of the south-side entrance, smashing open the door with a single swing. The shield bearer led the way inside, Jackson's hand on his shoulder, the commander's on Jackson's.

The first of two men running from the kitchen grabbed a shotgun from the wall. The second pulled a handgun from his waistband. Jackson dropped one with a pair of muffled bursts from his rifle. The commander took the second. A series of gunshots echoed from somewhere else on the main floor, followed by a series of pops.

"Clear!" someone shouted from the kitchen.

"Clear!" someone else shouted from the north side.

Screams echoed from upstairs—the unmistakable shriek of children. Jackson didn't wait for the all-clear.

He took the stairs two at a time, heart hammering against his ribs. He threw his shoulder into the door where the children were being held. The frame shattered, and the door burst open in a shower of splinters.

The snipers had done their job. The male guard was slumped against the wall. Half of his skull was sprayed across the bright-yellow wallpaper. But the scene wasn't clear.

A woman stood, pinned in the corner away from the windows. Four teenagers stood between her and Jackson. Her arm was wrapped around a young boy, no more than twelve. In the woman's other hand was a small handgun, pressed against the boy's temple.

"Stay back!" she screeched, her eyes wild. "I swear to God, I'll kill them all!" She pointed the gun at the other children before returning it to the boy's temple.

Jackson froze in the doorway, rifle raised but not aimed. The snipers could see what was happening with their thermal scopes, but it would be impossible for them to take the shot. Not without risking the lives of the children.

The woman's finger danced on the trigger guard. Too close.

"I remember you," Jackson said, not lowering his weapon. "From Maritime Workforce Solutions." It was the hawknosed woman who had lied about the workers not speaking any English.

"I want assurances," she said. "I'll tell you everything about the Fitzpatrick's operation, but I want complete immunity. Do you hear me? I'll never see the inside of a jail."

"We already know everything," Jackson said, raising his weapon. He dropped his voice to a low growl. "Put down the gun, or I'll paint the wall with your brains. Your choice."

"You don't know shit!" she yelled. "You *think* you know things, but I know *everything*. I know how they're bringing in the drugs and the people. I know who the suppliers are, and how the Fitzpatricks get past the Coast Guard."

"I will not talk to you while you hold a gun to a child's head," Jackson slipped his finger past the guard and rested it on the trigger. "Drop the gun, get on your knees, and interlace your fingers behind your head. I won't tell you a second time."

She hesitated.

Behind him, footsteps pounded up the stairs. The woman flinched at the sound, twisting her body ever so slightly.

That was all Jackson needed.

He locked eyes with the boy and dipped the nose of his rifle. A silent command. The boy's gaze flicked to his feet. Jackson took a slow, predatory step forward.

The woman shifted again, tracking Jackson's motion—

—and the boy dropped to the floor.

Jackson fired.

The woman jerked, gun falling from her hand, eyes wide with shock before her legs gave out.

Jackson crossed the room in three strides, kicking the weapon aside as the kids huddled together, their screams turning into gut-wrenching sobs.

"It's over," he said, dropping to one knee. "You're safe. You're safe now."

He grabbed the woman by the wrist and flipped her onto her belly. She screamed as he did. The exit wound on her right shoulder was leaking blood at a horrific pace.

"Call an ambulance," Jackson yelled at the commander who was standing behind him. "She needs to live."

The woman whimpered, clawing at the floor with her good hand. Jackson didn't ease up. He pinned her wrist, planted a knee in her back, and leaned in. The kids huddled together, eyes wide, defenseless. "It's over," Jackson said again, steady and flat. "You're safe. You're all safe."

Chapter Fifty-Six

Willow

They buried Mason two days before Christmas.

The family had considered postponing the funeral until after the holidays, but Willow didn't want to put the girls through that. They needed closure so they could start healing.

The graveside service was quiet.

Willow and her brothers stood on one side of the casket while the three girls stood on the other. Behind them, Jackson and his parents held leashes. Chief Stevens, Reeves, Thomas, and Anika stood slightly apart, keeping a respectful distance from the family. Further back, the police kept the media away. The death of two prominent members of Beaufort was big news for the local outlets, and the involvement of US Marine and Coast Guard personnel made it of national interest.

The wind cut across the cemetery, tossing Willow's hair against her cheeks as she stepped to the casket. She hadn't planned on speaking. Honestly, she wasn't sure she had the right. But Ivy had insisted that her father would have wanted her to. She cleared her throat.

"I used to think my brother was God-like."

A soft ripple of laughter moved through the crowd.

"He drove first. He graduated first, and he got married first." Willow's brow knitted into a tight V. "I was the only girl and the youngest of five. Growing up, my brothers made it their job to make my life difficult, and they succeeded spectacularly." A chuckle escaped her lips. "But Mason made sure they never went too far, but it didn't stop him from joining in the fun. *Fun.* Like when I was fourteen and brought home my first boyfriend. *Fun* wasn't exactly the word I'd use for that afternoon."

Another ripple of laughter. Colten and Cooper elbowed each other and grinned. Colten was fourteen months older than Cooper, but he could have been his identical twin.

Willow took an unsteady breath and continued. "I didn't realize this until very recently, but my big brother had always looked out for me. He made sure I went through life with my eyes wide open, seeing things for what they were and not as they appeared to be. I didn't fully understand that until it was too late, and I didn't get a chance to thank him."

The lump in her throat burned. She swallowed hard and beat her fist against her heart.

"I didn't know how much he trusted me, even after I had been a total bitch to him. He trusted me with—" The words caught in her throat as she looked to Ivy, Emma, and Sarah. Their eyes locked on Willow's, their cheeks wet with tears. "My brother trusted me with the three most precious people in his life. And I swear to God and to all of you standing here today, I will do my best to raise and guide them. Ivy. Emma. Sarah. I will never abandon you, and I will do my best to live up to your father's expectations."

She drew a slow breath, letting the silence settle. The ache in her chest swelled, but she pushed past it.

"I'll miss him every day. His laugh. His terrible cooking. His god-awful taste in country-pop music." Ivy chuckled and wiped at her cheek. "But mostly... I'll miss knowing he is always there for me."

She reached out, resting her hand gently on the polished wood of the casket.

"Goodbye, Mason. You did good."

Ivy stepped forward and scowled at the casket. "My dad was the best person I've ever known," she said, fury in her voice. "He died protecting his family and his friends. I'm angry he left us behind... but I'm grateful he loved us enough to lay down his life for us. If that's not the best role model in the world, then I don't know what is." She raised her eyes and managed a faint smile. "You've got big shoes to fill, Aunt Willow. Good luck with that."

Willow walked around the casket and wrapped the girls in a hug.

"I don't stand a chance," she whispered into Ivy's ear. "But I'll try."

***

Willow placed the last of the plates in the cupboard. It was the first Christmas that she'd shared with her brothers since before their parents had passed away.

The day after the funeral, Willow had sat Ivy down for a conversation about how to handle Christmas. She had asked Ivy if she would prefer the holiday not be celebrated, but her niece had instantly shot down the suggestion.

"Sarah and Emma need this," she had said, her voice strong and unwavering. "After mom died, Dad insisted that our lives needed to go on without her. He said that's what Mom would have wanted. Dad would want the same for us."

Ivy was the strongest person Willow had ever met. Her world had been ripped from her. People who were new to her, Jackson and his parents, were living in her home. For the past two weeks, police and federal investigators seemed to be at their door five times a day. Through it all, she remained stoic and unwavering.

"It was nice of your parents to come back and spend Christmas with us," Willow said to Jackson, hoping their presence would make a good segue to the conversation she needed to have with him, but was afraid to bring up. "Your mom has been a godsend, helping with meals and keeping our world sane. Your dad, too, but in a different sort of way. The girls seem to love them both."

"I think they've pretty much adopted the girls as their grandbabies. I hope they're not overstepping."

Willow shook her head and wrung the dish towel in her hands. "We haven't really talked much about... us. Mason's will was kind of a bombshell. He left everything to the girls but named me as their guardian and in charge of their trust."

Jackson tilted his head, confusion in his eyes. The action reminded her of Ranger, when she said something that he didn't understand.

"Do you still want to marry me?" Her heart stopped as she blurted the words. "I know you want us to have children, but not like this. I would understand if—"

"Huh," Jackson said, stuffing his hands into his pockets. "I was going to ask you the same question. For different reasons, of course. I didn't know if you'd want to still share your life with me, now that you've been gifted such a huge responsibility. The girls don't know me, and they might not want me in their life. I have no clue how to deal with children, or young women. I know dogs, and I doubt they're even remotely the same thing."

"You didn't answer my question," Willow said, her pulse racing.

"Of course, I still want to marry you." Jackson closed the distance between them and kissed her with enough passion to make Willow's knees buckle. "I'd marry you tomorrow if I could."

Willow's cheeks burned. "I'd marry you right now, but it's a little late to go down to City Hall."

"City Hall? You're joking right? Do you really think Momma's going to let us get married anywhere other than a church? The religion won't matter to her, so long as we speak our vows in the eyes of God."

"I think Maybelle will let us do whatever we choose to do," Willow said. "She's made it clear to me since the first day we met that I should be myself, and not the person she wants me to be." She patted his chest. "If you want a traditional church wedding though, I'm okay with that. It means I'm going to need a wedding dress, and a bouquet, and all that... stuff."

Jackson lifted a shoulder and smiled. "But it's going to have to wait for the right time. It seems wrong to celebrate our love right now. Maybe the timing will be better if we wait until the spring, like we planned?"

"Name the time and the place, Jackson Brooks, and I will be there." She tossed the dish towel onto the counter. "I'm going to need some time to figure out my next steps, career wise. I can't look after the girls and be an FBI field agent. It won't work, and I won't sacrifice my time with them."

"The FBI might not be in the cards for either of us, moving forward. Despite Alice's best efforts, the deputy director still wants our badges. During his press statement yesterday, he said someone needs to pay for what happened—and I expect that *someone* is us." Jackson held his hands up in a gesture of futility. "We got attacked and we bagged over a dozen felons, but *we have to pay?* He should be pinning a freaking medal on our chests."

"The man's a fucking asshat. I'm guessing he's got some sort of political aspirations. After the shootout, he's looking for sacrificial lambs. It never looks good when law enforcement shoot up a rich neighborhood."

"Ya," Jackson said with a laugh. "Forget him and the FBI too if that's how they feel about it. I don't need them. I got a job offer, but I didn't want to consider it until I knew you wanted me to stay."

"With the Beaufort PD?" Willow asked. "Janet asked me to join too, if I didn't want to stay with the bureau. The pay is going to suck, but she promised me regular hours."

"And?" Jackson pulled a kitchen chair over and took a seat. "What did you tell her?"

"I said I needed to talk to you about it. Who offered you a job?"

"NCIS, if you can believe it. Vicky and Greg are going to prison, and Matt will likely never return to work. They'd make me their lead investigator, and I'd have a team reporting to me. After what happened with Pratt, they want a larger presence at MCAS Beaufort."

"Fucking Pratt," Willow said. "He got what was coming to him. The dogs mauled him good. He's going to enjoy prison with one leg and one arm. Maybe Ex-officer Dade can be his bodyguard. I hear they'll likely end up in the same federal penitentiary."

"Well," Jackson said with a huff. "That's something, at least. You must feel good about Dade finally getting his comeuppance."

"It won't change the past, but yeah. His testimony is going to get him a lighter sentence, but he's still going to see significant jail time. Same goes for Fitzpatrick's executive assistant. It burns my ass that she's receiving any leniency, but she seems to have a shit-ton of information on their operation. Names, dates, everything. If her testimony holds up in court, she's going to put a lot of people behind bars."

"We can only hope," Jackson said. "And what position did Janet offer you to join the Beaufort PD? Will you get one of those snappy blue uniforms?" He waggled his eyebrows.

"Oh yes, wearing a flak jacket and a utility belt is going to be *super* sexy." She stepped closer, letting her hips sway with each step. "Janet wants to make me Captain and take over as their lead investigator. The position has been vacant since Janet was promoted to Chief. Apparently, the mayor offered to increase her budget to cover my salary plus the salaries of two new detectives and a certain mali-gator. I'm also going to oversee the PD's K9 unit, but only in an advisory capacity. I told Janet that Reeves and

Zeus had earned their stripes and that she could ignore the review we sent in. Honestly, I think they're ready for any scenario."

"That sounds amazing. You're going to make a great cop. But what about my opportunity? You didn't say how you'd feel if I took the job at NCIS. Even if my office is only twenty minutes away, I'm guessing the hours will be long—and the cases might take me away from home for days or weeks at a time."

"Of course I'm okay with it! I will miss you when you're gone, but you've already passed up a supervisory role for me once so that we could work together. I don't ever want to be the reason you're held back. You have a bright future ahead of you, and I want you to experience it to the fullest." She sat on his lap and kissed his neck. "I don't envy you the job though. The provost marshal's office is in shambles, and I'm guessing you'll have to root out what's left of the corruption. I'm sure there is a lot more on the marine base that has gone unseen."

"I guess it's settled then." He tucked a wayward strand of Willow's hair behind her ear. "We're officially moving to Beaufort."

Chapter Fifty-Seven

Jackson

Jackson slammed the front door as he stormed into their house. Well, it was the girls' house, technically, but until they were old enough to live on their own, it was Jackson and Willow's too.

"Calm yourself," Maybelle said, clutching her chest. "Ruby's sleeping, and you scared the daylights out of me."

"Sorry, Momma," he said, sucking a breath through his nose. "The immigration judge wouldn't even listen to us. Every one of the poor souls is being deported back to Haiti, children and all. He even tried to have Thomas arrested for marrying Anika, saying that he was trying to defraud the government to help an illegal alien gain permanent resident status. I had to give an affidavit to say that he'd risked his life to protect her, because he loved her, and not so that she could get a green card. Thomas yelled at the judge saying that if she wasn't welcome in the United States, then he would leave the country with her."

"And?" Maybelle asked. "Did the judge relent?"

"He did," Jackson said, shaking his head. Just thinking of it made his blood boil. "But he declared Thomas in contempt of court. He gave him a choice of thirty days in prison, or a ten-thousand dollar fine."

Jackson scrubbed the back of his neck. "He took the thirty days. He doesn't have ten grand to pay the fine."

"I could call my friend Grace back home," Maybelle said. "I'm sure she'd give Thomas an interest-free loan, considering the circumstances. She's got more money than she knows what to do with, and we both know how she likes to be a do-gooder."

"There's no way he could ever pay it back, Momma. Thomas doesn't even know if he'll have a job now that Mason's gone. People knew Mason and his dad by reputation. They don't know Thomas or the quality of his work."

"Grace won't expect him to pay it back." Maybelle rolled your eyes. "It would be a loan because Thomas won't take charity. He's too proud for that. But a loan that he can pay back whenever he can... he might be willing." She waved her hand dismissively. "Never you mind. Your father and I will look after Thomas. You have enough to do with your new litter of puppies."

"My what?" Jackson's head swiveled about. "Why didn't you say something? You should have called."

"Ruby had slipped off on her own," Maybelle said. "I only discovered the three new puppies because Ranger was barking. I guess he was celebrating the birth of his children. They're the cutest things I've ever seen."

"I need to tell Willow. Where is she?"

"Upstairs with the girls," Maybelle said. "I'm afraid Sarah has already named them."

A mortified look spread across Jackson's face. "She named her Dachshund Pickle. Oh, please tell me she didn't name them dinner condiments."

"No, she didn't, Mr. Smartypants. Your father has been reading her bedtime stories from his favorite novel."

Jackson groaned. "There's only three puppies. Which of the musketeers got left out?"

"Aramis," Maybelle said. "She named them Athos, Porthos, and D'Artagnan—but I suspect Dart is what will stick. Sarah struggles saying D'Artagnan."

"They're all males? Ruby had three boys?"

"Athos and Porthos are boys. Dart is a girl. Sarah doesn't care if it's a boy's name, and nobody had the heart to tell her differently."

"You're home," Willow said, striding down the stairs. "Did you hear the news?"

"Three new puppies," Jackson said. He was about to head up to see them.

"That's news, but it's not what I was talking about. How did it go with the immigration judge?"

"Not good," Jackson said. He didn't want to talk about it. He could fill her in later. "What news are you talking about?"

"That the District Attorney is not bringing charges against Liam Fitzpatrick. The DA's office could find no evidence of his involvement. Liam claims that his brothers were acting on their own, and that he had no knowledge of their activities."

Jackson clenched his hands into tight fists.

"We'll get him, Jax," Willow vowed. "He'll step out of line, and when he does, we'll nail his fucking ass to the wall." Willow grimaced. "Sorry, Momma. I really am trying to not swear in front of you."

"Your house, your rules," Maybelle said. "I don't ever want you to stop being you, because I love the you that you are."

"Me too, Momma," Jackson said, wrapping his arm around Willow's waist. "Me too."

"While I enjoy all the appreciation you're bestowing on me," Willow said, giving Jackson a peck on the cheek, "You have a pile of furry grandchildren you need to visit. If we leave Sarah alone with them for too long, she might start accessorizing them." When she saw the startled look on Jackson's face, she punched him in the shoulder. "Don't be so gullible. The girls are all keeping their distance from momma and her babies. They're children, not idiots."

"How am I supposed to know that?" Jackson said. "I've never dealt with children before, let alone girls."

"You said you wanted children," Willow said with a playful grin. "Welcome to the deep end of the pool."

"It's a good thing you've got a couple of lifeguards on duty," Maybelle said. "Your father and I won't let you drown."

"You're staying here in Beaufort? What about the house back home, and the kennels?" Jackson looked at Willow. "Did you know?"

"It was Willow who asked if we'd consider it," Maybelle said. "As for the house, we've already got a potential buyer lined up."

Jackson considered who she might have found so quickly. "Jason?"

"Who else would want a hundred-year-old house and an oversized kennel?" Maybelle said.

Dr. Jason Simmons was a behavioral vet and one of Jackson's closest friends. In his excitement to move to Beaufort, Jackson hadn't really thought about who or what he was leaving behind. He'd landed his dream job in Florence, helping to run an FBI regional office while training K9s for multiple law enforcement agencies. He'd made new friends and cultivated relationships within the Alabama Bureau of Investigation. Though he'd only been in South Carolina for a few weeks, Florence already seemed like a lifetime ago.

"Come on, Jax," Willow said, pulling him by his hand. "You haven't congratulated Ruby yet, and we've got some puppies to visit. I can't believe you're taking this long."

"Lead the way," Jackson said, interlacing his fingers with hers. "I'm with you."

The sound of their footsteps as they climbed the stairs matched the steady beat of his heart. In the eight months since he met Willow, his life had changed in ways that he couldn't yet fathom.

The coming weeks would be a maelstrom—new roles, new responsibilities, and a home life that Jackson wasn't afraid to admit scared the crap out of him. But with Willow by his side, they'd figure it out, come hell or high water.

Afterword

Thank you so much for reading. I hope you enjoyed the journey as much as I loved writing it.

If you want to be the first to know when the next case drops, join my inner circle for exclusive updates and early alerts on new releases. You can sign up instantly online at:

https://paulmouchet.ca/subscribe

If the story kept you turning the pages, I'd be incredibly grateful if you shared your thoughts in a review. Reviews on **Amazon, Goodreads, and BookBub** help other readers discover my books and allow me to keep writing more stories for you.

Even a few words make a world of difference. Your support means everything.

— Paul/PJ Mouchet

Also By

PJ Mouchet Novels

Brooks & Banks Series (Adult 14+)
Character-driven thrillers filled with high-stakes investigations, intense confrontations, and the human struggles that bind us all.

- Violent Echoes

- Deep Water

- The Crucible

- No Safe Trail

Paul Mouchet Novels

The Last Guardian Series (Adult 14+)
From unwanted outcast to the last Guardian of the Realm. Some paths are easier than others to follow.

- Rosemarked Assassin

- The Olander Legacy

- Realm of Arachnielle

Priest of Titan Series (Young Adult 14+)

Titan called her. The Temple forged her. Gods will fear her.

Life for Kit was difficult, growing up a Nomad human in a Berrat village. At the tender age of eleven, she travelled to a distant kingdom, and joined the Fist of Titan, a temple that worships a foreign god. The Temple priests trained her in the art of war. They taught her to deliver justice. They set her on the path to free their god, Titan. But paths have a way of taking you in unexpected directions and help you to discover things about the world and yourself. They can show you that meddling in the affairs of gods can either save or destroy the world. How can a teenage girl and her eclectic group of friends save the people and still prevent Ragnarök, the end of days?

- Call of Titan

- Hand of Titan

- Hammer of Titan

- Eyes of Titan

- Daemon of Titan

- Wrath of Titan

Fairytale Retellings (Young Adult 12+)

If you enjoy fantasy adventure with a touch of romance, then this is for you.

- Between Land and Sea: A Little Mermaid Retelling